IN THE HANDS OF MEN

A NOVEL

GIN SEXSMITH

Gilded Press
www.gildedpressbooks.com

ISBN 9798986466187 (paperback) | ISBN 9798986466194 (epub)

For all of the missing and murdered Indigenous women, girls, and Two-Spirit peoples, and everyone who loves them.

AUTHOR'S NOTE

This novel contains topics of sexual abuse, violence, and murder. It contains vulgar language. It contains feminine rage and desire. This book is necessary, for everyone. But it's not sweet.

We bring our past with us wherever we go

ONE

Polaroids lie scattered across the orange shag carpet, a slideshow of the night before. I stare down at myself, at the vacant eyes looking past the camera, and truly see what I was feeling. How the pleasure turned, as always, and left me feeling sick. Another failed attempt at saying no. Another mistake added to the list in the name of a good time. All to suffocate my boredom, to distract myself from myself, from *her*—Cedar—from who I could have been, from who she wants me to be, from this grief that never ceases raking its sharp nails along my insides. All in the name of instant gratification, much like the quickly developed images themselves. I think about placing them in the box in my closet but change my mind at the last second. I'm not ready to hide them away yet. I want the night to stay fresh in my mind.

I was already drunk when the breaking news skittered across the TV screen perched behind the bar, drowned out by the sounds of thirsty Thursday. A hush fell over the room as the piercing squeal of an amber alert possessed our phones, the screen flashing: THIS IS A TEST. The laughter and clinking glasses trailed off as the bartender turned up the volume.

"Women are being urged to stay home, to stick with buddy systems if they must go out. Men, worldwide, are suffering from rage outbursts, sudden acts of violence," the news anchor warned. "The cause unknown, stay tuned for further development."

Sounds like my father, I thought as a clip rolled of a chubby, middle-aged man taking a crowbar to a sleek black Nissan—the woman in the driver seat's face set into an open-mouthed look of fear and surprise, too similar to that Pikachu meme. The nervous tension that had begun to hang around our shoulders shattered once the laughter resumed. It felt good to laugh, to not think of my father's quiet, simmering rage and the looming sense that no matter what I do, I'll never live up to his expectations. It felt good to distract myself from this new hell that we are all racing towards.

We locked eyes over our beers.

He was attractive but lacked the kind of charm that would make him gorgeous. He didn't really like me; he was just the sort of man that rarely slept alone. I could tell, however, from the ease in which he spoke to me, that he had a big dick.

I intended on leaving after the first beer he insisted on buying me, but he sidled the next one up beside a shot of Wild Turkey. Cedar told me that there's a thin red line between brave and stupid before she turned in for the night, leaving me to howl in the face of danger all by myself. I think she knew, immediately, that I'd take him home.

A twinge of shame pricks my stomach. I stifle it as I stare at him, as if he's not just another man I've used in hopes that he'll make me feel full but instead a subject I can evaluate, pick apart. His breath is ragged: one deep inhale, one quick exhale catching in the middle, a quick inhale like he's gasping for life after nearly drowning, followed by a long exhale. It fills my small bedroom with the smell of his stale, whisky-breath. At least he's breathing. I glance around my room until I spot my camera perched atop my dresser. It's the one thing I always manage to keep safe. My nan would be proud, if only, of that. His arm is carelessly tossed across his forehead, dampened with a hungover sweat that gives his face an ill, reddish quality. Not blue. He's conventionally good-looking, his jaw jutting out even in slumber, blond hair falling across his forehead, full pink lips slightly parted by his breath. His shoulders are broad, muscle rippling down his torso and hiding beneath the covers. But he's ugly too. I take a step closer and take another picture, the camera whizzing and churning to the point that I think it will definitely startle him awake. He doesn't budge as it spits out a dark, developing image. I gently shake it in my hand, even though I know it doesn't make it come to life any faster. Even though I know it only makes it worse.

I have become a collector of sorts, of men.

Who would I be without them? I don't know.

My face tingles, the earliest warnings of a hangover.

Last night feels like weeks ago. It wasn't me who met him at the bar, who spilled into the cab beside him, my fingers fluttering like a bird to the fly of his jeans. It was the part of me that is the most in control when out of control, only living for the thrill. That much more intrigued because of the newfound hint of a threat. Maybe it was Cedar, experiencing moments that she'll never get to regret risk-free. My bed, and the man inside, are still enveloped in the comforter Cedar and I used to tell ghost stories beneath when we were kids, when we had our entire lives stretched out before us—before we became ghost stories ourselves. I try not to listen to the little voice that says part of me likes imagining my sexual encounters degrading me, raping me, killing me. A fated karma. That same voice says I like thinking of my sexual encounters pushing me towards a point of no return.

Despite my head feeling foggy, the night is still in one piece, some moments a little blurrier than the others. So many of my nights are lost forever, a looming black hole of mistakes and shame. It gives me a misplaced sense of pride. I glance at him again, remembering how his eager confidence was a pleasant change from the aloof, insecure boys with whom I so often spend my nights. Maybe I prefer them self-conscious and cruel. Maybe those ones let me see myself.

I can feel it still. His hand around my neck, the churn in my stomach, and yet the curl of my toes, the goose bumps that crept up my legs, my back, my arms until my scalp buzzed. *They're not dangerous as long as you keep them happy*, I thought, truly hating myself. I hate that I'd do anything for that rush, even if it leaves me a little more hollow than before. Even if I'm the one in control of my own erasure. Lately, the emptiness doesn't lurk around to slink into my bones the next morning; these days it hits during—as quickly as switching positions. I'm present and all of a sudden I'm not. I'm stuck in my own head, letting my body take over while my mind huddles in the corner and watches. I call it freedom. It's a lie, but it's less of a lie than what the women from the bar tell themselves. I saw them last night, the kind of women I can never meld into when they're in a group. Women who think their snarky looks are completely hidden behind sips of vodka-cran. A group who has probably known one another since high school, all married with children. Women who never miss a salon appointment or a spin class and do brunch with the besties on Sunday. Women who judge girls like me. Women who will never utter the words Intersectional Feminism, who *only* drop the f-bomb when saying, "Not to be a feminist, but ..." Women who will never admit that their husbands don't make them come or that their children were a mistake. Women who know that even if their husbands cheat, they'll never leave.

They're not free like me, yet when his eyes are on me, and he's pulling at my shirt and making me lie still while he stares, while he parts my thighs and inserts his fingers, I surrender every ounce of willpower I had when I was dressed. When he puts his wet fingers into my mouth and his grip tightens around my neck, I fully realize that to him—to them—I am an object. I'm nothing. I tell myself that he's an object too. *My* object. But there's a glitch, and I don't fully believe it. Or, even if I do, I don't think that being objectified will feel the same to him as it does to me. It doesn't threaten him.

It doesn't chip away at his potential.

Maybe I'm not free either.

Maybe we are all snared in different traps.

Maybe I don't like this lifestyle as much as I think I do. Maybe I envy those other women. Some of them must be satisfied, right? Maybe the lazy Sunday mornings and baby talk, the knowledge that there's someone out there thinking of me for more reasons than getting underneath my skin will fulfill me. Maybe if I could settle down into the cozy comforts and safety of a relationship, my eyes wouldn't wander to those of a stranger. I wouldn't feel him inside of me after one lingering glance. (But it feels so good.) Maybe I could halt the thoughts of someone else in moments of intimacy. Maybe I could know how I'm going to feel after and make better decisions before it's too late. But no part of me can stop once it's started. Instead, my eyes close, my head tips back, and a guttural moan escapes my parted lips. And his eyes are scorching.

Maybe they're all the same. Maybe they'll all leave me lonely. Maybe I'm no better.

Last night he winced as he came. Pleasure. Conquer. Accomplishment. I couldn't even speak. I rested my hand across my chest, but he quickly pushed it back to my side.

"Don't cover yourself up."

That part, I remember. The cringe of my guts. This ownership he already had after only a few hours and an orgasm. All I could do was laugh because what else was there to see? I give them everything. But he was serious. I hated myself as I let him push at my arms while he called me beautiful. And the entire time I knew it was more for himself than it was for me. I could be anyone, as long as I let him inside and made him feel like a man.

Welcome home. Make yourself comfortable. No need to take off your shoes.

What must that feel like? Women bending and breaking and shrinking before you? It must feel powerful.

The floor creaks beneath my weight as I slink to the doorway on my way to the bathroom. He lets out a soft snore gentle as the coo of a dove.

My sink has a soap scum ring that catches a little more dust and makeup each day. I could have scrubbed it when it started, but I let it fester. It's a theme of mine. This longing to deteriorate. The rest of the bathroom is clean, polished tub and toilet. The grime juxtaposes, as if I'm close to getting it right but won't let myself fully cross over the line to become responsible, sane.

There's a wickedness in my reflection.

She's someone utterly terrifying and hurt. Her eyes are too

green. The little line between her eyebrows gets the deepest when she speaks to me.

She calls me a slut the way all of my closest friends have. *Ex-friends*, the little voice hisses as I pretend that I don't feel silly and stupid and sad. Her eyes hold the same fire as theirs, these women who I thought knew me. I hate her with as much passion as I want her to love me. If I could flip the script and become her, I would. I've tried, but I can't.

"Well, good morning, beautiful."

I hear him before I see him. The jolt of surprise morphs into the heat of embarrassment as I drag my eyes from hers and meet his in the mirror. He's in the doorway, already erect, and I want to belittle him. But I don't. I feel the sickening, fake smile creep across my mouth before it becomes a conscious thought.

Has he ever had someone he loves cut him up into tiny, digestible, bite-sized pieces? He strides over to me like he hasn't. My eyes lock with Cedar's for a quick second—they're seething. She expects so much more than I'm willing to give. *I know you*, she says. Cedar is the only person I cannot lie to. She is everything I want to be. She feels like a kick in the ribs.

I watch my shaking hand squeeze too much toothpaste onto my brush. When I run it under the water a clump falls to the sink, becoming one with the grime. I shove my toothbrush too quickly into my mouth, the plastic banging against my teeth, and I want to smash the mirror when I see Cedar's eyes flicker—*You're better than this*, they say.

She wasn't always cruel. Life has a way of shaping us all.

She did, however, always have a bite to her.

My hygienist told me I need to brush softer. "We only get one set of gums," she said.

But maybe I like the taste of blood. Maybe I want to be all fang.

Maybe that's what Cedar expects of me.

He's looking down at my ass, this near stranger who I let inside. If I don't squat three times a week it dissolves as quickly as it plumped. But he seems to think I was born with it as he grabs a hold of my left cheek, shaking it like a gift.

"Fuck, you're hot."

I mutter a thank you amidst a mouthful of spearmint suds.

Men look at body parts the way little boys look at toys scattered across the sandbox. Eyes full of smug innocence and wonder. I always end up with sand in my mouth.

I lean forward to spit and the arch of my back must be as good of a welcome as any because he jerks my pyjama shorts off with one tug. My toothbrush falls to the sink. I place my hands on either side of the porcelain and don't meet my eyes. I can't stand the look of disappointment. I wish I could shed myself the way a snake sheds its skin, I wish I could shed Cedar too. *Where the fuck did you go?* the voice asks. *Who the fuck have you become?*

The news says that you'll be able to recognize the sickness. That it causes a lack of impulse control, but that's nothing new. I've seen much sicker.

Later today he will tell his buddies all about the slut he met at the bar. If he likes me, he'll omit the dirty details and tell them, "Man, this girl was right on." Tonight, I will romanticize how we fucked in my washroom. I will tell myself that I wanted it. Tonight, I'll touch myself as I think of it. I'll claim it. I'll whisper my own name as my legs begin to shake. I'll pretend that I've always been, and always will be, in control.

When he's once again dressed and as calm as a sunning cat— and I've cleared my throat four times and mentioned twice about having to work later—he finally makes his way out my door and down the apartment stairs.

He's bright and shining in the mid-morning sun, lingering on the front stoop of my apartment building. I want to call him Justin. But it could be Josh. Jamie?

"We had so much fun last night. You gotta give me your number so we can do it all again soon."

It could be cute, how he sandwiches our identities together in a plural pronoun, but it isn't.

"Eight-six-seven-five-three-oh-nine," I say with a smirk, wondering if he's old enough to hear Tommy Tutone in his head.

"Jenny, I need your number." His hand is outstretched, Samsung Galaxy resting in his large palm.

I type GIRL FROM BAR and hand it back. He doesn't take his eyes off of mine as he slips it into the back pocket of his Levi's. If I were eager, he would have left before I woke up. But there's an indifference about me that makes men constantly want to tear off their jackets and throw them at my feet. If for no other reason than to bring about a desire they can then reject. I come off as confident and cold and to the unsuspecting eye it looks like power. If I let them get to know me, they'll realize that I'm drunk too much of the time. They'll begin to see it for what it is: a weakness.

"I hope you have a great day," I say in lieu of a goodbye, my hand already on the door to steady myself from the dizziness of too much booze that the sunshine exacerbates. He places his there too.

"I hope you have a great *day*."

He could have emphasized the "you" but he didn't. His eyes are alight; he wants to knock me off my feet. Patronize me in a way only my daddy can.

What part of last night rests beneath his tongue? What part of me will tickle his subconscious for the next two weeks? Does he think of me as courageous? Rebelling against societal fear, letting him in the only way I know how? I look at the bubble gum pink polish on my toes, suddenly demure. It must work. He leans forward and tucks a strand of hair behind my ear, resting his fingers on the back of my neck until I meet his eyes. An attempt at tenderness that comes off as forced. He kisses me on the cheek as if he's off to work, mouth already salivating over the pot roast I'll have waiting for him at six o'clock sharp.

"I can't wait to see you again."

I remain silent, all at once taking our firstborn out of his car seat and backing over him in the driveway.

TWO

My apartment feels once again my own when I re-enter it alone. Men have this uncanny ability to overfill a space with their energy until you're thinking of jumping out the window. I burn sage and smoke a cigarette, unsure of whether it's medicine or poison that I need. I pull both kinds of smoke over my head and down my chest, exhaling the toxins and blowing my bangs away from my face, remembering the grey hair I found last week, cropping up like a cancer. As much as the humiliation of getting older causes an ache in my bones, it's also a fresh form of freedom—the fateful realization that I will not always be desirable. That I will have to be something more. That I will be free to be something more. Another wave of shame threatens to drown me, the admittance that I am *not* more. I have built my life around being coveted and even that will ultimately abandon me. I will be left with nothing.

It's these feelings that leave women scrambling. Breaking and bending. I remember hearing Aunt Cindy ask, "Who will want me?" after it came out that her forever cringingly, self-assured, obnoxious boyfriend had molested Cedar when she visited her mother that last March break when she was fourteen.

"Cindy, are you fucking serious?" my mother hissed, and I pictured the cord twisting around her wrist as it always had during difficult conversations. "You have to kick him out."

"I'm too old to start over," Cindy said, her voice low and defeated as I listened from the phone in my mother's bedroom, trying not to breathe and alert anyone of my eavesdropping.

"Who will want me?" she repeated, her voice shrill, bordering on a shout. "You don't understand, Evey. You have a good one."

"You didn't notice any suspicious behaviour? You just let your daughter become prey under your own fucking roof?"

Aunt Cindy started to cry then, short whimpers and gasping breaths.

"You fucking know better," my mother spat before the hard slam of the kitchen phone made me jump. I placed the other down as silently as possible knowing I only had about thirty seconds before she'd come upstairs and catch me in her room.

I hid in the hall that night, listening to the weeping sounds of my mother's voice as she told my father what happened to Cedar. "Oh, oh, that's terrible," he replied. "Someone should kill that cocksucker."

It felt as if a woman's existence was letting horrible things sink to the sediment, of picking and choosing what to bear.

The coffee pot dings twice. I race to the kitchen wanting it immediately but knowing better than to burn my tongue. I pour it into my favourite mug, orange with the face of a fox. In Indigenous folklore foxes are known to charm their prey before they kill. All I've ever wanted to be was a charmer. Its rich steam blends with the smoke in the air. I add a generous slosh of whisky, a desperate attempt to curb the anxiety racing through my mind. I cradle the mug into my bedroom, where I'm met with discarded clothing and the Polaroids. Oh, the Polaroids. The booze brought out an exhibitionism as quick as my tongue. I gather the photos of myself, hoping, praying, begging Justin/Jamie/Josh was cocky enough to think he'd be back again. That I am not a trophy but a possibility.

For me, he was neither. He was just a pastime. There have been others who I've spotted hitting on women too drunk to stand, with firm hands on soft shoulders and growls waiting to be unleashed from deep but gentle tones. There have been ones that I have made into souvenirs, examples of my own determination, strength, wit, insanity. I have photos of them too.

I pick up the last picture of myself and add it to the small stack, trying not to look at it too closely. If I could suck out the slip of fat that rests beneath my bellybutton and above the sleek curve of my pubic mound I would. I should. I'd inject it into my not-quite-womanly boobs. It vanishes if I go enough days without bread, but bread—like dick that doesn't belong to me—always pulls me back. I take the scissors and cut as if a surgeon, the film giving way and falling in blackened shards around my knees. I leave my face till last, my mouth parted, eyes dark. *Snip, snip, snip.* I toss the remnants into separate garbage cans. You never know what kind of pervs are out there with a glue stick and a dream.

The photos of Justin/Jamie/Josh I leave whole. The curve of his shoulder, the ripple of his back, the wet, anticipatory tip of his cock. He's disembodied. The way I want them. He even took one of himself: arm outstretched, stomach flexed, sloppy grin—the only one where you can see his face. I slip it into my pocket. It's almost wholesome. Almost.

I watch my hands as they pull the aging shoebox from the back of my closet.

These hands, that I want to call my own, look like Cedar's. I bend them at the knuckles, digging my short nails into my palms to remind myself that I am here, I am alive. "Kónnhe, Kónnhe," Nan used to wheeze as she got out of her chair. *I'm alive, I'm alive.*

The box is beginning to wear at the corners, its blue and white revealing its cardboard grey innards. Beneath the lid there are hundreds. Moments. Memories. Men. All in parts and pieces, their best assets only. The way they see me.

When I think of my destiny, all I see is this box, squandered and shoved amidst the discarded socks, hair elastics, and an out-of-juice vape. I drop the fresh photos in and place the lid on as quickly as I pulled it off as not to let anything escape. My nan said I have a gift, that the Creator made me spiritually inclined, but it lingers like a curse.

Why won't Nan talk to me when I beg her to? I've tried to get her attention, singing "Please Mr. Postman," laying down tobacco, even playing with Tarot and a Ouija board despite the fact that she never approved of those sorts of things. I thought maybe she'd come back if she were mad. It didn't work.

Before she died, Nan left all of her film for me. She had enough for a lifetime, but that lifetime was cut short.

"Capture everything," she said.

I plan to.

We plan to.

Part of me feels grateful that I can't feel her presence. I worry she'd judge these photos. She wouldn't be able to make sense of what I'm trying to do. She'd think me fickle and foolish, promiscuous and petty.

I hope she'd realize I'm trying to make sense of the world, that I'm trying to even the playing field.

I'm trying to teach them a lesson.

THREE

I'VE BEEN COMING TO THIS SAME CONVENIENCE STORE for the past four years, yet I'm still graced with precious anonymity. Anonymity is truly underrated. Or maybe the ones who don't appreciate it haven't come from towns of under two thousand people. They haven't felt the smile waiting to turn into a sneer. The animosity for merely existing as a woman in her late twenties, who isn't haggard from raising three children by two different men you could find on Tinder any given Friday—all flabby stomachs flexed to the point of hernia and photos of hooked fish. I've learned there's an acceptable bitterness, and it's not the kind that I possess.

The bellbottoms and bodysuit I wear are new, but my thigh-length, tan jacket, cuffed and collared with white faux fur is vintage. Thanks to the weather, my curls bounce as I walk. My breasts, small enough for training-bra jokes but with perky enough nipples to scoff at, sit high as if judging all of those around me who have yet to learn that yes, you can look good to feel better.

I pour myself a large cream soda Froster and wonder if I'm too old for this Lolita-vibe I so desperately seek. At what age does feeling the eyes of men climbing down the length of you become pathetic?

I feel fucked-up and starving for a nourishment no food can provide.

He's at the cooler with his wife. She's pushing a stroller. When he sees me, he averts his eyes, suddenly consumed between the ever-eternal question: Coke or Pepsi? I smirk as I grab a pack of condoms thinking of how he begged to fuck me at the club, how I denied him. The condoms are magnums. The box is black and gold, my favourite colours. Some stores around here have followed suit with the US and stopped carrying all condoms, not just the ones for those lucky men. First, they took away abortion and then they removed contraception. They use the pro-life argument as if women's lives are not lives too. I wish they would just be honest: we view women as little more than breeders. Women are less of a threat when they're saddled with children—they're more controllable, their attention divided.

I let him, and the little family he's made, go ahead of me in line. His wife gives me a warm, sleepy smile, and I peek inside the stroller. Their baby can't be older than three months. All pink and squishy and blissfully unaware that her screams reverberate off of every wall. Blissfully unaware of the agony she's been born into. She's still young enough to have no qualms with taking up space and making herself heard.

"Cute," I mutter. The woman widens her eyes apologetically and sighs before hushing and shushing and cooing to no avail. She glances at her man as he flips through the rack of phone chargers, and I wonder if she's thinking, *Darrel, you don't even have an iPhone.*

I think he told me his name was Darrel, but who knows? Sometimes they recreate themselves as much as I do.

"Honey," she says, and he looks up, startled. She gestures to the now empty register as he mutters, "Oh," and hustles up without meeting my eyes. I take a massive slurp of my Froster, feeling the stab of pain right between my brows. The wife gives me a shrug and a laugh. Sometimes it's difficult not to feel like it's my fault they are the way they are. I've let them get away with so much. I want things from them none of them have ever been able to give.

A reel of another attack plays on the screen behind the counter. The rage seems to be spreading like wildfire, singeing anyone who gets too close. Some men have been developing fevers, as if their anger is scalding them from the inside out. I spend half my time frightened and the other half snarking—of course men are ruining the world; absolute power corrupts absolutely. I am a set of teeth, always on the verge of gnashing. An over-played pop song cooing, *Duh.*

"Dad?"

"Abby?"

I glance as incognito as possible over my shoulder. I've always been a sucker for a good eavesdrop. She's ten and as chubby as I was at her age. Sparkly, Barbie pink-polished nails, chipped and lined with dirt, grip a bag of Cheetos. The crunchy ones. The best ones. Her eyes look up at her father. She bats her lashes for good measure, a toothy grin cracking her face in two. She's in her last year of being cute before adolescence sheathes her in awkwardness and spits her out beautiful.

"Put them back."

He carries milk and eggs and looks at her for a split second, only as long as it takes him to spew the words from his mouth.

It's awkward, like walking into the kitchen of a dinner party and hearing the hosts fighting about me spilling merlot on their crocheted table cloth that was handmade by a long dead grandma.

But I can't look away.

Abby twists her body and bats her lashes harder. I recognize her in-between stage as if it were my own; I sense it like the warning signs of a panic attack, a flutter in my chest, a lightness in my head. The scramble to get something back you didn't even realize you enjoyed. The way I felt when my uncle used to call me Skinny Minnie until one day he didn't—when skin and bones became slight curves and tender flesh. Abby's in that last year before she realizes what the world is really like. Why won't her father look at her like she's special? This world will chew her up and leave her for dead. The least he can fucking do is love her.

"I'm serious. Put them back. I thought your mother said you had a crush on that kid?"

I can picture him and his wife together in bed, watching some rerun of a family sitcom where the wife nags and the husband rolls his eyes as a laugh track roars. I can hear her spilling the tea about Abby's little crush and him nodding, maybe even muttering something about a shotgun. Abby's face falls and for the first time she notices me. Our eyes meet. I feel her humiliation slip all the way down my catlike body. Her ears redden.

"You gotta stop shovelling this junk, kid," he adds when he sees me, interjecting a comedic tone. As if that makes it better. She drops the Cheetos and stares at the ground. I wonder if she'll talk about this day when she's in therapy fifteen years from now. If she'll hear his words on the days that she hates herself. If she'll beat herself up for being so *dramatic* so *emotional* so *hurt*. I wonder if she'll be the type to know that she's deserving of therapy or if she'll be like me. If she'll look for therapy in all the wrong places. If she'll assign to the belief that she can't be saved. Our minds always jump to our big traumas, but sometimes I fear it's the accumulation of little moments that tarnish us the most. The little moments that we are told are too insignificant to ever mention.

"Next!"

I turn around as the door dings. Darrel rushes to his car ahead of his wife, who graciously doesn't look back at me as she manoeuvres the stroller out into the night. I set my condoms and Froster down on the counter before holding up a finger to the teenage cashier, his eyes locked and loaded on my nipples as if they have the power to cure his acne.

Abby doesn't look up as I saunter towards her, but she hears the crinkle of the bags.

"These too," I say to Aaron, reading his name tag and looking at the crotch of his black dress pants until he clears his throat.

I turn back towards the little girl and her dad who've lined up behind me. Abby's father is ogling now, performing a mundane assault. I don't give him the satisfaction of meeting his eyes. Abby's are wide as I bend forward, pulling out one of the two bright orange bags.

"Don't share," I say to her, loud enough for everyone to hear.

She gives me a small smile and I'm twelve again, being rocked on a camp counsellor's lap as everyone sings "This Little Light of Mine." My parents thought it would be a good idea to send me to summer camp after all that had happened that April. I've wondered since if it wasn't a break from them having to look at how my cheekbones started to jut from pale cheeks, my jeans slinking off of narrowing hips, lips blue—as if all that had happened was slowly killing me (it was). Maybe they liked the idea of me punishing myself away from them so they wouldn't have to stare into the ugliness of it all and bicker with each other. I wouldn't eat and my mom kept hiding her pretty pink razors. The nightmares of finding me dead wouldn't leave her alone. Maybe I had no choice in it. My father is extremely judgmental and my mother is extremely insecure; it was a perfect storm for childhood development even before everything terrible happened. Maybe it was just easier for my mom to pretend my dad was a good person when I was no longer in the house, making snide comments and staring at him with eyes permeated with hatred. Sometimes I convinced myself I wasn't willingly throwing up my meals—I just felt forever sickened.

Camp, with its tight-knit group of girls that I couldn't meld into, only made me miss Cedar more. The camp counsellor's name was Allison, and her long brunette hair skimmed the waist of her jeans. After Cedar impulsively cut her hair that spring, she vowed to let it grow. "Until it touches my butt," she'd say. I've always wondered if my parents had told Allison about what happened or if she just sensed it. I wish I could thank her for that one moment in time where I felt truly, unconditionally comforted. Mostly, I just want to ask, "Does my desperate need for love hang in the air like a stench? Is that why you held me?"

There's an older woman walking by, eyeing me warily. She looks familiar but I don't let my eyes idle. Her presence makes my once graceful movements jerky. I am suddenly an outsider. I can tell she thinks I'm cheap. I feel cheap. I am cheap.

I give Abby a wink and can hear her father scoffing behind me. Later, to his wife, he'll call me a bitch and she'll wonder if she doesn't need to keep an eye on him the way the media outlets are warning. Is he running hot? *He's always been a dick, though,* she'll think. *He's no worse than most.*

The early April air holds the promise of a chill, the scent of the years' first incinerated leaves as the retired prep their gardens for spring. This time of the year was my favourite when I was a kid, how it cradled the hope of new beginnings, signified the end of the school year and two whole months without bullying. But, like everything else, the scent of fresh mud and the early buds on trees can deceive you. Whenever I get excited after a long and brutal winter, I remember that it's easier to be devastated when the air is cold enough to freeze you to death. Sadness in the spring doesn't quite fit. It's as if the sun himself mocks you. Nature itself spewing clichés like, "It gets better," and "You'll be okay. Get over it."

The sunset seems to be saying that now as it casts its golden hue on my forest green Cadillac—my first purchase that made Daddy proud. My mom can't help herself from asking if it's broken down yet whenever I see her. She doesn't understand what would ever compel me to buy something without airbags. She doesn't understand the tickling risk of not being saved.

"Excuse me!" a woman's voice cuts through the cool breeze and brings me back to adolescence, to years better off forgotten. Her tone changes as I turn, warms with a touch of excited surprise.

"Delilah! I barely recognized you with that short hair," she says, eyes on my dirty blonde curls that hang an inch above my shoulders, bangs that skim my brows. It used to be long, halfway down my back, but right before I moved away at seventeen, I hacked through it with dull kitchen scissors when the rage and humiliation and ultimately panic struck. I hoped it would make me ugly, but it only made me look reckless which in turn held even more sex appeal. When that fades, I'm not sure what will be left. The thought fascinates me as much as it terrifies me. Will it feel like freedom or will I feel completely purposeless when the sight of me doesn't immediately inspire all the ways my body can be used for pleasure?

Deborah stands before me, hips squared and eyes alight. An out of place slice of my past. I watch in slow motion as she waves a photo of Justin/Jamie/Josh in my direction. "You … you dropped this."

Shame rushes down my calves. It's like flipping through pictures on someone's phone and accidentally passing a nude. Deb has hit a nude. But worse, she is also travelling back in time down memory lane. Am I jarring her?

"Oh, thanks," I say, my shoulders caving forward in a weak ass attempt of concealing my nipples. I seem to lose my agency the second I'm around someone from my past, reverting almost immediately to a timid, troubled little girl. Women my mother's age have always had the power to make me feel completely exposed. Who am I kidding? Women of any age. Girls too. No one can be as cutting as an eight-year-old girl on a power trip. Cedar taught me to be cutting, but I always seem to lose my edge when it counts. I've never been tough like her. Cedar says I'm wrong. She says I'm tougher. I don't believe her.

I snatch the photo from Deb's hand just as she's flipping it over, reading the scrawl of black Sharpie on the bottom: **YOU DON'T OWN ME**. Through her eyes it seems petty, childish, an exposed journal entry. I tuck it into my plastic bag.

"Art project," I say, trying to dismiss the Polaroid as nonchalant with a wave of my wrist. "How've you been?"

She nods, muttering, "Good, good."

"What are you doing here?" I blurt.

My sense of anonymity feels mutilated as I study Deborah. People from our town so rarely leave.

She chuckles. "I have a date."

In her hand is a bottle of Strawberry Perrier, and I ponder if the city's appeal doesn't represent something similar to her: delighted invisibility. You can't take a shit in our hometown without someone speculating what you had for dinner the night before, and after Angela left her the rumour mill ran wild. I was only ten, so I probably didn't hear them all, but the most repeated was that Ang had met someone online and Deb caught her with a thick, purple dildo and a webcam. My dad even joked that Deb would be frequenting Carpet Land, seeing as she was the only rug-muncher left in town.

My mother always remained silent when my dad made his jokes, but a small smile crept across her face when I told him that my little brother Theo or I could be gay and asked how he would feel if he was inadvertently shaming us into silence. I had been fascinated with women since first hearing Joan Jett's cover of "Crimson and Clover" when I was six. I kept that part to myself.

Deb's hair is cropped shorter than it used to be too, salted with grey along her temples. She's dressed in a button-down shirt tucked into tapered jeans, her style forever 1990's sitcom dad whenever she's out of uniform.

I follow her gaze as she eyes the thin plastic of my bag. Justin/Jamie/Josh lies on his side, wedged between the condoms and the Cheetos.

"I always buy magnums. Manifesting my future, you know?"

I hate myself.

She cocks her head to the side, registering my words. I long to show her that men mean nothing to me. Sometimes I feel pathetic for loving them like I do. Cursed for being attracted to women and men yet always, always, always choosing men—or rather letting them choose me. For loving them more than women, more than I love myself. For allotting them more freedoms than I allow other women, more than I allow myself. For wanting, more than anything, for a man to love me, truly, completely. To protect me, to show me that I matter.

I want to say, "I can use them the way they use me. They are not in control." I think of the two times she drove me home in the back of her cruiser: the first, my voice slurred and angry, shoulders arched towards her, eyes filled with determination and fire, and the second, completely silent, my hands stinging from splinters, nails digging anxiously into the thighs of my slightly bloodied jeans, eyes cold and cast out the window at the quickly passing night. I like to think of the days when I was as young as Abby, before Deb eyed me with cautious pity. Before everything horrible happened.

How would her eyes change if I told her what I'd done that second night?

Would the pity finally end?

Would it be replaced with pride?

I hunger for the acceptance of women like a starving mutt. Their disdain foams in my mouth. My panting repulses most; the kindest still slowly back away in confusion, careful not to corner me.

She lets out a deep, chain-smoker laugh and averts her eyes from my purchases to my car, taking in a whistle of breath. "This is a boat."

I smile and nod, hoping she doesn't ask me something I don't know the answer to.

"Are you still a cop?"

Deb pauses as if she's going to say something profound and

important. That she's sorry that she couldn't help me. That she's doing her best to find all of these vanishing little girls, these disappearing women, and that she hopes I stay safe. That I was right all along: strange men do come to our little pocket of land to ruin our lives. The abandoned child inside of me longs to babble and coo and spill her guts. But I've never been cradled when I cry, so I square my shoulders and narrow my eyes.

"You betcha. Going on twenty years."

I want to ask her if she thinks she's making a difference. I want to know her best and worst memory. Instead, I smile and nod politely.

"I like what you did back there," she offers. It's my turn to cock my head. I think of making the cashier squirm.

"With the, uh"—she glances back at the plastic bag—"Cheesies."

A shiver of validation runs down my spine. I think of how I'd storm into Deborah's office every day after school demanding more, more, more until I no longer felt like I deserved to demand. Until one day something inside of me burned out. Until one day I found Cedar myself.

"She would be proud."

We stand there in a tense silence, nothing but the past between us. I open my mouth to speak, but can't find the words to say. I want to say, "How dare you bring her up?" I also want to say, "Thank you for not forgetting her." Mostly, I want to say, "I found her. She's safe. I found her." But I suppose we'd both know that that isn't exactly true.

"We don't use half our power, do we?" she continues. They're Cedar's words. Words I have since come to realize represent both a pro and a con, causing the usual, ever-persistent tightening in my throat that always comes before the panic. I have to go. Now.

"Thank you. For the Polaroid ..." I open my car door. "Maybe I'll see you next time I'm home. Have a good date," I add, trying to scurry into the driver's seat, be free of the moment, of the tunnel vision blurring the corners of my eyes, the nauseating airiness in my stomach.

"Can you imagine if we treated men the way they treat us?" Deb nods toward the man from the convenience store, who's struggling to get Abby into the car. Her voice is faraway and I can't help thinking of all that she's seen.

I remember an afternoon I spent at the station waiting for Deb. A new cop, early twenties, broad shoulders from high-school football, called Deb's name.

"You woulda wished you were on call today, Hurston!" he shouted at her from across the room.

A flash of annoyance flickered across Deb's features, but her voice was light enough when she said, "Oh yeah?"

"Car crash." His face gleamed in a smile that he didn't even try to contain. "Twenty-six year-old mother of two," he said, still beaming.

Deb remained silent.

The man held out his left arm and made a slicing gesture across his neck. "Semi-truck cut her head clean off." His voice was full of the excitement my father's hunting buddies had after killing as many deer as they possibly could. "Real shame too, her body was fucking amazing."

While Deb searched for the words, all I could think of were those two little kids, their crying faces juxtaposed next to hungry cops feeling up the dead woman's tits, running their hands down the curve of her waist. I dug my nails into my thighs.

"Thought you woulda liked to take a peek at her."

Even though I could sense that it wasn't sincere, even though I could hear the tinge of disgust, she laughed. A seed of hatred was placed inside of me then, and I hoped to one day watch her face crumble. I wanted to hear her call herself a failure. To admit that she didn't become a police officer to protect women, she became a police officer to have the power of men.

I left the station without talking to Deb that day. It all felt pointless, and I began to worry that she really wouldn't find Cedar. I wondered what the cops said about Cedar when I wasn't there, if they longed to find her body too, to gaze upon budding breasts and long legs. I wondered what jokes they'd make, if she would be considered a shame too or merely a casualty. My mother used to ask me why I was so focused on Deb when the cop shop was ninety percent men. Deb was the only one I trusted would care. Her failure stung the worst.

The Cheetos are no longer in the little girl's hands. What if I ran up to his car, banged on the window, and yelled, "Where the fuck are my Cheetos! Did having control of the *Cheetos* make you feel like a man? Does deprivation beget power?"

I do nothing, my attention pulled to the storefront window.

There's a series of tiny photos of girls and women plastered all along the glass. All smiling. The man probably doesn't even consider that his daughter could be one of them. The privilege is subtle and sinister. Most of the girls have dark hair and eyes. *If you have any information please call: 1-800-222-8477.* All I can do is think of Cedar.

"Please stay safe. I don't want to see your face up there," Deb says.

When I meet her gaze it's one of guilt.

I pretend to busy myself texting as I watch Deb from the corner of my eye. She gets into her car and peels out of the well-lighted lot. Only then do I slip on a pair of gloves and pull another

Polaroid from the console. Only then do I walk to the window covered with the faces of all of those missing girls and women. Only then do I tape it up beside that sea of snuffed out opportunity. The photo is of a man's neck, the top of his muscular chest. The stab wound is a dark burgundy gash that looks almost black. In the white space beneath I wrote: **ARE YOU NEXT?**

Cedar gnashes her teeth.

FOUR

THE CLOCK ON THE DASHBOARD READS 9:39. A SONG about being young and chaotic blares from the speakers. I focus on the fluidity of my body as I mouth the words, urging them to pull me from places I don't want my mind to wander. We're all better dancers when we're alone, aren't we? When we're free from the shackles of potential humiliation. Here, in my car, I can be whoever I want to be. The past and the future can melt away. It's only the eyes of others that complicate things.

Seeing Deb has left my nerves raw.

When my cellphone cuts through the tune. I think of rolling down the window, of whipping it hard and fast against the cement, like a cigarette butt. Cedar always asks, *Why don't you do what you want to?*

The ringing stops. It starts again.

Nothing but streetlights and empty road stretches in front of me. I want to drive and drive and drive until I can become someone new.

"Hey, Ma, sorry I can't really talk. I'm on my way to work."

"You work this late? Is that safe?"

She has this innate power to change my mood, to induce a storm in me, with the slight patronizing tone of her voice. My mother is the magician—she alters my perception of self, making me feel little more than a child. I am merely her assistant.

"Have you talked to your brother? He's really nervous about the virus."

The real reason for the call. To check on Theo. For a second, I think of telling her what I've really been up to. To steal the spotlight from my younger brother once and for all. To hear her voice change from surprise to panic to what I'm not entirely sure. I want to tell her that I am capable of so much more than she's expected of me. I want to tell her that I am not weak, I am not delicate. Maybe, more than anything, I want her to be proud of me. Yet my longing for her love is a weakness too. I know it is.

No one can slice me in half the way she can. One glance and suddenly I'm reeling, awash with guilt and rage and longing for a drink, anything to escape my reality. She says it's all in my head. My dad says my generation has gotten too soft, falling apart if someone looks at us the wrong way. She tells me I need to learn to let things go. How convenient after a lifetime of making me relive every hoarded emotion so I can properly play therapist.

According to my mother, I've always been difficult. Dramatic. Selfish. She says I came out of her immediately judging the world around me, completely dissatisfied. I screamed every night for six months straight, and she says she couldn't tell my actual crying from the ever-persistent echo in her ears. She was beginning to believe that neither her nor I existed. Sometimes she still hears it, waking her up from a dead sleep in the middle of the night with a jolt. I used to apologize. Now all I do is stare at her blankly, resisting the urge to ask her if she wants a hero cookie for deciding to bring me into this world in the first place.

Everyone told her the second baby would be easier. Everyone was right.

Theo came along when I was two, and I still cried more than he did. I was jealous even then, my tiny fists clenched while his rested open at the sides of his robin egg blue sleeper. One of my first memories of Theo is standing in the doorway of his nursery, my mother rocking him against her chest. I hoped that something horrible would happen to them both—him for taking her away from me and her for abandoning me so simply. I've never told her that, and if I were to, she'd insist, insist, insist that I manifested his fate. "How could you?" she'd cry, as if I ran over him myself.

She'll never forgive me no matter how much I beg. I wish she would simply admit it. *I love you, but I'll never forgive you.* I think if she said that, I'd be able to breathe a breath I've been holding for seventeen years. She'll never say it. She likes to believe she's a woman capable of forgiveness. She likes to believe that she's a good Christian.

I once told someone how I really felt, and they told me toddlers don't have a sense of the darkness of this world. They had that same look in their eyes as my mother: *you're being dramatic.*

My naive hatred was no match for Theo. When my father insisted I sit on the couch and hold the baby, I was a goner with one glance into his dark blue eyes. His flushed cheeks wrinkled as he looked up at me, his mouth a tiny half smile. I held his hand in mine and sat in awe as his palm curled around my finger. If I wasn't already in love with Theo, I would have tossed him from my lap onto the cold hardwood floor when my father chuckled and said, "See, Lilah? He isn't so bad." But I was already in love.

Yet as much as I love Theo, my envy never completely vanished. If anything, as time went on, I just found more reasons to be jealous. Forever calm and sweet, my brother was also naturally funny and intelligent. He was free to play while I sat studying the same math equation over and over and still feeling as confused as I had been when I started. Friends gravitated towards him while people always seemed slightly repelled by me, as if something about me made them uneasy. When Theo got older and more popular, he could have treated me cruelly to launch himself even further up the social chain, but he never did. He was just as sweet as a ten-year-old as he was as a newborn, and it's that which I think makes it sting all the worse. This knowledge that bad things happen to the truly good while the bad go on unscathed.

"I'm almost to the office. There's a project I have to catch up on." I wish I had a flask in my middle console that I could chug before driving my car into the girthy trunk of a tree.

"Okay. I love you, honey. Call your brother, k?"

And report back to me. That's the part she leaves out. I haven't talked to Theo in over a month. When I text him, he avoids me and then will suddenly message out of the blue, never acknowledging the unanswered messages. Sometimes he says we avoid him (not true). That none of us have ever fucking managed to treat him the same as we used to (extremely true). His mood swings come on strong, a sudden change in tone and a hand slapping a table. My mother hushes him as if he were no more than a baby. It must be strange for him, being silenced so late in my life when he never cried as an infant.

He only lives down the street from our childhood home, a single-bedroom apartment over a garage that his disability cheques pay for. His living room window overlooks the bend in the road that changed his life forever. Whenever I ask him if he's thought about moving, he says no.

I try not to think of him overcome with rage, sweaty and chilled with fever. I like to think that his hypochondria will keep him safe, but no one knows what's causing it yet.

I toss my phone onto the passenger seat and watch as it bounces and falls to the floor.

My teeth clench around my index finger until I picture the flesh tearing, bone snapping, mouth filling with a rush of hot blood. I set my hand beside me on the seat and turn hard into the dingy parking lot.

My mom is right. I should call Theo.

FIVE

KNOWING FEVERISH MEN HAVE BEEN LASHING OUT AT
women at a higher rate than ever before, and that this male
violence has finally tipped the scales for what has forever been
considered *normal,* I think of buying out tonight. Of sitting at the
bar nursing a tumbler of scotch for dominance, sipping a glass of
wine for class, or twirling the cherry garnish from my sex on the
beach to prove that despite the subtle lines on my forehead I am a
helpless little girl.

But then he walked in and I craved a pedestal.

Ian.

The past, as much as you try to block it out, always finds you.

Jesse knows what song to play when I give him that look. I
hope it says: *I want to be a whore of biblical proportions. I want to be a
whore with the power to start a war.* But it might just say: *I'm kind of
drunk.*

I think of Ian making the hour drive to rescue me. To right his
wrongs. To love me. I picture him leaving without so much as a
text to his wife, letting her wilt and worry all alone. The little

voice in the back of my head won't shut up. It says he feels for Alice—this woman he *chose*—in ways that he'll never feel for me. He sees value and beauty and strength and substance when he looks at her. He sees purpose, the mother of his child. With me, he sees a release, a convenience, an ego stroke. A girl who will never stand up for herself and lets him come and go and do whatever he pleases, only reaching a breaking point sometimes after too much wine. But those nights don't count. The wine always reminds me of who I wanted to be and sets her beside who I am, mocking the differences with a crooked finger. I always take it too far and then apologize over and over and over as my anxious mind repeats, *He's never going to speak to you again.* But Cedar says, *You need to get a grip. When did you become this weak?* I know, like so many other things, I make this more complicated than it needs to be. With me, Ian sees someone he can fuck however he wants to. The little voice says, *Don't kid yourself. He fucks Alice however he wants to too.*

He's just one of those men that takes with such an air of confidence you convince yourself that it was your choice to give. You don't question it until you're once again alone, the essence of him a steady drip on a hardwood floor, one that will eventually rot it all the way through.

Sometimes I tell myself he'd love me if I let him close enough to know me. If I gained enough courage to be authentic and charismatic and the person I know deep, deep, deep down that I can be. *Love doesn't work that way,* the little voice says. *In order for someone to love you, they must respect you first.* Cedar says I make it too easy for him, that my desperation for love has always left me selling myself short. *Who hurt you?* she asks, as if she doesn't already know.

Ian sits far from the stage, asserting his dominance. He raises his hand in the air, signalling Chloe for a drink, and makes a point to stare at her tits.

While scientists struggle to keep up with an influx of information and hospitals fill with feverish men who have begun to thrash around as their skin breaks out in pus-filled blisters, other clubs have chosen to close. Some have been numbering their dancers instead of sticking with the tried-and-true tradition of stage names. Hera, our house mom, is heavily considering it for Club Eros.

"Maybe it will stop the men from getting too attached," she says, as if it's our names—all of which are names of Greek goddesses—that makes them fixate on us, lurking in parking lots and desperately trying to find out who we *really* are via social media.

Our names were her idea. She wanted Club Eros to be different. Her story was one of comeuppance, starting to dance as a high-school dropout at only sixteen thanks to a fake ID and eventually saving up enough to buy the club herself when the previous owner got nabbed for drugs and tax evasion. She prided herself on being a female entrepreneur who would protect her girls in ways she had never been protected herself. Thus, we goddesses were born. Before she was Hera, she was Bambi, and she says that the men saw a victim as soon as the name left her glossed lips. She didn't want any of us to be perceived as malleable, even if our livelihoods were based on being soft, sexy, mysterious, submissive, dominant—whatever the man in front of us needed us to be.

"He might disrespect an Ashley, but not an Aphrodite," she told me on my first night, showing me a list of names to choose from. "All of my girls have stage names that command respect and adoration."

And now, nearly eight years later, she's deeply considering switching from names to numbers. Hera doesn't meet my eyes when she says, "Maybe it will be for the best." She knows, like we all do, that stripping us of our names will essentially strip us down to nothing. Maybe she also realizes that she was wrong: a man will just as easily disrespect an Athena as he would an Amber.

Stanley, Hera's husband of seven years, thinks Hera should wait it out. "Club Eros won't make sense," he says, "without its goddesses. What are you going to change the club's name to? Room 769?"

He laughs about it, but I don't doubt he shares in my fears. If the men continue to lose control, it will be on him to protect us by force. It's already on him to protect us, but usually that's just escorting the handsy drunks outside.

When Hera engages with Stanley at the club, she treats him as if he is little more than security. It adds to the edge she's worked so hard to curate since her days as *Busty Bambi, the sweetest girl you ever did see.* She knows that being too mushy over her man would open a window she doesn't want any of us peering into; we don't even know her real name.

Stanley's been saying, loudly, that Hera, of *all* people, should be seriously questioning whether these new government mandates are for *any* of our best interests. Hera was the one who taught him to question everything—and it's her fire that he loves —yet the threats of fines affecting her livelihood and increased taxes are shifting her thinking. Lately, a dull tension has begun to hang around my shoulders whenever I'm in their general proximity. The changes to the club, and ultimately the virus, has created a new kind of animosity between them that all of the dancers feel. It's scary, our workplace safety in the hands of a feuding couple while our everyday safety is in the hands of bureaucrats who think this will all blow over if we just cover ourselves up and stay home. Hera calls Stanley a conspiracy theorist both to his face and behind his back. They've never been anything but a united front, but now that she's disregarding our well-being—especially in the eyes of a male-dominated society which she so often condemns—the happy couple is at odds.

I've already been fantasizing about my life with a number instead of a name. Some of the dancers think the numbers are an easier way to lose ourselves. To disassociate in ways we've never fully been able to before. It's a fire most won't fucking play with.

It's a fire I want to be engulfed in.

The ultimate disappearing act.

If we can choose, I'll choose the number Six. I like how it hisses. Tonight, I'm still Bia. Still sweet and sensual and slightly boyish. The goddess of force. And, of course, he's still Ian. Still ravenous and entitled and beautifully unfaithful.

At first, I debated keeping my own name, Delilah—exotic, erotic, and biblical. Hera put her stilettoed foot down, tapping a long, cherry red nail on her list of goddesses.

"I don't want to bury you, honey," she said with tender eyes and a nod of approval at my chosen deity. I felt a wave of emotion tighten around my throat, but I swallowed it down and smiled back. Cedar remained silent. The option of being buried is a privilege often overlooked.

My song starts and I mouth along the words to a pretty young thing clutching a sweaty twenty-dollar bill, tilting my head back and smiling as he sets it at my feet. The truth is I like to make Ian slightly jealous, and he likes watching someone think they can take something that belongs to him only to snatch it from them at the last second. He is a cat amongst mice. We all have our power plays. When Ian's here we both know I'll be dancing for him even when I'm seemingly dancing for someone else. I feel his eyes on me now, smirking between tight sips of his beer. I drop to my hands and knees and arch my back like a cat with a flip of my hair. I like to think I'm a cat amongst mice too.

Ian moves closer, sitting in a chair directly in front of me.

I slowly stand, only to quickly bend over in front of him in a way that would terrify me if we were alone, both hands at the base of my ass. But I come alive amidst the whooping and clinking of glasses, controlling the room with a slowing and speeding up of my movements, like the lunge of a snake, the flick of a tail. I caress the backs of my thighs and look over my shoulder, locking with his dark, unwavering eyes. I think of his cock hardening in his jeans instead of the way his averted eyes make me crumble. My greatest fear is that one of these nights I'll show up and he'll already be here, perched at the stage staring at someone else—or worse, coming down the stairs with a twinkle in his eye and one of the shiny eighteen-year-old girls at the end of his hand. He's always been the type to dangle my inadequacies in front of my face. I just hope he never does it here. The club is my safe place. The club is where I can be the best, most powerful version of myself. The club is where Delilah ceases to exist. I'm Bia.

Ian's silver wedding band shines in the purple and blue lights.

Maybe I'm no better than the little boys on the playground either, taking toys that are not mine. Don't we all want to possess something that can't truly be possessed?

He comes here most Friday nights, driving away from his real life. I like to think of myself as his home away from home. It sounds more romantic than it is. I slide back down to my knees and crawl towards him, sitting back to create the added illusion of hips and thick thighs that he loves. His mouth slowly parts, lips wrapping around the beer bottle. The image is seared in my mind as I lean all the way back until my hair skims the stage. I can roll over onto my shoulder, fanning my legs from side to side. This has become our foreplay. Dancing for him in front of everyone else. When I flip onto my stomach and grip the edge of the stage to slowly pull myself towards him, his eyes are dazed; it's the only time he truly looks fascinated by me, and if I could bottle it, it would be the only thing I would consume.

I'd shamelessly drench myself in it—his desire, his approval.

As the song ends and he stands, my stomach sinks. I can't let him see the pained rejection that will cloud my features if he turns to leave. The worst thing a woman can do is reveal her insecurities to a man, so I look instead to the hopeful eyes of the others and smirk before biting my lip, eyes downcast as if I'm shy. Then I run my tongue over my top lip as I look up, as if I'm confident. I can't look at Ian because sometimes he does leave like this, watching me silently without the hint of care or even a tip. A quiet dismissal that reminds me who is in control and who isn't.

But tonight, he does my favourite thing. My lips deepen their smirk as I watch him step to the stairs at the end of the stage, where he waits with a hand extended to help me down. I saunter slowly towards him, stopping for tips along the way, letting my eyes play upon the features of the other men. He likes to show people that I'll come when he calls, and I like to show him that I'm coveted. Of course, he only does these things when he feels like it. He never lets me get too comfortable.

SIX

With his hand wrapped around mine, I lead Ian upstairs to the room we've unceremoniously coined as ours. He stops me before I take the first step.

The headiness of desire has vanished, his expression sombre, eyes void of the glint he had in front of all of the other men moments before and much more frightening. He looks almost nervous, but not in a way that makes me feel as if I have him in the palm of my hand.

I offer him a smile and try my best to conceal my racing thoughts, willing my eyes to remain calm, clear. I take the first step, his clammy, calloused hand still in mine.

Ian looks at my forehead instead of my eyes, and I immediately picture him reading the expiration date between my eyebrows the way you would a carton of milk. But he doesn't pull his hand back or stop following me up the stairs. These little acceptances fill my lungs with a wash of relief. Every time with him feels like a second chance, a stab at redemption, an opportunity to show him that I'm worthy of love. Every time also feels full of the threat of the end, a finality that I'll play and replay as: The Last Time. It's constantly changing, water spilling through my clenched fingers. I want to ask him if he's afraid he'll get sick. Afraid of becoming something uncontrollable. Maybe he's worried that he already is. But he told me years ago that I'm his secret oasis, his little escape. I don't want to ruin it by talking about impending doom, the potential threat of his body betraying him. I don't want him to look at me as prey.

I pull the thick burgundy curtain closed, and the booth is immediately filled with tension. The set of his jaw, the emptiness of his eyes, the discontent writhing of his hands. I've never been able to garner what he wants the entire time I've known him. No matter how much time passes, I always revert back to the age I was when I first met him. The awkwardness that radiates off of me isn't sexy. It feels inexperienced. Virginal. On the cusp, just as I was years ago when I wrapped my body around his for the first time in that cool blue pool, back when he tasted like hope. My nerves exist only for him, like only he can reveal my innocence. Does he feel powerful knowing he turns me into little more than a girl?

I wish I would have signalled Chloe to bring us a bottle of wine as I watch him watching me. He looks at me like he's on the verge of saying goodbye. As if tonight will be the night that he finally tells me this ... whatever this is ... is over. I'm constantly scrambling between giving him too much and holding too much back, a desperate attempt at finding the balance that will keep him wanting me without getting so much of me that he becomes bored.

The cycle is vicious.

"Six," he says, reaching out his hands to clasp them around my bare waist. Lately, he's only been calling me Six. Never Delilah, never even Bia. I made the mistake of telling him about the potential name change after I'd had too much wine. Sometimes he makes me feel as if I'm losing my mind. I want to yell and scream and kick and tell him to call me by my name. To just give me this one single shred of decency. To give me the smallest inclination that I'm not purely part of his fantasy world, that I exist.

"Six," he whispers again, his voice raspy as if he needs to cough. I press myself down into his lap, my back arching and tiptoes sliding to the floor beneath me.

"You know what my name is," I say, staring down at his paper-thin eyelids with searching determination as I unclasp my bra and let it fall to the floor beside us.

"Six." His voice is still a whisper, a quiet power struggle.

"Can I touch you?" he asks.

"What do you think?" I whisper into his ear, my nipples grazing the soft cotton of his T-shirt.

He looks up at me then, eyes determined and heady with a hint of animal aggression. A flicker of threat.

"I want to hear you say it."

I lean myself back entirely, my fingertips teasing my nipples, head tipping back between his thighs as my hands slowly caress down my stomach to the top of my thong where I snap the elastic. My hands continue to move all along my body as I sit back up, grinding my pelvis as I say, "Yes."

He pulls me closer, his calloused palms inching up the sides of me until he cups my breasts. I can't help the moan that escapes my lips when he leans forward, sucking one of my nipples between his teeth and lightly nibbling. I'm hot and wet in his lap as I sink myself deeper, wishing I could disappear into him, that I could call his body home.

His hands slip down my waist and rest on my ass, where he squeezes and lifts me up and down and thrusts as if we're already fucking.

"Can I kiss you?" he asks, and my response is a wispy yes as his tongue swirls against my own, teeth nipping at my bottom lip. He kisses me until we're breathless but then abruptly stops. I'm panting, my hips still grinding up and down even after his have slowed to stillness.

I'm used to being looked at by men, but Ian has a way of looking at me that is totally his own. It makes me feel evil and powerful and addictive. A drug that has the potential to ruin his life. A bad little girl. A cocktease.

He looks at me as if he's in a dream, as if he didn't make the conscious choice to get into his car and drive an hour to get here. Any moment he'll wake, sweaty boxers soaked with cum. He's little more than a sleepwalker possessed by his need for me. Ian looks up at me as if I am a siren distracting him and pulling him into the dark crashing waves of the ocean. He is merely a sailor lost at sea while Alice sits at home with rocks in her gut and a child on her hip, twisting her wedding band until he returns.

It's always these moments that define what our night will become. I pull away from him, my feet finding the floor and carrying my body back, back, back.

"Come here"—he pauses, and I watch his eyes harden—"Six."

Ian reaches out and grabs me by the wrist, his entire hand clasping my fragile bones.

His eyes swim for a second in a silent apology, but as the tide picks up, he comes to the conclusion that I have created the storm. I am condemned by his gaze.

"Six," Ian says again, wanting me to beg him to stay, beg him to fuck me right here, right now. To tell him that this was all my fault.

But I won't. I hop off of his lap and turn around, pulling my G-string high up over my hips as I slowly bend over, letting my cold fingers travel to the slickness between my thighs. When I look back at him over my shoulder, he's back where I want him—the guilt and blame and shame and remorse have been stripped from his face. He is just a patron, and I am just a dancer.

For one brief moment I *am* only Six. No longer a girl or a goddess but a nameless vessel of desire.

It kind of feels the way I thought it would, the cozy comfort of disassociation. I like it.

I turn around slowly and let my fingers dip into myself, showing him how they glisten before placing them in my mouth.

"Can I fuck you?"

We're not supposed to fuck in the club, but I've never been able to tell Ian no.

"Only if you call me by my name," I whisper firmly into his ear as I lower myself back down onto his lap.

"Delilah," he whispers, voice deep and breathy—a moment of surrender as I ease him inside of me. His hair is long enough for me to grab a handful and when I do, I pull his head back so he meets my eyes. Right now, in this moment, the power is all mine.

He would give me anything during moments like this, and my fatal flaw is that I always think these moments will last. I move with him, dropping down with more force so he can get deeper, clenching myself around him as he does.

"I love you," he whispers into my ear, his hand on the back of my neck holding me tight against him.

"I love you too." My voice is husky in moments of pleasure. I rock my hips faster, letting my hand fall to rub against my clit as the orgasm ripples through me, my mind and body connecting and rewarding me.

"I'm going to come," Ian breathes, but I am too lost in my own world to pull myself off of him, and I feel the heat of him bursting inside of me.

We sit like that for a few minutes, bodies slack, breath beginning to slow. When I meet his eyes, the previous fascination has been replaced with impatience. I scoot back off of his lap, trying to keep from dripping. The difference in him in the seconds before and after orgasm are night and day. Even as he's coming, I see his infatuation with me slipping away, shivering off of him. And I know that his I love you was only said so he could hear it back.

"We need to talk."

These words, in this order, are my four least favourite words in the entirety of the English language. They are made exceedingly worse when combined with the sensation of his cum running down my thigh. The little voice in my head hisses, *Loser. Sucker.*

"You're going to have to give me a minute," I say with a bit of a laugh, exiting the curtained door and making my way to the dancer's bathroom at the end of the hall. My racing thoughts coupled with the booming music wafting from the main floor makes me feel dizzy.

I shut the door behind me and take comfort in the sound of the sliding lock. For a moment I rest my forehead against the door and close my eyes, taking one, two, three deep breaths. Ian hasn't changed—he's shown me that time and time again—and yet whenever given the opportunity, I jump towards him like a dog who's impatiently waited all day by the front door. A bitch.

Sitting on the toilet, boney elbows digging into soft thighs, I'm delirious. I look at my piss, stare at how his semen clumps together and sinks to the bottom. Fluffy clouds in a pale yellow sky. How we're separate, yet together.

The heat of the orgasm is still splattered across my neck, leaving a trail of pale red hives down to my chest. Swollen pink lips and hair that is perfectly fluffed. For a mere moment, before I meet my eyes, I feel beautiful, sensual. A creature deserving of passion. I cup the tap water with my hands and take a sip. When I look at myself again, it's her—it's Cedar—and she says that I am too old to still be this pathetic.

My eyes fall to the faucet as I switch the tap to hot, watching as it pours over hands that do not belong to me. Suddenly, the scalding registers and I pull back, slowly shutting it off and turning towards the door without another glance at the mirror.

I am radiant and Ian will see that too. I am radiant. I am radiant.

I am radiant.

When I get back, I will kiss him softly and ask if he wants to come over later. We'll order pizza and sit cross-legged in my living room, laughing as I rush through him with star power while we play Mario Kart on my N64. He'll tickle my back while we lie side by side, falling into the gentle clutches of sleep. I can hear him saying, "Good night. I love you," and his *I love you* is so much more meaningful because he isn't inside of me.

Ian's *I love you's* are no different than Justin/Jamie/Josh's *You're Beautiful's*. I'm the one who chooses whether or not to interject meaning into them.

But still, without fail, each time he says it, I reply with a desperate and relieved *I love you,* hopelessly reassuring that he only needs to give me the bare minimum and still I will love him.

I think of all the ways we lie to others in order to feel lovable. It's these thoughts that are truly dangerous—they say Ian and I are not so different. They hint at the possibility of us saving each other, of being able to make the other feel whole and worthy and pure. Interjecting layers and layers and layers of more meaning, building my own decrepit fairy tale. In my mind, in our own twisted way, we love each other.

I open the bathroom door and can feel the stupid smile playing across my mouth. This is the first day of the rest of my life. The crisp first sentence of a new chapter.

Distracted by my new beginning, I crash into Kara impatiently waiting for the washroom.

Kara and I used to be close once, but it feels so long ago now. It started with her ignoring me, but now I ignore her just the same, the fear of rejection causing me to always avert my gaze, strike up a conversation with someone else, anyone else.

"Excuse me," I say, my eyes on my toenail polish.

"You know your dude left, right?" I watch her lips, over-injected and coated in matte lipstick the shade of merlot. She knows who *my dude* is. She knows, from words I wish I could take back, what he means to me.

"What?"

Kara has always had the ability to disarm me. She's feminine in ways I've always lacked. She has the body we all want for Halloween and Christmas, and her skin gleams as if she's bathed in a milky temple of youth. She oozes sex even when she's fully clothed. I fear she has always been able to recognize how I look at her: not much different than how she's looked at by a man but with the added layer of jealousy atop attraction—as if I want to crawl inside of her to experience what it must feel like to be her.

She doesn't say more, just pushes past me, long brunette hair swinging behind her as she enters the washroom, leaving the scent of jasmine and cloves in the air. I take inventory of myself by way of a quick scan of my body before I push open the curtain. The possibility of humiliation has already shattered my confidence, and I hate the protruding of my stomach next to the extremely subtle curve of my boobs.

A small stack of hundred-dollar bills rests on the chair where Ian sat. The breath rushes from my chest as I grab the money, expecting it to morph back into the man I love or, rather, the man I wish could love me.

The money sets fire to the fairy tale I had been selling myself, one filled with love notes and road trips, movie nights and bacon cheeseburgers, delighted laughter at who we used to be compared to who we became, what we could become.

I wonder if Kara knew upon seeing me, or upon seeing Ian leave, that we had fucked. If she took note of my blotchy chest and raw lips. If the club will hum with talk of turning tricks and the classic *fucking slut* talk that too many of us are apt to spew behind each other's backs the first chance we get.

Tucking the five bills into the garter around my thigh, I race down the stairs, not caring who sees me as I run to the door, and scan the parking lot for Ian's pickup truck. I picture myself running out into the cold night, his money waving in my hand as if to pathetically shout, "Take it back! Take it back! I thought we were falling in love!"

The song switches to glam rock written for places like this. I head back to the locker room, ignoring the look Chloe shoots me from behind the bar. As I weave through the room, I don't idle at any of the tables of men who can't help but to turn their heads and let their eyes crawl all over me. I remind myself this is what I'm here for. This is what they're here for.

Cedar is laughing, and I long to slink to the floor, to clutch my ears and rock back and forth. To see which men are attracted to a woman coming undone. But I don't. I keep my head up and my stomach sucked in as I approach the freedom of the hallway, the bright white double doors of the locker room.

Ian's exit feels like a rush of air being knocked from my chest. A sob tries to work its way up my throat, waiting for someone to comfort me. For someone to look at the hollowness of my eyes instead of the curve of my hip.

I think of stopping at a table of smartly dressed, middle-aged men, of slinking myself down onto one of their laps just to spit into his tumbler of scotch and pour it into his mouth. To laugh in his face. To chuck the now empty glass against the floor and watch how it glitters in the purple and blue lights. I think of being both as seductive and as ugly as I possibly can be all at once, of smiling coyly at the flashes of fear and fascination, disgust and desire. I think of grabbing a piece of broken glass from the floor and walking calmly towards Kara, of slicing her smooth skin before slicing my own. Bleeding out as women scream and the men rush to their cars, wanting to be safely at home with their wives before the media crews get here.

Sometimes rejection makes me want to hurt those around me. Sometimes it makes me want to hurt myself. It always makes me want to inflict pain.

Cedar used to say that whoever caused us harm would have to pay. She said it with so much confidence it always convinced me that she knew some sort of secret, had some sort of trick up her sleeve. *Karma's a bitch, La-la-la-lilah,* she'd sing, tossing her long, jet-black hair over a frail shoulder. I long for an omniscient karma righting all of the wrongs I'm too afraid to right myself. Will I be righted too?

But I am a coward. I am as weak as Cedar says I am, so I do nothing except keep my head held high and eyes low as I make my way back to the locker room, wondering if Ian would attend my funeral while at the same time knowing that no, he wouldn't. He couldn't.

SEVEN

Mirrors line the walls of the locker room, and despite being around naked women constantly, I fight the urge to stare, to absentmindedly bite my bottom lip. In here, we're free of the arched backs and swaying hips. Here, we pick at blackheads and prod at our stomachs, the pooch of flesh that squeezes between our armpits and breasts, talking openly about how much it will cost to fix what needs fixing. The performance is over and leaves behind a dull vulnerability, a secretiveness over what we've each made. The money, that I am usually so proud of, feels dirty in my hands—an exchange that I did not agree to.

Even though the competitive air never fully leaves, in the locker room there's an insertion of reality that does not exist once we step out of this room and into our jobs. It's bittersweet, judging each other in ways that we all hope to never be judged ourselves while also feeling relieved that none of us here are perfect people with perfect lives. We've all been pushed, by circumstance or the drive to see how the darker aspects of society work. A longing to be welcomed into the underworld with open arms. Hello, Hades. Do you love to love me?

The longing for pure acceptance places me back in grade nine, changing quickly in the corner before gym class in an attempt to conceal every ounce of insecurity but knowing deep down that all I was doing was highlighting it. Othering myself even further. Cedar was gone by then; I would try to picture her soft palms on my cheeks, her sweet breath an inch away from my face as she told me that one day everyone would regret being cruel to me.

I've always judged myself harsher than anyone else ever could. It makes me untouchable—*Don't worry, you can't speak to me any worse than I speak to myself.* I'm responsible for the initial cracks that only let in more hatred.

Thinking of Ian seeing Kara as he was leaving makes my stomach twist. How her hourglass hips and spilling tits would look so lush after my almost childlike body. How even if he wasn't already feeling as if I wasn't enough, Kara's presence would highlight all of the ways in which I wasn't. But if he left without so much as a goodbye, he was already thinking that I wasn't enough. Paying me off in a way he knew would humiliate, in a way that would prevent me from following.

He was wrong.

I unfasten the buckles around my ankles and kick my white platforms beneath the counter, no longer wanting to feel the weight of them pulling at my feet.

Flipping my phone open, I scan the pixelated screen for a missed call, an apology text from Ian telling me to meet him outside now or asking if he can swing by my apartment later where we can make love on my balcony and drink hot cups of coffee as we watch the sunrise.

The call logs and little yellow envelope are both empty. The voice in my head laughs. *You're a loser, you're a loser, you're a fucking loser.* It's all I can hear. I ball my hand into a fist and want to smash the mirror where she resides, eyes alight, voice high and mocking. This girl I hate.

But as I look up with wild eyes, all I see is Lil walking towards me, dazzlingly beautiful and statuesque. Her voice pulls me away from the loathing of my own.

She looks down at my discarded heels with questioning eyes, a raise of her brows.

"Ya good?"

I giggle, as if she merely caught me lost in thought, zoning out.

I wish I was already in the silent isolation of my car, surrounded by the freedom of my own racing thoughts. Nails digging into flesh. Stomach writhing and threatening to spill its contents down the front of me. Lil's eyes soften as she watches me.

"Yeah, I'm fine, you?" The words come out too fast. I am an open wound, weeping with the pus of a burgeoning infection.

Lil lets me have this moment, even though I can tell she doesn't believe me for a fucking second.

"It was fun while it lasted, but you gotta stop giving your fuckboys my number once and for all." She sighs. "I opened a text in the grocery store today of a DICK. Derek almost smashed my phone."

I think of Justin/Jamie/Josh and feel another wave of shame. The fucking theme of the day.

Lil laughs, but her eyes are serious, dedicated.

Whenever I look at her there's a twinge of disbelief that I'm not staring at her on the cover of Vogue or National Geographic. She's striking in a way that looks wild, dangerous, completely unique and unattainable. Stunning like Cedar. Soft, honey brown eyes that dazzle with depth and mischief. She looks like she could take over the world. When she gives you a genuine smile, one that reaches her eyes, you feel as if you'd give her your life. Six-two in her heels with a jawline that threatens to cut me whenever I stare too long, she's better than Derek. A man who treats her as little more than an accessory. But those eyes shine just for him. They shine so bright I wonder what it must feel like to be him.

I started giving guys who I definitely never wanted to see again Lil's number out of a dull curiosity of what they would say. We would read them together and laugh. Then she would politely text:

Sorry, wrong number.

She loved it as much as I did, though for a different reason. She enjoyed living vicariously through my messy life and these messy men—the thrill of being single without the hopelessness of actually being single; I liked seeing how men talked to me without the anchor of needing to respond. There was always a risk that once I started playing the game of back and forth, I'd get attached if for no other reason than the dopamine rush of the message coming in, of measuring my responses, of waiting for the next.

Sometimes in a secret little compartment of my heart, I imagine Lil getting a perfect text. Something sweet and charming and just the right amount of hot on a day where she sees herself for who she is—powerful, radiant, intelligent, witty—after a fight with Derek where he made her feel pathetic, ugly, stupid, boring. It would finally click for her: she deserves better. It's manipulative, I know, but is manipulating for good the same as manipulating for evil?

"No, come on. We can't stop now. Someone has to keep Derek on his toes." I try to keep my voice light, but it still sounds childish.

Derek has been on a mission to get Lil to stop dancing. If it were purely risk related, maybe I'd believe it was for her safety, but his insistence started months before any hint of the virus. Last month, while Lil and I drank too much wine on my balcony, she whispered, "He says if I quit, we can start trying for a baby." Derek knows that the promise of a child is Lil's kryptonite and uses it as a pawn. Lil frets over how time seems to be speeding up the more she thinks about the life she dreams of. We've all heard her plot the years on a manicured nail. "School for two more years, then placement for a year, then we can start trying and hopefully I'll be having my second by twenty-nine, thirty tops." On nights when she's had a few glasses of wine to get through the hours at the club, she'll dab at her eyes as she whispers what age her firstborn would be. She takes the eighth of June off every year. Jayden's first birthday that he never made it to. To me, Derek's insistence is only about control, and it scares me. I'm afraid to lose her.

Lil rolls her eyes and grimaces. "I get it, ok? You don't like him."

It has long surpassed that.

"I mean he met you at the club," I say instead.

When you start stripping, you're always told not to date men from the club, yet we've all given it a whirl once or twice. But our initial sex appeal is quickly overshadowed by our normalcy. The fights always marred by whore and slut and gold digger in a way they never would be had they met us anywhere else. We call it an occupational hazard, but sometimes when we have a man between our tits saying he's never felt this way before we trust him. Later, he'll say, "I just couldn't fucking date someone all my buddies have seen naked."

If they fall hard, the first thing they'll ask is that you stop dancing. Derek says he'll pay Lil's bills the way all controlling men do. It predates the men we know so far back that it's not even truly their fault. Boys are only given the template for how to love their mothers, and when they fall in love with a woman, they want to turn them into their mothers. It's the only love and vulnerability they've truly been allowed to show. *And who would want their mom to be a fucking dancer, bro?*

Fucking a stripper boosts a man's confidence as long as he didn't have to pay for it. Dating one, though? Not so fast, bucko. You better turn her into a lady.

It's a slow death to have the men that put you on a pedestal take a sledgehammer to it. Deep down we want to believe he's breaking it down to rebuild it better. But we all know that's one of our favourite lies we tell ourselves. He'll leave us crippled. Lil is my only friend. I've never been a woman with many friends, always a person that people are intrigued by until they find themselves slowly backing away. I've let Lil scratch my surface, but barely. I've never even told her about Cedar. Or my father, my brother. I've even kept the most painful parts of Ian under lock and key, knowing that if I were to be completely honest, she would dismiss my pleas that she deserves better more than she already does. She would call me a hypocrite, and she would be right. It really feels as if it's too late to be completely myself now. For what it's worth, she thinks I started stripping to escape an abusive relationship too. Just like her. Just like so many of the women here.

Lil places her hand on her hip and looks me up and down. A shiver travels along my spine, as if she can see the sheen of semen that I meticulously wiped from my thigh. Suddenly, I feel inferior in my floor-length, satin, feather-cuffed robe that I ordered online at four in the morning when no amount of wine or weed would help me sleep. All of these addictions do nothing to satiate the bottomless pit of me.

I think of Justin/Jamie/Josh and feel a sudden yet acute sadness for myself that despite how reverently he tucked my hair behind my ear this morning, the first thing he sent was an unsolicited photo of his cock. Why am I surprised? If you let them in once, it feels almost impossible for them not to believe they own it.

The thought is highlighted by Lil saying, "I swear to God the guys in this club are better than the ones you take home. How in the hell is that possible?" For a split second her words feed my flood of self-hatred, but then she adds, "Gary came here straight from work again today, wah." She wrinkles her nose in disgust, and we're once again levelled.

Gaia and Bia.

Goddesses dancing for men who can't always be bothered to put on deodorant.

Goddesses who soon will be dwindled down to only numbers.

"I thought you loved that musk?" I ask, laughing as she zips her sweater up to her neck.

She sits down and piles her long, extension-riddled hair into a messy bun looking like royalty as she eyes me in the mirror.

I think of the days when we first met, leaving the club with our wallets full of cash. Our actual names still a secret from one another; I called her Gee and she called me Bee for nearly a year. We'd eat Whoppers and chicken fries in the Burger King parking lot and ugly laugh over how the men that worshipped us would never get to see us with mayonnaise dripping down our chin.

They'd never see us with anything dripping down our chin. Sometimes we talked about how our very livelihoods made it more difficult for all women, ourselves included, in the plight for love. On the edge of society, we were the threats.

I never told her about my dad's first affair. It felt Freudian and I couldn't quite stomach the disgrace of saying it out loud. I was only twelve when my dad told us he was in love with a stripper. Back then the idea of people taking off their clothes for money inspired little more than giggles. But after, my eyes would forever linger on windowless buildings, fascinated with these creatures of the night who had the power to destroy a family. These off-limit women who curated three of the most driving forces: lust, shame, love.

My parents think I work in an office, but my mother has always been famous for saying that everything comes out in the end. I'm not surprised my father chose a stripper. He'd always say that men are hogs but still asks, "Why do women wear yoga pants if they don't expect us to fucking stare?" He can't fight that deep down he believes we exist for them. That his own daughter isn't even safe from his belief that a woman's worth lies somewhere on the surface like a price tag.

My biggest fear has always been that I will turn into my mother—a man's comfort and home-cooked meals while he couldn't be further from mine. Meeting someone else's needs while completely neglecting my own. Yet there's this pull towards the only domestic life I've ever seen. One with a quiet, lonely woman grasping at straws and a robust man who always leaves her with the shortest one as if they're forever playing a rigged game.

I want to belong to no one while simultaneously being a man's whole world.

"You good, though?" Lil asks.

I think of the booth and how if I were to fuck someone for money, I would fuck them for more. Teenage girls sell their virginity, staking a claim on their worth knowing that it's only a thinning piece of tissue that keeps them from depreciating. Five hundred seems ugly, lowly, laughable. A slap in the face.

Ian's asked before if I turn tricks. I always tell him no, sometimes flimsily with a flirtatious giggle, more often firmly with unwavering eyes. He has to be my first for everything. He has to humiliate.

"Something really fucked-up just happened," I find myself saying to Lil before I give it a second thought, the words containing all of their hard edges.

Lil turns fully to face me, the humour in her eyes replaced with concern.

I'm retracing my steps, remembering how I felt special as Ian took my hand. Suddenly, I see the scenario through the men's eyes—Ian's alpha move to take me upstairs, to fuck me, to leave without saying goodbye as if the money redeemed him of any obligation. It reminds me of something a friend of his said when we were still in high school. "Ian uses girls to bust a nut. He calls them practice girls."

For a chronic overthinker, I pushed the words out of my head fast. I didn't even ask for clarification. Maybe because I knew he was only using me until he found the safe, sweet, simple woman he'd marry.

Over a decade wasted trying to make him eat his words, when in actuality it's just been a decade of letting him get away with whatever the fuck he wants to do.

I get so lost in seeing things how I want to see them that sometimes I never stop and look at things for what they actually are. Dismiss, dismiss, dismiss. I've lost track of my own life while being preoccupied with Ian's coming, his leaving, waiting for apologies that will never arrive.

"Ian?" Lil asks.

"I'll tell you later. It's stupid," I mutter, feeling eyes on me, voices on the brim of branding what kind of woman I am.

"You went upstairs with him, no? Is he okay?"

She's thinking it's the virus.

I'm wishing it was.

That the reason he took me upstairs was to tell me he felt sick. That he wanted to tell me goodbye and that he loved me in case this was his last chance.

Embarrassment passes over me like a cloud as I think of him calling me Six again and again and again. The rage boils up from my belly, only to be satisfied when I finally destroy him and everything he's ever wanted for his life. When he pays for all of these little and big humiliations. I will show him just how capable I am.

Ian has branded me without my permission, making me pant and beg and backpedal hoping that one day the tables will turn and I can get revenge once and for all. That one day he will want to love me and I will deny him.

I watch like a cornered animal as Lil widens her eyes expectantly, urging me to continue. Too embarrassed to tell her the truth, especially here of all places, I just sigh. She'll say what she always says: "You need to be done with him." Just as I tell her she needs to be done with Derek.

If I don't end it when the wound is fresh, it'll scab over and I'll convince myself that I played just as equal of a part in this charade as he has. That we're both cruel to each other. It's easier to believe that than stomach the truth. The lie grants me agency. He uses it to silence me, and worse, I let him.

When he comes back (will he come back?) he'll flag me over, tucking money into the string on my hip. He'll follow me upstairs without any sort of greeting. He'll call me Bee instead of Dee. And as we play this game of power, that's not unlike all of the other games we play, I'll convince myself that deep down, deep, deep, deep down he loves me. I'll convince myself that he wants to be done with me just as badly as I want to be done with him, but that we Just. Can't. Seem. To. Shake. Each. Other. Off. It's so romantic when I put it like that.

Cedar says I'm fucking weak. I fear that she's right. I am weak. Fuelled by self-loathing and a lack of willpower—or maybe, more pathetically, by hope.

A ragdoll forever pulling at the hem of control, never quite grabbing hold.

Sometimes I worry that the only thing I've mastered in this life is being docile. Ten thousand hours of silence and pretty smiles, extinguishing all remnants of who I once was, who I could have been.

Even Cedar has control of me most of the time. I'm still not sure if her control is to keep me safe or to convince herself that she has agency over her own life. If she's just someone else I'm letting live vicariously through me or if I've finally lost my mind the way I've always expected I one day would.

I pull myself back to Lil who's been overcome with the confused look that many people give me when I retreat to the make-believe world of my own mind. I mould my face into a big, fat, fake smile and add a curtsy for good measure. I think of being brutally, humiliatingly honest, of telling her that I just fucked Ian and when I went to the washroom and came back, he had left money by way of goodbye. I want to watch Lil's beautiful eyes go from surprised to full of pity to enraged. But at the same time, I really don't want to see any of those things, the things that will reaffirm my self-pity, fuel my self-destruction. What's worse is the possibility that she'll say I brought it all on myself.

"I think I'm done with Ian."

Lil's face cracks into a smirk, silently mouthing, "Okay."

She pauses, waiting for me to continue. When I don't, she asks, "What brings on this awakening?"

I think of pulling the curtain, of seeing the quaint little stack of hundred-dollar bills and the ache that it spoke to inside of me. I think of him driving away, driving home, with the scent of my perfume still on his clothes. I try to picture what station he'd listen to, if he'd drum his fingers along to the tune or if his journey would be one of silent contemplation. Maybe it would be neither and he'd casually find himself wondering what Alice was making for dinner, what he'd watch later on TV.

Maybe he'll fuck her tonight too, after a shower, of course.

Maybe I only exist for him in the moments that he wants me to.

"I think I'm getting too old to be fucking someone's husband," I say smugly, and the words do what I want them to do—they portray that I am the one in control.

"Ya think?" Lil says with a snort that makes me feel accepted opposed to judged.

The reality of never truly being seen causes a flutter of panic in my chest. I try to remind myself that I always come to regret the moments where I step out into the light, where I demand people to look at me, to fucking open their eyes.

"Besides," I say, my voice full of playful charm, "I have a date."

Lil knows me well enough to recognize the octave change in my voice, but she lets me have it.

"All done with dick pic?" she asks, waving her phone in my direction with a laugh.

How did Justin/Jamie/Josh expect me to respond to an image of his dick? I should have given him my actual number so I could spend lonely evenings building him up, breaking him down.

Nodding, I roll my eyes and it's honest: no part of me ever wanted to sleep with him, but I was bored and the night is long and alcohol is so freeing until it's not.

"Who's your hot date?"

His name is Jackson, but I leave that part out, in case he winds up missing. Tomorrow, I might tell Lil that he stood me up. This rage needs a home. It feels as if all I've been doing since twelve is trying to find a home for this rage and still it overfills space like a hoarder. Jackson is attractive in a subtle way that hasn't let him become too full of himself. I didn't get the chance to read him.

"I met him a few days ago … he was behind me at the bank."

She playfully pokes her head to the side to look at my ass, rolling her lips down and raising her eyebrows. "Does he know that you're an *accountant*?"

We laugh as if it's only us left in the room, but almost as if on cue, Kara walks in, cold and flawless and judgmental.

"He didn't ask. Just complimented my sundress and asked for my number."

"Phone or cattle call?" At the moment, we've been laughing off the looming numbers, making jokes about their ability to dehumanize us. I thought laughter was the best medicine, but my old therapist, on a day where he chose to actually do his job, told me that my self-deprecating humour was only highlighting my insecurities. "Delilah," he huffed, "you're announcing to the world: you can treat me however you want to treat me!"

"Phone," I say.

At the bank, I could feel Jackson's need to make conversation scalding into my back. We can instinctively feel a person staring at us from the days when we were hunted. Built-in gaze-detection to protect us from perceived threats. Instincts that have never left because we've never truly stopped needing them.

Jackson was watching.

They usually are.

As the world panics in news snippets, I feel more and more grateful for the instinctual anxieties women have never evolved from, that we've never been free to evolve from.

These instincts that will hopefully give us an edge.

"I think she can take you over there," Jackson said, as if I couldn't see the teller waving as she hustled back to her desk, hair pulled tightly to the nape of her neck, face free of makeup. I began to walk towards her without looking back, just to feel the weight of his lost moment fall to the floor. I turned five paces in, making sure my hair swung as I did, and offered him a smiling thank you. Women like us are becoming a thing of the past.

He cleared his throat the way all men do when you catch them off guard, when you catch them being boyish, when you catch them in a lie.

He called me sweetheart the way my dad calls checkout girls honey.

I'm not sure if he's good yet, but Cedar tells me he isn't. I believe that he could be. I am forever wavering between states of distrust and over-trust.

"Sundresses are like crack to these men. We should seriously consider wearing them here," Lil says, and I can't help looking around at all the mesh and G-strings, picturing us all in-nearly knee-length florals looking as off-limits as bridesmaids. She might be onto something. Maybe our assigned numbers will only work against us; we could trade Persephone and Venus for Mary and Rebecca—names of the good wives. The thought crumbles as quickly as it enters my head. If men viewed us as chaste, getting naked would make them uncomfortable.

"Their heads would explode from the Madonna-whore complex. In a sundress at the bank, he can pretend I've never seen one up close," I say with a smirk and a swoosh of my robe.

"Just be careful." Lil's voice is suddenly stern. She's seen it all. And yet it's about to get worse."Haven't you been watching the news? Is this really the best time for your weird little dates?"

Lil doesn't even know about the Polaroids, and I wonder what she would say if she saw photos upon photos of body parts. These men who really don't mind being my subject as long as I don't include their face. Some have been forced into silence after the photos have been taken—I've made myself the judge, jury, and executioner, and the funny thing is the unlucky ones never see it coming. They never view me as a threat until it's much too late. I say unlucky as if they didn't create their fate, but they did. Oh, how they did. The fear in their eyes is a drug.

Only one of them, one of the lucky ones, one of the good ones, has brought up the pictures in an uneasy text to Lil:

You deleted those pics, right?

She laughed and laughed and begged me to show her the nudes. Which I brushed off as an invasion of privacy, technically a crime. I could tell she didn't buy it, but she dropped it anyway.

The canister of pepper spray Lil gave me last month still

resides in its plastic casing on my bedroom floor. "Don't think these new laws will protect us," she said. "They won't stop until we're declawed."

"I'm always careful," I say, looking her directly in the eye. I would never tell her that there's a thrill that shivers through me when I think of putting myself in danger. When I think of people having to search for me, wondering if anyone would bother. Maybe this fear has nothing to do with me but instead with those who'd pace the floor crying over the last words they said to me. The ones who'd show up at my funeral with flowers and an ache in their gut.

Sometimes I think of being pushed to the point of survival, of having to come out on top. Of how I've tried to make the world a better place by taking it upon myself to cut the fat, to rid the streets of these men who only bring harm. There are just so many men who bring us harm.

I think of the men I've let leave the club and shudder. I think of the men I've killed, and I shiver.

Lil kisses me on the forehead before she heads back out onto the floor.

"Go home, babes, you look like you've seen a ghost."

EIGHT

I light Ian's favourite candles—pine and frosted cranberry—as if he's coming over. Even when he's not here I think about what it would be like if he were. They smell like Christmas and make him feel like a kid. It's these small shreds of humanity that keep me clutching onto him. Hoping that one day he'll let me know him. That one day he'll care enough to know me. I'll feel seen and wanted and understood. I can't count the number of times I've begged the people I love to look at me. I can't count the number of times that they've refused.

Yet I can't give up hope. If Cedar truly sees me, someone else will be able to too. The greatest effort someone can make is to take the time to understand you. To see you.

Cedar says my ability to go undetected is a blessing. She says the world was built around overlooked women. We are the salt of the earth, our blood its essence. We have learned to slink unnoticed, to be everywhere and nowhere. In it lies our strength. *You just have to choose it,* she whispers. She always wants more, more, more.

Instead, I find myself thinking of a world where Ian and I are in love, where my flaws are quirks. A world where the box of photos in my closet doesn't have to exist. An alternate reality where neither of us are monsters. It's a fantasy that always leaves me feeling emptier than before, but I can't seem to stop it from reoccurring. I've buried myself in it.

He'll never see it coming, Cedar whispers, but I'm not sure what she's talking about, and I don't ask for clarification.

I put The Byrds' "Turn! Turn! Turn!" on vinyl. I rescued my vanity from an apartment that stank of cat piss, lugging it down three flights of stairs, only breaking one bulb on the way. I had high hopes of it making me feel gorgeous yet devastatingly haunted, like that old picture Nan used to have of Marilyn Monroe, but instead it just helped illuminate the large oil-filled pores on my nose. I light a cigarette and watch my mouth as I smoke it, trying to pout my lips so they don't lose their lush. The building is non-smoking, but my landlord doesn't care as long as he gets the rent on time. His eyes always linger on mine a little too long, just long enough for me to know that if I made a move, he'd accept it. I picture fucking him monthly in exchange for my rent after he catches me masturbating on the couch when he stops by to fix the sink. Sometimes my mind wanders to the idea when I'm touching myself, and then after I've come, I ask myself: what the fuck is wrong with you?

As my mind traipses off to sordid fantasies, I bite my lip, my eyes sparkling as if I'm staring into a flame. I don't like that these fantasies often involve someone degrading me, making me feel worse than I already do, but I like the way thinking about it makes me look.

"I love you," I whisper into the mirror, my voice at once sweet and husky.

Cedar's eyes squint and I watch my hand grasp for my glass of makeshift rosé, feeling the clunk of it sliding down my throat.

You're a fucking loser, Cedar says, and I believe her.

We're opposites. She detests what I view as the best parts of myself.

The record begins to skip.

I let it, jolting up to yank open the closet door to peek at the possibilities. My other sundress, the one Jackson hasn't yet seen, is pale pink with dainty periwinkle blue flowers, mint green leaves. It falls a little shorter, mid-thigh. I bought it in high school when my hymen was still intact, before I knew that men can change your composition. Back when I thought that I would be different, I would be *better*, stronger, more powerful than all the women before me. It was this kind of thinking that weakened me the most, thinking I could rewrite the rules. Fuck as boys fucked. Twist and dip and writhe and claim whatever I wanted to claim. Have nothing stick to me. Boys—men have this innate ability to avoid judgment. We can know these horrible things about them and yet when they come into the room, they're allowed to be whoever they want to be. They aren't wearing their past the way ours is seemingly tattooed on our skin. They are not the people they fuck or the people they hurt. They are not the size of their clothes or the length of their hair. They are allowed to just be. My most foolish thought was the one where I told myself that I could break the mould, as if the blood that courses through my veins isn't that of all of the women before me who once shared the same juvenile thoughts: I will be better than other women.

It's those thoughts that fuck us up from the start.

I try not to dwell on it, the fact that I'm not the person I wanted to be.

Cedar reminds me to stop being selfish. A change of course is our inheritance.

Sónnhe. *You're alive.*

Besides, how many of us can say we are truly who we wanted to be? This world has its way of shaping us.

Now the government is saying that ABOVE ALL ELSE women should stay covered up. They say it's for our safety, but it feels deeply reminiscent of that day I wore a crop top in high school and was immediately sent to the principal's office and given his dusty cardigan from the back of his chair with the order to button it up; I walked around all day feeling scolded. It feels uncomfortably close to the days of asking women what they were wearing after they were raped. Of fining and imprisoning them for getting an abortion. Of telling us, without telling us, that whatever happens to us is ultimately our fault. That a pregnancy after a rape is an opportunity to learn love and forgiveness. It possesses all of the disregard for men and their impulses and evils. I am reminded of a cougar at the zoo, how it stalked back and forth, back and forth in its too small cage, its breath a huff, its eyes never leaving my body. But we are in the cage and the men are watching, and we are told whatever you do, don't fucking tempt them. They can come and go as they please. We are in the cage.

Don't ask for it.

I get dressed facing the bed, twirling back towards the mirror like I'm someone special.

Cedar doesn't think I'll fool anyone, that I've never captured her spark. My confidence is a cheap facade. I like the attention, but there's no substance behind the statement.

You need to prove yourself, she says.

I don't know Jackson, and she doesn't know him either. He

could be good. I always want to believe that people are inherently good. That we all start out good. That at the end of the day, all we truly want is to *be* good, but Cedar says this world was set up as a playground for men and that being good isn't any fun. Why be good when you have the freedom to be everything else, when the world is stretched before you like a long table of food, ready to be sampled and devoured and wasted and spoiled?

The world is a sea of opportunity for cis, heterosexual men.

And in order to capture the opportunity, you have to keep your eyes open, hands ready to snatch all of the moments that will come your way.

She says that even the good ones are still opportunists.

I should know that, the way men reach for their favourite parts of me after I've told them they can look but can't touch. How the *no* somehow makes them want it even more. How they giggle as if they can't help themselves. How they sigh. How they beg. How they touch. How they take.

I snap a photo, arm outstretched, smiling with everything but my teeth. It falls to the floor and I leave it, letting it develop facedown. The wine tampers with the edges of my brain. I picture black ink filling the folds. Wine is bad for me, I know it is, but it is also the only substance I've tried that lets me fully sink into myself until I feel whole. Until I fully accept myself for everything that I am. Cruel and desperate and hopeful.

My nan made me promise that I'd never try hard drugs, and I've never broken it. I'd love them. I'd get lost to them. I long to be one with the shadows, but Nan always called me her light.

The year before Nan died, she told me I should be cautious of my drinking. I was thirteen and met her words with an obnoxious laugh despite the tinge of acidic vomit on my breath. "I'm no quitter," I said, feeling cocky and dangerous and alive. It sounded like something Cedar would say, and I saw the realization flicker in Nan's eyes as she regarded me with a small bit of sympathy. Suddenly, I felt too young, as if everyone I came in contact with could see the naivety of a rebellious child grasping at the straws of independence. I felt pathetic.

I ruffle my hair and smile as if I believe I'm beautiful.

What the fuck are you doing? It's my voice but it's fleeting. I think of the many directions the night could go. Mostly, I think of Jackson looking at me and feeling as if he's won the lottery. I'm reminded of overhearing a table of men at the club talking about fucking insecure girls with daddy issues, someone muttering, "Ding, ding, jackpot."

"All she wants is someone to reaffirm the shitty things she already thinks about herself."

I wanted to stop by but didn't, twisting the thought around in my brain and wondering if it was true. If in actuality I wanted someone to push my face down into the dirt to make me feel as small and insignificant as I've always felt.

To hold me like Jesus and fuck me like Judas.

Once, when I was still convinced we were falling in love, Ian told me to stop being a cocktease.

To the average person, being called a cocktease might have made them walk away, but to me it felt comfortable in its familiarity where cruelty was care. It made me feel useful; he wanted something from me and he wouldn't think twice about belittling me to get it.

I was always trying to see what I meant to Ian but was too stupid to realize that he was always showing me.

Dropping to my knees, I'm greeted by the sting of the carpet as I flip over the photo. My mouth is smiling but my eyes are empty. I scribble: **DON'T BE A COCKTEASE.**

NINE

The lights of the city blur past the rain-covered window. My gaze settles on the cabbie's credentials hanging on the back of the passenger side seat. His name is Carl. Who names their child Carl?

He meets my eyes in the rear-view mirror as I tell him that he must, must, must try Johnny's Pizza with extra sauce and the garlic crust. The wine and my nerves have left me giddy. I don't ask him if he's ready for the end of society as he knows it. I don't care if he's feeling feverish.

"You're really pretty," he blurts as my eyes fall to my freshly-moisturized thighs, where my phone rests open. Ian never texted.

"Thank you," I say as monotone as possible, trying to be curt instead of coy to avoid giving him the wrong impression.

"Drinks with your friends tonight?"

"A date."

"Ouch," he says as if we were already on one.

Men like this will always take their opportunities when they have them. Was that part of the allure of this job? Getting perfect strangers from point A to B. The facelessness of it.

We are weaving through side streets, trees overarching like claws.

How often do women willingly get into the back seats of the cars of men they don't know? The radio has started to say we should look up the driver's name on the app before we confirm, cross-referencing to be sure he's who he says he is. I flagged him down from the sidewalk, not thinking of how he'd see me—short dress, jean jacket, winged eyeliner, tousled hair, sneakers—until I was all buckled in and the car began to move.

Wine makes usual fears flip around differently in my brain. Instead of being afraid of wild animals, it's as if I am one. I think of locking eyes with Carl in the mirror, mine doe-eyed and as innocent as the stepdaughters in the porn men like him watch. All angelic and equally shocked and smitten by the sight of a cock. I imagine myself a spider, weaving silken string from the waves of my hair to the polish on my toes, of wrapping him up, up, up, tight, tight, tight and then injecting him with my venom, letting him turn soft and vulnerable. Letting him feel as suffocated as I do when I walk down the street.

It isn't right to think like this. I know I should get sober. But wine makes me want to shed every aspect of myself that could be victimized. The buzz makes me feel at home within my razor-sharp edges. Like there's a chance I could still become who I wanted to be when I was little, before all of the bad things happened. It's my adult magic potion.

Cedar leaves me be when I act like this. I'm not sure if it's because she finally trusts me to be in control or if it's because this version of me frightens her. I like to think it's a bit of both.

I want to drink until I can't see straight. Until I can't

remember what I'm about to do, what I've done. I want to make a sacrifice. I want it all to be over. I want to make Cedar proud. I want to make myself proud. I want out of this limbo I've built for myself.

"First date?" Carl asks, bushy eyebrows raised in the mirror.

My fingers are inside my purse, thumbing the pointed ear of my self-defence keychain. "You wear it over your knuckles and aim for the eyes," my daddy explained when he handed it to me at twelve. I laughed, thinking, *You must be delusional if you think I would ever be brave enough to hurt someone.* Maybe he should have given it to Cedar instead. Maybe he realized that and that's why he gave it to me. Before it was too late for us both.

Carl turns back onto a brightly lit main road.

"We've been together for a year." My voice is girlish, casual. I wonder how many women he gets wearing short skirts in his back seat. I wonder if he's straining his senses to catch a whiff of me.

"I'm thinking he might propose," I whisper the last bit as if I'm letting him in on a secret—a deep, dark, white-picket-fenced desire. Showing him that maybe I'm more traditional than I look. I'm not that far from cherry pie.

"Wow, lucky guy."

I watch as Carl straightens up in his seat.

"Dumb, though, if you don't mind me saying that."

We both know that he doesn't care what I do or don't mind.

"A girl like you needs to get scooped up immediately ..."

I picture myself tightly squeezed in the back of a trailer, haunch to haunch with other prized cows, and see the smoke billowing from his ears. Hear him telling his friends, "She's probably dating a fucking douche bag. I'll never understand why women don't like nice guys." Or maybe he'd explain each of my body parts in detail, tell them how he just *knew*, just knew I was a slut. A fuckin' cocktease.

We've pulled up to a red light, and I focus on the sounds of the tires on wet pavement. I look out the window and think about jumping out. I always have thoughts like this, a little voice asking what would happen if I hopped out of speeding vehicles or took my keys out of the ignition as I'm driving on the highway? What would happen if I placed my palms upon the hot burners while I cooked dinner or spit my food in the garbage mid-chew or stuck my fingers down my throat or smooshed the butt of my cigarette into the flesh of my thigh? The light turns green.

Cedar doesn't understand. Her mind never wanders to her own destruction. Maybe it doesn't have to.

"Have you ever been to Cuba? I go every spring."

I focus on his ears, wondering if they were always that large or if he isn't slowly changing right before my eyes. Oddly enough, the news says that other than fever and blistering skin, all of the infected men have suffered from an enlargement of their ears, a deformity of the mouth.

He doesn't place his foot on the gas, and no one is behind us to honk.

"You can let me out here," I rush, my voice sticky sweet. The longer he idles, the more I think of what it would feel like to tighten my hands along his buttery neck and twist.

I hate these intrusive thoughts as much as the others. It reminds me of standing on a friend's balcony on the twenty-first floor nearly in tears; everyone looked at me with laughing eyes until they realized I was serious … or, rather, having some kind of psychotic break. I was no longer confident my body wouldn't betray me for the final time and chuck itself over the railing. I stopped smoking weed for six months—a different kind of personal hell when the insomnia returned, those precious hours of sleep riddled with nightmares.

Carl eyes me again in the rear-view mirror and looks at the GPS on his dash.

"But you're still two blocks away," he says it as if he wants to tack *silly* on the end. Men do not know when they should be wary of women. It's an instinct they've never had to develop. High cholesterol is scarier than we are.

"I forgot I had to pick something up. It's no worries, really."

I watch my hand edge towards the door handle. Carl slowly pulls the car to the curb but doesn't place it into Park. He knows he has only so many subtle advantages. I tell myself not to show fear, never to show fear. Do not show rage, never show rage. In this strange in-between the only thing I show is passivity.

He wouldn't show you mercy, Cedar whispers, her voice low and raspy yet still so, so sweet. She shows me a dirt road on a cold, wet night. I hear the squawk of a vulture, the coo of a raven. I feel incredibly cold.

"Can I give you my number? You can give me a call if things don't work out with your *dream* man."

Is he calling my bluff or pinpointing my fears? *We both know all you're good for is a sneaky weekend placed on a different account than the one the wife checks.*

I giggle by way of a refusal, hoping it still shows that I'm flattered.

Flattery makes them kinder. Flattery gives them hope, cushions the blow.

My mind flashes to a dingy swamp in the middle of nowhere, surrounded by thick brush and spindly branches. I watch from above as my body is wrapped tightly in a tarp, weighted down with rocks, as Carl drives away unscathed.

If I made it to the papers at all, they would read: college dropout, exotic dancer, short skirt, out alone, alcohol in her system, didn't register her ride on the app; bad place, bad time, bad girl. Stupid, stupid, stupid. Eventually, after the shock and horror and sadness of it all wore off, my mother would insist that she knew—she just fucking knew—that I was lying about my job. She would say that she raised me to be cautious, that I knew better. My father would clear his throat.

The cab already smells of Carl's sweat, and it makes it easier to picture each disgusting droplet pinging onto my forehead in an unholy baptism. I'm flipping between my death and his when he turns and places his hand on my knee like a claim. There's a hunting knife in my purse with a bone ivory handle that fits in my palm like an extension of myself. It's much more useful than the self-defence keychain. Don't tell my dad. Beside it are six Polaroids that I intend to post in high-traffic areas, places where they won't be missed.

"I feel such a spark with you, I can't explain it."

Opportunists.

I jerk my leg from his grasp and quickly retrace my giddiness over extra saucy garlicy pizza, my wine-induced "How's it going tonight?" and "Oh, I love this song," knowing all the while that it doesn't fucking matter what you say or what you don't. How kind or how dismissive. What you're wearing or how you look. They decide, not us. I know this. It doesn't matter.

I think of pulling the knife from my purse, of sinking it into the fat flesh of Carl's neck, of wriggling it up and down before pulling it out. But, instead, I fucking giggle.

We've learned it's the easiest response, haven't we?

When all pleasing fails, we tease.

Please, please, please.

The giggle doesn't do it for Carl.

"You could just say no thank you. You don't have to be rude. Jesus. You must think a lot of yourself."

I open my mouth to speak, but I can't find the right words to say.

It's one of my father's favourite sayings, and I hate when horrible men remind me of him. But I've heard him mutter it my whole life. *She must think a lot of herself.* I've always wondered what it is about a confident woman that sets him off the way it does. Perhaps seeing a person so comfortable in their own skin illuminates all the ways in which he is not. And when that person is feminine, encompassing the ability to emote without shame, to hold space for those they love, to be both sensitive and strong— all of the traits he has been told are a weakness—it twists the knife, makes him feel worse about himself. He is always more cutting when his insecurities are running rampant through his brain, his self-hatred spewing from tight lips and beady eyes. Sometimes I sense him waiting in the wings to slice me in half during moments of joy. I've become accustomed to hiding it from him, those glimpses of happiness. I can't count all of the ways he's broken my heart. But maybe it's not his fault. The trickle of self-hatred flows easiest to your children, these little monsters who resemble you.

One time, in one of Theo's outspoken moments, he told me that it wasn't our fault Dad didn't love us, it was just that he hated himself so much he couldn't look at us and not hate us too.

Theo's words made sense, but the groundwork had already been set. I had already learned that above all else, if I wanted to be worthy in my father's eyes, I must never think too highly of myself.

It felt way more real, more tangible, than Nan's

"Yakonkwehón:we i:se." *You are a Mohawk woman. You are powerful.* Slipping into the wallpaper felt like a more realistic existence for me.

I've never felt powerful. And whenever I have, my father—or men just like him—have always been there to remind me that I am not. It's only the wine and Cedar that try to convince me that I am, and I don't think either can be trusted. And the things I've done to regain control? I spend too much time wriggling away from them, palms firmly pressed against my eyes, refusing to look. I fear time and time again I've let Nan down.

I wish I could go back in time back, back, back to the days where men first decided that they were the judges of women. When they turned a blind eye on who it was who carried them within her body, who gave them life. I want to tell Carl and my father and every man that dare judge me that I do not exist for him or anyone like him. That I exist purely for myself. But I keep my mouth shut. Because it's just not worth the breath, the energy.

I set a twenty-dollar bill, four dollars over my fare, onto the seat beside me. Looking into Carl's eyes once again, I am no more than a dog lying on her back, revealing her velvety soft, pale stomach. He finally places the car in Park, and I nod in thanks as I hop out.

As I'm shutting the door, I hear him mutter "cunt" beneath his breath.

For a moment I consider asking him to repeat himself, the sweetness of my voice stripped, shoulders squared. The wine and Cedar don't care about logistics, but I do. He squeals away before I'm fully on the sidewalk, muddy rainwater sloshing up at my pretty pink dress.

I should have led Carl on. Told him that I felt that spark too.

It's crazy, isn't it? We barely know each other and yet … you just seem to … get me. I wish I would have had him pull over so he could squeeze his body into the back seat beside mine. I would have taken his ruddy face between both of my palms and looked at him as if he was beautiful. *You. You are beautiful.* I'd run my fingers up the thigh of his (polyester!) pants until I felt him stiffen beneath my touch. *I don't usually do things like this,* I'd say, watching his eyes fill with awe and fascination, nervous excitement and impending joy and entitlement.

I'll get a condom. We don't want to start our family too soon, right? I'd look at him with Bambi eyes and soft lips. *No, no of course we don't want to start our family too soon. We want to have fun, really enjoy each other for a while.* I would have lingered on the word *enjoy*, dragging it out until it painted a mental picture of all the things we could do to each other, all the things he could do to me. I'd be fast enough that the delirious glint in his eyes didn't have time to fade. That he didn't have time to fully register the smooth ivory in my palm instead of the crinkle of plastic foil. As I lowered myself down onto his lap, so close that I could smell the assorted sub on his breath and the hint of fresh, excited sweat, I'd stab him to death. I wish that his blood was on my dress instead of the dingy splotches of dirty rainwater.

I laugh amongst the empty street.

Maybe I don't want to give up violence. Maybe I've earned it. Maybe I've become it. I raise my chin to the sky, basking in the fat droplets of rain as they splatter across my cheeks.

With Carl's car no longer visible in the distance, I begin to head in the same direction we were driving. I'm actually four blocks away from the restaurant, but walking seemed safer. The night is still young. The streets aren't yet barren. A man and woman walk towards me, hand in hand and quietly comfortable in slick red rain coats and boots. I think of all the women who will lose the men they love to what is now being coined The Change as scientists work to figure out what's causing it. I wonder if they wake in the night to stare at their man, brushing fingertips against familiar cheeks and praying that he be spared.

As the two get closer to me, I watch the woman's eyes trail down my bare legs to my muddy sneakers before she looks at her man with wide, mocking eyes. He snickers. She looks like a traitor. I picture them sitting on a couch and calling women on TV whores. I bet they never make eye contact when they fuck, but he'll fuck her best friend on their kitchen counter while she's at work.

Cedar takes it a step further and shows me the woman being chased and nobody stops to help her. Sometimes it feels as if she hates the women who judge us more than she hates the men that hurt us. I feel the same way, but I think women have just been conditioned to act like men in order to protect themselves from the same scrutiny, to make themselves more desirable. *Stronger.* More *chill.*

Just as suddenly as it began to pour, it stops. The vibrant orange sunset careening through the clouds is nearly blinding. I fumble for a cigarette, flick, flick, flicking it to life and inhaling as if it's my last breath. Daddy would blame me. "If you don't want unwarranted advances, then don't go out alone wearing short skirts." He'd tack a *honey* on the end. The pet name would only work to make me feel worse, as if I'm incapable of taking proper care of myself, as if I'm dumb.

Mom would say, "But what did this cabbie actually do?"

I'd think back to Carl and wonder if I was losing my mind and it was obvious to everyone except me.

Theo would meet Mom's eyes and his would be alight; they'd

roll them in unison. He'd repeat our mother's question a little louder, a little more rudely.

When we were kids, he was always so much more polite and sweeter than I was, and I hated him for it. The cliché is true; you just don't know what you've got until it's gone.

"Yeah, what did he try to do, Delilah? *Fuck* you?" Theo would laugh too loud, hand slapping down and rattling the kitchen table.

My mother would meet my eyes, and I would see that she was also remembering a different Theo, one that I was yet to fail. She no longer adds how Theo was never brash, never angry or impulsive. He was *never* rude. She doesn't sigh or dab her eyes or ask me, "Why did you let him go?" Now, all she has to do is give me that look. The one that says I failed her baby, that I failed her.

If Nan were still around, I know she'd say that women deserve respect no matter what they're wearing. She'd say that we're powerful. She was always trying to remind Cedar and me of that. On days where she seemed temporarily lodged in the past, she'd say that she was too young to feel powerful when her girls were small. That she regretted not instilling strength in them. Cedar and I would squirm, forever awkward when Nan talked too whimsically about our mothers. As hard as we tried, we could never imagine them as young as us. We could never picture Nan as a mother, as a girl or a childless woman in her own right, only as a nan. Only as our nan.

The ownership we place over the women who gave us life must feel like a prison.

Cedar says the longer I fail at asserting myself the faster I'll disappear.

They brought this on themselves, she whispers with a little giggle. *You'll see.*

She shows me the mucky edge of a swamp at dusk. I hear the

guttural hiss of turkey vultures as they fight for the best parts of a fresh kill. I press my thumb and index finger into my wrist, feeling for my pulse until she stops.

I squeeze my phone in my hand and hit his name even though I know I shouldn't. It's supper time, and I know never to call him first. But the cigarette isn't working to pull the panic away from the edges of my vision.

I want him to stop me from who I'm about to become.

I want him to say, "I'm so sorry. I love you. I'll be right there."

I'm insane. I want him to be someone entirely different from who he is.

"Hello?" Ian's voice is a breathy question mark. I hear the slide of a screen door and know he's outside with his dog Marmalade (I came up with the name when he first sent me pictures of her at eight weeks; he calls her Marm). I picture his wife, Alice, smiling over from the stove, the kind of peace you're awash with when you believe you've bagged a *good one*.

"Hi— I-I'm sorry. I'm just having a shitty day and was wondering if you wanted to meet up later? Was everything okay yesterday? You left in a hurry."

I take the gentle way out, choosing not to acknowledge the humiliation, the panic, the money. His silence propels me to keep talking, my voice a nervous rush. Does he know me well enough to sense my mania?

"I was just in this cab and this guy, the driver, he put his hand on my leg and called me a cunt and the news says to cross-reference with the app, but, well you know, I don't have a smartphone and—"

"Wait, let me get this straight. A man put his hand on your leg and called you a cunt?" I can hear his smirk through the phone, silently asking, *Isn't that just another day in the office for you?*

"We've been over this. I told you I'll call you," he continues.

"I know, I'm sorry, I just. I just thought."

Last time I saw him, really saw him, was a Sunday outside of the club where he picked me up and we drove away from the city until we hit the backroads that reminded us of home. A day where he called me Delilah and looked into my eyes when we parked. A day where he asked, "What did you want to be when you were a kid?"

And I said, "A wildlife photographer."

"Like taking photos for National Geographic?"

"Yes, exactly!"

"That's really cool."

I felt, for a second, like I could fly. He made it even better when he told me that he and his best friend, Will, used to dream of being firefighters when they were little, before they realized the kind of money to be made from the trades. His voice caught in his throat when he said Will was his favourite person. I watched his eyes, wishing I could peer into his skull and see what version of Will he was seeing, what childhood memory was running through the fields of his mind. Knowing all too well that he was omitting any and all memories that we both share.

Will had been found dead in a park the week before. Stabbed six times.

Ian was unravelling in a beautiful way.

His grief, his panic, were marinating him in an appreciation for those still breathing. As if Will's death truly showed him, for the first time, that nothing is promised. After we fucked, we lay in the bed of his truck and stared up at the night sky, more starless than home but not empty. I curled up against his chest, and he began to cry into my hair, his vulnerability freezing me to the point that I feared if I moved, I would break the spell he had fallen into. If I spoke, he would suddenly turn cold. Still, I whispered, "I'm sorry," and he hushed me with soft kisses along the top of my head, my forehead, my cheeks until I was crying too. In that moment, he was the Ian I always dreamed of: tender, broken, in love with me. An Ian so different from the one at the club, who stared at me with glassy, empty eyes. Who said, "We need to talk," while his cum dripped out of me and then decided that I didn't even deserve a conversation while I pissed the rest of it out.

"Are you okay?" he asks.

He doesn't wait for a response.

"You're going to be okay. I wanted to tell you yesterday that this, whatever this is, needs to end. I'm starting to feel really sick about it all."

I can't take a breath and picture suffocating to death, cold and alone on the sidewalk. All dolled up for my demise.

"Babe?" I hear Alice's voice off in the distance.

"Is that your mom? Tell her I was able to get Stacy to cover for me so I'll bring potato salad on Sunday, k?"

"For sure, babe." He speaks it into the phone, giving the babe three *a's*. Just for me.

I pull a Polaroid of him from my bag. I want to tell him what I'm about to do. I want to tell him that it's all his fucking fault, even though it isn't. It goes deeper than that. In the photo his head is tilted back in the early evening sun, and he's laughing the kind of candid laugh I convinced myself belonged only to me. It's the second Polaroid I ever took, after I built up the courage to dig out Nan's old camera and all of the film that had before always made me sob and scream and forget to breathe. But then there was Ian. The first taste of happiness since everything had gone so, so terribly wrong. And Nan would be so happy for me. And eventually, so would Cedar. And I would tuck it into a shoebox at the back of my closet and look at it when he came home grumpy or made me cry. I would look at it and I would remember what happiness felt like, in the beginning, when he made sure to talk to me every day and his eyes would follow my every move as I walked off the bus, and when he left someone else for me because I was special. I was special.

I wish I remembered the joke, what was making him laugh in such a way as my finger touched the shutter. I suppose I didn't think it was important because I imagined a lifetime of making him laugh like that. When I look at it again, it's as if he's laughing at me. Maybe that was the joke.

I don't know what to write on it yet.

TEN

JACKSON'S CUTE AND UNASSUMING, AND I CAN'T BRING myself to do it. I watch how he dabs at the perspiration on his forehead with the thick, black polyester napkin he places back onto his lap. Is he feeling feverish? Is he worried about turning into a monster too? He doesn't look it. Just nervous ... of rejection, abandonment, those true-blue human fears that connect us all. He pulls his phone from his jacket pocket, checking the time; he's sent me two texts.

One, twenty minutes ago:

I'm here, sitting dead centre, you'll see me.

And the second, five minutes ago, a slightly insecure:

Did I mix up the days?

Now he's scrolling, scrolling, scrolling as the waiter comes over to refill his water, offering another beer while he waits, which he turns down—he's a man who likes to keep his wits.

The restaurant is cast in a golden hue, each table glowing with a tea light. Most are unoccupied. Dating, it seems, has quickly faded into a state of near nonexistence. For years, we've been ordering each other up like pizzas, sloppily taking each other home after one too many drinks without knowing much about each other than what we've chosen to disclose. In the land of casual dating, we can be whoever we want to be. We share our bodies and little else. No wonder why we all struggle with panic-inducing trust issues. We are the stars of our show and we don't give a fuck who gets hurt as long as it isn't us. And now, what are we doing? Pairing up for the end? Showing up at three in the morning after an hour of back-and-forth arm-extended nudes and *tellmewhatyouddotomeifiwasthererightnows* no longer seem safe. I've always preferred fucking exes for this very reason. Stick with the evil you know. And yet here I am while the news rattles on about first dates possessing a new edge of danger.

For women, there's always the subtle threat of feeling indebted to a man after he buys you mozzarella sticks that you barely touched, too worried of the swell of your stomach or the chance that the cheese would bring on a sudden wave of the shits. There's always that chance you'll just fuck him because he was nice and you wanted him to stay that way. But now, BUT NOW there's the chance he could have a sudden rage blackout in the middle of your mains and lunge at you from across the table snout first. And he doesn't realize it yet, but there's also the risk that the pretty, unassuming woman sitting across from him could be sizing him up and deciding whether or not he's worthy of breath. Whether or not he's part of the problem in this bigger picture.

Jackson picks up the menu for what must be the hundredth time, flipping the pages too quickly to read a single thing. My hair is matted down and my eyes are wild, and I can't bring myself to push open the double doors. I can't bring myself to be who Cedar wants me to be. To be who I know I can be.

The knife rests heavy in my purse as if it weighs twenty pounds. I think of how the blood pours from the necks of pigs as their throats are slit, thick and beautiful as decorative icing. Jackson has traded scrolling with intently watching his twiddling thumbs in his lap. Is he just sweet and lost and insecure?

They're all sweet until they're not, Cedar says. She wants me to open the door, to sit down, to talk and laugh and flirt and watch his true colours unfold before me. I bite my bottom lip to stop it from quivering.

Cedar likes the idea of killing strangers. Men who I've had no time to seriously get to know, no memories to look back on too fondly or remorsefully.

Remember, they don't need a reason, her little voice coos. *Men don't need a reason.*

But I can't bring myself to order a bottle of red and a bottle of white and laugh at his jokes or ease his mind. I can't bring myself to catch a glimmer in his eye when he talks about his mother or his dog or his fifth-grade birthday party when no one showed up or his horrible haircut in high school or how he's always feared that no one has ever really loved him. I can't allow myself to feel the stirrings of a crush. I can't bring myself to give him hope and then be the one to take all of that hope away. The calm, cool, collected version of me that he saw in the bank has all but vanished. I can feel the blood pumping in my wrists, my temples. Can The Change affect women too? Will all of the rage rise up like high tide and wreak havoc on all of those who get too close to me, my short fingernails morphing into claws?

I'm running out of time. Time to prove what kind of person I am before I'm left to be digested by everyone else.

Time to experience love.

It's love that makes the world go round.

Sometimes, I fear that Cedar doesn't even believe in love anymore.

Sometimes, I fear that I don't either. Lately, I've been having trouble seeing the good in people. Love lets us see the best. I hope Cedar knows I love her. I tell her and tell her, but I never seem to be able to get through.

She used to say it back. She didn't used to be so hateful. She used to tell me she'd love me forever and ever and ever, her warm hands on either side of my cheeks. Sometimes, I worry the voice isn't hers at all. She never used to be cruel.

I try to tell her to trust, to breathe the way Nan told me. Don't you remember Nan, Cedar? Where *is* Nan? She doesn't listen. Our relationship feels like a one-way street.

I've always longed to trust, and sometimes that longing makes me trust too fast.

My mother used to say it wasn't our fault for trusting, it was their fault for betraying—but that was years ago. "You can't control who hurts you," she'd say. "You can only control how you handle it." I hated it, this idea that we couldn't get through life unscathed. She sounded so wise and positive and downright giddy back then. I suppose that was before my father broke her in irrevocable ways, back when conversations about trust were little more than hypothetical. She says now that it's easier to talk about things when you're not directly in them, that no conversation can prepare you for the long haul of a real relationship. The thought makes me panic. No matter what I do, my pride could still be shitcanned in a matter of seconds.

My gut tells me to trust no one, to hurt before being hurt, to fuck and fight and run. To be the villain instead of the victim. Cedar says it's another example of me being weak—too passive to ever tell someone how I really feel. Too afraid to cut the cord and be on my own. I tell her I could be on my own if she'd just let me be. She shouts, *Ding, ding, ding, another lie! You need me.* Sometimes, she acts more childish than others. She is a child, though, isn't she? She has that excuse.

Looking through the glass, I tell myself this is an experiment. I will let myself get close enough to people in order to see their true colours and then, only then, will I act. She's appeased. Jackson looks up just as I push open the doors. His eyes immediately lighten when he sees me.

I self-consciously toss my hair as I approach his table, my voice a rush. "Hi, I'm so sorry I'm late. I had to walk. The cabbie was being a creep." I wave towards the window with an air of nonchalance.

He flattens his palms on the table, pushing himself half up. "Oh shit, are you okay?" He looks out the window, scanning for a car. It reminds me of my father, the kind of take charge, protector attitude that makes me feel cared for immediately even as I dismiss it with a laugh.

"Yeah, of course, just a little dishevelled." I glance at the empty pint and water glasses.

"Have you been waiting long?"

"Oh no, not at all," he fibs. "Do you want a drink?"

I nod as he signals for the waiter, who genuinely looks surprised when he sees that Jackson is no longer alone.

"Can I get three-quarters of a glass of red with a splash of white? House is fine."

"I'll do the same. She sounds like she knows what she's doing." Jackson chuckles. "I was actually getting worried about you," he adds as soon as we're once again alone.

Sometimes, I fear that Cedar is right. I am weak. I will forever be unable to care for myself, always begging for scraps. I want to cut open the top of his head and peer into his brain to see if he was actually worried about me or if it just sounds better than saying he was anxious over the humiliation of being stood up. Was he thinking of me dead in an alley or raped in the back seat of a car as a consolation for his bruised ego? *At least it wasn't her choice to miss our date.*

I think of Jackson pretending to be my fiancé, pulling Carl from his car by the neck of his ill-fitting T-shirt and punching him repeatedly in the face. Studying his features, I feel nothing that lends to thoughts of the rest of my life. He's just a guy. I imagine he's only feigning concern until his chance to slide his hand onto my thigh.

Opportunists, opportunists, opportunists. The little voice sounds like my own.

Then Cedar says, *If you go on a rampage, you'd be doing more good than bad.* She asks, *Why, why, why won't you seek revenge? Why, why, why do you have to wait until things get worse? Men don't need a reason to kill us. Men don't need a reason.*

She's coming undone. Maybe I am too.

This is the beginning of the end, she says. *Things are going to get worse quick, real quick.*

What she doesn't say, but what I always feel, is that it should have been me instead of her. The thought makes me want to drink until I disappear.

A seer once told me that when I drink, my soul leaves my body. *Awesome,* I thought. My soul is decrepit. My soul is the root of all of my problems. It remembers all of the things I'd rather forget, reminding me of the days before everything was ruined, back when I had a real shot at happiness. I like when my soul fucks off and leaves behind a dull, simmering rage. If my body was a cage, I would crack it open and set my soul free. I like when my eyes narrow to violent, judgmental little slits and I lose compassion for everyone and everything. There's a freedom to anger, isn't there? There's a freedom to selfishness.

Alcohol makes my testosterone spike, and in that state I can understand how men think, how everything is viewed through a filter of propelling themselves forward, of doing what they want to do when they want to do it. They don't even realize it's wrong —it's all they've been shown. They've been told it's where their strength lies.

My soulless mind reminds me that I am powerful. Yet when the intoxication fades, the alcohol working through my system in its morose, hopeless way, I lose my edge.

I tell Cedar that I think I have a substance abuse problem. Like her mom, like our grandfather who we barely remember. She tells me, *Hush, hush, hush. The world is changing in a way that views any coping mechanism as an addiction if it isn't yoga or therapy or green juice.* Aunt Cindy used to say the same thing, that people could get addicted to positivity too and that it was just as detrimental as booze or smokes or sex or what have you. Nan would always roll her eyes. Sometimes she'd mutter, "But yoga won't leave you choking on your own puke," to which Auntie would say, "Not so fast, Ma. Have you ever tried the plow pose?"

The thing that Cedar doesn't want to admit to me is that she likes me better when I'm drunk because I'm more impulsive. She can worm her way into my mind easier when it isn't already all filled up with soul.

Cedar longs to be in a position of power, and when I'm all fucked-up, she can convince herself that she is. Sometimes, it doesn't feel that different from the men that would take advantage of us whatever chance they get. She feels opportunistic too. I try to keep that from her, but I know she feels it.

Life is a constant struggle for power until one day accepting that no matter what, you will never be in complete control. Maybe that's why old people are so content sitting in a chair all day, watching the world around them from their front porch; they've learned to relinquish control and found that is where peace lies. I've never been peaceful.

Sometimes, I think it's not who I am deep down that I hate—it's this body, this vehicle that always betrays me in one way or another.

The waiter drops off our glasses of wine, and I have barely spoken. Jackson watches me the way someone watches a wild animal they've stumbled upon in a field. He's not afraid because he's still in his parked car, free to silently observe without the threat of an attack.

"You'll love this," I say, clinking my glass with his.

He takes a sip and raises his eyebrows, nodding his head in approval. He's a beer drinker and looks like one: large hands, the hint of stubble, an easy laugh. I like that he's drinking wine for me.

Tomorrow the remnants of rosé will demand I drink more, and if I refuse, I'll envision kneeling before my vanity and slashing my wrists. I'll debate skipping my wrists and going straight for my throat. The lost grey matter and lack of serotonin will use the little voice as a channel and it will repeat, *You are profoundly sad. You always will be. You are a burden, you are a burden, you are a burden.* It will say it enough that I'll believe it. I won't be able to remember a single moment of being blissfully happy, not even content. But I don't think of any of that tonight as I sip every thirty seconds until I need a refill. The first memories the wine kills are of how I always feel the following day. It says if I just stayed a little drunk forever, I would always be my best self, the real me. I would be in control.

Tomorrow, I'll think of Aunt Cindy and her talk of being addicted to positivity. When you're drunk you always want to belittle those willing to go through life sober with all of its rough edges and jaw-splitting emotions that leave you raw and ragged and so, so thirsty.

"It's good," Jackson says, and I don't know him well enough to discern if he's telling the truth. He takes a big sip for emphasis, and I think of a father making airplane sounds as he hovers a fork in front of a high chair.

As the waiter approaches the table, clutching two bottles of wine by their necks in the nook of his palm, I can't help it and ask, "Do either of you think you'll change?"

If I were a man, I don't think I'd continue going to work. I don't think I'd date. I'd live exactly how I always wanted to in this tail end of society.

I watch them through eyes beginning to narrow as they give each other a quick once-over. These two men who have been in each other's presence for the better part of an hour have yet to silently evaluate each other.

The waiter shrugs but Jackson says a definitive no. How could he know? What gives him this confidence, this certainty? *He answered too quickly, with too much assurance,* the little voice says. It shows his privilege, that he doesn't feel unsafe in the company of men. That he feels untouchable even by a virus that doesn't seem to see age or skin colour or socioeconomic status—the only common denominator that I've heard of so far is that The Change is only affecting cis-het men.

It's little, tiny, seemingly insignificant moments like this that cause the most rage in me. I often think that if men were willing to fucking look (look!) at the capabilities of other men, the world would cease to rot. It is men who have the power to change other men, but they don't bother. They listen to each other as they dwindle us down to body parts. They laugh and snicker even if the conversation leaves them feeling uncomfortable, even if they complain about it later to their wives—women who can't help feeling let down, realizing that they've married a coward who would rather protect his popularity over the well-being of women.

The more Cedar demands a sacrifice, the more I realize how far she has always been from peace. With the angst of a teenager, she doesn't care if she ruins my life. Hers is already destroyed, I suppose.

The guilt thrashes. It's the same guilt I've felt for seventeen years. Cedar is my best friend, but I want her dead.

Jackson has all but lost the smug confidence he showed me at the bank. The man seated before me buttering a piece of bread is undeserving even if he is ignorant to the faults of his gender.

"Would you like some?" he asks, offering me the basket as panic begins to pulse through my brain. Can he tell by my rampant sips that I have a problem?

Can he see the darkness taking over my eyes, sense my soul leaving my body?

His eyes are on my mouth as I tear into a hunk of bread with my teeth, rabid.

"Do you know what causes it?" I ask, mouth full.

Cedar has told me, but I'm not sure if I believe her. She might just be trying to rile me up. She was laughing as she said it, sounding more unhinged than usual. Even as children, she had an innate ability to terrify me until I begged her to stop.

"I heard 'roids," Jackson says. "A bad batch of a popular brand."

I think of the popular boys in high school, the ones who went from lean and lanky to too-buff in the span of a summer. I fucked them all. Or, I suppose, they fucked me. They were so similar in bed: anticlimactic, quick, afraid of eye contact.

"Hmm." I nod, pondering.

Jackson is fit but by no means buff. He catches my eyes lingering on his arms and laughs. "You've got nothing to worry about here."

In that moment I like him, a level of self-deprecation that doesn't cross over into depressing or cringe. One that simply humanizes until I can see him looking over himself in the mirror with a small twinge of insecurity. I can imagine him going over conversations in his mind and feeling like an idiot. It's these thoughts that tell me to get out. I become attached too fast and then before long, I'm seeing the ugliness, knowing that I should have left at the first sign of a flutter. Most people are nice when you first meet them, and the rain made my hair really cute. Does Jackson believe his own words? Is he as certain as he sounds about not changing? I don't think they always mean to manipulate. They tell themselves that they are good boys just as their mothers used to.

"No one is a villain in their own story. Everyone believes that they are inherently good," I say.

Jackson takes a gulp of wine, clearing his throat and muttering something about it going down the wrong tube.

We all have our reasons for being bad.

My second glass is empty, and I've yet to open the menu. I'm not sure if it's been fifteen minutes or forty-five. I desperately want a third, but the waiter is at the end of the bar trying to hide that he's texting. His secrecy takes his full attention. I imagine him rearing his head and being different, frightening, while Jackson's bottom canine teeth protrude from his lips. The last news clip I saw was of a man who had been kept in a padded cell and monitored by video surveillance, fed from a tray slid through the slit in the door. Jackson's gaze falls to my left hand and I realize how tightly I'm gripping the wine glass. I want to bash the bowl against the edge of the table and shout, "I can't do this!" while brandishing an ironic weapon of choice. A warning, a demand. "Back, get the fuck back." His lips are exactly the same as they were, and his teeth are not visible. His eyes are kind, gentle.

His voice is sweet as he asks, "Shall we order?"

I picture taking the jagged edge of the glass and gouging into the sinew of his neck as Cedar and the little voice speak in unison for once. *Yes, yes, yes, yes.*

"I-I can't do this." I scoot my chair out from the table with an obnoxious squeal. The waiter looks up then, tucking his phone into his dress pants, standing. I need to be out before he approaches the table. If he beats me to it, I'll lose my nerve. I know this about myself. Jackson watches me with curious, frazzled eyes. They're medium brown or maybe hazel—pretty. He's leaned forward on his hands as if he's about to get up himself. As if I'm aware of something dangerous behind him that he can't yet see. He doesn't realize that he's been making eyes with danger. Men have no instincts when it comes to being cautious of monstrous women. Their biggest threats are smoking too many cigarettes, eating too much butter, texting while driving.

Cedar has me by the throat, and she's saying, *Just chill, just chill,* and the little voice is saying, *Stay for one more glass, another ten minutes. You're okay. You're okay.* I know them well enough to know that they're manipulating me. A shadow dances in the corner of my vision, and my stomach feels hollow except for the swirling of panic.

"Stay safe," I spit.

Jackson opens his mouth to formulate a question, but I don't give him the chance. The little voice counts my steps loudly, my body ricocheting with a sigh of relief as I make it back out onto the cold street before the waiter gets to the table, before I lose my nerve and say, "Fuck it, keep 'em coming." She's always counting and I'm always racing. I never want to know what will happen if I fail to do something in time. Jackson is nearly to the door himself when the waiter must call for him, thinking that we're dashers. Jackson is nothing if not conscientious, aware of appearances. He makes his way back to the table, palms forward and lips moving in explanation. They both look out the window at the same time, but I drop my gaze before I can register what either of them is feeling. I don't want to do something that I'll regret. Cedar tells me that once I was gone Jackson muttered, "Fucking crazy bitch," to the waiter, and he gave him a beer on the house. I'm not sure if I believe her.

Like I said, I don't trust anyone.

ELEVEN

Do you ever think of the number of men that go out and kill women?

I do.

And when they're caught—if they're caught—and interviewed, sometimes they say that their mom used to beat and belittle them or they couldn't live up to their father's standards, their first girlfriend cheated on them, or their dick is just so, so small.

It's all bullshit. Nothing gets them as hard as curating fear, of terrifying something innocent. Of peeling the wings off flies and tearing the legs off spiders. Of drowning kittens. Of putting a woman in her place.

Demons are said to be most attracted to our fright; the energy of our terror lets them *be* something. I don't think men are that different.

It's our fear and their force that keeps them in power.

They say not all men, and I say that they're right. I've never known a trans man who fed off my fear. I've never known a gay man to leer at me as if I'm little more than a meal.

Just these heterosexual cis men who this world was built for, who it was built by.

They don't seem to need a reason to hate us. As a society, we accept that there's a little murderous rapist in most of them. Something he needs to get out of his system like the thigh-clenching need to come. It's why we tell our daughters to cover up, to keep an eye on her drink, to call when she gets there, to smile, to watch her mouth. But we tell our sons they can be whatever they want to be—as long as it's something masculine!

Men are hardwired to spot vulnerable women, knowing just what to search for. They've been conditioned since birth, like wolf pups watching and observing how to be a predator. Social structures that reveal how to hunt with the greatest ease and practicality.

They seem to sense these girls no one will realize are missing. These women who society already views as a lost cause destined for turmoil. As if she was just put on this earth to satisfy a man's blood-thirsty need.

My father once said, "Think of all the missing women," with laughter on his breath. Laughter that always seemed misplaced. "There must be a lot of men out there who've never gotten caught. Men who've just killed once, just to get it out their system, just to get a taste."

"You sound fucking insane," I said, hating that his words lingered with me.

I began looking at all men, searching for their monstrosities. Wondering immediately if they wanted to fuck, kill, or marry me. Which form of power assertion salivated between their lips? When they'd choke me in bed, I'd coo, "Fucking kill me," just to feel how hard it made their cocks when I acknowledged that they had the power to end my life.

Always a little ashamed of how it made desire blossom inside of me too.

I wish my mother never would have told me about that doctor's appointment my dad went to when Theo and I were little. "I just keep having this fear that I'm going to beat my wife," he said to the doctor, fessing up that he needed some kind of medication. I've often wondered why he told her, if she took it as a threat, if he meant for her to.

His anger had always paralyzed us all. That knowledge of his inner thoughts gave it an added edge. When I'd catch him muttering beneath his breath—one voice fast and rabid and furious, the other small and scared and reasoning—I'd picture he was arguing with himself about all of the ways he could harm us. An internal struggle of the pros and cons. There were always two voices. An argument that couldn't stand to stay in his head, he had to let it out. As if one part of his personality was trying to win over the other.

Did he fear that he'd inherited rage too?

Theo and I never met his father. He died drinking and driving when our daddy was only ten, a night when the kids weren't with him so no one was able to sit on his lap and steer. I've always wanted to ask my grandma if she was relieved—he used to kick the shit out of her.

How much of that violence runs through my father's veins? In the early days, when my parents were little more than teenagers, that rage made my mom feel sacred.

"It's good to feel wanted," she told me with a raise of her jaw and a hint of a smile. Men's violence truly seemed to represent how much they cared. *Our* innate power? We could make them lose control.

Before they got married my father grabbed my mother by the

throat when she threatened to leave. During another argument, he kicked down my nan's door when my mom wouldn't let him inside.

"I was so stubborn," she said with a laugh, "Why didn't I just open the door?" Would she laugh if a man kicked down her door for me?

"Wasn't that a red flag?" I asked. "Wasn't Nan mad?"

"Your nan's always loved your daddy," my mom said with a dreamy-eyed smile. "Your nan's also always known how difficult I can be."

She's always been testing people, pushing button after button to see how much they can take. To see how much they care. His aggression showed her that she had him in the palm of her hand. It was a different rage than the rage she was used to from her own father. My daddy's rage said that he'd kill her if he couldn't be with her. Her daddy's rage said I'll hurt you because you're mine. It was different. But then again, it was the same too. She felt loved.

I suppose all of these stories were my earliest glances at love. Violence and rage and stubbornness and jealousy and control all braided together that I dubbed romantic once I found their stash of Valentine's and anniversary cards. Gushing words that sometimes even crept to the back with an arrow directing my mother to flip it over. Words that proved he truly saw her in ways that weren't always obvious in their day-to-day lives. Publicly he'd say, "Your mom was the prettiest girl around and I got her." Privately, he'd write: I could never imagine waking up without you.

The cards let me understand their relationship in ways I'd never been able to in true-blue waking life. I thought of his muttering voices and wondered which one this was, this one that was so romantic and tender and sweet and in love. In writing, he spoke to her in ways she had always dreamed of. She could return to them always, telling herself that this was how he really felt. Never mind his actions, which you can't catch a hold of, these words were timeless and so tangible she could grip them in her hands. In a way it made his anger and tension and what happened later bearable because she had proof of how much she was loved in his messy, boyish handwriting. There were pictures too. From before Theo and me. They looked so happy in matching jeans and jackets with poufy sleeves, their hair equally floofed, grins equally dazed. She was a difficult woman, and he loved her for it. She didn't realize then that in time he'd make her docile. He'd train her.

I'd stare and stare and stare at my father's boyish smile, his sparkling, slightly shy eyes and wonder if he had wanted to beat her then too. Or if he was equally surprised by his hands around her neck, his steel-toed boot through the door.

I long to ask him if he still wants to beat her now. But I don't. I never do. He has this way of slipping into his shame. In a lot of ways, it makes him worse. Maybe that's why he found other ways to hurt her.

My mother exasperatingly holds her hands to her face when she hears me talk like this. "Oh, I just wish I never would have told you anything!"

I suppose my takeaway feels like a betrayal to her; she was hoping to gloat in the romance of it all and all I can see is the abuse.

When she asks me what the hell is wrong with me, I come up empty-handed. Everything? Nothing? I don't know yet.

Yesterday, there was a news clip that warned of graphic content and disturbing subject matter. It showed dead bodies out in the street and talked about Russian soldiers raping Ukrainian women in front of their children, sometimes cutting out their tongues so they could no longer speak. None of these soldiers were in the clip, just lifeless bodies, some of which had been burned. But at the back corner of the screen there was a creature of some sort. Something that maybe once had been a man but was now hunched and salivating with enlarged canine teeth and protruding ears. Clothing ripped and skin blistered and filthy, hair bristling from its knuckles and down its cheeks but thinning across the top of its head. The Change is spreading like the common cold amongst soldiers in war-torn countries. It must be the escalated testosterone.

Shoot-to-kill orders have been issued amongst their own soldiers at the first sight of symptoms, skipping the earlier attempts of quarantining. It's already backfired, falling upon the leaders who put them in place, their executions swift upon sickness. The twenty-seven countries with female leaders are being praised, free from the chaos of a sudden internal power shift and a complete lack of leadership. In New Zealand, the prime minister is ruling mass extermination of any man over eighteen showing symptoms. I read a story of a woman who hid her nineteen-year-old son and his friends in her basement. When she stopped returning calls, a close friend found her brutally raped and murdered by the boys which now resembled a pack of beasts. The incident spurred a publicized warning from the prime minister to her country and the rest of the world: these boys and men are not who they once were, and there is no evidence to show that they will ever return to who they once were.

In Finland groups of women have escaped to the forests with their young sons, hoping to raise them free of their fathers, free of the influence of the men who are ruining the world.

Canada, as always, feels almost innocently safe from the atrocities of the world. A blissful ignorance while the rest of the globe seemingly falls into inescapable turmoil. Lil says that people on Twitter are condemning Americans and their surging statistics of devolution and violence with the kind of ignorance that says Canadians are not the same colonizers who wiped out most of the Indigenous. They're not seeing the forest through the trees—it's here. The creatures are already hunting.

I figure we'll have to develop a similar taste for violence if we are to survive. I can't shake the feeling that we'll have to beat them at their own game. That we have the tools, we just have to gather up the courage to use them.

It's not our fault they've ruined the world. If the tables were turned, they wouldn't think twice about ending us. They never have.

I'm losing my ability to see good. Childlike wonder slipping further and further as reports of violence become unavoidable. As I watch the subtle tactics of control. As I feel the leers in the street, men waiting to rip me to shreds more than ever before. Are the unchanged hoping to change? Are they hoping for permission to be as heinous as can be?

They don't need a reason to kill us. And yet here they are, destroying everything, and we're stuck still discussing who they could have been when they were children—before this world got its paws all over them, before they were trained by the alphas.

It's as if we've forgotten that we can be alphas too.

She's been whining at the door for too long.

My skin itches with the thought of letting her out.

Part of me thinks my past prepared me for this. Part of me thinks I'm doomed because of it.

TWELVE

My phone dings twice. Jackson asks if everything is alright. If he said something wrong. If I was sure I was okay from whatever had happened with the cabbie. If I got home safe.

I long to tell him that he's lucky. That he's safe. That I'm sorry for thinking I could hurt him. I'm sorry for dwindling him down to what women are dwindled down to every day: an opportunity for violence.

I tuck my phone back into my bag without responding, wondering if he'll look for my face in the posters that line the sidewalks. Beside the posters, I tack up another Polaroid—the back of a man's head. He lies facedown in an inky pool of his own blood. On the bottom, with my right hand, I wrote: **I ASKED YOU TO STOP. I STOPPED YOU.**

The streets reek with the smell of trash and piss. Each year, it seems to get a little worse. The earth is getting to a place of no return. She will shed us like a cancer. She will rest. She will revive. We will all die.

Looking around, I expect to see bins piled at the curb, but they sit beside their assigned houses and apartment buildings, lids closed. Ian has texted me twice. Only question marks which I'm supposed to decipher as: where can we meet so you can suck my dick?

Men, if they do it at all, often rush through eating pussy like it's the final bite of dinner before they can go and play. Yet they look at women sucking dick as the main event. As if we wake up in the morning and think: Gee, I really hope I can suck some cock today.

Dinner must be over, and he must have changed his mind about us being over.

Alice is either watching trashy reality TV or giving their daughter a bath. He tries not to text me anything incriminating. My name in his phone is Samuel. If I were to see my man texting nothing but question marks, I would know. Maybe women who've never been the other woman don't know what signs to look for. Or maybe she's just a fan of blissful ignorance. A true Canadian. Maybe she's weighed her cushy life beside her husband who fucks around and has chosen the cushy life.

When I start listing the amount of times I've been the other woman, I could throw up. All of the times I have paid no mind to fucking someone else's man. All of the times where I have found it charming! Funny! Commendable! Listening to the lies a man will spill in order to sleep with someone new with a smirk on my face and their cock in my hand. I have worn their infidelity like a satin robe. I have let it convince me that I'm special. And now, when I realize what all can happen in an unaccountable hour, I have horrible, crippling, god-awful trust issues. Jealousy that fills me with so much adrenaline I could kill. Because I know what people are truly capable of. I've tasted it. I've built my livelihood around it. I see it every day.

Is it because of my lies that I expect everyone else is lying too? Will I ever know?

I don't tell my mother about what it feels like to be the other woman. She calls me a knife twister. Little does she know my hand isn't even resting on the handle; the knife isn't even drawn. I don't tell her how everyone is full of shit. How we're all living these double lives. We're all victims of the lies we tell ourselves.

I can't tell her about my occupational hazards when she thinks of me spending my Mondays to Fridays, nine to five, in an office, sometimes returning late to finish a project, to make that bonus. She takes pride in it, how hard I work. I like that she does, even if it's misguided. Even if she wouldn't if she knew the truth: that most of my money is made from married men. Men like my father. Men who have altered her life. Men who will always, always, always, always put themselves first.

When I think of the commonality of it, how often we all betray each other, I always come to the same conclusion: polyamorists know what's up. The thought is quickly followed by the fact that my jealousy brings about images of jamming forks into eye sockets. I couldn't willingly share. Like so many others, I want to have my cake and eat it too. Frosting smeared all over my face. I'd rather cheat than tell my man that I want to fuck someone else; both things shatter the vase, but one of them allows you to pretend that it's still whole. Maybe I'm just terribly afraid that trust will lead to humiliation—it's all I've ever seen.

The night is young. I let my finger hover over Ian's name willing him to send me a third text. Ask me to meet him halfway, a perfect thirty-five-minute drive for each of us. I want him to apologize for earlier, for yesterday, for everything, to ask if I'm okay and mean it. To tell me that he was stupid for thinking he could ever let me go. I would accept anything other than a singular punctuation mark. But all he ever sends anymore is this secret language. He has me trained. I hate it as much as it sends a tingle up my thighs. Sometimes, all I send back is the letter *k*, as if telling him that I am no different. I don't want anything more than his body, these little shavings of time and pleasure. He doesn't know me well enough to know when I'm lying (that would take too much effort). When the wine spills over inside of my brain and tears pour from my eyes and the truth spills from my lips, we leave it be. Me, buried beneath comforters the next day, willing myself to die. Him, getting caught up in his life—the life he chose, one where I don't cross his radar and if questioned, he hasn't seen me since high school.

Sometimes, I daydream about what kind of woman Alice is. If she's the type to chuck his clothes out of their beautiful bedroom window, to cry openly and ugly on a Facebook live, or if she'd merely have an extra glass of wine each night and not mention what she thinks she saw for twenty years. I flit between: she must know and she can't possibly.

Is he gentle with Alice in ways that he's never gentle with me? He must be.

Knowing someone's darkness is knowing who they genuinely are. I know him, I know him, I am the only one who truly knows him. To her, who is he? What is he?

I have to believe I mean a lot to him, that he thinks about me when he wakes up and when he falls asleep and when he sees something particularly funny on TV. I can't accept the truth. That she makes him happy, and I am only extracurricular. Fun and games. A pastime.

I like to play pretend and call it controlling the narrative. I like to tell myself that if I took the pussy away, he would beg and plead and cry and pour his heart out to me. The idea of it is too fulfilling to shatter. I can't risk knowing otherwise, that if I took away the milk and honey, he would stop texting entirely. That the only reason he remains tethered to me is out of convenience; he knows that I need him more than he needs me. He knows how I twist the secrets between us, how I've let them vine up the sides of me until they look beautiful.

A THREAT OF STAY-AT-HOME ORDERS ARE BEGINNING to circulate across the world. The virus is spreading too quickly for anyone's safety—no buddy system can protect women and children from sick men who have ganged together with a common goal of rape, kill, eat.

Newscasters, now mostly women, talk into cameras with eyes that dart about nervously, the soothing calm of their journalism-degree curated voices wavering. Reporting has become scarce after too many women have been attacked while the camera's still rolling, once even by the camera man himself. Discarded with a clang, the scene off-centre as he ran towards her shouting that this was all her fucking fault.

America's lockdown starts on Monday. Women shout, "Fake news!" on media reports of The Change, saying that all this boils down to is fear mongering, another means of coercion. *It's CGI*, they write on Reddit. Others say that if it's true, it was probably invented and released from a government lab. A science experiment gone wrong. A way to frighten us into submission that backfired and now has men morphing into beasts at a remarkable rate. Cedar laughs as I research, her voice shrill and hyper as she squeals, *Karma, karma, karma.*

Women have begun to be fined for being out alone. We're too tempting.

"We are doing this for you," conservative leaders shout. "Please, just listen!"

I don't like the idea of bodies of men in control of my every move.

That's where this all started, isn't it? A crackpot idea of reclaiming power?

We were getting too powerful. Flaunting all the money we could make by twerking our asses and sticking out our tongues. We were becoming fearless.

And we were, even though there was never a time that you could turn on the news or the radio without hearing of an attack, an online date gone wrong, a parking-lot gang rape that was recorded and uploaded. Snuff porn went from a disturbing, shameful, dark web niche to a mainstream category between *Big Tits* and *Gang Bang*. Men no longer want to only see a woman gagged or choked or crying—their orgasms relied on a steady escalation of violence. They want to see a woman fucked to death.

There has been an uprising of men rallying towards women going back to traditional gender roles: having more children, cooking, cleaning, tending to their husband's beck and call, mending the nuclear family. It really kicked into full force when not only was abortion once again criminalized, but contraception as well. It's a war against women. While cis women and trans men are being denied reproductive rights, trans women are under fire for being as subject to The Change as cis men, despite the fact that there has yet to be a case of a trans woman showing symptoms.

The virus seems to be a vehicle for the political boogeyman, conservatives spinning stories to point gnarled fingers at women instead of admitting that this is somehow the universal karma for the patriarchy itself. Men becoming unable to hide their mutations any longer. I like to think of it as mother nature's revenge.

"They'll change too!" republicans shout, using the end of civilization as we know it to punch down at trans women—as if the virus is completely linked to possessing a cock and balls. It reeks of ignorance. Ninety percent of the reported Changed have been heterosexual and cis, but what is this atrocity if not an opportunity to further strip women of their shred of power and decency?

I learned from a young age that things can always get worse if there's room for them to. This world has become a playground for degradation.

Men have always had the potential to be animals.

Their wildness has almost always been looked upon with innocence. As if the world is nothing but a conservation area for wolves. Women, us young, pretty unassuming women, released like rabbits.

I make my living off of men. Off of their wants and needs and desires and fears.

Like Cleopatra and all the powerful women before me, we're taught that our main source of power lies within our sex. Yet we are shamed for utilizing it. Shamed for admitting that we want more. But I'll admit it: I want it all.

Cedar comes alive like a ringing in my ears. My senses perk as if I'm a deer nearing a highway.

Their voices are hushed, quick snippy whispers followed by loud guffaws.

"That's fucked, man," the voice behind me says, trailed by another laugh. I lower my head and quicken my pace.

When I first went to college, my mom got me a rape whistle that let out a shrill scream when you pulled the clip. I refused to bring it with me. The sound made me go to a place in my brain I never wanted to return to. A reminder of the first silent time and all of the silent times that followed. I think of Lil's pepper spray, how I smirked at it as I set it on my bedroom floor. I wanted something that would maim. Stupid, overconfident, I wish I would have tucked it into my purse like she told me to.

I walk a little faster but refuse to run. Refuse to make myself prey.

The knife in my bag, shiny and sharpened, can be used against me. The strap of my purse twisted around my neck. My Polaroid camera in the hands of someone who will take photos of me, dress torn, lips bloodied, eyes empty. I hear laughter again—it sounds almost nervous.

The street ahead is barren, long shadows from the buildings on either side stretching in front of me.

I can't tell if their footsteps have become louder or if I'm just hyperaware. My adrenaline spikes, palms wet, as I picture a large hand grasping my hair and slamming my face into the brick wall of the alley. Without a smartphone or cable, my knowledge of what is actually going on is limited to regurgitated stories from the women at work and a long late-night Google search on my lagging laptop after Lil told me to educate myself.

Do they have a weakness? Other than enlarged ears and mouths and aggression, what are the other telltale signs?

My mind races, thinking of a childhood spent in the bush. If you spot a black bear, appear big and loud. If you spot a cougar, hold eye contact and walk backwards slowly. If you spot a grizzly, play dead.

Are men more like cats or bears? If you turn and run, will it force them to chase? If you shout and wave your hands above your head, will you entice them to engage? If you play dead, will the fun of the pursuit be stripped from them or will they still prod and huff and take, take, take?

All I've heard is that when you see one, you'll know. I sniff the air, hoping for the overturned outhouse stink of a bear in the woods, the acrid urine scent of a cat. I smell nothing except the sour sweetness of garbage juice.

I take a deep breath and pull a cigarette from my purse. The first drag creates a relaxation over my shoulders, a steadiness. This is a bad dream. It's only a bad dream. Cedar's whispers are relentless—low and raspy and viciously frightened.

"Are you okay, bro?"

The men behind me have grown quieter, but I can still hear the sound of shoes slapping pavement.

"Come on, leave her alone, man." The voice is definitely nervous, which frightens me more.

The laughter has all but stopped as they whisper amongst themselves. I strain my ears to try and make out what they're saying in their hushed, concerned tones, but I can't.

Suddenly, one of them is beside me. He's younger than I expected and shorter than I am. Maybe twenty-five, fully grown yet not fully matured. Both of his hands are shoved into the pockets of his bomber jacket, and his eyes follow my cigarette, a small smile playing across his lips. His eyebrows are scraggly and his nose turns up in a slight peak that was probably only cute in childhood.

"Hi," I say, forcing my voice to come out confident, secure yet not rude. Never rude. I strain my ears to hear the others, but I don't. I immediately think of the coyotes back home. How you're safer when you can hear them all behind you than you are when you suddenly only see one. They've had the chance to surround you by then. When I turn to look over my shoulder, expecting to see the others hunched and ready to pounce from the shadows, I see something worse: the backs of their jackets as they hurriedly walk in the direction from which they came.

"Want one?" I ask, craving the rush of calm that will fall over me when he starts speaking.

His hands have yet to leave his pockets.

"I want something else." His voice doesn't seem to match his mouth. It's strained and hoarse and oddly grotesque. I glance behind me again, hoping that the other two are still here. The shiver traipsing down my back says there is nothing scarier than when men are afraid of another man. They've seen the ugliness they all possess rise to the surface like curdled milk in a cup of coffee and have let him go rogue. They've decided to turn a blind eye, save themselves as if this sickly little man is contagious.

As his left shoulder leans into my right, I realize he is gently pushing my body into the alleyway beside us.

"I want to taste your cunt."

The alley is bone quiet except for the synchronized slap of our shoes on the cement, together yet so far apart. For a second, I think of how hot it would be if the words fell from Ian's lips while his calloused hand tightened around my throat. Sometimes he says, "I'll kill you if you don't fucking come right now," and the orgasm always ripples from my body, pleasure possessing every nerve ending. I am powerless when it comes to him. The revelation hits fast and heavy and brutally true. That's why he likes me. I make him feel like a king.

Ian is tall and self-assured and disguisedly unkind. When he threatens me, part of me believes him. This gremlin of a man beside me, with his shoulder pressing into mine and the smell of stale coffee on his breath, bits of spittle in the corners of his thin-lipped mouth, longs to be a man like Ian. Maybe it's that longing that's pushed him into this shedding of who he once was. He looks like he was made to rub a woman's feet, not rape her in an alley. Maybe the news has spurred on a different change in him, a longing to be vicious for the end of the world, to grab hold of whatever he wants, whatever he feels he's been deprived.

"I want your fucking cunt," he repeats, voice unwavering gravel.

I picture slicing it from my body, handing it to him dripping in blood. *Here you go. Here is the softest, most sensitive part of me.*

"I'm going to take pictures of your cunt," he sneers to reveal janky, overlapping teeth.

Cedar's voice is a quick succession of whispers, words I can't make out. A prayer beneath her breath.

I see an abandoned dock and hear the crashing of gentle waves. A backseat, my pale legs splayed open in the blue dashboard light.

I feel the seat beneath my ass, chafing with each thrust.

I smell Axe body spray and the noxious new car scent you can buy at the dollar store. The once-soothing scent of a wood stove.

I taste the blood from my own tongue as my molars sink in and my vocal cords lie still. My tongue somehow comforted from the pressure of my teeth.

I shove my shoulder into his and stumble forward. There is no one on the other side of the street. I don't even know if it would matter if there was. My voice is trapped deep in my throat as if this is merely a bad case of sleep paralysis. And who knows? Maybe if there were others around, they'd also choose to hurry away, to turn their heads. We used to make jokes about not getting involved in domestics when we heard shouting through a wall; now men record it on their cellphones when a woman gets assaulted on the subway. Society has become a red flag, but we've become too self-consumed to notice.

He grabs me, thick hands wrapped around my shoulders. His mouth, filled with protruding teeth once in desperate need of braces, is ravenous. Features rat-like and homely, angry that he didn't grow up beautiful, that women are not his bounty when he's been told since infancy that he was a little ladies' man. Eyes penetrating yet impenetrable. I picture my body twisted and bloodied, exposed.

"You're a fucking coward," I spit between gritted teeth.

His response is a tight fist, knuckles slamming against my brow.

My knee shoots up, stabbing him in the groan and biding me a second of time as he releases me.

Cedar says that when you get chances, you take them. She tells me I shouldn't be sorry. She tells me that they'll leave us for dead. *You know that*, the little voice whispers. *They'll leave you for dead.*

It's as if I am watching myself from above. A dreamlike state. One of my nightmares that I'll jolt awake from, tangled in sweaty sheets, inches away from the ice-cold fingers of death. My mom used to say that if you died in a dream, you died in real life. I picture myself as a fawn hurrying through the forest. Pure instinct. Mind and body seamlessly connecting in a way they never do in waking life. Nothing but a dream.

His breath is a pant behind me, this new world of monsters and men.

I wonder where the other two went, if they're circling back to relish in the kill. If they're sipping coffee and avoiding making eye contact with one another. If little voices of guilt are running around in their minds, regret bashing its fists against their insides. Or maybe, they're jerking off, playing around with the idea of being wild and ruthless like the man they left. The man who's hurried steps are getting closer. Closer. Closer.

He's laughing now as he runs. A maniacal squeal.

Cedar's prayer intensifies. It tells me that she can't help me. We only pray when all other hope is lost, a result of being raised with religion even though we've never been believers. It reveals there's still a shard of faith that God may split the sky and show us a miracle.

I'm sorry, Lilah, I'm sorry, she coos, her voice small and helpless. I don't know why she's apologizing.

I scan for an open store, another person, but the streets are dead. I envision his sour breath on the back of my neck, his dark beady eyes locking with mine when he pulls me around to face him. I can almost feel the heat of him. Can already smell the hints of his chicken-soup sweat. It reminds me of visiting a farm when I was small, of the thick glisten that coated a horned-up pony, his erection comically large and frightening and gross.

I see my body, lifeless, slack, passed from lap to lap, and men are laughing and moaning and laughing.

Cedar tells me to focus. This is not a time to let go of my hold on reality. *You are real, you are real. Sónnhe, sónnhe. You are alive.*

When I round the corner, it's the cherry of a cigarette I see first. It glows orange like a beacon of hope, and I am once again myself, running faster as the footsteps slow behind me. Men in the presence of other men are always on their best behaviour, even amidst their unravelling.

"Pretend that you know me," I hiss into the darkness as I inch up beside him. "I'm being followed."

His boyishly dark brown curls frame high cheekbones that

protrude through porcelain skin, eyelashes curling away from deep, dark eyes. He's not much taller than I am, his stature almost delicate, and for a second I wonder if he'll be able to protect me, or if he'll be hurt too, because of me.

"Long time no see," he says, his voice velvet.

My heart pounds in my ears, and I want to crawl beneath his skin.

There's just something about him.

When I work up the courage to look over my shoulder, the man has slowed his pace, as if I am deranged, as if he is only out for a stroll.

THIRTEEN

"Fuck, are you kidding me? He was right behind us? We should have circled back, kicked the shit out of him. Are you sure you're okay?"

His skin is the colour of fresh cream and makes his olive eyes appear nearly black as they glimmer in the moonlight. He licks his lips, and without meaning to I lick mine. I find myself staring at the curl of his lashes and the sweep of his dark brown shoulder length hair before I remind myself to speak. Many people in the city don't start their sentences with a *fuck*, but I like it. It's not classy. It reminds me of home.

My breathing has steadied, and I let out a loud guffaw, the breath breaking into a sob at the end.

I place my head in my hands, peering at him between the slits of my fingers, humiliation washing over me. For revealing fear or for putting myself in danger, I'm not sure. I hope I'm not just trying to be cute.

He reaches out, a gentle touch against the back of my hand as he begins to peel my fingers one by one from my face.

"You're okay," he says softly.

Cedar has calmed down from the run-in with the man in the alley and is now judging my crush. She says I need to take my life into my own hands. That I sicken her. I silently beg her to leave me be, wishing it were that simple.

"I'm okay," I say. "Thank you."

He steps closer to me, so close that I can smell him—vanilla, smoke, and something darker—holding his hands up, palms forward the way you'd approach a horse. *Easy, easy.*

My hands have stopped shaking, but I can still feel my heart pounding in my ears. His fingers are cold as he tenderly grips my face, turning my chin ever so slightly towards the streetlights.

There is a throbbing in my left eye where broad knuckles hit socket. He eyes it with the steady concern of a father.

"Is it okay?" I ask, my warm breath radiating off of his cheek. He tuts once, twice, and then steps away from me.

"You'll probably lose the eye, but I think you'll live."

His furrowed brows raise and his mouth cracks into a grin.

"Phew," I whisper. "Delilah," I add, offering him a cold hand.

He envelops mine within his own, eyes alight. "Elijah."

I thumb my eyebrow, pressing down against my flesh in hopes of stopping the pulsating pain. We stand in silence.

"That was fucking crazy," I say finally.

"I see you're not abiding by the buddy system." Elijah looks around into the dark night. He glances down at my bag. I want to snap a photo of him, this first moment, stare at it before I go to sleep.

"I like to be in control of my own life," I say. I can't tell if it's a lie.

"Who would have thought we'd go from women getting slut-shamed out of court rooms, to tracked down and murdered after an incel found their address via Only Fans, to *this*? Remember when the world was proper?"

I can't help but laugh as he continues.

"God, remember the good old days? When all men did was innocently yell 'grab her by the pussy!' at *freedom* rallies?"

He meets my eyes with his own sarcastic glint. A matching expression that says that everyone else is fucking foolish for not seeing this coming.

"Can I buy you a coffee?" I blurt, wanting to drag it out. "You know, as a thank you?"

"Hmm ..." He stops walking and rocks back onto the heels of his black combat boots. "Certainly." His face breaks into a grin revealing charmingly crooked teeth.

My lips part and I don't want to fuck him. I want to kiss him softly, unwrap him slowly. I want to savour him. I want to be sweet. The feeling is carnal and cosmic and all-encompassing.

We walk for two blocks through the dingy streets in a comfortable silence. When we reach the diner, I follow behind him, watching how his shoulders slink like a mountain lion as he slips into a booth. How he's at once refined and lupine. I slide in across from him, slowly pushing my hips back and placing my chin on intertwined fingers to look up at him.

"What can I get for ya?" the waitress asks, her mousy grey hair pulled harshly into a bun at the nape of her neck. She lets her eyes fall to the muddy hem of my sundress, and I sit up straight.

"A little cold out, no?"

I tug at the dress, a blush rushing to my cheeks.

"I'll have a peppermint tea," Elijah says, pulling her attention away from me.

"Me too," I add, giving him a smile as she wanders back behind the counter.

"Will you turn that up?" the cook yells from the kitchen, and I watch as the waitress grabs the remote.

Breaking news flashes across the screen over Elijah's head, but I can't keep my eyes from his. He stares back at me until it feels like a game. I trail my eyes along his thick eyebrows, to his long nose and full lips, and then back to his greyish green eyes, careful not to blink.

He's effortlessly beautiful the way I've always wished to be, like Cedar, like my mother.

His eyes drop to his folded hands. I watch him as his confidence slowly crumbles, until I can see a gentle insecurity that makes me want to trail kisses from his head to his toes.

"Why are you staring at me?" he whispers.

With his chin tucked towards his chest, his high cheekbones stab through his cheeks. I visually remove his mesmerizing eyes and creamy skin to see what his skeleton would look like.

I continue to stare as he raises his square jaw and peers down his long nose until his eyes sparkle with mischief, his mouth breaking into a slightly insecure grin.

"Because I feel like I know you," I whisper back as the waitress sets our spoons and white mugs of tea down with a clatter.

"A pretty young thing like you will need to be careful," she says, turning her body fully towards me and raising her brows knowingly.

I look past her to the TV as footage of a man shouting at a teenage girl behind the counter at a McDonald's in Alberta blasts across the screen. He back swipes the cabinet containing muffins and pretty pastel donuts and begins to maniacally laugh as it smashes. The laughter is so similar to that of the man in the street I can't help but turn quickly and gaze over my shoulder as if he changed his mind and followed us both.

The banner along the bottom is again advising women to stay at home until further research is conducted. I meet the waitress's eyes that look at me flatly before trailing down at the neckline of my dress.

Elijah doesn't stop her this time, and I wonder if she's right, if I am somehow asking for it. I hate the thought as quickly as it enters my consciousness, what it suggests.

A scientist with her long hair pulled back into a low ponytail looks sombrely into the camera as she says, "The research has been steadily pointing towards a breaking point like this. It's just with this career being a male-centred field, a lot of the studies were underfunded or ignored."

Elijah drums his long fingers on the table. The scientist has my attention, but not more than he does.

"I don't think she wants me hanging out with you," I say slowly once the waitress is seated at the end of the counter, gaze glued to the TV.

"Discrimination," Elijah says with a smirk. "You must be brave, though," he adds, looking me up and down in a way that makes me never want him to stop. I feel like art.

I tilt my chin and narrow my eyes. "This world has always been a dangerous place for a woman. It doesn't matter how we dress. If this is the end of the world, I want to dress for the occasion."

He laughs, curling his lips down in mock thought. I'm again awash with a sense of familiarity, as if I can't imagine a day before today, a day that I didn't know him. I have to pinch my thigh, reminding myself that I *don't* know him. That all I'm doing is building expectations off of chemistry.

"This world isn't safe for anyone," he says finally.

I want to spout off facts. Tell him that the biggest threat to a man's life is heart disease, while the biggest threat to a woman's life is a man, but I don't. I like him. I want him to like me. He's younger than I am. I know that for sure. I don't want to appear bitter. I will reveal glimpses until I'm sure-sure-sure that I can show him what I'm really made of.

Nan used to tell me that men didn't have it easy either. She'd say that this entire world was sick while Cedar and I dropped lumps of dough into a frying pan sizzling with oil and rolled our eyes. Theo wasn't warned to stay away from our uncles the way Cedar and I were. These sick men who couldn't be trusted to change a baby's diaper.

I want to ask Elijah his age but don't want him to ask me back. I don't want to risk him being one of those younger men who feels sudden, inexplainable repulsion from a woman dangerously close to thirty.

My mind wanders to previous crushes, how seeing their true colours felt like sand in my eyes.

How some pushed me to points of monstrosity.

I pinch my thigh again to stop my mind from wandering and stare back at the boy across from me. He looks like a purpose instead of a distraction. He looks like an escape better than booze. He looks like sex that wouldn't leave me ashamed.

I've always wanted to vanish into the woods with someone I love and create a life that no one else needs to know about. Free from the stress of the things society grinds down on our shoulders. I've always wished there was a plane ticket I could buy that would let me depart from who I am. I've always dreamed of starting over.

"Do you ever think of running away from it all? Creating a new life away from everyone and everything?" I ask, immediately embarrassed.

He doesn't seem phased and quickly answers, "Every day, but I have to admit, I'm fascinated by this virus."

I shiver.

Cedar says that men make me weak, but sometimes I think she's just jealous over the fact that she is unable to make connections the way I can.

I can usually pick apart what kind of person a man is within seconds, but Elijah holds a mystery that I want to sink into like bathwater.

When we leave the diner, he drapes his jacket over my own, and I know somewhere deep down between my stomach and my ovaries that I could love him. Boyish and unassuming, he tells me he's lived here his entire life, flitting between friend groups like a chameleon. He's only twenty-three.

I tell him I'm a small-town girl and we hum "Don't Stop Believin'" before he asks, "Wouldn't you be safer in your town?"

"I'd rather see perfect strangers change than the men I know."

What I don't say is that if I'm attacked, I'd prefer it to be violent and unexpected and perpetrated by someone completely unrecognizable. Being hurt by people you know feels like an extra layer of violation and betrayal even when it is not particularly violent.

"The *Change*," he says, making jazz hands, dragging out the *a*.

"Aren't you scared?"

My mind travels to the days of mad cow disease and Theo crying as he watched the TV, the cute black-and-white calf straining against the rope tied around its neck, its tongue lolling, eyes wild. Theo refused to eat beef for an entire year.

"Terrified," Elijah says solemnly. "But like I said, also completely fascinated."

I want to ask him if he thinks he'll change, but I don't want to ruin the fantasy where Elijah is soft and sweet and gentle and always will be.

"I've been steadily searching the web, seeing if I can figure out what's causing it."

"I heard men earlier tonight say they thought it was a bad batch of 'roids."

Elijah scoffs, smirking with a roll of his eyes.

I laugh too.

"I mean, they're probably onto something thinking that it stems from some form of toxic masculinity."

Hearing men talk about toxic masculinity is an aphrodisiac to me. Too often I've watched eyes glaze over as if I'm referring to unicorns.

"I guess if I'm being serious, I want to figure out if I'm going to change too. And if so, can I stop it?"

"What have you found, Professor?"

The word gives me a rush, an educated *daddy*. I picture him sitting in front of me, eyes wide and adorably anxious. I imagine sliding my knee between his jean-clad thighs.

"Too many articles debating the legitimacy of The Change happening at all. A lot of shit on it being a hoax as a means to control cis women and illegitimize trans women. The steroids belief has already been disputed. Men have changed who have never before stepped foot in a gym. Medical histories are all over the place, same with race, location, age. I saw this one video of this little ninety-year-old man mid-fever; he no longer had his own teeth so he didn't develop those sickly protruding canines, and his ears were already huge—ears and noses never stop growing, you know?" Elijah pauses to chuckle before clearing his throat and continuing. "But he was making this horrible animal whimper, and his eyes were beady and violent, his neck hunched forward in a way even scoliosis couldn't be blamed."

I think of the man from earlier, the gravelly ache of his voice, yet his teeth only looked like the result of a lack of dentistry.

Elijah gazes off into the distance, lost in thought.

"So far, men who've been hospitalized mid-change have been so diverse that no commonalities have been found, other than, of course, they're all straight, cis men. Thank fuck I'm bi. I guess, maybe it's my saving grace."

"My favourite people are bi," I say, "but then again, I'm *biased*."

Elijah rolls his eyes again and grins.

"Want to watch something?" he asks, hand fumbling inside the back pocket of his jeans. For a second there's the ever-steady fear of dropping my guard, but then he pulls out his phone. His eyebrows raise, as if asking the question again.

"What is it?"

"I've really gone down the rabbit hole. It's fucked. I mean, trigger warning and all." He holds the phone between his thumb and middle finger and dances it from side to side. I take a deep breath.

The video is a little shaky, the phone held from an unsteady hand. The man in focus initially too close to the camera to make out any features.

Elijah reaches forward, pressing down a button on the side to turn the volume all the way up.

"I'm sorry, I'm so sorry," the man's raspy voice repeats from the phone speaker. Cedar stirs. My stomach clenches.

Suddenly, I see him. His once-thinning hair is now buzzed close to his skull. His eyes are littered with crow's-feet and paper-thin wrinkles. His teeth are just as yellow, but his canines are beginning to protrude, creating tender, reddish spots on his thin, cracked lips. He was ugly before. He's much uglier now.

"This shit is wild," Elijah whispers, eyes glued to the screen.

The man lets out a barking cough, and his spine jumbles forward. He holds the phone beneath him so it feels as if we're looking up into his face, those wet, blueish eyes.

"God, please spare me," he croaks.

Cedar laughs her favourite snarky laugh. A knowing laugh. A laugh of chaos.

He falls to his knees, the phone wobbling for a second before refocusing from his outstretched arm. I glance at the site, dark web and niche.

"Seventeen years ago ..." His voice catches in the middle. I swallow hard, hot bile rising up my tightening throat. The media was a huge fan of this snivelling little boy act during his trial. He breaks into a full sob, eyes falling from the camera as if he can't bear to look, can't bear to reveal his guilt. These same eyes that feigned innocence.

"I can't," I spit, shoving the phone towards him, my vision a vignette.

Just listen, just listen, Cedar whispers as my stomach twists.

"I raped and—" Elijah turns it off. I look back at him from the edge of the sidewalk, my heart rate beginning to slow, the panic subsiding.

"I'm sorry." Elijah lets out a rush of breath but then smiles. "It's fucked, I know. There're all these videos like this. Confession videos ..."

Perspiration dots my hairline, and I try to take a deep breath, but I'm about to vomit onto the pavement beneath our feet.

"I've found other videos since, but this was the first one. It came out two weeks ago," Elijah says. "He's long changed now."

Glen Belvedere. But I refuse to say his name. I finally manage to take a deep breath, holding it in my lungs for a silent four count as I fumble in my pocket for a cigarette.

Justice, Cedar whispers. But this doesn't feel like justice.

I wanted to be the one who got him myself, but men like Glen are like mosquitoes, revealing themselves only when you decide to swat.

"I'm sorry," Elijah says. "That was dark. I just ... I had a feeling you would appreciate the hypocrisy of it all. I've watched so many things I've become a bit desensitized."

"Yeah," I answer, my voice sombre.

"So, when are we running away to the woods? You gotta give your two-week notice at work." His subject change is swift. I can see the apology in his eyes, for thinking he's subjected me to too much.

I think of telling him if I didn't show up tomorrow, another girl would be hired by the end of the week. That only Lil would put up flyers. My regulars might ask about me for a month and then move on to the next dancer.

"I didn't even tell you that I wanted to go to the woods. How did you know?"

"Because you've already taken the midnight train ..." His lips twist into a goofy smirk, and his eyes crinkle at the corners, hardly able to finish the line.

"And where am I going?" I smile my coy smile, the cutest of all my smiles.

"Anywhere?"

We burst out laughing, and I'm floating.

"Let's go in two weeks then," I say. "You got any outdoors knowledge?"

"None at all. But I'm a fast learner."

We stand still, gazing at each other like kids.

"I'm a bit of a lost boy," he says, and I picture us in matching racoon hats, our favourite belongings strapped to our backs. "I don't think I've found my purpose yet. And don't even get me started on my daddy issues."

I've never really heard a man speak with candid vulnerability without their face buried in my little tits. It's refreshing. He feels nostalgic, like a favourite movie from childhood that you've forgotten about until it's on and you realize you know every single line. For a moment, I think of opening up. Of telling him just who I am. But then he checks his phone and my heart falls to my stomach, sizzling in its acid, bloodying the toilet when I shit it out.

He steps from one foot to the other, a grin spreading across his face before he bites his fist.

"Okay. So, I really didn't want to tell you this ..." He pauses and I touch my face, feeling for a booger or lipstick on my teeth. Worse, I think of a stunningly beautiful and kind yet bitingly funny lover waiting for him back home. "But I'm late for work. Gotta put in my notice, you know?"

My heart begins to beat again, blood rushing back into my cheeks—the birth of hope.

"Go, go, I'm so sorry."

"You know when you're thinking of winding a conversation down, but you never find the perfect moment? And you're thinking, 'This is it. I'm going to die in the frozen food section of No Frills.'"

My eyes widen, shocked that he'd say such a thing, such a thing that we all think but never say out loud.

"Oh no, I'm one of those?" I bite the side of my thumb,

smiling in childlike wonder. This moment feels wrong after seeing Glen. Selfish and sick and sad.

"You are," he says, taking two steps away from me and widening his arms, his oversized black sweatshirt stretching like wings around his frame. "But, in like, the best way."

I grin and twirl on a rain-soaked sneaker.

He comes closer, and I want to roll in his intoxicating scent.

"Can I have your number? And we can do this again sometime?"

My heart drops again, but only halfway, realizing that our jokes of escaping were only jokes.

"Save my life?"

"Minus that part, hopefully. I do feel really bad that I can't walk you home. Try to stay alive, k?"

"I'll try my best," I say, the giddiness of my voice too much for the severity of the subject. He turns then, leaving me smiling in the street, watching him leave.

"Wait, your jacket!" I yell after him, beginning to pull it off.

"I'll get it from you next time," he hollers over his shoulder.

I spend my entire walk home desperate to know when the next time will be.

I hate myself for being pretty pink putty, already moulding myself into the kind of woman a boy like him would want.

It's thoughts like these—hateful, true thoughts—that make me want to rebel against who I am, be more like her. More like Cedar.

Can't you see? Cedar asks. *Can't you see what I'm trying to show you? Can't you see what I've done?*

I think of how my mother and I watched with bated breath as Glen was interviewed in a little windowless room. The last footage of Cedar was taken from outside the only convenience store in our little town. We watched the tape of her getting off her bike and leaning it against the pale yellow siding; this strange man, Glen, approached and grabbed her handlebars. Cedar's sinewy arms jutted out as she rested her hands on her hips and straightened up to her full height of 5'5". We couldn't help but laugh as we watched Glen step back, palms forward. How Cedar always had this ability to make herself look larger, tougher. Later, during questioning, he said that he noticed something askew with her bike and he was only trying to help. The bike was never found.

FOURTEEN

I can't go home. When I think of those four walls, my feet pacing the floor, mind racing, I can't do it. There's a bar up the street, its sign illuminated in tacky neon green. Aging beer posters sun-stained in the windows. O'Sheas. The front porch calls upon memories when we could all smoke on patios. Days where nothing seemed to matter as long as the bartender accepted my fake ID. Upon opening the front door, I'm hit with the smell of spilled beer permeating every single sticky crevice of the floor. The air is heavy with grease from the steady churn of french fries. I wish Elijah were with me, anyone to distract me from myself, from Cedar, from Glen and the past bubbling up like bile. There are less women out at the bar than there used to be, but the ones here self-identify as dangerous. Skirts slit high up the thigh, highlighter so glowy it could be seen from space. Women who are not disillusioned: men have always been a threat —now, they're just revealing themselves faster. I order a pitcher and sit in the far corner, where I have a perfect view of the entire bar and also the front door.

My eyes linger on the men casually shooting pool, laughing with their friends because they know the looming lockdown won't be applied to them. A table of women, all dolled up and laughing loudly, animated hands dancing to the tales of their gossip as if this is just a normal night. Only one of them eyes the group of men warily, seemingly unable to meld into the conversation that has the others enrapt despite her ruby red lips.

A couple on a date, barely talking, the space between them dark and vast. I wish I was closer so I could overhear the few words they share between long sips of beer for him, vodka water for her.

I want to get obliterated.

The only other woman here alone is perched on a stool at the far end of the bar, her burgundy boots kicking at the bottom rung. An empty shot glass and three limes sucked dry sit in front of her. She taps her shot glass along the dark brown oak; it would be rude if she wasn't so cute. The bartender turns with the bottle and gives her a smile as he tops up her glass. She knocks it back quickly without so much as a wince.

"He fucking left me for his ex and then had the *au-dac-ity* to ask if any of my friends were single when I wouldn't take him back!" She sucks in her laugh with a honk and places both hands flat on the bar to steady herself before asking for another. I pour myself another beer, the foam frothing nearly a third of the way down. I drink it anyway.

She kicks her feet more aggressively, her voice a little louder after each shot.

There's a man at the other end with his back to me.

He's been watching her the entire time I've been here. Who knows how long she's been here?

She orders another shot, and he approaches, sitting two barstools down as if he just arrived. He tips his glass her way and nods his head. He's not unattractive—tallish, full head of hair, dark eyes. But there's something strange about his mouth. He looked over his shoulder at me briefly on his way over, oblivious to the fact that I've been watching him watching her.

"Megan!"

Her introduction sounds over the breaking of billiard balls. He moves to the stool right beside her, close enough so their shoulders touch as he points to the top shelf of liquor.

"Oh, you're fancy huh?" she asks as the bartender grabs the bottle of tequila.

He slides his hand to the small of her back. His voice is too low for me to hear his response.

"He had the audacity to ask if he could have my friend Emily's number." She laughs again as if it didn't make her stomach sink. As if it didn't make her want to risk it all by going out alone.

He leans closer to whisper something into her loose waves.

"Stop! Stop right now!" Megan scream-chortles. He nods and smiles and whispers something else.

His teeth look nearly too big for his mouth, and the bartender eyes him as he dries a glass.

In the wee hours of this morning, sick of waiting for Ian's apology, I cut off a man's dick and shoved it down his throat. In my defence, he followed me all the way back from my middle of the night coffee. I pretended not to sense him until I had him alone, his footsteps staggering, breath reeking of booze. He fell over with my first shove; it was almost too easy. I put those Polaroids outside of a hockey arena. I might be jaded when it comes to hockey players. My friend Theresa dated one in high school. Brock. We were at a party where I had two beers and a puff off a joint and instantly felt sick. Theresa told me to lie down, and when I did, two of her boyfriend's friends entered the bedroom. I was too out of it to speak, my limbs suddenly cement, but Brock barged in and asked them what the fuck they were doing.

Later, I wondered what would have happened if I hadn't been Theresa's friend. How many of us are saved based on who we know? How many of us aren't?

"No, no, I'm waiting for a friend," Megan says now, tilting to the other side of her barstool so her shoulder is no longer resting against his. Has she positioned herself as a perfectly digestible booby-trap like I would? He whispers something else and she obnoxiously laughs.

I've been pinning up new Polaroids every single chance I get. Warnings. Threats. Omens. The newspapers are calling them THE WAR AGAINST MEN, but I've only been getting the ones who bring it on themselves. Then again, the newspapers have been telling us to stay home. The rhetoric no different from: What were you wearing? How did you speak to him? How much did you have to drink?

For lifetimes, the responsibility of not getting raped has been in our hands. It's still in our hands, but consequences have a way of revealing themselves in time. Cedar says, *It's not too late. I'm making it easy for you.*

The man orders two more tequila shots and a beer for himself. He pushes both shots Megan's way with a raise of his eyebrows, a challenge. She drinks them both and lets out a theatrical thirst-quenching sigh.

"It's time for you to go, buddy," the bartender says. Well-built and stern, but not a threat to us because he's gay.

He stands up and runs his fingers along Megan's arm as he does. The bartender squares his hips.

"My friend will be here any minute," she says again, her voice smaller than before.

The bartender nods and gestures to the door.

It won't be long and bars will close down like they have in the States. Alcohol makes men worse. It gives them an excuse. Last year, the courts tossed out all sexual assault cases where booze was involved. More than half of them.

He nods, letting go of her arm and trailing his fingers along the bar instead. The hair on the back of my neck stands up the way it does before anything bad happens.

I can't help but lean forward as I watch. The leg of the bar stool disappears beneath his grip, and the splash of liquor explodes from the bottles as he chucks the stool at the shelves. Megan screams before he pushes her head against the corner of the bar and runs out into the dirty, rain-soaked streets.

I follow, but these monsters have gotten faster.

Megan comes stumbling out of the bar with the bartender behind her. She's furiously apologizing as he shakes his head and places a firm hand on her shoulder.

"Are you okay?" He carefully touches the red mark above her temple.

"My friend—my friend really should be here soon."

I watch as she looks up and down the street and then looks at the phone in her palm.

"She left … she left forty-five minutes ago, and we don't lie about that kind of thing anymore."

Lighting up a smoke, I watch them both with my back against the old brick building. There's a sense of calm, the way some element of normalcy slips through during the worst moments of life.

"I can walk you home," I say, watching as they both turn, almost startled by my presence. I've become wonderful at slinking unnoticed. I've grown around it, the shadows.

The bartender looks at me as if he's seeing me for the first time: cute dress, muddied sneakers, unwavering eyes, oversized jacket.

Megan steps from one foot to the other. "Umm …" Her eyes on the verge of brimming, the tequila has fully permeated from bad bitch to baby. I'm quite familiar with the feeling.

"That was fucked," I say, twisting the butt of my cigarette beneath my shoe. She nods, looking back at her phone.

"I live … I live really close to here."

"You're drunk though." My gaze flickers to the bartender, silently judging him for over serving although I fucking hate when I get cut off myself. His eyes drop to the ground. He pats her on the shoulder, mutters something to her I can't make out.

"She lives across the street," he says, absolving himself. She must be a regular. "I … I gotta go back in." Looking from the door back to Megan, he asks, "You okay?"

She offers an overdramatic, drunken bobble-headed nod, and he heads back to the bar.

"I'm good, really." She points a baby blue tipped nail to a building across the street.

"I'll wait 'til you get in safe."

She smiles, nods, looks both ways before she crosses the street then waves from the front door of the nondescript building.

"Megan!" I yell across the empty street. She stops, the door half ajar. "Always carry a knife, babe!"

She grins, bites her bottom lip, and disappears up the stairs.

I see Cedar everywhere.

I go back into the bar, order another pitcher. Keep watch.

I didn't choose this life; this life chose me. There would be no justice if women didn't create their own. Trauma is a woman's inheritance and we're not supposed to be mad about it. Yet I can't sit pretty and let this life chip away at me. We're diamonds, us women, made powerful from pressure.

This world is deserving of our wrath. We have the right to be angry. We have the right to be angry. Don't let anyone take that away. Of all the deadly sins, that one is Cedar's favourite and she is mine.

My wrath came to fruition when I was only fourteen. It had been brewing for years before that though. Don't discredit teenagers—their anger has the power to engulf the world.

I had lost all that mattered most two years prior. It felt as if I lost everything, and sometimes it still does. It was October 5 when I changed, and it was a beautiful night. There was a full moon, not too cold yet. Sometimes, I want to blame it on the moon lighting up the night and making the crazy crazier. Sometimes, I want to blame it on him, Richard, this man who got in the way of my wrath. Sometimes, I want to blame it on her, Cedar, who only ate justice. Who only came back for justice. Always, I blame Glen, who took her away from me.

Saying October 5 was the worst night of my life would be a lie because it was the night Cedar came back, and that will always drape it in the scent of her strawberry bodywash and sweetgrass breath and something that felt like hope or maybe connection.

Before that night, I always thought of the life of girls and women in the terms of The Before and The After. Statistically speaking, only one in five women have been raped, but I don't think I've met a woman who hasn't experienced sexual violence at the hands of men. I knew what The After looked like from all of the women around me. One in five, my ass. Unless maybe, my family is just cursed. Because of that, I never thought I'd need to know it up close and personal myself. But there are some things in this life that we don't get to choose, I suppose. Entering The After is never our fault. It's never our choice.

As soon as I could talk, my mother had been warning me of men. Men who drove too slowly beside you as you rode your bike. Men who approached you with free candy or asked if you wanted to see his puppy. Men who knocked on the front door and asked if your Mommy or Daddy were home. Men who asked you to keep a secret. Men who tried to tickle you or touch your privates. I learned that these men could be anyone anywhere: the fathers of friends at sleepovers; strangers in the street, in cars, at Walmart and the fair, mall washrooms; uncles or cousins or grandfathers at family functions. My family tree's roots sprawl out rotting in every which direction. A different uncle molesting a different niece or nephew. A different father molesting a different son or daughter. Maybe the worst uncle of them all, feverishly jerking off at his new apartment, in the picture window, facing a daycare.

I couldn't see my cousins, my aunties without thinking of The Before and The After. How they walked around with their loud cackling voices and chatted with heavy sarcasm and had families of their own when all the while they were in their After. I wondered if they taught their children about what to watch for, who to avoid, to hold onto their bikes. They laughed as if they hadn't, swatting at each other's arms and telling their inside jokes. I began to think that maybe my mother had made it all up.

Until Cedar got back from her mom's.

I knew something was wrong as soon as Cedar stepped out of the passenger seat. She didn't jump or dance or shout, "Holy heck, did ya miss me?" She didn't say anything at all. And that laughter that was always in her eyes, even if her lips stayed comically motionless, was gone.

She didn't race up the porch stairs and take my face in her hands, wrists clasped beneath my chin, squealing, "I missed you," or "What's good?" or "La-la-la-lilah."

She didn't run into Nan's hug, nearly disappearing amongst her ample chest and fleshy arms.

She walked past us both, not even stopping to put down her checkered duffel bag. Not even stopping to run to the stove and lift the lid off the pot to breathe in the simmering sauce.

Nan told me to follow her. To bring her a plate of food. To see what was up. But I couldn't. My dad stood at the front door, shrugging like he always did. Nan muttered something about PMS, and I thought of my mom and how she said we were just at different ages, that things would iron back out in a couple years. But the thought of a couple years felt like forever, so I didn't go upstairs. I didn't bring her a plate of spaghetti with her ungodly mountain of Kraft parmesan. I just went home with my dad because I knew. I knew, I knew, I knew. I knew she was in her After.

And maybe that's my biggest sin—that she was in her After, and I didn't go up the stairs to sit beside her, even if she wouldn't speak to me, even if I was hurt, even if I was afraid. That I let myself be selfish because I was hurt, because I was afraid.

That was still two and a half years away from October 5. From the full moon and the night that I entered an After of my own.

I really thought I was untouchable. I sucked at math, but I was good at spotting a dangerous man. Maybe that was the biggest indicator of my pride: this undying faith in my own abilities to keep myself safe.

Before my After, I had the nerve to be angry with Cedar. She told me it was us against them. She told me that women only used half of our power. She was supposed to change the world. We were supposed to be the generation that changed it all.

Maybe that's why she came back for my After.

Life is nothing if not bittersweet.

FIFTEEN

Maybe putting too much faith in my instincts let me drop my guard. I thought I knew everything to watch out for. I can't believe that I was wrong. I can't believe that a life of preparation still led me to failure.

As women we're not supposed to say that we like attention, even though our clothes, our makeup, our hair, our push-up bras, our giggles, and our silences all lead to it—despite the fact that we're raised to believe the most important thing we can be is desired. And when you first get a taste of being desired from someone you think is cute and mature and worldly, funny, interesting, attractive ... it feels so good.

My mom never warned me about that part. Or maybe she had, talking about infatuations with adult men when she was still only a girl. Of charming first dates with men who brought flowers and opened car doors. Of men with exciting careers and huge social circles and love notes. Men with good hair and gorgeous smiles and a list of women who wanted him all while she was failing grade ten algebra.

I was yet to decipher the good from the bad when it came to those kinds of men. Maybe if Cedar would have still been around by the time I was fourteen, she could have helped me. She could have added onto my mother's initial training with lessons of her own. But she didn't make it back in time. And anyway, even before she left, her After had stolen her spirit.

A lot had happened in the two years from Cedar's After until my own. Maybe the doctors were right—I'd starved myself to the point my brain cells were dying and I wasn't paying attention.

Maybe I wanted to be hurt. Maybe I wanted to be loved.

Maybe I had been on the edge of reality for so long I wanted to fully slip. Maybe I brought it on myself.

Maybe I wanted revenge.

If it wouldn't have been Richard, it would have been someone else.

Men like Richard have impeccable timing. Men like Richard know precisely when you're looking to be saved. I'd be a liar if I said part of me didn't hope Richard would save me from it all.

Sometimes, when I think too much about Cedar's After, I wonder if that was what created this fascination with eating less and then nothing at all. If somehow I didn't subconsciously correlate puberty to our body's first betrayal. If trying to prevent myself from going through it at all wasn't a last-ditch effort to blissfully remain in my own Before forever—that if I stayed childlike, I'd stay safe.

As much as I fought it, my long legs glistened in a golden tan. I loved them so much I wore short shorts, liking how I could make men sputter and stare. I twirled cherry red suckers between highly glossed lips, and my boney shoulders looked waifish beneath my long golden hair. My cheekbones jutted to reveal knowing eyes. And it was my eyes that betrayed me last. For it was my eyes that Richard looked into. It seemed as if it was only my eyes that he noticed. I felt ethereal. I felt wise. I felt seen.

No one warned me about that. Or maybe they did, and I just chose to ignore it.

Maybe thinking of being looked at like that and actually being looked at like that are two completely different things. Maybe I was just so, so lonely. I was only fourteen. I barely had any friends. It was an accident.

I'd met Richard a week before, when he stumbled upon me and Jenny and Alyssa, two sisters who lived down the street from me who kind of seemed like they liked me but kind of made fun of me every chance they got.

They had dark hair and bright eyes like Cedar. They were beautiful. It was my awareness of their beauty which made Richard's attention that much sweeter. The first night we met him, he strolled up to us while we passed a water bottle half-filled with the skimmings of Jenny's father's liquor cabinet between us, giggling and sputtering as the concoction burned our throats.

Alyssa tucked the bottle behind her back as he approached, black leather jacket, blue jeans. Longish hair and a jaw line that cast shadows on his neck beneath the streetlights.

"You're all good," he said with a laugh. "I was just wondering if I could borrow a lighter?"

He looked at me as he spoke. Then again, I was the only one out of us three who smoked.

I'd recently found my mom's secret stash, Vogue Menthol Slims, hidden in the third drawer of the kitchen cabinet beneath a plush stack of tea towels. The pack was half full and beside it was a bright magenta lighter. I slipped two from the pack, peering over my shoulders at any creaking of the house. I placed a bottle of Calgon Hawaiian Ginger body spray in my bag and decided that if she asked, I'd say one of my friends smoked and the scent got stuck in my hair; I'd crinkle my nose and twist my lips in disgust. I'd let my mother keep her secrets as long as she didn't stumble upon mine.

"You shouldn't make a habit of this," he said, watching my cigarette travel from my lips to the end of my delicate fingers.

"You should say the same for yourself," I said.

He took in a deep puff, jokingly burning his dart a third of the way down. Jenny passed the water bottle back to me, and I took a sip without gagging. Richard looked at us as if we each had two heads.

"Are you not nineteen?"

Jenny and I were fourteen and Alyssa was sixteen. We told him so with nervous laughs.

"Could have fooled me," he muttered as he finished his smoke, refusing Alyssa's offering of the swamp water.

"I have a six-pack in my trunk, if you want a beer?"

I was the only one who said sure, nonchalantly, choosing not to catch the look that Jenny shot Alyssa.

Cedar had taught me to chug two years prior, Nan's skunky beer stinging my nose as it spurted onto the floor to a backdrop of Cedar's sputtering guffaws.

His sleek black car and how he spoke told me he was city. I smoked his Belmont Kings after I'd finished my second stolen menthol. He said he didn't usually smoke, only when he was away working. Said he couldn't believe he had forgotten to get a lighter. I told him he could keep it. I didn't have any smokes left anyway.

He thanked me, his green eyes lingering on mine in a way that felt different from how anyone had ever looked at me before, but handed the lighter back, along with a smoke of his own, tucking them both into my palm and closing my fingers around them.

Jenny, Alyssa, and I had been taking photos of each other with my camera. Richard held up the palm of his hand when I snapped one of him, his long pale fingers obscuring his face. I wished I would have snapped it faster, caught him candid.

We all called him a dinosaur after he left, and I didn't admit that I thought he was kind of cute. The next day the rumours started. Everyone heard I had blown a grown man behind the bleachers. That was the day people started calling me a whore. Whore felt so final. I didn't even think I had been flirting. I didn't even know how to flirt. I felt so awkward, so young and gangly. Skinny in the wrong places. Fat in the wrong places. Richard said he'd never met a girl like me before, and I loved how his words made me feel.

"You're wild," he kept saying, taking drags of his cigarette and slyly shaking his head.

Later, I'd realize that he was searching for girls like me whenever he was away from his wife and children. Maybe teenage girls made him feel like a teenager himself. Maybe teenage girls made him feel like a man. Maybe there was a neediness to me that made him feel wanted.

That first night, before the rumours, as Jenny and Alyssa went one way and I went the other, I felt weightless. Cedar and I used to race from the fork to my front yard, keeping our eyes glued to our shoes as we ran. Never daring to look into the woods on our right and certainly not into the cornfields on our left. As terrified as we were, we could never stop trying to summon Marybeth. Aunt Cindy told us Marybeth had been killed decades before, and her body was dumped amongst the dried stalks. That during the full moon you could say her name three times and she would begin to follow you down the road—if she caught you, you'd never leave her side again. "She's just so lonely," Auntie said.

Cedar always shouted it first. I always whispered it second. Neither of us ever dared to utter the third. Always running flat out at the first sound of a leaf crunching, the wind whistling through stalks, so sure that we heard Marybeth in there somewhere, humming old Indian songs our mothers never taught us.

But that night, for as far back as I could remember, I didn't feel scared.

The moon seemed to shimmer, and I felt giddy.

Amongst the cornfield full of secrets, I felt calm.

"Marybeth!" I called, my voice rising with laughter.

"Maaaaarybeth!"

Feeling alive, I looked from the darkened maples to the swaying stalks. I pulled Richard's cigarette from the pocket of my jean jacket and marvelled at how it glowed against the darkness— white like resurrection. As I smoked, I pretended I was breathing him in. The smoke tickled my throat and made me feel grown-up, sexy. Destructive. Glamorous.

For the first time ever, I felt fine on my own. Fine without Cedar. Fine making my own choices. I whispered the third Marybeth. The breeze blew across the cornfield and whistled against my jacket, tickling the back of my neck and sending a sea of goose bumps cascading down my skin. I laughed puffs of smoke.

I wish I could have stayed like that forever, confident in my Before. When everything was good and new and exciting.

SIXTEEN

IF I COULD STAY IN THE NUMBNESS OF THE BAR forever, I would. But it's closing and my hands rattle against my quickly emptying glass. The bartender looks exhausted, having spent the last hour sweeping up glass.

And Cedar … Cedar's singing in my ear. She's downright giddy. Maybe because she can feel it—I'm losing my grip. I'm becoming something else.

Once I'm alone again, my mood plummets. The shadows of the streetlights overarching like hungry limbs threaten to pull me into their darkness. I've always been this way, tumultuous and fast-changing as the ocean. Empty and hateful and profoundly sad without stimulation.

I think of Elijah, his easy smirk and the way he made me feel more like myself.

You're doing it again, the little voice says. *You're playing make-believe with a stranger.*

This is what I did with Richard.

It made more sense at fourteen than it does at twenty-nine, back when the world still seemed somewhat vast and I still felt somewhat full of untapped potential.

Cedar has turned in for the night. Left me to walk home all alone. Sometimes, I wonder if it isn't her propelling me towards the darkness, a point of no return, a final escape. Sometimes I wonder if she wants me to join her.

I want to blame her for my After. That if only she would have been more careful herself, I wouldn't have had to get lost within myself. I try to hide these thoughts. She scoffs, says I owe her my second chance. That I should be grateful she gave me strength.

But it all feels like wrong place, wrong time, wrong girl.

It all feels as if I brought it on myself.

Maybe that's the downside of being overly prepared. When you fail, you feel as if the only person who can possibly be blamed is yourself.

Richard would have found someone else. Who knows how long he was finding girls like me? Girls like Cedar. Tough little girls with difficult pasts who tell themselves daily that they are untouchable. That they are wiser and quicker and more aware than other girls. Girls with angry or absent fathers, occasionally one and the same; their anger takes them away even when they're right beside you. Girls with bright eyes and fiery souls and misguided hope. Girls with ruffled socks and messy hair and lip gloss. Girls like Persephone.

I officially had no friends the next time I ran into Richard. I'd taken to spending my lunch break in the pizza parlour parking lot across from the school, away from the smoker's pit and the kids with eyes that lingered on me and voices that whispered. I smoked alone, taking to stealing gold ring smokes from the bags my nan kept in her freezer. Each day, I told myself I was on a road trip. This town was a rest stop that meant nothing to me. All the people there were strangers who meant nothing to me and would never know me. My skin stopped crawling for those brief moments, concentrating on my inhale, pausing for a second or two to hold the smoke in my lungs before I released it with a languid exhale. I didn't realize it was Richard approaching me until he spoke, so accustomed as I was to letting my eyes glaze over, of pretending that I was somewhere else, that everyone around me was unrecognizable.

"Fancy running into you, kid," he said, his hand on the pizza parlour's front door.

My mind caught up as he walked towards me, and I nervously nodded a hello. He asked me if the pizza there was any good and I shrugged. I didn't eat lunch. I barely ate at all.

"It has great reviews," he said.

I shrugged again, glancing back across the street at the ringing of the bell. "I'm going to be late for class."

"I hated school too," Richard said, and I felt seen. He knew it too, by the smile that instantly lifted the corners of my lips. Without booze, talking to him made me nervous. For a second I wished that Jenny and Alyssa were still with me so they could see I was just as shy. That I wasn't a whore.

"Get extra sauce," I said, wanting him to think of me as he dug his teeth into slice after slice, eating until his stomach hurt.

I was halfway across the street when he asked if we could hang out again.

"Meet me where we first met. Tonight, 8:30?" He looked boyish in the bright afternoon sun.

I thought of making up an excuse, saying I had plans. I liked the thought of being unattainable. But in reality, once I got home my evening would only consist of trying to get from the front hallway to the sanctity of my bedroom in as few words as possible between me and my parents. A dismissive "homework" to my mom or "cramps" to my dad. So, I said yeah, sure.

In math class, I tried to figure out if I should change my clothes before meeting up with Richard or if that would show too much effort. If I should toss my long hair up in a bun to prove just how little I cared. If I should try and snatch a couple of beers from the crisper where my dad kept his Busch Lights. By the end of class I had decided I would change and even put on a bit of makeup. Thinking of it made me feel less alone, these little rituals, these little gateways into womanhood.

I did my eyeliner like Cedar had shown me, dark black flicks that made me feel feline and powerful and older. I wore a small baby blue tank top and tight blue jeans, a cropped zip-up hoodie. I spritzed myself with my mother's perfume and then layered on some Hawaiian Ginger so I still smelled like me. I didn't tell my parents where I was going, and they didn't ask. They'd become preoccupied the last couple of years, distracted, morose. Sometimes it felt as if they also played the game of five-words-or-less with me. Looking at me made them uncomfortable, as if they were face-to-face with someone they had forgotten to grieve. In a way, maybe we were all grieving the death of our whole entire family. I walked the gravel road to the park alone and the entire time I wished that Cedar was with me, even if it meant that Richard liked her more. Boys always liked her more. I guess men did too.

But she wasn't there, and she hadn't been for two years. My nerves ramped up as I walked towards him. I wished he wouldn't have noticed me so soon, each step threatening to trip me up.

Cedar would have glided, basking in his eyes on her slight hips, but I wasn't her. We weren't at the park for long before he asked if he could show me his favourite spot. I slid into Richard's car, and soon the nerves were replaced with the first stirrings of control as his eyes traced my every move while I crossed and uncrossed my legs in his leather seat. I criticized his country station and changed it to classic rock with a swirling finger and a daring, "Let's listen to some real music."

No one had ever shown interest in me before, and I wondered if he was right: I was an old soul. Wise beyond my years, mature for my age.

He had a knack for smelling the ache in me, like all men do. But I liked the sound of those things better than the reality. Cedar was gone and Theo would never be the same and love wasn't real and each Tuesday I had to go and sit in a forever too-cold room while a fat, middle-aged therapist told me it gets better while his tongue darted out and over his thin, cracked lips.

Richard and I came to a compromise and listened to pop. I watched him as he watched the road. I thought of how mad my mother would be, how she had told me since I was a toddler to never, ever, *ever* get into a car with a stranger.

Yet here I was, willingly hopping in without a fight. I felt rebellious, but it gave way to glimmers of anxiety as Richard's tires left the road and sunk down into the soft earth. I was grateful how the radio drowned out the pounding of my heart as I strained my eyes to see through the shadowy trees, awash with relief at the first hint of waning moonlight glimmering on top of the water. He hadn't spoken in five minutes, and I was years away from learning how to speak to men. How to get them to warm to you, to become attached, to long to protect you.

"Here we are." His voice was calm, joyful. "My family had a cottage here," he added, waving his arm back towards the trees.

He led me over to the dock as I muttered that it was a cool spot. I racked my brain, wondering if he mentioned the cottage to Jenny and Alyssa while I peed in the bushes. If I just didn't hear him over their tight gulps of swamp water and nervous laughter.

"There's something about you," Richard said, breaking through my thoughts as we watched the waves crash against the littered shore.

"What's that?" I asked, pushing my insecurities to the back of my mind, letting myself feel as if I was in a movie. A leading lady. Someone to be pined after. Wanted.

"You don't know how beautiful you are."

"Imagine how dangerous I'd be if I did," I whispered, a hint of nervous laughter of my own on my lips.

I didn't mean it. It just sounded like something a beautiful girl would say. It sounded like something Cedar would say. Nan said she was as cunning as the coyote, as sly as the fox. I was as gentle as the deer. I wanted to cry whenever she compared us like that, whenever I realized how obvious mine and Cedar's differences were. Nan only laughed as I sulked.

Richard had another six-pack of Budweiser, and I was happy it was just him and me there, that he hadn't asked me to send Jenny and Alyssa a text to join us. I took a tight sip of the beer Richard handed me and willed it to make me present. But as I looked out over the dark, mesmerizing water, I couldn't stop thinking about Cedar. I couldn't stop wondering where she was. Wondering what she'd say if she were here. Maybe it was the waning moon, the crashing waves, and what happened next that made her come back. Maybe she knew how desperately I needed her. On that night, I was able to think of her freely for the first time in two years without my heart racing.

Before, when I thought of Cedar too much, my vision would darken around the corners of my eyes, so I tried not to think of her at all. When I did, my legs would suddenly feel as wobbly as a newborn colt. Sickly, feverish sweat would drip down the back of my neck, and then everything would go black and she would be inches from my face—so close that I could smell her cotton candy lip gloss and Dove conditioner. Other times, she'd just be leaving a room and I'd be getting up to trail after her. Sometimes, she would be calling my name from a darkened hallway. Always, when I came to, the vomit would spill hot from my mouth and a numbness would creep into my bones. Nan gave me her abalone and a bundle of white sage when the panic first hit, while my parents put me into therapy that they couldn't afford.

"She's a little girl," I'd heard Nan whispering to my mother after the first attack. "Cedar was like a sister to her."

I could hear my mother's short, whimpering breaths, and they filled me with animosity. She didn't love Cedar. Not the way I did. Before everything happened, when Cedar first began to drift, she told me it was probably for the best if I made some new friends.

"Cedar's going to be trouble," she said, and I could see twenty years of jealousy in the lines around her mouth. Jealousy that always reared its head when my mother compared herself to her younger sister, when she compared her daughter to her niece.

"It's just a panic attack," Nan said after I'd first fainted. She lit a small piece of sage, and I watched as clouds of sweet, thick smoke billowed from the iridescent shell.

"I was going to wait until your first moon"—she waved the smoke over my head, pulled it down my flat chest—"but you need it now. It will clear the energy. And when you're really panicking, count in for four breaths and out for four." I watched as her tissue paper cheeks puckered in and out as she counted. She gave me a kiss on the head, and I thanked her without meeting her eyes.

Whenever I smell that sweet smoke, I think of her, my nan. I think of how she tried to make sure Cedar and I would have better lives than our mothers did. I think of how her failure killed her. The sage didn't help, but its scent did conceal the cigarettes I'd begun to blow out my bedroom window.

Therapy wasn't helping either. The only thing that actually helped was the splash of cold toilet water when I quietly rid myself of whatever dinner my mother had made. I liked looking at my vomit, something delicious and whole that was immediately ugly and grotesque. I enjoyed the delicate game of control, what went in my mouth, what came out. The simple habits of a girl preparing for womanhood that felt equally luxurious and disgusting.

As limiting as it was liberating.

It was the luxury of me that enticed Richard, I could tell as I slipped one of my mother's long, thin cigarettes between my lips. I stole two more from her for the occasion.

"Bitch sticks," he whispered into the chilly early fall air. I felt decadent, something to be consumed, digested, wasted.

He slid his warm hand onto the thigh of my jeans, and my stomach churned. I wondered if deep down I wanted to be just like Cedar. If I wanted to taste darkness. If I was Persephone stumbling into a crack in the earth, if I was seeking it out.

"There's just something about you," he said again, his breath warm on my cheek. "I can't stop thinking about you."

I gave him a smile but checked the time. His compliments were all I needed, a sense of approval, a sense of control that felt more fulfilling than chewing a bite of food forty-five times before spitting it out. I told myself my mom would be worried, and it felt better than the reality that she didn't even know I was gone. His hand grew hotter on my thigh, the perspiration from his palm bleeding through my pants. The nervous tingle in my stomach turned into a dull ache, and I suddenly wanted to be alone. The moment felt too real, time passing too fast.

"We'll have to do this again sometime," I said, crushing my empty can for emphasis, butting out my cigarette.

There was a flutter in my stomach different from anything I'd ever felt before.

A hyperawareness of my every ounce of flesh, a tingle in every nerve ending.

"You're trouble," he said, lips curled into a smirk with a shake of his head. His face inched closer to mine, his stubble brushing my cheek.

His hands moved up an inch.

"Maybe," I said, my spine straightening, giggling as I looked down at my hands.

"You can't play innocent now." There was a hint of laughter on his voice, but his eyes were unwavering. Serious. Set.

Richard's hand fell from my thigh, his fingers trailing up to grip my chin instead, turning my face fully towards him. "I want to kiss you."

His breath smelled like beer and cigarettes, and his tongue quickly darted against mine, unwelcome. This was it: my first kiss. Our teeth knocked awkwardly, and I thought it shouldn't feel like this, even though I had no prior reference. I pulled back and laughed, nerves rushing out of me and escaping into the night air.

"What? Not up to your standards?" Richard asked, his voice suddenly snarky.

"Just different," I said, going to stand. I thought of the long, winding dirt road he'd driven to get us here. I thought of the half hour walk home in the dark. I thought of Marybeth. Would being stuck with her be worse than being stuck with Richard?

A desperation radiated off of him, breaking the spell I'd nearly fallen into, illuminating the crack in the earth. My mom said never to play with a man's ego, but it wasn't until then, that nervous laugh of mine, that I realized how fragile they were. Men will ask you to break in ways they wouldn't even consider bending, and I love to pick at them like scabs. There's something about their quick bursts of temper that show me just how weak they are. That show me just how powerful a woman can be.

I like to relish in the desperation that oozes from them, that demands to be heard, seen, touched, tasted, fulfilled. But I was just a kid back then.

"I'll give you something that you'll like," he said.

I laughed again, even though his voice was completely stripped of its humour, its charm.

"I really have to go. I told my mom I'd be home for ten."

I sounded immature. Far from the femme fatale I wanted to be, but I couldn't help it. My stomach churned, gurgled.

"We won't keep her up too late."

Overlooking those jet-black waves, I heard Cedar speak to me. She said she loved me. Then asked, *What are you doing? Lilah, no.* It felt so good to hear her voice after two years of silence.

Richard turned and placed both of his arms on either side of my thighs, his body a cage around me. He kissed me again, open-mouthed and panting. I put my hand on his chest the way I'd seen in a movie once. Cedar said that I needed to go. Now. Her voice felt like a warm blanket. I looked over my shoulders, nearly positive I'd see her standing in the trees at the base of the dock, her clothes dirty and hair long, cheekbones more prominent than ever. Yet when I turned I saw nothing except the long shadows the moonlight was making of the pines.

"Did you used to swim in here?" My voice was higher than normal, revealing my nerves.

"What?" Richard pulled back from me, eyes hooded.

"Did you used to swim in here? When you had a cottage?" I asked again. The water contained the run off from Lake Mazi; everyone on the rez and the neighbouring town knew how polluted it was. I used to picture one-eyed fish and creatures evolving in sick and twisted ways in order to take a breath.

"Oh yeah, all the time," Richard said, his voice a rush.

"Why would you lie about having a cottage here?"

"What?" he asked again, face still close to mine.

To make you feel comfortable, Cedar said. *Only to make you feel comfortable.* I wanted to get lost in her voice. To never hear anything but. I turned towards the trees again, hoping, praying, begging to see a flash of her face, but still, I was alone.

"Are people not supposed to swim in here or something?" Richard leaned back on his hands, looking out across the water.

"It's polluted."

"Fuck, well I turned out fine." His eyes danced over my lips, down to my tank top. I imagined Richard with only one eye, scales jutting from his neck, moving in and out as he struggled to breathe like the fish I'd seen my father let flop on the floor of our dingy little row boat.

I sat frozen, looking out over the dirty water as he watched me. He tucked a fallen strand of hair behind my ear.

"Where do you work?"

"Ah, come on, you don't want to talk shop. I thought we were here to have fun." His hand reached up again, resting on my knee.

I've always wondered if deep down I didn't seek the situation out. If I didn't want to vanish too. I wanted to see darkness all for myself, to be able to try and make sense of it. It looked like a big, warm, cozy bed, and I was so, so tired. Instead of being coveted, maybe Richard was drawn to me like a moth to a flame, a girl longing to be snuffed out.

A girl longing to flirt with danger and lose.

A girl longing to flex her strengths for the very first time.

A girl longing to hurt.

Cedar's voice was husky and stern when she said I needed to go. But if I listened, I was afraid she'd stop talking. She would disappear forever. The only place for me to move was back. My hair fell through the cracks of the dock, dipping into the water beneath. And Richard hovered above me now, his breath warm on my lips, my cheeks, my chest. His eyes dogged yet his mouth curved with the hint of a smile.

"I'm not ready," I said as I heard the jangle of his belt buckle.

"Men don't work like that," he said. "You can't stop them once they've started."

He grabbed at my sweatshirt and my tank top. The cool breeze hit my stomach as he inched it up my skin, his face lowering to trail his tongue below my belly button then dipped it inside.

"I'm scared." It sounded better than "No, I don't want to." My voice, high and wispy, barely sounded like mine. I sounded sweet, innocent. I was. I thought maybe he'd turn and see me as the child that I was. Richard didn't pay it any mind as he whispered into my waist that there was nothing to be afraid of, that he'd be gentle.

I placed my hands on the dock beside me, scooting up with my triceps. Richard's head slipped from my stomach, his chin cracking on the dock beneath me. When he looked back up at me, his eyes were black holes. His hand reached up and tightened around my thigh while his other staked claim on the fly of my jeans, tugging to reveal my blue and white underwear.

Cedar's voice had dulled to a whisper, raspy and fast and fluttering like the panic in my chest, but suddenly it was clear. Dedicated. I was sure this was it. I had fully lost my mind.

Grab that rock, Cedar said.

I noticed it suddenly, inches away in the grass. Richard's eyes were downcast, watching as his fingers fumbled along the waistline of my underwear as if his hands didn't even belong to him.

"Please, stop." I made my voice smaller, sweeter, the rock jagged against the palm of my hand. I could see my After laid out before my eyes, this new wave of emptiness just waiting to slink into my delicate bones. I knew I wouldn't survive it.

"Stop," I said again as his thumb rubbed through my underwear, searching for the heat of me.

His breathing was boorish, and he made no attempt to respond, to stop. His tongue tickled my thigh, his back arched like a lion. It was as if he couldn't hear me at all. Had my voice somehow deserted me like everything else?

Swing, Cedar whispered.

I thought of her running as my bat cracked the ball, her screams gleeful as she skidded to home base. I swung once, the rock slamming against his temple with a thud. Awareness entered his eyes, looking up at me as if I had awoken him from a dream. He kicked at my legs, and for a second I pictured myself falling, Richard clamouring on top as his blood and sweat trickled down onto me. I whacked him again, the meaty sound echoing across the water. His voice was a disillusioned whine as I lifted the rock again.

"Stop, I have two kids," he muttered as I swung once, twice, three times, four, grunting with each thud, the sounds reverberating off of the surrounding trees. Like him, I pretended I couldn't hear as I thought of every ounce of happiness that had slipped through my hands. It was easy to blame Richard, this nondescript man, for all that had gone wrong. My legs were warm when I looked down, and my grunts broke way for a sob as I saw what was left of him: his dark hair matted as if he had just been swimming, blood pooling from his temple onto the aging dock, his skin bright white beneath the night sky.

Richard's lifeless fingers still clawed around the edges of my underwear. I scooted back quickly, a gasp escaping my lips as I chucked the rock still clenched in my hands into the water beneath us, willing it to sink like a secret.

It created a splash before it sank with a plop of air that felt final. I tried not to look at him as my legs strained to push, push, push, until he was no longer on me, until he belonged to the dirtied water.

Water that he swam in anyway.

I knew that he'd float within days, so I did my best to wipe down the door handle of his car, the dial of his radio.

On my walk back to the road, I peered towards the abandoned cottage, its windows broken and front stoop sinking into the soil. How many times had he brought girls like me to this little oasis in the middle of the woods? How many girls had shivered as they thought of overarching trees and crashing waves, of docks that should have filled them with a sense of adventure but only left them numb? Did he let them leave, let them carry on with their memories of him and his car, his smooth voice, his hungry mouth, his determined cock? Did these girls tell themselves that it was their fault? That men can't stop once they've started.

I wondered if Richard believed his own lies.

I wondered if Richard felt a sense of peace as his blood pooled and his consciousness wavered.

I wondered if he could hear Cedar too.

I wondered if he could see her.

I wondered if he felt remorseful, wherever he went, for showing me my strength.

SEVENTEEN

AND SO, I'VE BECOME SOMETHING I NEVER WANTED TO be. That's a coming-of-age feeling, though, isn't it? The world moulding us into people we never thought we'd be. Nothing has felt as good as the choice I made that night. Of being the one with the power to snuff another out, to create another's erasure. Men, they don't seem to notice how their actions subtract us from ourselves. Worse, they don't seem to care.

I'm over-intellectualizing. Maybe I just stumbled upon killing. I never wanted to be a killer. It's just one of the choices we are never told we have.

The message to women has always been to stay home, to hide out, to do everything to keep ourselves from danger. To not get ourselves into *trouble*. Don't attract the wrong kinds of *attention*. My mother has barely left the house for years, and I don't blame her. If her lessons have traumatized me, her pain has traumatized her.

My mind wanders to the men who will become monsters and

the women who will disappear. The ones we'll search for, the ones we'll discover bloodied and broken and free, and the ones who will remain intact—except the light is missing from their eyes. Women like my mother. The missing glow only noticed by those who were aware of its shine, who long for its return. Somehow, the latter creates the biggest ache in the pit of my stomach—those still with us who float through their lives like ghosts.

Like my mother, the media says we shouldn't be vengeful. It's just biology that's made us soft, a gentle mixture of nature and nurture. It's just biology that made them callous.

The statement rests in my psyche like a rock.

When I think of all that's gone wrong, I surprisingly don't think of Glen, or Richard, or Aunt Cindy's boyfriend, or even my father—all I think of is Ian. And when I think about Ian, when I really think about Ian, my heart feels like a pus-filled wound, forever infected.

He never lets it crust over. How could he let it heal when I let him rip off my bandages, stick his dirty fingers in my tender gash? After enough times, it's as if I've given him permission, as if he has an all-access pass to me that will never expire.

Sometimes I think if I made everything right with him, if he loved me, it would all be worth it. I would no longer crave love and escape and violence and vengeance. I would feel whole. His love would erase all of the instances of his indifference that I've accepted as love.

We met on a Tuesday. I was already a murderer, but I was still a virgin. My After looked very different from the women who'd raised me.

I was at the front of the high school, waiting for my mom's green minivan to pull up and take me to Doctor Harrison's office.

Inside the doors as per her wishes. Ian was on his way to the principal's office. He had always seemed mythical to me, this tether to a different life. A better life, where Cedar was still a phone call away, a bike ride away. The very first time I had seen Ian was on Cedar's computer three years before. A Facebook message that read:

Sup?

Cedar and Ian shared English the second semester of grade nine, and he waited a month to message her. She squealed and playfully bit her nails as she showed me his profile.

"He's cuter in person," she said, a little sheepishly which was unusual for her.

Ian was taller than anyone I'd ever seen, and his neck was garishly thin. When he walked past me and said, "Hey," he sounded nervous. I liked him immediately. Cedar was right. He was cuter in person. I'd seen him in the halls, but he had never acknowledged my existence. He was in grade eleven, and I was not one of the grade nines that got scooped up by Thanksgiving. I barely had tits.

"Hey," I said, breathy and foolish, and it showed my hand—back then, I didn't know how to hide it. I hadn't felt giddy since Richard, but that crashed and burned. Even thinking of Richard made me feel irrevocably broken, dirty, damaged, monstrous. My baby steps into womanhood had ended as abruptly as they'd begun. I was gun-shy.

But Ian just smiled and two days later added me on Facebook and, since Zuckerberg was yet to defeat Gates, asked for my MSN. I was ecstatic. I secretly always longed to take something that Cedar wanted. I wanted to be the coveted one.

The screen in front of me looked dreamy and mythical, as most things did since Richard; I'd started drinking every day. First stolen sips from my parents' liquor cabinet, which sat mostly unused except for that grey area between Christmas and New Years when there is little to do other than drink. I never bothered to fill anything up with water, always sampling a different bottle each afternoon. Before school, two quick shots of mouthwash would make me present, but three would make me feel as if I was floating through life, and that was my favourite. Drinking made it easier to ignore all of the things that had gone horribly, horribly wrong. Drinking made it easier to ignore the sadness that was more often than not in the eyes of every single person I loved. Drinking made it easier to ignore the urge to slip into my parents' room while they slept and take a hunting knife to my father's stubbled throat while he snored, sprawled out as if he deserved to be there. Drinking dulled everything until I felt almost normal. All I longed for was normalcy.

Ian looked like an escape into a normalcy better than intoxication. Ian was worlds away from the voices that kept me up at night and gurgled up my esophagus. He wouldn't want a girl who got drunk off of Listerine and longed to kill her father and herself and was afraid that one day she would be caught for killing a near stranger. He wouldn't want a girl with guilt nibbling away at her insides, threatening to leave a bloody hole. Ian would want someone calm, cool, sane. Someone like Cedar. And I could do that, couldn't I? Pretend?

His message rolled in with a ding. I bit my nails as I first messaged him back. I never bit my nails, but I liked feeling like Cedar. Wearing her eyeliner and clothes, messaging the boy she liked, trying to speak the way she did: cocky, calm, fearless. Maybe

I thought it would make her jealous enough that she'd come back. Maybe I just wanted to feel what it felt like to be her.

I sat in the dark living room, my face glowing in the artificial light of the family computer as I stared at Ian's name on the screen and repeated, "Message me, message me," beneath my breath like a spell.

His "Sups?" were lazy, and he probably sent them to a lot of other girls—but I didn't think that back then.

I would just stare at it for a couple of minutes, his name flashing down at the bottom of the screen before I'd slowly type:

Not too much, you?

The conversation never blossomed much further than that, yet nearly every day I'd get one as soon as I logged on after school. When he didn't message me, I'd log off, watching the clock for ten minutes before I logged back on so he'd see my name flash again and think of me. Fingers crossed.

It happened slowly and then all at once, the way these things do.

One night he invited me skateboarding, and when I got there I realized he had a girlfriend from another school. What initially felt like a letdown rested into a firm stroke of my ego; it was my first example of how he asserted himself in plain sight. He had invited another friend, and initially I thought he'd planned a double date without my knowledge, but I kept catching him taking peeks at me when he thought I wasn't looking. Maybe he wanted his girlfriend to think we were on a double date.

The warm June air held the promise of summer, of new beginnings, of better days. I wanted Ian's attention more than I'd ever wanted anything before. I wanted him to fall in love with me.

His girlfriend was gorgeous with tan skin and waist-length jet-black hair (kind of like Cedar), but he didn't seem fazed by her. She was a toy he had tired of. I could see that even then. He was more attentive to me, and I felt like I mattered as her voice went from whiney to indifferent, until she stopped talking altogether, shoulders slumped while she texted quickly with the tips of her tacky, fake nails. Ian continued to talk to me, and it made me laugh louder, this little game of *fuck you* that I'd never gotten the chance to play before. My voice shook as I wobbled on the skateboard. Ian held out his hands to balance me.

"You're doing good," he whispered reassuringly.

I placed my full weight on the board for a second or two before hopping off in a fit of embarrassed laughter. When I went to leave, he flicked my ponytail and said, "We should do it again sometime."

His girlfriend shot me a dagger and I liked it, that sizzle of power. A stab of envy that confirmed me as a threat—a woman in my own right. I thought of Jenny and Alyssa calling me a whore and realized they must have been threatened too.

The next evening on MSN he typed:

Last night was fun.

And I typed:

It was.

And then before I lost my nerve:

It's stupid hot. I wish I had a pool.

I KNEW HE DID AND WATCHED RAPT AS THE SCREEN said he was typing. I pictured the bright blue water against the navy sky, us sharing a forbidden kiss in the pool. Him breaking up with his girlfriend. People talking negatively about me at school in a voice that almost resembled awe. Holding hands in the halls before class, driving me around in his car at lunch.

He'd say there was something about me and not immediately reach for the fly of my jeans, the zipper of my sweater. We'd be in love. He would be my vehicle away from tragedy, away from mental illness. Ian would normalize me.

Theo idled in the doorway of our living room, shattering my picture-perfect fantasy. He kept coming back every five minutes for the last twenty to ask when I'd be off. Practising patience had been difficult since the accident. He was more childlike at thirteen than he ever was at ten. We had become less like best friends and more like exasperated roommates. Sometimes, I talked to him slowly just to hurt him, always thinking it would somehow make me feel better. It never did.

I waved him out of the room with a promise of five more minutes, and he let out a groan as Ian's message flashed across the screen:

Come over then.

I wanted to shut off the computer, make an excuse tomorrow at school about my mom needing to use the phone, Theo freaking out as Theo sometimes did.

But instead, I just wrote:

Okay.

When I got to Ian's house, his charm was replaced by the awkward jerk of nerves. For a while all we did was sit silently on the deck, our toes dipped into the lukewarm water, surrounded by the soothing scent of chlorine. His cologne was like breathing in a bag of freshly opened marshmallows with a hint of cloves.

I asked about his girlfriend and he said that she was moving away soon, that they didn't want to do long distance. He sounded so grown-up when he said it. He didn't ask me much about myself. He didn't mention Cedar and their fling three years before, when they were both fourteen. I was happy that he didn't. I felt nervous and giddy. If there were warning signs, I missed them all.

His parents' bedroom was on the second floor of his house. We were extra quiet as we slipped off our clothes and sank into the water. Sitting on the deck, I'd felt the inches between our thighs like a current, but he slipped his arms around my waist as soon as we were submerged into the initial shock of cool. Chilled skin and silky water quickly became my two favourite sensations. He had this uncanny ability of melting my past with a look, of turning me into someone prettier, funnier, better. Undamaged. I tightened my legs around his waist and felt weightless as I looked into his eyes, dark blue and flecked by the yellow lights. He kissed me then, his tongue a frightened snake that scurried from the garden when I helped my mom pull weeds in the spring.

I felt my hips melt forward, a warmth in my stomach I'd never experienced before—on the edge of dipping into an awakening. The moment was instinctual, natural, freeing. The world seemed to vanish as he carried me around the pool. The hitch in his breath when I pulled my hot mouth from his felt like power.

He was hard against me, throbbing and hungry and powerless. I ran my fingers down his face, as soft as the leaf of an African violet. All at once I felt gorgeously innocent and animalistic, demurely wild like a mythical creature you'd only watch from afar.

"I'm a virgin," I whispered. For once I felt free of the shame that I felt at school as I overheard talk of birth control and bittersweet, milky semen. Free from the ache in my stomach as I heard girls my age talk about desire.

The daze in his eyes changed for a split second then. His hands moved from my ass back to my waist, grip firm and tender and precious.

"Your first time should be something special," he whispered, breath warm on my cold earlobe.

I didn't want it to be special until he said that.

I thought of the girls at school who cried in the halls over silly, cruel teenage boys that they had been tricked into giving everything to. Girls who I never wanted to resemble. In that moment I wanted to tell him the truth. Of another moonlit night so different from this one. I wanted to tell him that he was redemptive and beautiful and so fucking hot. That he made me feel like someone precious, but that I wasn't precious. That I was bad. That we didn't have to wait.

I had always wanted to fuck the way boys did. Before Richard, I had wanted to suck the juices of life, feel a passion that didn't bind me into thinking it was a love that would last forever. A passion that didn't mar who I was or who I could be. I wanted to be like a boy, mouth lapping at experiences yet never changed by them. It all felt so manageable and realistic before I was changed myself, before I became a killer.

I didn't want a boy to feel as if I owed him any parts of me. I wanted him grateful. I wanted a boy who didn't look at me like a slut as I was wrapped around his body. I wanted a boy to look at me as a gift, a privilege. Ian felt like that kind of boy. Wild in his own right, he wouldn't even view me as promiscuous. Nan used to say that in traditional Indigenous communities, sex was something sacred. Cedar and I would blush and scoff and laugh. We never got the chance to discuss how we wanted to be sacred. How we one day hoped to be matriarchs. It's funny, looking back, and thinking of how sweet Ian was with his throbbing cock and his gentle hands and his lying mouth that said my first time needed to be special.

I smiled all the way home, even as my pussy pulsed with want for him.

His unexpected care for me convinced me of the blossoms of love. I was no longer satisfied with only fucking him. His desire to wait made me want more, more, more.

Life is a series of events that chisel you into something else completely.

IT'S A DIFFERENT WALK HOME AS MY EYES SCAN THE street ahead of me. I walk down the road, stepping to the sidewalk only for the passing of cars which there are only two. However, each one leaves me veering tight to the shadows, wishing I had a bike to clutch onto. Just last week a woman made the mistake of walking by a man who was parked on the side of the road looking for something in his trunk, and as she passed, he tossed her in.

There are rumours of unchanged men beginning to kidnap women for their changing friends and relatives. Our flesh satiates their violence if only for a few hours. It appears the changing prefer to stay on foot, abandoning their vehicles to sneak along alleys, beside rivers, through fields. Watching, waiting, hunting. Inside of every man, there's a voice that tells him he might be God. That he can control who suffers. He is a descendant of Adam, and as descendants of Eve, we have been made just for him. It is us that tempt his evil. It is always us.

I think of Elijah, humble and attentive despite his magnetic beauty. Lacking all of the entitlement that's rotting the men around him as he deep dives on the internet in search of information that resembles nightmares. My intoxicated state resembles confidence but can easily stumble into the dangerous drunk of carelessness. I feel light on my feet.

I long to hunt the hunters.

I always have.

Deep down I think I've always known that men would ruin the world. They're haunted.

I want to play their own game and win. Men have taught us they have no remorse, feeling bad only when they're caught. Bad, cruel men and men I've loved with all of my heart. Men that I've so desperately wanted to believe are inherently good. Men like my father.

I think of Glen's desperate, watery eyes, his raspy pleading voice. Only sorry once he's unable to twist away from the consequences of his own actions, now that he's at the end of the line.

Women internalize our shame. We tell ourselves we deserved it. It's all we've ever been shown. We know that even the good ones will make selfish mistakes. When my father finally smashed the delicate glass that our seemingly perfect family was encased in, my mother said, "Even the good ones mess up. Even the good ones are selfish." As if it was men's right, their human nature. I hated her for it. I pity her for it. That she can't untangle herself, but then again, neither can I. They've made me a ghost, weighing expressions and struggling to decipher intent all while the present is passing me by. They've prepared me for the end.

Half a block ahead of me a woman travels from post to post with a stack of bright white papers and a staple gun. She stops, facing a telephone pole. The stack flutters at her feet as she staples one up with a punch. The click sounds menacing from afar. It keeps them away. I'm sure that's what she's hoping. The wind whistles over my shoulder, flurrying half her stack along the road. She lets out a howl. I rush over and grab a few that have been picked up in the wind and hand them over to her. She jumps as I approach and quickly tightens her grip around the stapler. I can't help but laugh.

"Shit, sorry," I say, composing my chuckle and stepping back with an arm outstretched, waving her flyers towards her. She lets out a tight sigh of relief, but it's only a second until she glances over her shoulders again.

"I didn't hear you." The realization that when it comes down to it, she can't trust her own senses clouds her features. Her instincts are off. She is not a predator.

After her darting eyes confirm we are alone, she looks down at the thick stack of papers extended between us. I follow her gaze until our eyes are both staring at a black-and-white photo of a little girl. She's missing her two front teeth, and all I can hear is my nan singing "All I want for Christmas (Is My Two Front Teeth)" from an old family video.

"Your daughter?"

She nods as she stares past me at the photo pinned to the pole. "She really wanted to go to school last week for a spelling bee. I've been wanting to pull her out. I'm at work when she gets off the bus

—" The woman's eyes are distant, watching a different, better life play out behind her sockets. "I knew as soon as the news started talking about girls and women staying home in other countries that I should be vigilant. That it would only be a matter of time." She looks down again, her thumb grazing the grey ink of her daughter's cheek. "But, she's a little girl. She's just a little girl," she whispers.

The heading of the sheet reads MISSING in big, bold letters.

I don't ask her how long it's been. By the weight of her shoulders, the purple shadows beneath her eyes, it has to be over forty-eight hours. The hysterics in her voice have morphed into a sombre monotone that to the unexperienced ear might even be mistaken for indifference or acceptance. But I know it's just a lifelessness. It reminds me of my nan, how her light, twinkling voice suddenly dimmed. Her expressions shortened. Her health deteriorated.

The woman in front of me has an expiration date, the decay already beginning to settle into her bones. It reminds me of my own. I want to drag whatever man responsible by his hair, lay him at her feet tortured and begging.

Grief has the power to change our composition too.

I follow her like a shadow as she continues to poster each pole. The pain radiates off her like a smog in my lungs. She's lost to a non-reality that doesn't sting. This dreamland that begs you to step foot in it.

She begins to cry as she staples the final poster, taking a step back to look at her daughter's face in dull black and grey ink. This kind of grief deserves solitude, and I have never been a comforting person. My inability to get out of my head for the needs of someone else makes me feel selfish. Does she want to disappear too?

"Can I walk you home?" I really want to ask about the child's father. Has she lost him too? Will I lose my own?

If I ever went missing, my daddy would burn the world down. He'd search tirelessly. He'd strangle whoever hurt me with his bare hands, kicking them until their body was mush. My father loves me so much he would kill anyone who harmed me, but he's never thought twice about how he's hurt me. He'd slit a man's throat if he ever hurt my mother.

The men we trust, it's their job to hurt us. They are very territorial over it, who inflicts our pain. My father acts as if he doesn't know that his selfishness will always reside in my bones like marrow. He used to say fucked-up shit like if a man ever wanted to kill a woman all he needed to do was go out West. Men look at murdering us as an experience, something to scratch off a bucket list. They look at killing us similar to how they look at sleeping with us: their choice. He would never say anything about women killing men because it so rarely happens. Women killing men is considered hysterical, impulsive.

He can't see the link, the subtle, constant objectification of women and the violence inflicted against us. How men have been conditioned to believe that we're here just for them, vessels for their judgment, pleasure, and hatred. And since we're here just for them, we can be treated however they deem acceptable. The funny thing is, my father says he's completely against violence towards women but then tells me I need to learn when to shut the fuck up.

It all makes me feel so incredibly alone.

The woman shakes her head, sighing as she places the heels of her hands against her eyes to aggressively wipe her tears.

"I don't mind, really. I could use the company." I want to tell her that I can protect her. That I have a knife, that I'm ready to kill.

"No, that's okay," she says too firmly for my fragile ego. I stare at her for a split second too long, my mouth partially agape. The rejection stings my eyes. I despise this insatiable need to be wanted.

"Okay," I say, too quickly, too aloof, too high, too fake. She turns to leave and I add, "You'll find her." It sounds too similar to "I'm sorry" at a funeral. I regret it the minute we lock eyes.

Cedar wants me to hug the woman, to hold her tight to my chest. The initial hours of the mother's search have settled into a monotonous numbness, and I know that feeling all too well. As the days pass you go from picturing their smiling face to picturing them pale, frightened; dirty and bruised to empty-eyed yet still breathing; to bloated and lifeless. Eventually, all you want is their body. The closure that comes from laying them in the ground and placing a few flowers upon the freshly turned earth. It's then that you don't feel too different from the men that started the ugly chain of events in the first place, only wanting a body. But you'll never be the same—he treated her as if she wasn't there when she still was, you want her free.

The woman walks off into the inky night, her staple gun swinging at her side, pathetic yet charmingly brave. Maybe she's hoping for it all to end tonight. For her own face to smile back from telephone poles next week. The police have been absolutely swamped with missing persons reports, but the men filing the reports are careful not to reveal the fact that they're more concerned over whether or not the virus will get them than they are the vanishing women and children.

The rage that boils up in me feels ancient, instinctual, necessary. This world holds us hostage—controlling how we carry ourselves, what we wear, how we feel about ourselves when we're alone. How we're searched for when we're missing. Who gets searched for at all.

Dictating which ones of us are deserving of justice.

Our lives are ruled by *just in case's* and *be careful's*, and then comes the blame: *What were you thinking? What did you expect?*

The snickers over our bodies, our brains, our choices, our lives. Guttural grunts and hateful laughs and lies. Lies to get us, lies to keep us, lies to leave us, lies to harm us.

The slurs, the dismissals, the pain between our legs.

The broken trust, the slamming doors, the blackened eyes.

The hungry children, the tortured animals, the dirty water, the toxic air.

All flesh fed, homegrown and raised on toxic masculinity.

This rage is ancestral.

I think of those sweet ones, the Elijahs. The fear and rage rumbles like bile, the anxiety that he is just another kind of monster. The kind that you hope will save you from yourself.

The wind bites against my cheeks, pushing Elijah's coat tight between my legs. I'm grateful for the sudden kindness, yet wish he were still here for me to dissect. I long for men to let me alter their lives the way they have altered mine. To let me give them wings if only to clip them and watch them writhing around on hopeless spindly little legs.

Cedar says I shouldn't sell myself short. I've done that, I've changed lives. She tells me to be brave. *You're not bad like them. You're better.*

I wear this rage like a second-skin. It races through my veins, hot beneath my flesh.

We have always had the ability to be wild. In Mohawk raónha is *male* while akaónha is *female*. Yet aónha, *animal,* is the root of us all. When I see him seated alone on a park bench, his neck beginning to curve forward so viciously that within days he will be unable to ever again look up at the sky, to see the sun or the stars or the migrating geese, he looks like hope. The fear I felt from earlier, as his shoulder pressed into mine, has been replaced by a dull anger. An acceptance. A promise. A gift. A becoming. I pull on a pair of gloves as I ask Cedar to please show me what his last hour held. Her response is a whimpered, *No.* She knows I already know.

The creature's nails are chipped and tainted with dirt and blood. Blood that had so much potential to be my own.

"What did you do?" I ask, heavy with the weight of disbelief. I pinch my thigh hard. This is not a dream.

A cell phone rests on his thigh, the screen coloured with tan skin, light skin, dark skin, a grid of photos of unsuspecting women. I watch from the shadows as he tries jamming a swollen knuckle against the screen.

I will take pictures of your cunt. It's his kink, and it predates the virus. I see him for what he is. His body is just catching up.

He has yet to see me as his breath becomes increasingly frustrated like that of a huffing, overworked horse.

I think of the lives he's marred, ruined. Cedar's right. There is nothing wrong with cutting the fat, culling the creatures.

The streets are barren except for us, two monsters amongst the shadows.

His bomber jacket is tacky and shiny beneath the streetlights. The handle of the knife in my palm is heavy with potential, my mind suddenly clear as I approach him quickly.

A jaw that only hours before was still clenched and human has dipped, leaving room for his protruding canine teeth and a slack stupidity. Eyes, which might have been the first aspect to change, hold nothing but a dull exhaustion, the want in them stripped. There is blood on his fraying jeans, and I know it's not his. Maybe that's why he looks calm. Maybe, like men, sex depletes them. He remains silent as my blade presses firmly against his jugular. I wonder if he hates his existence as much as I do as I slice, the metallic scent wafting up at me in a rush of warmth as his spirit escapes to wander forever, aimlessly.

I wipe his blood against the skirt of my sundress, not caring that it ruins the periwinkle flowers, the mint green leaves, the innocence of it, how it tarnishes my own sensuality. It becomes hidden quickly amongst the heavy, navy blue fabric of Elijah's coat.

In his choking, gurgling struggle, he falls from the bench, twisting his body into fetal position on the dirt. I think of his mother, the joy she felt when he was first placed in her arms, pink and soft and wriggling, the shame and anguish she'd feel now.

My camera whirs to life and he isn't yet dead, but he won't live for long.

I will take pictures of your cunt.

I laugh as I think of his words, so confident and entitled and disgusting.

"You are weak," I whisper to him, this dying thing that longed to inflict pain upon me. This stranger who showed me no kindness. How many others have there been? This rage is ancestral.

I take two photos. One for myself and one for the world.

Something about his eyes is almost peaceful, and I think of the people who love him, the ones who saw only the good. The ones who would be surprised by his change. Shocked voices saying, "I don't believe that," or "But he was just so nice."

Beneath his photo I write: **HE CHOSE THIS.**

I place the Polaroid in his slack hand. He chose this. I want the world to know that he chose this.

For the first time, in what feels like a lifetime, Cedar is proud of me.

I might even be proud of myself.

He chose this.

EIGHTEEN

from Elijah:

Did you make it home safe? It was nice to meet you.

I stare at it but don't respond, my stomach twisting in guilt even as butterflies flit about. The blood on his jacket reminds me that I'm tainted, that in knowing me he'll be tainted too. I should protect him. Save him from myself.

That thing I captured on my flimsy piece of film and left in front of the park bench all cold and bloody and alone wasn't the first monster I've killed. It would be justifiable, killing only once they revealed their monstrosity. But then there's Richard, in the cobwebbed corners of my mind, hovering inches above my face during those nights of booze-induced sleep paralysis. And when I see him now, I can't move, I can't swing, and the worst part about it is the anger that once clouded his features during our last encounter has been replaced by a face full of sadness. A face that tells me I should feel guilty. I close my eyes until the weight of him passes. The others don't haunt me the way he does, this first man who made me what I am.

You can only feel guilt for so long until it manifests into something else. Be it numb. Be it rage. Be it entitlement. Be it satisfaction.

I wish I could know for certain that if Richard were still here, he would be changing. I wish I knew that ultimately I did a good deed however premature. Back then, I was just a scared little child who got the opportunity to swerve. Now, I see it clearly. How I swerved, how this world makes us swerve. But what have I lost along the way?

I like to think that I'm growing into my own. Filling out my skin. Becoming.

Even if I'm becoming less of myself.

Even if I'm leaving.

Even if I'm making room for someone else. Cedar shushes me. *You're okay, you're okay, you're okay.* She believes I've saved others. I don't know if that's true.

That little man in the alley fills me with a sense of pride. That he died between ignorance and the realization he was slipping into monstrosity. That he never had to fully suffer for his sins. That a lifetime spent thinking that he was one of the good ones boiled down to his final hours accosting women in the street. That his last moment was spent victimized by a woman he longed to have under his thumb, under his tongue, beneath his hips. That it was ultimately his entitlement that led to his demise. I can't help feeling accomplished, and I hope that his brain was still firing in a way that he knew he facilitated his downfall.

The feeling of pride, like all of my feelings, is fleeting.

What if stooping to their level makes you one of them? I feel my forehead for hints of a fever.

Stripped of my clothes, it's my turn to lie in fetal position. I twirl thick strings of shag carpet between my bleach-stained fingers. The smell of bleach has always been soothing. Like all of my favourite things, it reminds me of a bright white nothingness. Today, the lingering scent seems sinister. My heart pounds in my ears, veins jutting from my jugular. Fresh guilt bangs against the inside of my ribs, begging for release. There's nowhere for her to go. I wrap my arms tightly around my waist, gently rocking back and forth as a low groan hums from my throat. I am good. I am good. I am good.

We all think we're good.

I look at my pale hands, the white, pruned tips of my fingers. The hands of a girl who has just scrubbed a kitchen, a bathroom. That shiver of accomplishment, I shrivel it. A proverbial *la la la* to the memories and the little voice and Cedar who all say that I can take power back. I can make them beg. I can leave them lonelier than they've ever been. *Remember when the guilt faded and you fully realized what you were capable of?* the little voice asks. And asks again. Showing me facedown on a different floor, looking at pale, bleach-stained fingers.

We do what we have to do.

Sometimes we have to fight, Cedar whispered. *Fight for me.*

I begged for Marybeth on the walk home from the lake that chilly October night. I wanted to stay fourteen forever, to stay with Cedar wherever she was. I thought maybe Marybeth would understand me. Maybe she'd hold me and hush me and keep me with her. I thought of our individual loneliness cancelling each other out. I thought of her being proud of me. A little white-washed Indigenous girl who got away.

My wrists felt weak. I clenched and unclenched my fingers but my hands did not feel as if they belonged to me. Turning them over, palms up, palms down, they glowed blueish white beneath the night sky. I thought of slitting my wrists and wandering between the blowing stalks. I wondered if the pain would make me present. If the pain would make me realize that I was always me all along. I am here. I am here. I am here.

The glowing headlights had the same effect. My initial thought was of Richard, soaked and angry and after me. My second thought was of Cedar, hopping out of a stranger's car with a nonchalant laugh as if she had never left, her hair waist length and shiny, the way she always wanted it. I clenched and unclenched my hands again as panic surged up my chest, these guilty hands that belonged only to me.

I glanced down at the dainty traces of Richard's blood on my pants. I tried my best to scrub them clean with the lake water that held the earthy stink of dead fish. In the darkness my jeans just looked wet. My sweatshirt and tank top were miraculously still the bright baby blue they had been hours earlier when I felt full of hope and butterflies. I stepped onto the shoulder of the road, turning my body towards the cornfield, careful not to be in full glare of the beams of light.

I thought of running into the field as the car began to slow, its tires hitting the shoulder with a soft thump and brake lights that beamed red. I wondered if this wasn't my karma delivered swiftly.

"Do you need a ride?"

The cruiser came to a complete stop. I would have recognized Deb's voice anywhere. It was the second most important voice I longed to hear whenever I raced to the kitchen to answer the ringing phone, sometimes waiting and crossing my fingers and uttering a small, "Please, please, please," beneath my breath before saying hello. It was never her on the other end. It was usually empty air, the warning before a telemarketer begins their spiel.

"I'm fine!" I called, careful not to meet her eyes, not to reveal mine swollen and crazed.

"Dee, it's cold and it's only a five-minute drive."

"Exactly. I'm super close to being home. I'm fine."

I kept my eyes glued to the small patch of dirt road ahead of each of my steps, trying not to let my mind race to the blood on my jeans, the potential state of smeared eyeliner that was once so perfect.

"Okay, okay, thank you," I said as Deb opened her car door. My vision threatened to fail me, and my voice sounded as if it were coming from outside of my body, from somewhere small and crouched within the field.

Deb kept her eyes straight forward as I hopped into the back of the car.

"You could have hopped up front," she said with a laugh on her breath, shutting her door and sliding the car into Drive.

"Old habits die hard." I tried desperately to keep the trepidation from my voice.

"Are you okay?" Deb asked, craning her neck to glance at me over her shoulder.

I said a silent prayer of gratitude that she was only choosing to look at me after the interior lights of the car had shut off and I was once again cloaked in darkness. I muttered something that sounded affirmative. Staring out the window at the passing trees, I wished I could tell Cedar that Marybeth didn't come for me. That Marybeth didn't exist. I clenched my eyes tight hoping to once again hear Cedar's voice, but I heard nothing except the low hum of the radio and Deb's tires atop the dirt road.

"How's your brother?"

It was that question that led to me getting escorted out of the cop shop. Deb had told me to focus on Theo, that it was a miracle he'd recovered the way he did. That I should count my lucky stars and focus on someone still here, someone who needed me.

She cleared her throat as she careened the car down the dark road. "Your mom and dad? They good?"

"Yeah, yup, everyone's great." I could see the light from my front porch. "Thanks so much, eh?" I said quickly as she began to slow, placing my sweaty palm on the car door the second she parked, my legs swinging out before she could turn and really see me.

I shut the door quickly as she rolled down the passenger side window.

"Delilah? Are you okay?"

I desperately wanted to cry. To tell Deb what had happened and let her comfort or punish or understand. But mostly I didn't want to pass out in my driveway. I didn't want her to wake up my parents or take me to the cold, quiet station.

When Richard's body was eventually found bloated and bludgeoned, and the reports rolled in of his work trips and his affliction for budding, tormented girls, I wondered if she thought of me damp and distressed and alone and reeking like a rotting fish in the sun. He was found by a man walking his dog, his body amongst the garbage-lined beach. A news story ran later about a sixteen-year-old girl who came forth and said that the dead man on the news had raped her three years before. It was that story that began to mould my guilt into something useful.

That night my eyes seemed darker, my skin brighter. My hands gleamed powerful as I wrung them together over and over, fascinated by the remnants of Richard's blood beneath my chipped nail polish. I flipped them over, staring in awe at my capabilities. I almost didn't want to wash them, but when I did there was something almost sensual about scrubbing and scrubbing and scrubbing yet never feeling clean. There was something sort of metamorphic about the scalding hot water and the discarding of my clothing. I stood naked in front of the bathroom mirror and knew that I would never be the same. I was forever altered. I had forever altered myself. The thought was somehow freeing after an adolescence of attempting (and failing) to grip onto some semblance of control. I had created my very own After.

I told myself I would never kill again, and I believed it.

The little voice whispered, *You don't know yourself.* Cedar added, *But didn't it feel good?*

I drank half a bottle of Listerine. I went to sleep listening to the gentle sounds of Cedar's voice that I had missed with every fibre of my being.

I'm proud of you, La-la-la-lilah.

Tonight doesn't feel so far from that night.

NINETEEN

There are subtleties to violence.

Little lies that pave way for larger hurts.

Men won't think twice about lying to us. It is their world. Their entitlement is inherited just as much as our rage. They have to make the conscious choice to respect us, and even the best sometimes lose sight of what that even looks like.

The guilt that rots against my ribs is reminiscent of all of the harm I have inflicted, all of the lies I've told.

It took me two months to stop looking over my shoulders whenever I was out of the house. The remnants of Richard's blood had been meticulously scrubbed, but still I checked beneath my nails, sure I'd see specks of rust. I took my clothes, double wrapped in grocery bags and tucked into the bottom of a black garbage bag, to the curb the night after I killed him. Yet a stench seemed to emanate from my closet as if I'd never disposed of them at all. I was a monster. I felt numb. The only feeling I could dredge up was one of cheap defiance. Richard brought his fate onto himself. I kicked myself for not cutting off his dick and stuffing it into his mouth. I would not be a victim of this world the way every other single fucking person seemed to be.

I think of the stranger's body becoming stone cold overnight. Of being found tomorrow morning as someone goes to sit down with a coffee and their cell phone. What kind of person will find him? Someone brave enough to look closely and see the Polaroid clutched in his hand like a gift from beyond? Or someone who only screams, calls the police from thirty feet away, until they convince themselves that maybe they didn't even see what they thought they saw—maybe he's just passed out.

The thought makes me feel powerful, someone stumbling upon my dirty work.

My hands travel down my hips to my thighs, and I wonder why no one ever takes the time to caress the subtle, most beautiful parts of my body.

They say that nature's aphrodisiac is grief, but what if it's guilt?

What if shame fuels our sex?

With its slippery sweet distractions and its ability to freeze time and empty our minds. Alter our impressions of ourselves. At least my guilt has always made me feel as if I am in control of my own downfall.

I think of the women who'll smile when his photo flashes across the screen, when he's marked as murdered. The ones who will appreciate my Polaroid for what it is—art.

Will he get any coverage at all? Neck slumped, teeth yellow and protruding. Will his killer be marked an anonymous hero? Or will the TV flash with a photo of him before? Will they list his achievements the way they did when Glen was questioned for Cedar's disappearance? Will they light candles? Will the park bench be adorned with a plaque? Will the police say wrong place, wrong time?

Will they say that someone stole his strength?

Will they suspect a woman?

Will Deb see the Polaroid on the news and know that it's me?

Will she secretly agree with Cedar? It's time to take our power back the only way they've shown us how: violently.

The second Polaroid of this ugly stranger lies in front of me on the floor, bloody and lifeless. Will anyone be proud to have known me? I glance at the abalone shell with its twigs of sage and feel a desperate urge to free myself from myself. I long for the smoke to rise up and clear my own energy, extinguishing it into the abyss like an exorcism.

Will people say they never saw it coming the way those who loved Ted Bundy or Cary Stayner say they have a hard time believing he could have done all that he did? *He was just so loving.*

If society kicks around to turn this into a film, will mine be flirtatious and exhilarating like *Extremely Wicked, Shockingly Evil & Vile*, cutesy like *My Friend Dahmer*, or drab like *Monster*?

Because I'm a woman, I think we already know the answer. Aileen Wuornos had one of the shittiest lives imaginable: her father sent to prison for raping a seven-year-old girl, mother abandoning her and her older brother and leaving them in the care of her parents who were both alcoholics, her grandfather sexually abusing her and allowing his friends to abuse her further —one of his friends even getting her pregnant at fourteen. Aileen said that her six cases of homicide were perpetrated against men who all raped or attempted to rape her, and yet that's still met with severe doubt. But Bundy ... Bundy was just so *likeable*. So *funny* and *well-educated.* Why can't we just call it what it is? This world hates vengeful women. We need a good reason to murder, and even if we have one it isn't enough.

But men, especially white men, don't seem to need a reason to murder us.

They are our biggest threat, but when we've succumbed to the hatred that men plant inside of us, they call us evil.

We are not charming. We are not promising. We are not troubled. We are not worthy of redemption.

But that thing last night, with his fist to my brow, proved he wasn't worthy of redemption even before his body began to morph.

I hope, like the first time, I won't be caught.

I don't believe in God, but still I pray to be spared as I light up the sage and pour a heaping glass of wine.

Save me.

TWENTY

There's a moment of peacefulness upon first waking up no matter how fretful your yesterday was. It's as if the sun is peeking through the curtains even if you're in a windowless room. Whatever nightmares that jolted you awake are on the other side of the fence in your psyche. And yet just as quickly as the tranquility sets in, it is ripped away.

There's a hole in the fence, and the creatures are in the yard.

My knees involuntarily rush to my stomach, and I clutch them as if I'm holding myself together. There's a throbbing in my head, the remnants of wine. I clench my eyes tighter, praying—begging —for the possibility of more sleep, but my heart has begun to pound as if someone is knocking against my pillow from the inside out. It bangs through my back and into the mattress beneath me until I'm positive that it must be shaking the entire room.

I pull the covers over my head until I fear I'm not the only one under them. I throw them off with a gasp and peek over the edge of my bed. The Polaroids still litter the floor.

In death, the gnarled mess of him looks halfway between monster and man. Pale and unsure of what he's to become. I stare at the photo I snapped with a shaking hand. He's almost cute drenched in blood. I want to show Elijah and say, "This is what was after me. This is what you saved me from," even though the picture itself is proof that I can save myself. I don't know why I long for this gut-wrenching need to be saved, to feel delicate. I picture Elijah's smile, his large hands squeezing around my shoulders as his eyes lock with mine, as he tells me he is proud of me, his approval an aphrodisiac. We could fuck atop my Polaroids, these bits and pieces of men I've murdered in their states of most vulnerable—they have a one-track mind once they're hard; it's honestly too easy. And when we rise from the floor, we'd laugh, peeling them from each other's backs. Elijah wouldn't call me a slut or a sociopath. He'd look at me as if I am a goddess, a goddess of force, of destruction. I am fucked-up. In reality, he would probably look at me in fear, the wide-eyed realization that I am insane, dangerous. I would scramble, spewing excuses and trying to recapture the rope.

Dropping to the floor, I squeeze the picture between my palms, afraid to look. I am a dog who has yet again shit on the floor, with guilt-ridden eyes and a snout that keeps twisting away from its own filth. *Look at it. Look at what you've done.* The hangover creates a nervy twinge inside my brain. It feels like something dislodging.

On the morning after I killed Richard, I awoke early and wondered what his morning routine would have looked like. Thinking of him alive, living his day-to-day, seemed to distract me from the nauseous flipping of my stomach, the rapid pounding of my heart. I pictured him drinking coffee in the car, texting with one hand. He would look handsome with hair still damp from his shower. His cologne would be fresh, spicy, bringing a hint of danger to the comforting scent of the fabric softener his wife used. Sometimes, the dirtiest ones shine with utmost cleanliness. It's how they pass.

I try to picture the man from last night's morning routine. A stuffy apartment, the slightly sour smell of old cereal bowls beside the mattress on the floor, hardened socks and fruit fly-filled poutine containers. Will anyone miss him? I look towards the old shoebox, wondering who my decisions have touched. *Their decisions,* Cedar whispers. *Their decisions. You'll see.*

When it came out that Richard Clark had an affliction for young women (the media never likes to say girls even though that's what we were), I pictured his wife shutting off the TV with a swift click and clatter. I pictured his young daughter not fully understanding, of yelling, "Mommy, turn it back on!" I pictured her growing up and one day feeling spared. That he only got to witness her sexless, sticky-faced, and innocent in those awkward years before beauty sets in—if it's going to. Maybe his wife would be relieved; she had accidentally chosen the wrong father for her children. That in death she was granted a second chance at saving her babies from this world.

I imagined Richard strolling into his office with a sense of purpose yet chill approachability. He'd say hello to his secretary professionally but then send her a text to ask if she was wearing any panties. There is no word I hate more. I always say underwear, but it's what Richard would say. I know, because he muttered something about the little blue bow on mine.

If I would have let him live, he'd have become the type to spend too many hours with his thumb sliding over the EXPLORE page on Instagram, resting on young girls with arched backs and bucket hats, glowing skin and butterfly clips. Girls with daddy issues. Girls who look like they smell like spit and vanilla. Girls like me.

He'd be the type to complain about how much young women can make on OnlyFans. It would give away how much he cared, how much his thoughts were tormented by them, these little money-hungry harlots. The man last night was probably like that too. The type to tell his friends he was dating a stripper when in reality he just had a bad habit of spending too much of his rent money at a club on a girl who looked like a girl he loved from afar in high school.

Richard would handle meetings with a bullish charm that could only be regarded as assertive.

At lunch, in his car, he'd slide his hand onto his secretary's thigh the way he'd done with me. He'd say, "There's just something about you."

She would be equal parts turned on and afraid. She'd only been there a month; was she okay with being a cliché? She'd look at his dark eyes and the want that she brought out in them. She'd part her thighs. She'd tell herself that this was power.

On his drive home, he'd take a longer route. One that took him by the park where the bad girls snuck cigarettes and made out with older boys. His children would be waiting for him, standing by the large picture window, closing their eyes and counting to ten. Richard would walk through the door as soon as they reached ten. I created that game when Cedar first left. I'd count and when I got to ten, the phone would ring. Cedar would be safe.

By then I knew what it was like to lose someone who you thought you'd absolutely die without. If I'm being honest, I was happy that I'd created more people who would share my same unbearable sense of loss. The parts of me that should have felt remorse only felt bliss—that what would initially sting would hurt less than the agony their father would have continued to inflict had he lived. How long would it have been until his secretary wound up pregnant? Until a young girl made it to the cops? Until his daughter hit puberty? Or was he better than that?

I play out the life of the man from last night as if I would have let him fully change, head painfully curved, beady eyes downcast, nose upturned and frantically searching for a scent to follow, to hunt.

I'm too full of rage to curate feelings of remorse. I hope, for his family's sake, that the media will announce the truth: that he was in his early stages of fever. He was never going to be the person they loved ever again. This was unfortunate, but at least it was over quick. Later, maybe, they'll call it painless the way people call a fatal car accident where the driver is decapitated. Instant. Painless.

As if they fucking know for certain.

The man last night showed his true colours. He took it too far and didn't care. He pictured my body beneath him, legs splayed. But he didn't know that I am the grim reaper. I am radiant. I suppose now he knows. I can feel him quivering.

When I look into my vanity expecting to see a monster, I am surprised by the face of a frightened little girl. For a moment, I feel almost beautiful. But the wickedness never stays away for long. I tuck his Polaroid beneath my others, a scene of pain amidst all of the pleasure. I regret taking two photos. That sickness inside of me that needed something to peer upon, something hard and real and gruesomely tangible that said: this is who you are; this is what you're capable of.

That said: you are strong; you are in control.

Slamming the lid back onto the shoebox, I shove it to the back of my closet. Nan would say that I've trapped his soul, but then again, she also blamed the little people whenever she misplaced her keys.

I like to think that men like him never had a soul to begin with.

Maybe the bad ones extract them directly after childhood in order to survive. They lose them in hockey locker rooms and frat parties and hunting camps. Maybe other, older, cooler boys extract them with repeated taunts of *little bitch* and *pussy; faggot, wimp.* Maybe this has nothing to do with women. Boys are just brought up to prove themselves to other boys, and we are the easiest vehicle in which to do so.

Closing my eyes, I press my forehead against the heels of my hands, breathing in one, two, three, four, and out one, two, three, four. I have built a life of hiding in plain sight, and this will be no different. I tie up my hair into a tiny little bun and pad to the washroom, where the hot water scalds my skin. I wash my body without looking at it and towel off with my eyes glued to the chipping green paint of my bathroom wall, careful not to look down and risk crumbling into a bout of self-loathing.

I apply makeup without meeting my eyes, focusing on the features I need to conceal. I need to sheathe myself from the mania of my gaze. To hide from my own vicious mind and a conscience that says this is not who I was meant to be. That I have only grown around being whoever I needed to be in the moment, none of these versions resembling who I truly am. I pull on a cozy, oversized sweater and a pair of well-worn jeans and wonder if any of these versions of myself are lovable. I don't rest on the thought for long. Instead, I focus on zipping up my boots, of stepping outside into a bright and shining day. Mother Earth seems completely avoidant of the problems brewing. The birds chirp as if everything is okay. And I suppose everything will be okay, once humanity is re-envisioned. She must know that. Maybe this is her doing.

Cedar laughs.

There's a small coffee shop around the corner that's resisted the city's urge to turn pretentious, to sell out into the caramel macchiato stench of gentrification. It offers coffee, tea, and occasionally, cellophane wrapped sandwiches and has zero options when it comes to plant-based milk. It always makes me feel as if I am stepping back in time, the rich smell of strong coffee and freshly baked cookies, and Carole, a busty cashier with big eighties hair and a townie accent. Carole, most of all, reminds me of home.

But today there's a man behind the till.

And the TV hanging on the wall marks how different countries are handling The Change. China is under lockdown too while Russia is letting its men run wild, the casualties left mostly unreported. Despite government restrictions, all over the world the rate of suicide is skyrocketing. Men who fear for their slipping morality and women who fear for the same thing, offing themselves before the end. The current story is one of a white-picket-fence murder-suicide, almost Shakespearian, romantic and tragic. He killed her before killing himself. These nearly perfect lives left to crumble as the man of your dreams shows the earliest warning signs of monstrosity.

"Just a black coffee," I say to the unfamiliar man behind the till who watches me as I watch the TV. "Can you believe this shit?" I offer him a smiling thank you as he sets my Styrofoam cup down in front of me.

He remains silent, averts my gaze.

The story changes with a warning of graphic content and

suddenly there he is, the thing I killed, and what flashes next is my Polaroid, the near-twin to the one in my shoebox back home.

His name was Kyle. Of course, his name was Kyle.

I step from one foot to the other, trying to force my face into a look of shock, grateful that the man behind the counter is watching the screen instead of me.

The newscaster is asking for tips.

The man behind the counter finally meets my eyes. My stomach sinks as heat travels up my neck. I hastily grab my change to pay, pulling out a toonie and loonie (Canada, forever wondering why we'll never be respected by the world when we've chosen such cutesy comical names for our currency) from the pocket of my jeans.

Kyle's mom blubbers on the TV screen above us. "He wasn't sick. He wasn't sick," she cries, face pinched and puckered and similar to his—the same mouth and nose. The monsters are always the star of the show. I learned that from Glen, from Richard. The cash register dings, but the man before me remains silent.

I look back to the TV, resisting my initial urge to hurry away, trying to push thoughts of last night far, far from my mind. The screen reveals a smiling photo of Kyle a few months ago.

When Cedar went missing, the screen flashed with an unsmiling photo of her in the upper left corner. The day after she didn't come home, I had brought an envelope full of pictures of Cedar to the cop shop. I pinned my favourite and the most recent —her hair neatly shorn yet her face beaming in her trademark smile as she sat on Nan's front steps—to the front with a paper clip. I screamed at the TV screen when I saw the photo they chose to use. It was her school photo, eyes glassy and dark. An image that curated images of juvie.

I figure once the autopsy comes back to reveal that Kyle was indeed sick with the virus, the media will go on a bender talking about how his death was painless and a blessing, that he didn't have to sink into the worse sufferings of sickness.

Only when the TV goes to commercial do I turn to leave.

"Thanks," I say, trying again to meet his eyes as I grab the warm cup. "Have a good one."

He remains silent even as I turn to leave. It makes me feel as if I am losing my mind. As if I am dreaming or dead or have slipped into a state of in-between. As if I am truly alone in the world, my karma for a childhood of convincing Theo that everything was all a dream and laughing when he began to panic and insist that I stop.

Is this a new rule to keep everyone safe? Are men not supposed to speak to women? Maybe we're supposed to stop speaking first. Maybe they're told to ignore us, keep their eyes averted the way you would with an aggressive dog. Do not make eye contact, do not engage. As if it's our fault that the world is turning rabid.

The coffee doesn't taste as smooth and robust as it once did. It splashes lukewarm against my tongue. Bitter. I think of Carole, her big hair and bigger tits and biggest personality. Her ability to make me feel alive and loved and charming via a five-minute conversation about our days. The lemon scones that she'd toss into a brown paper bag on the days she deemed I needed a pick-me-up. *"You're looking too skinny,"* she'd say without an ounce of judgment or praise. Voice thick with the warmth and humour of someone who cared. Loud and fancy and femme as she stated that it was a shame she was a lesbian, when God had gifted her two man-manipulators that only gave her back pain.

"Don't get me wrong, women like big tits too," she'd say, "but it's not the only thing they see, y'know?"

Where the fuck is Carole?

I look back towards the coffee shop window feeling sick.

"You gotta girlfriend yet?" she used to ask me, perhaps joking, perhaps able to see me for the parts I hide. I'd blush and shake my head or sometimes flirt yet always wish I was the type of person who could just be myself. I'm not even sure if I've been judged or if it's all in my head: those long-ago years of confiding in Cedar about having a crush on a girl in my class and the next day hearing Nan say, "So, I heard you're gay," with that disapproving tone she reserved only for gossip with the other old hens at bingo.

At the sound of the bell, the man behind the counter meets my gaze but still remains silent.

"Where's Carole?"

If I'm honest I was hoping to tell Carole exactly what I did.

I killed one, Carole. I killed one.

I wanted to see her chest heave and her eyes water. To feel her soft pudgy hands against my crying face. I wanted her to tell me that everything would be okay. To hush, hush, hush. Snidely, I wanted her to ask me if he deserved it and I wanted to tell her, "Yes, yes, yes."

He stares at me and I think of hurling my body over the counter, of grabbing him by the hair and slamming his face down against the cool ceramic.

His voice is soft and sweet and scared, but he still doesn't meet my eyes when he says, "It wasn't safe for her here anymore." When he finally does look me in the eyes, I realize that his aren't indifferent. They're frightened.

TWENTY-ONE

The club hits different in the daytime.

No bachelor parties. No groups of guys who've brought their *cool* girlfriends to stare at me as if I am a zoo lion. Instead, it's everyone who doesn't want to get caught walking into a building with blacked-out windows. The man on the business trip. Your neighbour. Your dad.

It's here where they reveal their vulnerability as graciously as I reveal my skin. They're safe to be themselves. And they say it, how their wives never get to see these sides of them. How everyone is such a snowflake these days. How the world would see them as a perverted old man just for looking at us.

He'll say, "But you want me to look, don't you?"

And I'll make my voice soft and sultry yet shockingly innocent as I tell him, "I love the way you look at me."

A lot of them are dumb and or delusional enough to believe me.

Dancers swap info on the men who will try to get more than they paid for. We've learned that sometimes the men we think will be creepy are completely harmless whereas the ones we think will be decent are absolute pigs. We lean into our instincts, knowing that behaviour can change once the curtain is closed. And now, knowing that the man himself could change too, I don't even reveal a nipple until song three. More than ever, I want to gauge patience, making sure the man in front of me is in control of himself before I let myself become too vulnerable. A lot of the girls have stopped drinking entirely. I can't. The booze lets me become someone else—Bia.

We know we can have them tossed out with a snap of our fingers if the DJ is paying attention or Stanley is close. We keep our eyes hyper focused for early signs of sickness. The clammy skin of a fever. The scent of cum. Men with enhanced curvature of their spines are denied entry at the doors. It's too tough to distinguish scoliosis from a gradual inability to see the sky. Those who are steadily changing are past the point of caring about the death of society, the death of a dream.

No one comments on misogyny in the club. Our very livelihoods are built around objectification. Some of the men, these patrons, disrespect us every day but our bank accounts grow. Some of them treat us like the goddesses we are. Either way, our confidence blooms—in the club we are fully permitted to relish in the power of our sexuality. Here, the men are under our control. If I bite back in the club, it's looked at as little more than charm; he knows he'll still see his favourite parts of me if he ponies up and I let him. Out there, with this job, I'm something less. In here, with hopeful, hungry, lonely eyes unable to look away from me, I'm something more. And now, as women abandon their makeup and tight clothes and strip any suggestiveness from their voices, I'm something else. If I was exotic before, I'm endangered now. We're rare. Temptingly taboo. That much more coveted yet also, of course, criticized.

Clubs have been closing by the week. Men will have to go back to bottling their emotions or trying to connect with wives they've all but checked out on for the last decade. We've convinced them they deserve more from life. What will become of them when we're taken away? Coming here, seeing us, all of us, has become their God-given right as red-blooded, hard-cocked men. A few of the girls have been breaking the carnal rule and giving their favourite clients their numbers, a backup plan of income when Hera shuts her doors too. No one talks about how strip clubs are sex work lite, but what will happen when we lose the safety of the club's walls? Maybe we're all just trying to soak up the blissful ignorance for as long as it can last, taking shots and shaking our asses and pretending that the news is lying—men are not changing into near animals and women, especially women like us, aren't disappearing by the day.

If it took courage to have this job before, it's nothing like the guts it takes now. I hate when people say, "Wow, that takes balls." There is no weaker body part than a dangling pair of testicles, bodies keeling over from a hard flick. We walk in like warriors, baring the parts of us for as long as they're deemed worth being bared. I float through life in a haze, only coming alive when I step foot in the club and am praised for the delicate violence of me.

Today, I keep my hood up and my eyes down. My violence is no longer delicate. Instead, it's abrasive, obvious, threatening. The men I've killed before haven't gotten coverage so quickly. I also haven't ever left them right out in the open. A side effect of coming undone is sloppiness.

I thought this would be the one place where I felt safe. But I fear they'll smell it on me: a fox in with the hens.

The room is already abuzz with stories of the man found beneath the park bench, how his spine was beginning to arch and his mouth looked *different*.

One of the dancers even knew him. "We went to high school together," I overhear her whispering, voice laced with the awe of knowing a celebrity before the world got its hands on them, rimmed with emotion as if they were closer than they were. Death casts the most forgiving glow.

"The Polaroid was fucking creepy," a small spitfire of a dancer, Aphrodite, says with a laugh and a toss of her bright copper hair. "What was he like when you knew him?"

The other girl sniffles twice before muttering she didn't know him too well, but he seemed really kind.

I clear my throat to stop myself from scoffing as I think of him demanding to taste my cunt. The bruise on my brow throbs. The little voice whispers, *Breathe, breathe, breathe,* and God how I wish it was my nan's.

"He was changing, wasn't he?" I hope my voice only conveys fear of the virus.

The two women look up at me. We've barely spoken before, and I watch their expectations of me flickering behind their eyes.

Aphrodite shrugs.

The other one shakes her head, and I think of the clip of Kyle's mom inconsolably crying, calling him the sweetest boy. They regard me for another second before the other dancer quietly changes the subject, their shoulders turning in a way to let me know that our encounter is over.

Has Kara already spilled the tea about Ian and the booth? Or do I just make the other girls uneasy all on my own? I glance into the mirror and don't know who my eyes belong to.

Usually, even before The Change, I did my makeup here. I like the ritual of it, sprawling my creams and powders and tubes across the counter as if I am applying war paint. It keeps me present. At home, I can lose hours. But today, my skin is matte, the bruise buried beneath perfectly blended foundation that I had to watch three YouTube videos to master. I wonder if the other girls noticed my face is put together but my eyes are those of a cougar pacing in too small of an enclosure.

Lil hurries into the change room, a black vinyl G-string pulled high on her hips, her bronze legs ending in a pair of silvery platforms that she quickly kicks off.

"We have to get out of here!" she yells at everyone and no one in particular. Her eyes, always vibrant and assured, are red-rimmed, pupils dilated from fear. There is a gash across her sinewy stomach, burgundy and violent. She locks eyes with me for a moment while the other women's voices morph into panic. I am filled with the sickening sense of being late, of running out of time. I watch her in a stunned silence as she grabs her duffel bag from her locker and crouches down to pull out sweatpants, a hoodie. She holds a delicate hand to her stomach, the baby blue of her sweater immediately turning a purple.

I pull my attention from Lil as the door swings open and Derek bursts in. Some of the girls scream, covering themselves, crowding together. When I look closely, Derek doesn't look any different, but his eyes are angry, zealous. Hera is on his heels.

"Okay, okay, you know you can't be in here!" Hera quickly shouts at Derek before turning her attention to the rest of us.

"Girls, there's a bit of a situation out there. I need you to all get dressed. We'll leave out the back."

The chaotic rush of shrill voices and the clank of locker doors opening and closing, bags being unzipped intensifies. Derek makes no move to leave, his mouth trapped in a sneer, eyes cold and dedicated and hyperfocused on Lil. I look to his hands but they are free of blood.

"See what you brought on yourself, Lilith?" he spits, using her real name which she has worked to protect at all costs. I eye the door, overcome with the eerie stillness before a crack of lightning tears open the sky.

"Derek, you heard Hera. We have to go." Lil's voice doesn't quiver, even though her eyes well with tears.

She piles her hair into a bun on the top of her head and meets my eyes in the mirror. They're firm, hardening into something between strength and acceptance. *I love you,* she mouths.

Love you, I mouth back, hearing Cedar whisper it in my ear. She sees herself when she gazes into Lil's amber eyes. Lil makes her feel like a shy child longing to fit in, something Cedar never was.

"I should have known you were fucking lying," Derek continues, this monologue amidst the bedlam that he must feel won't impact him.

Lil closes her eyes and places her well-manicured nails to her temples as I think of the times she's mentioned Derek's insistence that she stop dancing. Her solemn voice that she hasn't saved enough. That she needs at least one more year. Her dismissal that he only says it because he cares.

The door swings shut as Hera leaves and all of us women know that within a minute Stanley will be here to physically remove Derek. Without the authority of Hera, Derek comes closer to Lil, his body moving quickly, sturdy muscle beneath taut skin.

I think of the thing bloodied beneath the park bench and wish that it were Derek. His once piercing blue eyes emptily set on the afterlife.

He turns his attention to me. "What the fuck are you looking at, Delilah?" I bite my tongue to stop myself from telling him he is pathetic.

"Leave her out of this," Lil says, her voice stripped of any emotion. "I told you I wasn't done yet, you just refused to listen."

"I told *you* that if you *didn't* quit, we were *over*. And now look at you." He glances down at her soiled sweatshirt. "Now, look at what you've done."

Her eyes stay downcast on her bare feet.

"Derek," Lil whispers, her voice pleading, "let's go home."

"Home?" Derek's laugh is biting. "*We* don't have a home. I want you out."

Lil pays half of the rent, but Derek talked her out of putting the lease in her name for income tax reasons. The other dancers don't know that, and I can tell from the set of Derek's shoulders that he's saying it for them, even though the other women are disinterested in a lover's spat.

I watch Derek, the bulge of his shoulders and crane of his neck, viewing him for symptoms. He used to parade Lil around like the most beautiful woman in the world, but when it faded, six or so months in, it faded fast.

In two steps he is over her, his large hand firmly clenched around her bicep, maniacal eyes peering down into hers. As his grip tightens, Lil's gaze is unwavering, their jaws similarly set. He inches his face closer to hers so that whatever he mutters is for her and her only.

The look on Lil's face is not one of fear: it's the death of a dream.

"Derek!" Stanley shouts as he barges in, veins jutting in his neck, and it's only then that Derek drops his hand. "Everyone left in here, get your shit. We have to go out the back. If you didn't drive here, pile in with whoever did. Lock the doors as soon as you're in the car." Lil looks down at her arm but makes no move to stroke her skin; it's as if she's enamoured by the faint finger prints. Shocked. Tainted.

"You can come with me," I tell her.

She stands still amongst the chaos swirling around her. I long for Cedar but feel completely alone. A fat tear falls down Lil's cheek as she swings her duffel bag over her shoulder. Stanley pushes Derek out into the hall. Derek obliges, although not without muttering something beneath his breath, the word *whores* cutting through the dead quiet of the dressing room.

As the door slams shut, Lil remains trancelike, pulling on her socks, tying up her pristinely bright white sneakers.

"The thing—it wasn't human," she says, voice solemn, the indifference of shock.

I think of Lil when I first met her. Bitingly witty and intimidating. Confident from taking her life into her own hands and excelling because of it. Fierce and independent and seemingly unafraid. It was that spark that drew Derek in. He met her here, after all, buying her shots for the entire duration of his best friend's bachelor party. I wasn't surprised when he first asked her out; men are always trying to take us for drinks, to get us on their turf. I was, however, surprised when she said yes. I pictured Lil going to barbeques with Derek at his newly married bestie's house. I thought of how he was the type of man that eventually wouldn't be able to handle that all of his friends had seen his girlfriend's tits. How the ego stroke would deteriorate into an ego attack.

I watched with bated breath between a slit in my fingers as her *I's* became *we's* and she let me in on her tucked away secret: her biggest dream was to be a wife and mother.

Selfishly, I wanted to tell her that I loved her, but I couldn't.

How long was it before her days off were spent drinking beers with Derek's friends, her homework undisturbed in her backpack? In the early days, she used to chew him up and spit him out. Before long, she guarded her words when he was around, and her smile … her smile is not so different from the one she uses in the club.

Now, she stays silent as if her very voice is kindling.

I gaze at myself in the mirror, my skin never looking more flawless, and resist the urge to hiss. I think of the man last night, bloodied and broken beneath my fingers while Cedar sings, *He had it coming,* her voice both girlish and raspy. Derek isn't too different from all of the men we hate.

The women are emptying out, leaving me alone to beg for Cedar to tell me if this is the end, but I can no longer hear her.

"Let Gaia be a lesson to all of you to keep your relationship drama at home," Hera said a month ago after another one of Derek's visits.

Lil has a history with men like Derek. At eighteen she was fired from a hostess job at an upscale restaurant she couldn't afford to eat at. She'd lied about the job to her boyfriend Tony, three decades her senior. I don't remember the exact lie, but it boiled down to saying she was hanging out with a friend, who accidentally outed Lil's new job when Tony messaged her on Facebook, seemingly innocent, asking what time she thought Lil would be home. Tony showed up already drunk during her second shift, keeping his eyes glued to her every move as he ordered whisky neats two at a time. Looking back, she said she wishes she would have pretended she didn't know him, that he was just some egotistical middle-aged man with a drinking problem. Instead, she had told her manager that he was her boyfriend and watched how the woman's birdlike eyes crawled over her body as she came to her own conclusions on what kind of teenage girl was with a man nearing fifty. The manager told her that it was nothing personal, the business just steered clear of drama. When she got home, he was waiting at his kitchen table in the dark asking why the fuck she lied to him.

Tony was recently divorced and had the Porsche to prove it. His wife had left him and sometimes, when he was only a few drinks in, he would say that he never fucking hit that lying cunt; other times, when he was seven or eight whiskies deep, he would cry and ask Lil over and over and over again if she thought he was a good man. She always told him that he was, even when she didn't fully know what a good man was or truly believed that one existed. We're cynical, she and I, comparing good men to leprechauns, yet seemingly unable to untether ourselves from them, forever searching for that pot of gold.

I think she always knew Tony would one day hit her, but that night was the night. Two quick slaps in the face that hurt her dignity more than they hurt her flesh. The sobs choked up his throat, and his hands clenched too tightly around hers as he whispered, "I'm so sorry," and "It will never happen again," and "I'm just so afraid to lose you," as his tears soaked through her T-shirt until sleep steadied his breath.

She told me all this after a bottle and a half of redneck rosé. His morning-after bended-knee begging made her feel like a queen. His watery-eyed remorse created a pool in her. She chugged down the rest of her glass and quickly changed the subject before I could pry. I wanted to tell her that I understood, but I stayed quiet.

I thought of my mother gauging violence as an indicator of love. In that moment, I wanted to tell Lil everything, like the vulnerability junkie that I am, but just as fast as the moment arose it disappeared again. I told her that I thought she was incredibly strong. Her back was pressed firmly against my wall, feet flat on the floor, knees up. She parted her legs ever so slightly and raised her jaw towards me the way I hoped she always would, and I lunged forward like an animal, my fingers sliding into her jeans with ease to find out that she was already dripping wet. It felt powerful to initiate and watch a woman respond with the arch of her back and a gentle sigh of breath, her legs falling open further to let me in deeper. How could men ever leave us as unsatisfied as often as they do when making a woman come feels like harnessing lightning?

I wondered if she had thought of me before, the way I had thought of her. Or if it was just the wine, just the candy-coated shame that is most easily silenced with sex.

We only fucked once.

She had been seeing Derek for a couple months by then and the guilt that shadowed her features the next morning stopped me from telling her that I loved her. It took us another three months to fully be able to look each other in the eye, and by that point she was in love with him.

I long for the love of women the way I long for my mother. I am denied just the same.

I've always hoped she didn't take my silence as judgment. If anything, it was only shame. Perhaps we were both wading through pools of our shame, using sex as a life raft.

Our bodies had found each other in the night, and we awoke stuck together in a soothing sweat. We stayed that way for five minutes, in the delicate freedom of silence with our eyes gently closed. We didn't discuss our hungry mouths as we sipped coffee on my balcony. She mentioned that she was meeting Derek for dinner once he got off of work, her voice holding the casual acknowledgement that nothing had changed. I didn't need to ask if she would tell him. I knew she wouldn't. I told my boyfriend for fun, delighted by the tone of his voice over the phone, the mixture of pain and arousal.

I want to tell Derek now, to humiliate him in front of the others, to watch him squirm, all the while knowing that it wouldn't make me any better than a man who brags about fucking another man's girlfriend. That by bragging I'd be stripping Lil of her own agency, her own desire, her own wickedness.

Lil started stripping to curate freedom from Tony. Derek met her here and it was hot until she realized he didn't want an independent woman either. Few do.

And maybe, in comparison, Derek feels like hope. Maybe she convinces herself that his concern is merely protective, caring. He wants to save her from the end of the world.

He wants her all for himself.

The prospect of love and acceptance is as blinding as mace.

Then, the screaming starts.

TWENTY-TWO

As soon as I open the change room door, I'm hit with the stink of goat, the almost-human stench of pig shit. This is why the clubs have been closing. The proximity of changing spurs on more changing. Half of them still walk upright, however laboriously. The rest are on knuckles and knees. Jesse cuts the music, accentuating the screams of the dancers who were already on the floor, the grunts of the creatures. Saliva dribbles out of garishly slack, frothing mouths. Curved necks and torn clothes and exposed erections barbed and vicious.

They can smell us.

Stanley stands at the front door, arms raised. "I tried to stop them. I tried to stop them. They barged right in." He's sobbing. We've been warned that we should all stay home behind double-locked doors, but we chose blissful ignorance. The pseudosafety of continuing to come to work as if the world isn't crumbling around us. The self-promise of just one more day. The comfort of our gentle, sweet regulars. Men so appreciative, so tender. Men who make us feel cherished.

We don't speak much about the regulars who we haven't seen in weeks. Most of them were the ones who continuously overstepped, and the club has been more enjoyable in their absence. But here they are, their eyes still shockingly human even as their ears protrude, even as their vocal cords tighten to only permit grunts and groans. They have no more self-control than animals during mating season.

The unchanged stand frozen, taking inventory of their fellow men as they rip whatever women they can sink their teeth into to shreds. Do those yet to change feel it tampering at the edges of their psyche, coursing through their veins? Can they feel the fever heating their hairlines? Teeth and cock beginning to ache?

This is it. The devolution.

I can't hear Cedar. I can't hear her at all.

Stanley's voice cuts through the commotion, his typically soothing tone teeming with anguish. "Beverly!"

I follow his gaze to the stairs, where three of the things have Hera cornered: two blocking her from running past and one on the stairs, its body hunched and contorted as it snarls.

"Bev!" Stanley shouts again, pushing his way towards the stairs as the creature pounces, humanoid claws lashing out to grip Hera—Beverly—by her long auburn hair, her neck snapping like a branch in the forest, body dragged behind the stairs where the sounds of panting breaths and smacking jaws blend harshly with Stanley's inconsolable howls.

Creeping behind the bar, I try to steady my breath to keep the tunnel vision from taking over. My fingers dig into the ever-present bruise on my thigh as the sounds of screams are replaced by the rhythmic slapping of flesh, the damp, carnal splatter of fat and muscle, knowing that my safety is completely reliant on whether or not there are enough half-dead women to pacify their need to fuck and feed.

I think of the days spent in the woods with my dad. How I'd never be able to completely enjoy it, always afraid of bears bursting from the tree line, cougars emerging from rocky cliffs. Afraid that I'd forget what to do in the moment, afraid that I'd be eaten alive. This is worse. This is worse than I ever imagined. I think of how peaceful the woods really were, the sun careening through the tops of trees. I think of my hand fully enclosed in Elijah's, his smile drenched in light. I hold the image in my mind before looking back around the club, this living hell.

It is a hell that even Cedar cannot grasp.

I can see her, in the corner of the club, watching like the frightened child she is. My eyes close, tears stinging my lash line, willing Cedar to show me where I'll wind up. Willing her to help. She has left me all alone as the smell of ammonia and rancid meat wafts towards me. My stomach spasms in a gag. The stench combines with the invasive heat of an animal's pant, the sound of its thumping heart and shifting weight as it approaches slowly, carefully. As if my actions have triggered an instinctual fear, as if it realizes I am somewhere between predator and prey. I open my eyes.

There's a raw remorse radiating from its dark blue gaze, something so sickeningly *human* I almost start to cry. The protruding teeth look almost comical, jutting from bitten and bleeding lips that I loved to kiss. Its snout gnarled as the cartilage tore skin in order to morph, nostrils raised to catch scents with enhanced ease, the upper base of ears ripping from scalp to extend outwards and ending in a jagged point. It moves closer, so close that I can feel the moisture from its breath. A dull whine reverberates from its throat. Eyes glued to mine, it barks low and choppy, some kind of warning I don't understand. I thought staring it in the eyes would cause it to attack, would cause it to prove its dominance, would end it all here and now, but it drops its head, saliva dribbling to the floor from its deformed mouth. I am overcome with a sense of recognition as I stare at the dark blonde hair along its scalp that now grows from its jaw and ears. I reach out my hands and the creature jolts back, movements quick and jerky, still getting used to its new body that changes by the hour. A body truly ugly after being truly beautiful. It steps closer, sniffing at me with gentle huffs. I place a palm on either side of its face, ruddy, hardened cheeks sprouting coarse hair that was once so soft and promising.

"I just wanted to be special," I whisper, meeting the cobalt eyes. Eyes that I've forever longed to look at me like this. Eyes that only look gentle now, now that its body is anything but.

Where were these eyes when Ian picked me up in the middle of the night a week after we spent time together in his pool? As we sat parked, his hand inching a little higher up my thigh. I looked away from the window and looked at him. Like Richard, he was watching his hand as if it belonged to someone else. I felt oddly removed from the situation happening between his wandering hand and my still leg, so I leaned in and kissed him. His tongue was cold as if he'd just taken a gulp of water, and I hoped he was nervous, that I made him nervous. I leaned back, pulling from the kiss to look at him, but his eyes wouldn't meet mine. Here I was at the locked door of intimacy, too afraid to knock loudly.

He grabbed my hand and placed it on the lap of his jeans, puppeteering it back and forth in a haphazard stroking motion. My wrist felt weak, the dead hand of a dummy.

"I thought we were going to wait," I said. In reality, after day three of not hearing anything from him, I figured he was uninterested after I had outed myself as a little inexperienced virgin. I wondered if telling him the truth would have been better: I killed the last man who tried to fuck me.

I was too young to realize how men long to stake their flag.

Ian groaned into my mouth then, as his hand still manipulated mine, muttering, "Fuck that feels good," against my teeth.

I pulled my mouth away from his and leaned back in his passenger seat, half-chuckling as I removed his now sweaty palm from my thigh and placed my hand on his. The outline of his boner through his jeans made me feel awkward. My only attempt at breaking the tension was laughter. When his eyes jerked up and narrowed, I realized immediately I had done something wrong. Again.

"Sorry," I said quickly, my voice still light. "I just thought about what you said, and I think you're right. My first time should be something special."

"I get it," he said, his eyes set somewhere above my head. "You're just a cocktease."

I let the word replay a few times in my head, the solid two syllables of it striking like a slap. I wanted to go back in time to the previous week, when I could feel him firmly pressed against my thigh and he had said my first time should be special. He had kissed me sweetly when I left. His eyes were so different from the blue marbles that glared at me now.

His expression didn't soften as he kissed me, biting breaths, stubble rubbing against my soft cheek. Cedar always left me when I was with Ian, and I felt powerless without her. His hips ground into mine, moving back as his lips slid down to my neck, trailing teeth and tongue. The breath on my neck and the rubbing, I can't say it felt bad, but it felt as if I were watching it happen to someone else. I could feel myself get wet, my thighs quivering. It was the first time my own body betrayed me.

Still, I pushed his hands off of me and squirmed in a way that I was half sitting up, my pants still on.

"Sorry," I said, seeing him again through my own eyes. The determination of his brow confirmed he was a teen even if he was older than me, even if he had a car and an erection. His tongue squished against mine, silencing it so my words were nothing but muffles. His fingers clawed down my sweatshirt, thumb and forefinger finding my nipple. I had never been touched like that, and the ache in my stomach didn't align with the shiver in the core of me that made me lean forward and sink myself into the seat beneath. I groaned and it was as if my voice betrayed me too.

"Ian," I said finally, pulling back and catching his dazed eyes.

"Please." His voice was raspy, almost tender.

I didn't know anything.

I moved to straighten my sweater, looking out the window at the starry night.

"Maybe we could go for a walk?" I asked.

His response was a whoosh of breath somewhere between a *huh* and a *nah*. I pictured strange looks in the halls. Of how I would no longer be excited to get home and log onto MSN. How I would no longer take the hall pass out during each of my classes to wander the halls in hopes of bumping into him.

Then I heard the crinkle of the wrapper, the snap of the latex. His weight was once again on my thighs, and he was yet again not meeting my eyes.

I slid myself back into the passenger seat and told myself that I wasn't special. That it was my fault for letting my expectations swirl and dance.

You thought you deserved better? It wasn't Cedar's voice this time.

It was my own. I think she was the meanest of them all. Snarky and biting and honest.

It didn't feel that bad, but my sprawled legs looked ghostly in the blue light of the dash. With his face so close to mine, I could make out the pores along his nose, the light dusting of redness on his chin from where he'd shaved too close. His eyes remained on my forehead, and I wondered how I could feel this far away from someone who was literally inside me. His grunts grew steadier, thrusts faster, deeper, deepest until his body trembled against mine and became slack. For a moment I lay there, feeling foolish and out of place, listening to the buckle of his belt, the opening of the car door. I remembered hearing somewhere to always pee after sex, so I hoisted my jeans mid-thigh and stepped out into the cool air, squatting beside the car to rid myself of the experience. Ian was doing the same, his back to me while he pissed into the trees. The next day at school he didn't speak to me. I don't know why I thought he would, but that night, when I curled myself around my pillow and shut my eyes tight, tight, tight, begging for sleep, I told myself a little lie. And the little lie was that one day he would love me.

I don't know if the eyes staring back at me right now are filled with love or remorse, but I can't dwell on it for much longer. Two other creatures slink around the corner of the bar, clouding me in the fecal scent of rotting teeth, the sour milk stink of smegma. Their shoulders are taut with thick muscle, mouths bloody slashes from their jutting canines and the odious feast on the other side of the room. What was once Ian barks deeply. I feel the bass of his voice in my chest. The other two continue approaching. Ian turns away from me, squaring his shoulders to guard from the other creatures' approach. I want to break down and slam my fist repeatedly against the floor as I shriek for answers from a god I refuse to believe in. But maybe some things never change, so instead I stay silent, watching as Ian lunges his lankily misshapen body towards the others, voice nothing but an anguished squeal. The others square their shoulders, cocks bloody. They attempt to peer around Ian with hateful stares set on me as if I am merely a consolation prize for their condemnation. Ian looks over his shoulder one last time as the others attack. I pull myself up onto the counter still littered with half-full beer bottles and folded twenty-dollar bills under glasses wet with condensation. I try to tune out the sound of claws tearing into leathery skin, teeth snapping in a testosterone-induced contest. Instead, I look upon another horror, the smearing of blood atop cream tiled floors, the stink of disembowelled bodies donned in sweet-scented lotions. The mangled mess of ripped out weaves, body parts torn from joints, picked apart. Some of the creatures sleep, fresh blood still lingering on what were once faces and hands, elongated cocks soft and benign. Ian barks again, but I can't look at what he's become. I step down onto the devastated floor, my socked feet immediately soaked with spilled beverages and blood. I try not to make out what's left of any of the women's faces, these women like me. These wild, fearless, spirited women. Tiptoeing around the wreckage and the peacefully sleeping creatures, I am undeservedly Daniel in the den. Light streams in through the front door, abandoned ajar. The two behind the bar smack their teeth as they feed, grunting and breathing heavy amidst jaws full of what was once the man I longed to love.

After peeling off my socks, I carefully step into the redemptive late-afternoon sun. My eyes dart from left to right and back again, neck craning over each shoulder every couple of seconds until I reach the safety of my car. If any women made it out, they are already gone, but the lot is still predominantly full.

I think of Lil.

I debate turning back, but I don't.

Speeding down the empty streets, I let out a barking laugh, thinking of who I was this morning, guilt rising up inside of me like bile as Kyle's mother sobbed on a screen, the aching fear of being found out. I feel too far away from the girl I was an hour before. I feel the way Cedar has always wanted me to feel: self-assured of my own violence. It's not in spite of the fear, it's because of it.

TWENTY-THREE

I MAKE IT HOME SAFE. EVEN THOUGH I COULDN'T STOP glancing over my shoulder into the emptiness of the back seat. Even though I had to rub the sweat off of my palms onto my jeans to stop them from slipping off the wheel. Even though I was one of the lucky ones who was still dressed and not already out on the floor. Like the society crumbling around us, the women the most scantily clad were the first attacked.

The hallway light is off when I enter the communal front room with its dusty stacks of mail from past tenants or maybe those who have gone missing or have become sick themselves. My keys fall through my shaking hands when I reach my apartment door at the top of the stairs.

I'm safe, but I don't hear Cedar. I think the evening's events spooked her.

My blinds are closed and I check the locks on every window, the balcony, and front door. I check them again and set my knife and pepper spray in my bedside drawer. I have a baseball bat under the bed. I call Lil six times. I send ten texts. Silence. I even text Derek and call him twice, envisioning Lil answering his phone in a panic, saying that he's holding her hostage. *Ayuda, ayuda.*

Thinking of Ian, I romanticize his death, grateful that he won't show up here once he devolved beyond reason, possessed with hunger and want. Ian, this boy who always took too much, is gone. Is this my Saturn return or am I just fed up?

Cedar's fed up too. *It's all because of me,* she whispers with a little giggle. I don't know what she means. I smoke half a joint, knowing that if I smoked a full one my paranoia would be unbearable, I wouldn't be able to sleep at all. With half I can try and let my mind empty as I stare at the ceiling.

IN THE BITTER SHREDS OF DAYLIGHT MY HANDS RATTLE like a lid on a pot that's about to boil over. Taking my time to make myself look beautiful, meticulously covering the bruise that's now a shade of greenish yellow, does little to distract me from my phone that hasn't rung. I stare back at my empty-eyed reflection like an idiot, powdering my face, spritzing on perfume as if looking pretty and smelling nice matter. There's this fear of stepping outside and being lost forever.

My hair is teased and sprayed and shines like a golden halo beneath my vanity lights, my lips pale pink and ladylike. They turn slightly purple in the middle as I sip a glass of red wine. I try not to think of the carnage of the city streets. Of Ian. Or Elijah. I try not to condemn myself for this longing to let men show me how I should treat myself. I crave to be held.

"I'm afraid if I hug you, you'll cry," my mom used to say when

I was upset, standing back from me with hovering arms not quite high enough to provide an embrace.

I always felt as if there was a part of her that was slightly afraid of getting too close to me, as if my sadness was contagious, as if she'd see parts of herself she tries so hard to ignore. Whenever we fought, she'd say she kept seeing a black shadow in the corner of the room, something low to the ground and fast and wispy. "I don't think it's trying to frighten me," she'd say, "just alert me of its presence."

Cedar has always wanted my mom to see her for who she is.

Tears brim to the edge of my eyes as I take another sip. I look at myself the way you look at a puppy that's beginning to squat in the house. *No, no, don't you fucking dare.* I glance down at my body, the fat smoothed and concealed in some places, pooled and pushed in others. Never plump or flat enough. My feet are still bare, tinged with blood. I drove home without my shoes, my belongings discarded at the back of the club. I couldn't bring myself to walk back to the locker room, to risk what kind of madness lingered there. To have to relive walking out of it for the last time, of seeing the blood and gore and remnants of women who were only trying to laugh in the face of danger. To see defeat sneering back at me.

If the club is searched and my wallet is found, I suppose whoever finds it will figure that I didn't make it out alive. I pinch my thigh—hard.

The tears betray me, creating pathways in my concealer for the mascara to fill. Revealing the blueish bruise on my left brow as I rub my eyes, dispersing the fear and rage that pools together and overflows. I wish I would have killed more. I wish I would have listened to Cedar.

Amidst the chaos, the creatures that I recognized were all once horrible men. Men who tried to slip fingers inside of us while we danced. Men who Stanley repeatedly had to remove on booze-drenched Saturday nights. Men who this world is better off without. Men who I could have lured away from the club months, years ago. Men who I could have snuffed out, who I should have snuffed out.

I don't remember the last time I cried. I seem to schedule it the way you schedule a dentist appointment. I watch my mother's favourite film, *Bridges of Madison County*, and I sob. I sob for the silent agonies women allow ourselves to call living. My brain screams, "Leave!" So what, your children hate you for a year? So what, your husband has to cook his own dinners? We all knew he'd go to the diner every evening for the daily special until the waitress took him in. Until he became another woman's fixer-upper. Another woman's tender arms and doting words and pseudosafety. Shit, I'd think, maybe you're robbing him of *his* Clint Eastwood by keeping your loneliness all to yourself. Ever think of that? Does anyone think they're fooling anyone else when their passion has turned into the Sahara Desert? When planning the meals for the week or leaning up against the tumbling dryer is your only distraction? When a dry kiss goodnight feels like the kindling that set the house on fire with everyone in it?

I used to watch my mother from the corner of my eye as the tears slid down her freckled cheek and could see all of the ways she lied to herself. We all see ourselves in our favourite films, hear our struggles and thirst in our favourite songs. We condemn narcissists as if we don't all have the capacity to become them. We should be our favourite person—we are the only one we can control. Instead, we live in the shadows, the tiny pockets of joy amongst the never-ending stretches of dissatisfaction. We live as if we'll get a do-over. But what if we don't? What if the afterlife is nothing except being glued to the shadows, floating fast and feathery throughout rooms we used to roam? Trying to get a point across again and again and again yet always managing to fall on deaf ears like a toxic relationship. What if the afterlife is lonelier than the living?

"I will never get stuck," I said, watching Meryl Streep weigh her choices during the length of a red light: the man she loved or the man she felt indebted to; the man who saw her or the man who took her for granted. My mother's sobs turned into whimpers, the sounds of her own childhood love stories dying beside me on the couch. She was twenty-nine then. Wrinkle-free and more stunning than I'll ever be. Maybe she wanted me there. Maybe she wanted to rub my nose in the wrong choice. To tell me that if she had it her way, she'd disappear into the night. Her decisions always revolved around men, sordid conversations about ex-boyfriends who she swore she'd always love. I fear I'm not that different. I wore her decisions like a cloak. I was her best friend. I was her demise. It's those first children that change a woman's life forever. Motherhood is a full-time and eternal job, and I know she tried her best, sacrificing herself without a second thought. Maybe I needed to see her take her life into her own hands. Maybe that's all I've ever wanted.

She and her sister both had children too young. Unlike Aunt Cindy, my mother will never admit all that I stole from her. She chose me. And she's never been one to go back on her choices. She chose my father. She chose her life, even if at times it's proven to be agonizing. When you choose something, it's easier to overlook the flaws. She chose us.

She could have chosen better though, couldn't she?

I think of all the women who've stood by their men, who've built homes of comfort and safety and joy for their children even if they haven't truly felt it themselves. Those shrinking and silencing and refusing to start over. Those staying, even as their men stray and patronize and change. Men … men are truly free to change their minds. To strive.

The shadows haunt my father too, but maybe he's just seeing his own ghosts, his own demons manifesting to run rampant throughout our family home.

I think of the men, or what was left of them, at the club. "A girl is only good if you can save her," a pot-bellied sixty-something man said to me once as I clamoured all over him to the sound of a sultry classic rock song that will unfortunately always remind me of that dance. When I told him I wouldn't go home with him for the fourth time, he finally—begrudgingly—nodded before saying, "Remember what I said though." And I nodded with a roll of my eyes. "What was it that I said?" he asked, his tone incessant that I indulge him.

"A girl is only good if you can save her," I said.

He clucked me under the chin like a grandchild and said, "That's right."

I found it fascinating how the saving only extended to women, not the men who sat there night after night, begging us to take off more, to please, please, please let them touch.

Did Lil pass the creatures on her way out? Did she get out? Derek's car was no longer in the lot when I left. A seed of hope.

It's been twenty-two hours and still nothing from her. For a moment I debate calling my mom, of begging her to pile in the car and hole up in my apartment with me until—what? I'm not sure. I think of finally telling her about Richard, the stranger last night, and the men between. I long to ask, "Have you been watching the news?" I want her to know that Ian saved me. *Am I lovable, Mom? Do you think this means I'm lovable?* The sob rattles from my chest with such force it's as if something inside of me is breaking, shifting, dying. On hands and knees, I crawl to the base of my closet, crouching inside and curling amongst the clothes long ago fallen off of their hangers. My fingers search the carpet floor for the shoebox—these games that I no longer want to play after Ian's body was devoured beside me. He saved the raw beauty of his ugliness for me. I think of his soft skin beneath my fingers, the down of a beast. His blue eyes gazing at me for the first time with a look of compassion as his body betrayed him.

I should have known he was somewhere close when Cedar left. When she left me all alone with him as she always has.

"Cedar?" I whisper.

"Cedar?" I whisper again.

"Cedar?" I think of her like Marybeth, materializing from the shadows to wrap me up in her surprisingly strong, skinny arms.

My ringing phone startles me with a jolt, and I scurry out of the darkness, praying for Lil.

ELIJAH flashes across the small, pixelated screen. I hold it in my palm, knowing that men have a gentle knack for altering your route. Knowing that I will let Elijah alter mine. I answer on the fourth ring, hoping he was starting to worry.

"Hello?"

"Delilah."

His voice is chipper and contrasts brightly against the gore of yesterday, of the night before. The screams still echo in my ears. I crawl to the window, watching as two birds flit together, blissfully happy that it's spring.

"You're alive," he continues, letting out a deep sigh.

I think of saying *barely*. Of breaking down, letting my choking sobs slam against his eardrum until he has to hold his phone from an outstretched arm.

"Did you hear about that man killed close to where we met?"

"No, I didn't. Was he starting to change?"

"Turn on the news. His picture is everywhere. The virus has arrived. It's in full swing. We don't need to go on the dark web to see confessions … Men everywhere are out in the streets begging God for forgiveness."

I peek out my window again. My street is barren except for the birds.

"Is this a dream?" I ask, staring at the pinkish, orange sky outside my window, a gorgeously deceiving backdrop.

"It's a nightmare."

"Do you want to come over?"

There's a pause, and I immediately feel foolish, desperate, weak.

"Do you trust me?"

I don't trust anyone.

"Fifty-seven George Crescent."

I pull the shoebox from its hiding place, toss off the lid, and pick Ian's photo from the mess. I write: **I'M SORRY**. But it feels wrong. I scratch it out.

I flip over the photo of Kyle and think of the clip I saw at the coffee shop: a month ago at his college graduation, beaming smile, lopsided cap. The camera lingered on that image more than this one, the media forever obsessed with a man's potential instead of his reality.

I did him a favour. Today, the skin would have torn from his knuckles as his hands curved inward, his chin bloody from the pressure of his own sharp teeth.

I dial Lil again. The phone rings and rings and rings and then catches, giving me a wave of hope before her voice comes across, "You've reached Lil. Spill it after the beep."

It reminds me of those early hours I spent slouched in the hallway of my childhood home, phone cord wrapped around my wrist as I called Nan's house, my heart sinking lower each time Nan answered and told me, "Delilah, honey, we need to keep the lines clear. We need to keep them clear for Cedar."

I hung up and sat alone in my forever cold living room. My parents were both at the hospital, and by the time they came home, I had melted into the wallpaper. They let me melt into the wallpaper. They asked, "Any news?" and I shook my head. I asked about Theo and instantly regretted it. If he was okay, he'd be home. Dad grimaced and Mom kept her spacey eyes on the floor until I wondered what kind of better life she was picturing amongst the carpet.

To rid myself of the useless feeling, I called my nan again. I counted it as it rang, envisioning Cedar running inside from the front yard, the screen door slamming behind her.

"Babes, what did I just tell you?" was all Nan said, knowing that it was me even without Caller ID.

A text jolts me from the memory. Elijah is at the front door. I glance out the peephole before I turn the lock and hustle down the stairs to the front door, where I check another peephole before letting him in.

My feet have been scrubbed and the bruise is covered again. I thought of leaving it all, of showing him that I was coming undone. Of telling him, "I didn't have to watch the news. I did it, I did it, I did it," but I lost my nerve.

Elijah has a bouquet of scraggly wildflowers held out in his hand, and his eyes lock on mine as he says, "Have you heard that the changing can't hold eye contact?"

I don't tell him about Ian and that last lingering look. The last thing a man wants is to hear a word about another man.

"You look radiant," he says.

TWENTY-FOUR

Elijah lies sprawled across my carpet, lanky arms propped behind his head, mesmerizing eyes set on the ceiling, a stark honest vulnerability that makes me feel as if I've known him forever.

"You're a brave one, little mouse." He sings it to the tune of *The Grinch*. We are a bottle of wine in and our lips are equally tinged as Elijah pulls up videos from local news stations on his phone. Stores are being looted all across the city, the unchanged greedily clutching onto whatever they can. Men armed with crowbars and baseball bats, and one with a three-pronged garden hoe, causes us to burst into a fit of drunken laughter until tears stream from our eyes.

Canada, which has been on the brink of lowering its gun laws for the last five years, now resembles an open-carry state as those who've begrudgingly kept their weapons in cabinets now keep them strapped to their chest and hips. More frighteningly, yet in no way surprising, gun shops have been looted as well, the mass shootings in America climbing to numbers so high they must be made up.

"It's not the guns that kill," lobbyists say after news of another massacre involving school-children—mostly school-children, but sometimes movie-goers, music lovers, or people waiting to order a burrito at the mall.

The pro-gun are also very anti-abortion. "The shootings are abortions fault."

"Women, these nasty murderous sluts, show the greatest disregard for human life. It's women who set the precedent." They say this with straight-faces, although all of the mass shooters were men.

I've always likened a cock to a loaded gun.

Like the gun when children's blood winds up smeared across schoolroom floors, it's not the cock that meets any criticism when a woman needs an abortion. It's as if the gun and the cock are immune. Equally inanimate. Society, in its end, always searches for a woman to blame.

Not the gun, not the cock. The Change will be no different; they're already searching for a cause. A woman, with the power to inspire lust and rage, is to blame.

"We cry out for you. We pray for you!" Conservatives say the same thing to a woman walking into an abortion clinic as they do to a family burying their child who was shot during math class.

"We cry out for you. We pray for you!" I want to say that to a man as the fever hits.

If we can fully disengage with reality, we can convince ourselves this is all the fault of women. North America is built on nothing if not disillusion. Patriots screaming of freedom on lands drenched in the blood of the Indigenous, built upon the backs of African slaves. Blood on the hands of countries that pride themselves as the best in the world. Canada's catchphrase, "I'm sorry," is equally as empty and meaningless as a man who's apologizing for raping you the night before. The changing, and progressively changed, roam the streets, most in packs of two or three, some solo.

Elijah's pulled up articles on Kyle, zooming in on pictures of the Polaroid so I could take a closer look, seemingly for the first time. "Oh my God, that's him I think," I say, pointing out the ripped bomber jacket, the wiry stature.

"I wish I would have killed him myself," Elijah mutters before setting his phone down again, only to pick it back up when another Change-related notification dings.

Elijah is self-proclaimed obsessed with the illness, his notifications turned on for any and all news stories, the alerts linking to the most recently published YouTube videos. While he's distracted, I peek at my phone.

My father has texted me twice:

You should consider coming home.

Do you need me to come get you?

I've left both unanswered, cruelly, hoping he thinks I'm dead. Wondering if now, he'll believe in ghosts. Any interaction with him more often than not leaves me inconsolably crying the second I'm once again alone, the unconscious hum radiating from my throat reminiscent of an animal dying in a trap. I hate him as much as I want him to love me. I thought I'd outgrow the feeling by now, this desperate need for him to know me and be proud of what he finds. He's forever sickened by the emotional pleas for connection, poo poos the gooey complaint of emotional trauma.

There have been times when the pain has been visible in my mother's eyes, that she chose a father for her children who is incapable of love, but she pushes it down as quickly as it arises. I feel problematic when I blame her for the emotional divots my father has carelessly carved into Theo and me, yet it's too easy to overlook a hapless man and blame an emotionally intelligent woman: she should have wanted more for us; she should have wanted more for herself.

My father makes me want to flee yet halts me at the same time, a nervous flutter in my chest while my body seems incapable of movement. His energy is depressive, a weight pressing down on my shoulders. Cedar always thought my issues with my father were trivial; she never had one to love or hate, resent or respect.

"You're lucky," she'd say. "At least your dad wants to make sure you are safe and always have money in your pocket."

Before she moved in with Nan, Cedar had grown up without. I had grown up too comfortable to ever completely appreciate the security and warmth of money. I knew better than to explain that money was near meaningless to me, how I'd trade all of his financial help for one day of him truly seeing me, for knowing me. I knew I was lucky for being unable to relate to poverty, to have only gone hungry by choice.

I can feel Cedar storming about the apartment, angry that I am allowing myself distraction.

"Is your family all in the area?" I ask Elijah, refilling both of our glasses knowing that I'm down to my last two bottles, but I care less about rationing than getting to a state of euphoric obliteration.

"My mom and sister, yeah, they've been talking about heading up to our cottage"—he stops and flutters his hands in the air—"you know, *away* from it all."

"And your dad?" I pause, wondering if his father is out running the streets, if he's chained up in a basement being delivered raw chicken breasts and bowls of water from a safe distance.

Elijah takes a gulp of wine, emptying half of his glass. "Are we to this part of our relationship yet?" He flips onto his stomach, pulls himself towards me.

When I think of relationships, I think of them ending. That hollow thump in your chest, the empty ache of your stomach. How your limbs seem to pull you to the floor as if they no longer want to belong to you either. Their only purpose is to drag you down, down, down. Keep you anchored to your bed. And yet even as your cemented arms and legs hold you prisoner, your mind races with all of the best moments—the moments you felt free to die during, the moments you were happy. The moments you believed you were fully seen. You've consumed the poison and fallen face-first into a daydream where you'll be loved forever, unconditionally. You'd prefer a cheese grater to the skin than the reality that it was all a farce, all for nothing. A waste of time.

Feeling fully seen makes the heartache that much worse. You can't look back and say, "I never truly let them in."

No, you showed them everything. Maybe that's why they left.

I like to know all the ways a person can inflict raw, searing emotional pain. I like to act first.

"I suppose not," I finally say. The slight warmth of his breath hits my cheek as he approaches me and grabs the bottle of wine beside my thigh. "What have you found, Professor?" I ask, wanting to keep him close as he retreats to sit cross-legged in his same spot on the carpet, a safe distance from me.

A howl pulls us from our conversation and reminds us that we are not telling campfire stories, we are in one. Our eyes dart to the window, but I keep my arm parallel to the ground, signalling Elijah to crawl. The only sound is the thumping of our hearts as slowly, slowly we raise our heads until our eyes can just barely see the sidewalk beneath.

The creature is across the street. It's in its final stages of walking on hind legs and keeps dropping back down to scraped and bloodied hands and knees every few steps, its outcry anguished, piercing. I glance down the street in both directions, letting my eyes attempt to careen down the alleyways, scanning for others.

From a distance I can see how its thighs morph into hindquarters. Its hands gnarl into hoofed claws, the toes and feet melding together in a way that makes me realize women's high heels were based off of animal hooves, manufactured to dehumanize. Downcast face, neck inverted and mangled as the spine juts. I can't make out its features other than teeth that have managed to puncture through stubbled cheeks. Its blonde patches of hair.

"Holy fuck, they're uglier in person," Elijah whispers, and I quickly nod, careful not to make a sound myself. Careful not to think of Ian. Not to morbidly wish that it was him out there, coming to see me once more.

The thing howls again, so shrill I feel it in my stomach.

I watch it dart across the street as I hear pounding on the front door.

TWENTY-FIVE

The aftereffects of too much wine on an empty stomach has me swaying as I stand. I wait for one, two, three, four seconds as the blackness fades from my vision and my room comes back into focus. The pounding gets louder.

Elijah pulls the baseball bat from beneath my bed as I glance again at my phone, hoping for some kind of indication. If there was ever a time to call before you pop by.

"Do you want me to get it?" Elijah asks, his voice a rush.

I shake my head, holding up a finger to tell him to please wait as I unlock the chain and twist the deadbolt. From the top of the stairs I can see the front door rattle with each knock, accompanied by a soft yet frantic, "Please, please, please."

I rush down the stairs, envisioning tripping, breaking my neck at the bottom as the front door remains locked. The voice catches and it's her. I know it's her.

The lock turns with a satisfying pop, and her eyes are frazzled, cheek bloodied. But she's standing. She's okay. In her left hand is a rifle, and I step away from it before I notice the tranquilizers.

"Lil," I breathe, looking behind her at the sidewalk where a thing lies twitching.

The air rushes from her chest, her face cracking into a sob. I realize that this was nothing but a desperate stab at survival. She did not think I would be here. Maybe she didn't think I would be alive at all. She is in the same oversized sweats she was wearing yesterday when she left the club, when she'd seen firsthand how men can morph, the blood stain on her sweater a dark, rusted burgundy. Her eyes widen and she begins to murmur a quiet yet constant, "No, no, no, no" as her gaze falls over my shoulder.

"It's okay. You're okay." I hear Elijah before I've turned my head, picturing his mouth beginning to hang slack as his jaw breaks from the pressure, his hair patchy and growing in tufts down skin that was just so smooth. Yet when I turn, he's the same with his large pale hands held palms forward, eyes soft, chest gently heaving in breath.

Is Lil picturing herself torn to shreds, devoured by one of my bad dates? Her eyes lock with mine. I nod with an expression that aims to reassure, but it feels as if it falters halfway and winds up apologetic that I'm not alone. I'm never fucking alone.

She fully steps inside as I recognize the half-torn jacket on the creature crouched on the sidewalk. Derek's growl is hoarse and pained.

"That was Derek. That was Derek," Lil repeats, her voice frantic, as I slam the door behind us.

"It wasn't, babes. It wasn't."

As the lock slides with a satisfying click, I gesture for her to head upstairs quickly. There are a group of men who live in the apartment beneath me, the bass from their music booming every Friday and Saturday, long-weekend Sundays, and oddly enough, every single Tuesday without fail. Sometimes, one of them or one of their friends has been out in the hall when I get home in the early hours of morning. Red Solo cup in hand, voice slurred but still assured as he asks if I want a drink. I picture them all, behind the thin walls, changing. I haven't seen any of them for a week. I've never been neighbourly enough to learn their names.

"Come on," I whisper to Lil, waving my hand again.

Lil stops, as if transfixed, and places both of her palms against the frosted glass of the front door, peering out into the early evening glow at the man she loves as he eases himself off of the sidewalk and looks around with the gentle innocence of a fresh fawn.

"We have to go, Lil. Now," I say as Derek slams against the door with the strength of a bull. Elijah follows behind us, and I wonder if she's envisioning the same thing that I am: a man half-changed trailing after us like a lost puppy.

After double locking the door, I peer through the peephole. My fretful eyes scan the dim hallway for movement, sure that I will see the silhouette of what Derek has become in the dimly lit hallway, his smooth entitlement replaced with force.

"It wasn't Derek," she says as if in awe. It's the lies we tell ourselves that keep us sane.

The thrashing at the front door continues, and Lil jumps, a tiny squeal escaping her lips before she crawls to my bedroom, peers out the only window facing the front of the building. I follow. Beneath, Derek rests in a crouch, limbs jutting out in a way that is no longer human.

A laugh rattles up from my chest, bordering on manic. *It wasn't Derek. It wasn't Ian. He wasn't himself.* We've said things like this before, haven't we? I let out a rush of breath and only then am I aware of the fierce pounding of my heart—the way you don't notice it until after you've come. The thought makes me laugh harder. Elijah's smiling from the doorway, a look of amused disbelief. Is he measuring my mania? How long before he leaves?

"Lil, that wasn't Derek." The more we say it, the more it sounds like the truth. I lead her back to the kitchen, hand clasped around hers, away from the window, away from reality.

Her head bobs and bobs like that of a sleepy child. She sinks down to my kitchen floor, her body crumpling forward, bloody hands clasped before her, chin resting on tile as if she's begging for forgiveness from a cruel king. I can hear her heart thumping too.

Exhaustion lingers behind my eyes. I picture scooping them out of their softened, rotting sockets with a melon baller. The fatigue feels tangible, a cancer that could be removed. Lil watches Elijah from the corner of her eye as he stands up, pours himself a glass of water from the tap. She's weighing him the way we do men in the club. Used to. Realizing that all we thought we've learned has only taught us that we can't tell the good from the bad. There are too many grey areas. Too many hidden agendas behind seemingly genuine compliments, moments of tenderness. I can feel the rage in Lil blooming, searching for a home. Cedar can feel it too. She longs to be held by her.

Lil raises her jaw towards Elijah, her eyes narrowing. "What's your deal?"

Elijah steps from one foot to the other, takes a sip of water. Sets the glass down. Clears his throat. Picks the glass back up again. "My deal?" he asks, not rudely, more with an air of anxiety. Perhaps a biding of time to find the right words.

"He saved me the other night," I say, and it's not a lie, but it doesn't feel like the complete truth either when I think of Kyle's throat slit, how his body quivered at my feet. When I think of Cedar hissing that I don't need saving.

A flash of similar disappointment clouds Lil's features.

"What? You didn't say …" She looks down at her hands.

"Everything happened so fast yesterday—" I think of the creatures feeding upon the flesh of our fellow dancers, the gash across Lil's stomach. Derek. Ian. "I didn't get the chance."

"Do you want me to leave?" The glass of water is back on the counter, and Elijah's hands lie clasped in front of him. He keeps his eyes set on Lil, who closes her eyes and rubs her temples.

"I'm getting a fucking headache," she mutters.

Elijah looks down at the waist of Lil's shirt, where the blood has soaked through, crusted over. She follows his eyes, looks up at him from beneath the ridge of her brow.

"Women can catch it too," he whispers.

Lil drops her gaze again. He stands up, pours a fresh glass of water, and passes it to her. She bites at her lips, figuring out how to respond. "All I know is I lost the man I love to this virus and he's … out there!" She glances towards the door. "I saw, I don't know, a dozen fucking others foaming at the mouth last night and none of them were women."

"I'm sorry." Elijah takes another sip, and I can tell he wants to say more; he wants to ask questions, but he doesn't. And I'm grateful for it, his silence. "I'll go." He turns towards the door. "Take care of yourself, Delilah."

Without thinking, I'm on my feet, barricading the door in an act reminiscent of those breakups in my early twenties, the tears and wine, and I can't live without you's.

"I'm the one that showed up here unannounced," Lil says, wobbling a little as she stands.

"Yeah, chased and covered in blood." Elijah extends a hand to her to tell her to stay.

Please, I mouth to him, hoping I'm not rolling over, that he's not repelled by my soft white underbelly.

He pulls me in, two hands clasped at the back of my neck, his eyes locked on mine. "She's right. Neither of you know whether or not I'm dangerous."

I think of Ian between my legs days ago, beneath me yet leaving me feeling so far, far beneath him. If Lil wasn't here watching me, waiting for my response, judging me from the floor, I'd say, "I'm willing to take the risk."

"You can't. Derek—" I hate myself for using his name. I don't look at Lil before I continue. "He could still be out there. It's not safe." When I drop my eyes from Elijah's, ashamed of the abandonment I feel so soon, I hate myself even more.

"When you two leave, bring weapons," he says, pulling a switchblade from the back pocket of his jeans before he drops the chain, slides the deadbolt. I resist the urge to roll my eyes, as if we'd leave here without the tranq, without my knife.

I don't breathe until he's out in the hall. A thrashing makes us both jump. I picture Derek just outside the door, lunging at Elijah. I picture Elijah, spine twisting, jaw cracking, lips splitting, coming back for me, becoming one of the pack.

"Don't," Lil says, crab-crawling backwards towards my living room. I'm still not used to seeing her frightened. I don't like it. It makes me want to scream.

Reaching for the door, my fingers clutch the lock as it pushes back open. And it's Elijah. Still Elijah. He slams it behind him and turns the lock again, slides the chain into place, leans against it with all of his strength until I imagine something bursting through at any second.

"Yup, that thing ..." He looks at Lil between rushes of breath. "Your-your boyfriend? It got in."

Lil's body twists as if she's in literal war of head versus heart.

"Don't, babe. He's gone. He's gone."

Her eyes narrow into slits, and for a moment I don't know what to do, what to say. She has me paralyzed.

Elijah runs his hands through his thick dark hair, pushing back the fresh sweat that's begun to accumulate against his forehead. He leans up against the door, letting out a biting laugh.

"Do you mind if I stay here a little longer?" he asks.

The creature thrashes against the door, its voice halfway between a whine and a squeal, and I'm sure, I'm sure that I can smell it. It reeks of want.

Lil looks past us to the shaking door. She inches back a little further into the living room with each of the creature's thrusts. I want to grab my hunting knife from beside my bed, but I fear the second I leave the room the thing will burst through. I won't look like I was defending, I'll look like I was fleeing. Just like in the club. I grab a steak knife from the block on the counter, stifling a small laugh, knowing that I bought the set from the dollar store and they aren't even sharp.

Cedar laughs too. Maniacal and panicked. The laugh she'd do before orange pop spurted from her nose and poured down her chin. Childish. Wild.

"If only you had a garden hoe," Elijah mutters, and I laugh the way I laughed when an ex avoided a head-on collision by a quick jerk of the wheel, the car spinning with the risk of flipping. It's an accepting laugh. The laugh of death.

Lil's wild eyes watch us both. She scoots further into the living room, stifling whimpers with each thrash, each huff of breath that I swear I can feel oozing in from around the doorjamb.

"Fuck this," she mutters, hopping up and grabbing the tranq from the kitchen counter.

Elijah steps closer to the living room, gestures for me to stay where I am—straight ahead of the door, yet far enough that when it opens I won't be struck. He slinks until he's nearly in the other room, and I understand. The creature will come for me, and that's when Elijah can pounce. But he'll only have a second before I'm in its grasp, before my neck is snapped, legs spread too wide. Before Derek gets me. I stand back, knife shaking in my sweaty palm, like a cliché babysitter movie.

How many more thrashes will it take? I watch the shaking door. I close my eyes, preparing for the moment of action, of finality. It feels almost blissful, knowing that it won't be much longer until I'm dead. Until this nightmare comes to an end. I'm almost excited for it. Will I see Nan?

"Derek!" Lil begins to yell. My head snaps towards her in panic as the thrashes become harder, more determined. She gestures with a toned arm for us to move back.

"Lil, please," I whisper, but she just squares her hips. The door rattles, the fury of a dog with rolie polie puppies. I watch in awe as she undoes the chain.

"What the fuck?" Elijah steps back further into my hall. I follow him, every shred of control drifting from me like dust.

She turns the deadbolt as he thrashes again.

She turns the doorknob.

Cedar murmurs with glee.

Derek's shoulder is bloody from where he banged it against the door, his breath a pant. He stumbles into the apartment on all fours, neck tossing from side to side like an angry horse. I think of Ian.

"I wanted more for us, Derek," Lil says to the creature in front of her on the floor, its blood leaving smears across my tiled floor. Her voice is too calm. She's slipped into shock and will be the reason for our demise. "You were supposed to be one of the good ones, remember?"

The creature snarls, its lower register so similar to Derek's speaking voice. I watch Lil step back for a second, disillusioned. Face-to-face with something that no amount of dark web or smartphone notifications could prepare him for, Elijah remains silent beside me.

"I loved you," Lil whispers as the creature lunges towards her on gnarled hind legs. She fires a dart. It lets out a small whimper but doesn't stop. Suddenly, Lil is buried beneath bloodied, sinewy flesh and taut muscle, flailing claws. I hear the tranq fire again, a dull *pop*. Derek's body finally slackens, but my feet are cemented to the ground as I watch the scene play out in front of me. Elijah rushes forward, pulling the thing off of her. Lil's eyes are wild as she kneels over Derek's body. She strokes his cheek, touches the tip of her finger to the sharp point of one of his teeth.

The monsters will reveal themselves, Cedar whispers. Lil's head jerks up, and for a moment I want to ask her if she heard Cedar, if she can sense her, but I don't. Of course she can't. Lil scrambles to her feet and yanks open a drawer, utensils clattering. It's the knife I use for chopping sweet potatoes, carrots for stew. She stares at it in her hand, as if the hand doesn't belong to her, as if she's watching herself from above. She turns to me and smiles before dropping back to her knees. She places a small kiss on the creature's forehead before she begins to stab messy jagged gashes into Derek's neck.

Lil has never looked more radiant. Elijah vomits into my sink, lean shoulders shuddering with each retch. My fingertips move to my temples. Cedar is still laughing, and it hurts. It stabs. She loves nothing more than a woman coming undone.

Realizing their strength, she says between guffaws. *Realizing your strength!*

Lil looks up at me, fist firmly clenched around the black handle of the knife. She beams.

"Let's get him the fuck out of here," she says, voice alight. I hurry to my feet as she stands and further kicks open my door.

"You better help too," she says to a clammy and pale Elijah, who hasn't moved far from the sink. He pushes his sweaty hair back with a large, shaking hand but with his foot he helps us heave Derek out the door, to the top of the stairs, until finally, with one last shove, his body clatters down.

I slam the door shut as we step back inside, re-locking the deadbolt, sliding the chain until it sits safely in place. Lil's laugh is manic. It ends in a sob.

Suddenly so tired, I walk to my bedroom in a trance. Darkness falls around the street, the streetlights looming long shadows. I slump to the floor, grateful that I can no longer hear it, the wet nightmare sounds of horror.

Lil curls up beside me on the floor, her breathing fast and uneven, hands and clothes coated in blood. I place two hands on her shoulders the way my nan used to do with me.

"Breathe, breathe," I whisper into her sweaty hair. "It's okay, just breathe."

The cry breaks free from her throat, high-pitched before it ends in a deep groan. She leans so deeply into my arms I wish I could absorb her, provide her with the utmost comfort. Elijah waits at the bedroom door, his back to us, taking deep breaths of his own. I know he's listening. Waiting for more monsters to crash up the stairs. I think of the club, how they exhaust themselves, how they sleep like cats, or post-coital men, unable to keep their eyes open, pussy-dazed and content. I think of Derek decomposing in the hall. Soon, we'll have to leave.

"Everything will be okay," I tell Lil as if I'm speaking of monsters beneath the bed, the boogeyman.

Lil's breath rushes from her chest. Her shoulders continue to shake. "I'm pregnant."

The thing at the bottom of my stairs, twisted and broken, is finally free of the smugness that always hung around the corners of Derek's lips. I open my mouth to speak but can't find the words.

"He wasn't who I thought he was."

I place my hand on her shoulder to steady her. I want to tell her that they so rarely are, but I don't. I stay silent.

"Derek got the tranq gun for me," she says with a stifled guffaw.

"Did he know that he was changing?" Elijah asks, stepping gingerly to sit closer to Lil, cross-legged, hands folded in his lap. The colour is slowly returning to his gaunt cheeks.

Lil shakes her head, but her eyes look unsure. I hear what he's asking: *Were the signs as telltale as they said they would be?* I push down the urge to laugh again, forever unable to cope in situations where screaming seems to be the only answer. This sickness creeps up upon men the way men creep up upon women in an alley, revealing themselves only when it's too late. I think of Ian. Guilt thrashes inside of my stomach. His eyes and trembling hands, the money on the table. Were his hands any hungrier than usual? His voice any deeper? His mouth any crueller? Did he know? Did he know? Did he know? Untapped emotion that I can't begin to process, I want to tell Lil that he saved me. I want to tell Lil that it wasn't all for nothing. But there are no words. There are no words.

The sky opens up with a furious rain. Lightning shimmers like a flickering switch. Childishly, I wonder if I've caused it. If the Creator is permitting me to cry.

"I haven't read anything about the virus being reversible," Elijah says solemnly. "And I've read a lot." His chuckle is half-hearted.

Lil's long fingers massage her tiny stomach, still free of any sign of life, nails digging into smooth flesh. I want to tell her I'm happy that Derek's dead. That she's better off. Does she realize it now? I want to tell them both everything.

We're only as sick as our secrets, the little voice says.

Elijah excuses himself to go to the bathroom, and for the first time it's only Lil and me.

"I'm so tired," she says to no one in particular, her features softening.

The response is a howl.

Another lost boy out in the streets.

Cautiously and low, we look back out the window, trailing our eyes back and forth, back and forth, along my weed-riddled walkway. We duck as a creature attempts to raise its head and sniff the air, unsure of what will transpire if we lock eyes. But as the deterioration continues, it must catch another scent.

We hear the howls of others, the startling *pop-pop* of gunshots.

I wrap Lil's hand in mine, squeeze twice.

Her shoulders shake as she places both of her palms on the cool glass of my window, her face staring out with the agony of a child being sent away. Staring out at this fresh hell that has the power to change everything. I think of the cluster of cells taking form inside of her and can't help the shiver that grips me. I silently beg Cedar to tell me that everything will be okay, but she's chosen apathy. *It is what it is. It'll be what it'll be.*

Lil quickly looks over her shoulder, startled, and meets my eyes with a gaze full of terror.

"Did you hear that?" she asks. How do I respond? She bows her head and begins to sob again, cries stifled in her hands as she tries to stay as silent as possible. "I'm so tired. I'm so fucking tired." She presses her palms against her temples, keeping her eyes on the floor. "I think I'm losing my mind."

TWENTY-SIX

It's disturbing how quickly you grow accustomed to the sounds of gunshots and squeals, flesh being ripped from bone. How these nightmares become nothing more than a backdrop.

"Do you think she's going to be alright?" Elijah asks the nook of my neck as Lil lies sound asleep, curled up on top of my duvet.

Every noise made her jump even though her eyes quickly fell back to their dazed state, lids heavy. Three times I covered her with my favourite throw, hand-knitted by my nan for my tenth birthday, but she keeps kicking it off. Before sleep embraced her, I cleaned her wound with cotton pads soaked in peroxide, recalling memories of the scraped-knee freedom of bike rides with Theo and Cedar. I coated the gash in a thick yellow layer of Rawleigh's salve then covered it in a long strip of gauze, medical tape on either side. Elijah found the first-aid kit beneath my sink amongst hopeful hair products and blackhead scrubs. I threw her sweatshirt in the trash, not wanting to wash the bloodstains we all knew would never fully fade. I gave her two Motrin and three puffs of a joint, hoping that sleep would wrap her in its arms before the realization struck that we are all living inside of a bad dream.

"The scratch is only surface. It really doesn't look too bad now that it's cleaned up. It stopped bleeding."

"I don't mean the scratch," Elijah says, and I follow his unwavering gaze, how it rests on Lil with a kind of caution that too easily resembles fear.

"Women have been contracting it too," he whispers without looking away from her. Lil's eyes flutter in sleep like a baby, soft hands pressed palm to palm beneath her smooth cheek. "Do you think that was why she had such an easy time killing it? Why she kept stabbing and stabbing?"

Guilt pools in my stomach. I want to tell him about the rage, about what happens when you accept it.

"Where did you read that?" I ask.

The internet is littered with just about any opinion you can come up with. As the media becomes more and more rogue, fact-checking is finally being acknowledged for the privilege that it was —a privilege so many took for granted in society's Before.

Elijah grabs his phone from the floor beside him, sliding his password with his thumb and clicking rapidly before he hands it over to me. The sounds she makes are jarring, a high-pitched throaty shriek that reverberates in my core. I quickly turn the volume all the way down, my eyes darting to Lil who barely budges.

The changing woman's long, straw-coloured hair hangs in clumps, her scalp riddled with bald patches. The delicate bones of her shoulders cave in as she thrashes against a linoleum floor. When she looks up, her eyes narrow towards the camera with the intensity of an animal that realizes they have their prey exactly where they want them. A dark confidence. She sneers with a mouth of sharp teeth, a living demon.

I click off the phone and toss it back towards Elijah facedown.

"They don't know what's causing it. Just like the men. This woman," he says, shaking his phone as if she's inside of it, "had a history of mental illness, filed a claim against her father for sexual abuse."

My stomach gurgles and my face feels hot, the sudden surge of panicked blood.

"Lil will be fine," I say, more to myself than to him, this man who's already asking that I choose him.

"This case in the UK is a breakthrough. Not only because it's of the first reported change amongst women, but also because of her documented list of mental illness and abuse."

I want to light up a cigarette, but I don't want to wake Lil with the sweet swirling of nicotine.

"She doesn't have a history of mental illness." If I meet his eyes, I fear he'll see the shame in mine. He'll see that I don't remember a time when I wasn't mentally ill.

"There has to be studies of all of the changed men that disprove this has anything to do with mental illness," I add, hoping I don't sound as if I'm grovelling, attempting to manipulate.

"The men vary from each other across the board, but men are more often undiagnosed."

It's true. Men are four times more likely to kill themselves.

"I've read that suffering sexual assault correlates with dementia later in life for women."

This longing to forget becomes terminal. My voice contains a hostility that stalls Elijah. My brain is like a maze; trauma creates winding pathways that are then suddenly barricaded, the memories irretrievable.

I think of the stories of doctors and cops, teachers and homeless men. Athletes, musicians—many of whom famous and absurdly charming—gas station clerks, high-school students, suddenly equal in their devolution.

I shake my head.

"The other possibility is a bite," Elijah adds, eyes locked on the oversized Molson Canadian T-shirt my dad got out of a case of beer that swims over Lil's small frame.

I square my shoulders. "This isn't a fucking zombie apocalypse."

As if on cue, sounds of shouting from the street and the deep rally of voices of the unchanged combined with the sharp squealing of the changed fill the room. Gun shots and grunts.

Lil's eyes bulge open in panic. A small whimper escapes her lips.

"Derek?" For a moment she's forgotten where she is. I watch the realization, the anguish cloud her features as her eyes wince tight.

"You're okay, you're okay, you're okay," I coo, rushing to her and brushing the damp hair off of her clammy forehead. Elijah watches us from across the room. I pretend not to notice, choosing instead to watch Lil as her lids close and begin to flutter again, even amongst the tears that rim her thick lashes.

"You're okay," I say again, still seated on the floor. I rest my head beside her on the pale tangerine duvet, stroking her smooth arm with its large owl tattoo that seems to stare through me. Can it see me for who I truly am? I can hear Cedar whispering my name from outside my locked bedroom door. It echoes soft and sweet and familiar as sleep presses in with a gentle vignette.

I AWAKE IN THE DARK, IMMEDIATELY UNSURE OF MY surroundings until I notice the outline of my desk from the warm glow of the streetlight outside my window. I go to sit up but my body is pinned to the floor. The only thing I am able to move are my eyes, and they dart sporadically amidst the darkness until they settle in the corner of the room where a large shadow lurks. It turns its head quickly, and I realize that it's an owl, its glare knowing and ancient like the one on Lil's arm. And behind it stands Richard, his hair soaked and dripping against his face, his lips pressing wider and wider—unnaturally wide—into a sneer. The owl begins to spin its head too fast. I open my mouth to scream but can't force out a single sound, my hands clutching the shag carpet beneath me, frantically twisting the soft strands. The owl gets bigger, its shadow looming over my body, obstructing Richard from my view, but I am unable to turn my head. I can't fucking turn my head. I don't even know if I want to. Something is beside me. Heat radiates off its body inches away from my side. My vision tunnels, heart pounding until I pray to pass out, dip away from the overwhelming fear pooling inside my consciousness. I picture Richard's weight upon my chest, his smooth voice telling me to relax, relax, relax. Is this it? Is this what the men see before they are forever changed? I'm burning up.

My phone begins to ring, sharp and piercing. I sit up with a cry, the rush of breath finally finding its voice. Lil is still asleep on the bed beside me, her features soft. Elijah sits cross-legged on an old beanbag chair in the far corner of my room. His wakefulness soothes me even if his eyes are still on Lil. No Richard, no looming owl ready to transport me somewhere I'm not ready to go. Just Elijah.

We are okay, we are okay.

My phone rings again, and I crawl towards him to peer upon the flashing screen alight with the word MOM framed in little pixelated hearts that I placed one day when I felt as if I loved her more than I will ever love anyone else. Elijah looks up at me but stays seated, stays quiet.

"Hello?" I whisper, untwisting the lock on my bedroom door and stepping out into my small living room cluttered with books and dried remnants of plants I long ago forgot to water.

She's crying, her breath catching in her throat and escaping like the coo of an infant.

I've heard her cry like this only twice before.

"We can't find Theo."

"What do you mean?" I ask stupidly, a cheap excuse to find the right words.

My mother sucks in a sharp intake of breath before her sobbing voice rattles into my ear. "We thought he should stay here. We want you both here—" Another rush of breath. "He wasn't answering texts."

Theo goes from bouts of answering within thirty seconds, his phone glued to the palm of his hand, to responding in weeks if at all after the texts have reached an amount to induce panic. There has never been an in-between.

I wait.

"I had your father pop over."

My stomach feels as if I've swallowed gravel. I picture my brother's body riddled with the virus, his bones morphing painfully, his expression confused and feverish and starving.

"Your father didn't come back." She stops, steadies her breathing. "When I went over, the front door wasn't even closed. It was just left ajar and inside it looked like there had been a struggle."

"Do you think—" I don't finish the question, just leave it as is, dangling. She's silent save for her frantic breath. A sense of guilt overwhelms me. Cedar stirs.

"How was Dad when he left?" I think of my father's darkness he's always seemed so apt to step into.

"There's been no exposure," she answers quickly, coldly, regaining a stern sense of composure. I long to tell her of the last forty-eight hours, the squirming wasted pit of what's becoming of men, of the creatures out in the street, Derek's crumpled body at the bottom of my stairs, the hopelessness that fills me.

The news they've been watching must speak of it like a zombie apocalypse, spreading through diseased flesh, sexual intercourse. I think of my feverish body tightening around Ian just three days ago and think of what's left of him now.

From the corner of my eye, I see Lil sit up, too quick, small hands clutching at the fabric of my well-worn T-shirt. She keels forward, her body leaning off of my plush bed, the juxtaposition of cozy innocence and stark, biting reality as she vomits—pale yellow and acrid.

"Ma, I gotta go."

"Honey? Are you okay?" It's an afterthought I want to drape over myself like a blanket.

"I'm okay, I promise. I'll see you soon, k?"

Lil retches, shoulders stabbing forward through the thin cotton.

"Everything will be okay. I'm sorry. I love you. I love you so much."

"Delilah?" I close the phone just as Lil leans further forward, fingers gripping the duvet as she gags.

I grab a towel from the back of the orange patent leather chair at my desk. The carpet, that took me six months to find, is drenched in bile.

"You're okay," I say, rubbing her back to find the T-shirt soaked in sweat.

Elijah watches us from the corner of the room, either keeping his distance or fearful of a moment that seems purely feminine.

"Do you want some water?" I ask her as Elijah comes back with a glass, a blue blob floating near the bottom, and a roll of paper towel.

"For the carpet," he says. "Peroxide and water, bit of dish soap."

"It's okay," I say, more to Lil, as I grab a paper towel and begin to dab at the sour puke, turning my head to try and keep myself from gagging.

"How long have you known?" I ask.

"I just found out three weeks ago. It's still so early." She wipes her mouth with the back of her hand and then looks down at the floor in disgust. "I'm so sorry." Lil glances towards the window, a tear splattering against the grey T-shirt. "This was all I ever wanted," she says without turning her gaze away from the window, "but not like this."

I'm grateful for Elijah's presence, how he awkwardly pours his makeshift cleaner onto my carpet, how he stays quiet. Male energy that keeps me from having to be vulnerable.

"Do you two want to get out of the city with me?"

I look from Lil's face to Elijah's, wanting to ask, *If I let you in will you leave?*

"My brother and father are missing," I tell them both.

TWENTY-SEVEN

The police stations are overwhelmed. Reporting someone missing, be it a man or a woman, is laughable to different extremes. Still, I call, hoping to hear a voice that will soothe me even as it carries me back to the bleakest time of my life. Deb's voice. But the phone only rings and rings.

"You've never mentioned your family," Lil says, voice equipped with a layer of accusation. I don't tell Elijah and Lil about Theo's brain injury. I say that he is a sweetheart, but that he is also blunt. I don't know how to tell people that sometimes when you love someone so much but know they're in pain it's easier to just not speak of them at all. I don't know how to say it without it sounding selfish and immature. It is selfish and immature. I don't know how to articulate it properly: he needed help and I failed him.

Maybe I should have put in more of an effort to stay close.

How can I tell them about my family when I moved away in order to escape them all?

And Theo. Theo. My first best friend. How do I tell people the things that I drink to forget? What would be the point? To create more eyes that watch and judge, more mouths that snicker and whisper. Because we all do that when we hear something horrible about someone we do not know, tiny jokes in order to process.

"My family's a bit of a mess," I say to Lil now, hoping she won't pry. "My brother, he was in an accident as a kid, and so my mom's really freaked out."

It's an understatement. These words that I can't find to match up with the severity of the non-reality that we're living in.

"My father … I don't know if my father will be okay." What I don't say is: I don't know if I want him to be okay. "I know that it seems silly to look for them," I add, embarrassed as I think of what's left of Derek at the bottom of the stairs.

"If I had a father, I'd want to look for him." Lil's words tear into me.

"Me too," Elijah says, and I look at him, remembering his mention of daddy issues the day we met. Wondering if like Lil he has excluded his father from his life to the point that he says he's without one or if he's just never had one at all.

"We don't know what's causing it," Lil says. "Your dad, your brother … they could be okay."

I love her for this, this little reassurance that she guts herself with. I nod solemnly, eyes on my bare feet as I think of who Theo would run to, who he would run from.

I POUR THE POLAROIDS ACROSS THE FLOOR AS THEY sleep. The carpet is now free from stains. I sift through them like playing cards, the artistic licence making all of the body parts look dismembered, even the ones that aren't. I wish I would have taken full pictures of each of the men so I could look at them fully and make my assumptions. I've always waited to strike until the moment they're sure they have me, that dazed, half-lidded look of lust. There are many within the pile I could have loved—sweet boys who walked me to work, who knew I like my coffee black and my bagel with butter and extra cream cheese. Boys who grew distant once I grew fond. Boys who weren't bad, if only a little selfish. Boys who looked at me as if I was a goddess, but then grew angry when others did too. Boys who didn't question where their possessiveness was stemming from, yet who refused to except mine. Are those ones all okay? I hope so. At the same time, I know that even the best can surprise you with violence. Even the best can surprise themselves.

All of them, both dead and alive, bring about similar feelings of emptiness, an insatiable hunger. When I took the photos, I was attempting to curse them all—even the ones who left after kissing me goodbye. I hate this about myself, this inability to trust, this need to see the bad. To marinate myself in the bad.

Richard's photo rests next to the one of Ian. The only two full pictures, even though Richard's hand obscures his face. I can still see his expression in my mind's eye, the carefree smile, the charm. For a moment I remember the butterflies he gave me, how interesting he made me feel.

Ian laughs back at me from the glossy film. The next one to make me feel so interesting, so special. The next one to show me that I could not trust my own judgment.

I write a message on each Polaroid, on what I can remember, the most important take away. Many men don't seem to realize it, but to fuck someone is to know them. They reveal themselves to you. I can tell the type of man someone is by how he looks at me, from his foreplay: either rushed so I can't say it didn't happen, or long but delivered from a smug mouth—a mouth that says this isn't for me, this is for him. A mouth that's building a reputation. I can hear insecurities or pseudo confidence in his moans, feel his hatred or shame as he gets up too quick, as he walks to the washroom without meeting my eyes. I can feel his hope as he lingers in bed, tracing patterns on my damp skin, how he kisses me goodbye.

Anguished howls of beasts pierce the silence, but it's no longer jarring. It's as if we've all become conditioned by the howls yet not of the screams. The screams of women and children who are without a safe place. I'll leave my door unlocked when we make our escape, hoping those in need will find shelter instead of my once beloved apartment becoming a monster's den.

Some of the media outlets are down, some taking the time to wave goodbye, sign off with their same studious voices as if this is only a practical joke. Other channels just went black and YouTube ... YouTube has lost any semblance of control on what can and cannot be uploaded. It's not for the weak of heart. It appears some men, those unchanged, have begun farming the changed. They've been capturing women, most likely under the guise of protection—the unlucky ones and the ones who cannot let go of the idea of men equalling safety. They've been feeding them to the changed. Uploading videos of fucking and feeding alongside voice-over narratives of this being our ultimate punishment, that we turned our backs on God and He is teaching us a lesson.

"He had to teach us a lesson," they say, Christian women and men alike. The creatures, they elude, are the soldiers of God. They treat them like pets yet are extremely cautious to never get to close, God forbid they fall into the receiving end of the lesson.

The videos are called Farmtime. Cute, isn't it? And the

channels increase by the day. I've told Elijah I don't want to hear anything about it. I've begged him not to watch.

"It'll be a matter of time before one of these idiots changes too," he says, filled with a sick curiosity that I can't seem to shake.

Without the media, the virus is left to speculation. Besides, neither of us trust the media much lately. We've all seen how it panders to its audience. The main audience that seems to matter being the Conservatives they've brainwashed with faith. People praying and scream-crying. Yelling that they saw this coming while Cedar mutters, *No. No, you didn't.*

We've kept the videos from Lil, not wanting her to see the father of her child in every rippled spine and deformed mouth. Not wanting to remind her of the night she refers to as a fever dream. She's been saying, "I can't believe I did that. Who am I? Who the fuck am I?"

Her words remind me of my own. I want to show her the Polaroids. The pictures that she's heard mention of before, but whenever I decide to, I lose my nerve. It's selfish to put my own wickedness on her shoulders while she's already under immense stress. What if she felt fear instead of camaraderie?

Instead, we speak of hope. We talk about her baby as if they are already here.

We talk about how we need to leave, how I'll hold her hand as she steps over Derek's body. How I'll be her eyes until we are outside. We're running out of food, and she is already too thin. The morning sickness rattles through her in the evenings too.

She cradles her stomach as if she's already showing. It reminds me of Cedar with a baby doll up her T-shirt, laughing and keeling over as she said, "Ouch, ouch, the baby kicked!" I want to tell Lil about Cedar, about those good memories at least. But I don't know how to share the good without the bad without upsetting her further. Maybe, selfishly, I want to keep Cedar all to myself.

Last night, we heard something in the apartment beneath us thrashing around, but it has since stopped. I've asked Elijah if they can die like a house cat without water. The thought makes us snicker, these monsters that are able to hunt yet may be unable to get out of a locked apartment. We think of the world, the amount of single men, basement dwellers, those pseudo-intelligent who have devolved into creatures amongst their sickly-orange ringed Kraft Dinner dishes and gaming headsets. Their snouts struggling to jam into glasses of water on bedside tables, of how they'd lap it from the floor as it spilled, tonguing their shit-tinged toilets. It reminds us of the days of mocking incels. Those mouth-breathing bastards who thought that women were their God-given right. Who saw gorgeous plus-sized women on TV and cringed as they said, "I don't want to have sex with her," disregarding their own ample stomachs and fleshy arms, completely confident in their belief that women—all of us, cis and trans alike—existed to please them and that if we didn't tickle their fancy, we weren't deserving of even pseudo-respect. We hope it's men like this who are being affected.

Elijah has me take his temperature daily; we chart it in a little black book beside my bed. It's never been higher than ninety-eight.

"If it ever reaches 101.5, kill me," he says, his voice unwavering, eyes serious.

"Do you have any reason to suspect that you'll change?" I ask, thinking of his ringing notifications, all of his open search engine tabs.

"No, but what if I'm wrong?"

I already can't picture my life without him. I want to curl

around him, a snake around a sword. If Lil weren't here, I'd tell him that I'd let him kill me, and I suppose then we'd fuck while I muttered, "Kill me, kill me, kill me." But I can't bring myself to say it out loud, to risk looking that weak. Besides, we haven't even fucked yet.

TWENTY-EIGHT

The tender hints of morning look like hope opposed to danger, so we decide to leave at dawn. We've packed anything useful from my apartment in an oversized hockey bag; I never played sports, but it was three dollars at Mission Thrift, and I used to have high hopes of travelling the world: the ultimate opportunity at recreating myself, becoming whoever I needed to be. Shedding who I was feels better than accepting who I have become. There's something about going home in a crisis. A dumbfounded belief that your mother will always be able to save you, shield you. That she'll let you revert to being a child, even if she's never ever really treated you like a child. I wish I could leave Cedar here. I try to push the thought from my brain as soon as it enters, in case she feels it, but it keeps popping back up. *Just stay. Just stay.* Maybe she wants to go home. Maybe she's already there. Maybe she never left.

I've noticed how Lil stares into the hall when Cedar lingers by the doorway, wanting desperately to come in. She turns on every light in the apartment when she walks to the other end to use the washroom, starting up a conversation in hopes that I'll follow, that we can keep talking through the door while she pees. I've longed to ask, "Can you see her? Are you afraid of her?"

Lil hasn't been sleeping properly. "It's just the hormones," she says when I've noticed her jump.

But I know it's Cedar, who's never gotten to spend this much time with her, who feels fascinated by the curve of her cheek and her long jet-black hair. Who dreams that she could be her. It makes me jealous, almost, Cedar's obsession. How she wishes she could be Lilith. How she sees herself in her in ways she has never seen herself in me.

Cedar always daydreamed of being a mother. While I coloured pictures of cats, she pushed around baby strollers and pretended to breast-feed beneath a soft, crocheted blanket that Nan had made for her when she was born. She wanted four kids, and she never wanted them out of her sight. It could be the life growing inside of Lil that fascinates her the most. Cedar never understood how it was so easy for her mother to leave her with Nan. That her father hung up the phone when he heard of her growing existence. I used to think that was horrible, about Cedar's father, but as I've gotten older, I've almost viewed it as a blessing that he was never in her life at all to ramp up her expectations. That she could always see him for who he was, an empty seat at the table. I know Cedar wishes she always would have stayed with Nan. That Aunt Cindy's guilt-induced few weeks a year to play mommy fell off while she was still a child—that she could have avoided her After for a little longer.

This is no world for a child. I try to muster excitement for Lil, that at least she has this little life while everything else crumbles, but I just can't. Won't she see Derek when she looks into her child's eyes? It's said that babies especially look like their fathers when they're first born, a biological trick to try and convince fathers to stay.

"What do you want to name the baby?" Elijah asks as we fill plastic bags with the final remnants of my cupboards, canned pea soup, bags of rice. We plan on bringing it all to my mother's. We don't say that there's a chance we won't make it there at all. The end of the world is lived in snippets, moment to moment. There's no time to dwell. It feels as if the baby is the only thing giving us time to think of the future.

"I'm not sure yet," Lil says with a twist of her lips. "Derek and I"—she clears her throat and I avert my eyes—"we always liked the name Eden."

Elijah nods, and I love how he tries to relate even though, like me, children must be the furthest thing from his mind. Trauma shapes us differently. Some of us never want to risk re-traumatizing the next generation, while others dream of giving a child a better life than they had. Last night when I asked Elijah if his daddy issues came from a father he knew or if his dad was always absent, he said his family seemed perfect for quite a while, but his dad turned out to be a piece of shit. I didn't pry out of risk that if I did, I'd have to share how I knew that feeling all too well.

I haven't been home since Christmas, a near silent turkey dinner other than Theo getting too heated about the relationship of two podcasters he watches daily.

"Whatta fucking whore," he kept saying, despite my mother's winces, his mouth full of mashed potatoes.

Later, over a beer, I asked him if he got so mad about these celebrities because it was easier to hate strangers than our own father, and he looked me dead in the eye and said, "I love Dad." I opened my mouth to explain, to say that of course I love him too, but it's not absurd to think he created a crater of trust issues in us. Theo brushed off the conversation, saying it was silly of him that he got overly invested in the relationships of strangers. I hadn't meant to make him feel silly. Instead, I guess I wanted him to validate the ache in me.

"They were happily married for a long time, Delilah," he said with a sigh. I heard my mother's voice within his.

Mom tried to invite me down a few times this year. The idea of it is always better than the reality. As much as she wants me there, I think it's also easier for her if I stay away. I think I remind her of too much. I think she wants to want to have me around. I don't think it always translates once I'm there, when she can no longer visualize her favourite parts of me. Instead, I'm present, asking her if she's okay. Being the eldest and only daughter feels like a lifetime spent wanting your mother to be okay. A lifetime spent asking her if she is and knowing that she's lying to you when she says yes.

I don't know if anyone else asks her that.

Maybe she doesn't want to be asked it at all.

I try to push down my anxiety, to prevent myself from asking Elijah and Lil if they have any other suggestions of where to go. We do need to get out of the city. Anywhere with high populations will provide the biggest bloodbath, and out of the three of us—four I suppose—I'm the only one from elsewhere.

"My family's really nice," I say.

It isn't a lie; they are lovely to other people. They are only cruel to me in small and sinister ways. Ways you can't quite put your finger on. Ways that feel dramatic if you bring them up at all. Like insisting you come over for dinner and then complaining that you ate too much. Sometimes, after I've seen them, I'll find myself lingering with a knife in my hand as I do the dishes or idling on the side of a busy street. I want to feel real pain. I tell myself never, never, never will I beg for their love again. Then I won't eat for three days, not wanting to admit to myself that deep down I'm hoping they'll notice the jutting knobs of my spine, hoping that the thought of losing me scares them. It doesn't work. Sometimes I think I keep a steady pulse of men around me because men prevent me from looking inside of myself too deeply—they are nothing if not a cheap distraction. Their semen a mind-numbing substance. When I'm with them I can avoid myself. They never let me truly be myself anyway, so it's simple. I envy them. How nothing seems to touch them too deeply. I envy the freedom of that.

Life would be so much easier if I were born a boy. I linger on the edges, performing femininity rather than being. I tell myself femininity was built to be a performance, entertainment for men. I've always felt like an imposter: not Native enough or straight enough or feminine enough. Not enough of anything to firmly stand on my own two feet and insist this is who I am. I'm not anything fully enough for it to stick. I'm a faint shadow on the tree line.

When I look at the Polaroids, all of this raw masculinity, I'm reminded of how much I love the subtle, soft slope of my hips. The gentle rounding of my chest. I am reminded of how much I love to be a woman, even if I've never been a woman that's completely accepted as so.

Men must not feel this guilt, this shame. They have so many more options of what to be they don't need to be attractive to take up space. They are free. Free to be depraved.

Yet I will always be able to hide in plain sight. There is so much power in this femininity, even if I'm only on the edges of it.

TWENTY-NINE

The night before we leave is sleepless. I listen for breath, none of it steady. Too many deep sighs. Too much rolling from side to side. I reach for Elijah's hand, where he lies beside me on the carpet. We gave Lil the bed. We could have slept on the couch, but as we were leaving, she whispered that she didn't want to be alone and we couldn't leave her, not then.

I wish Elijah was asleep so I could pour my Polaroids along the bottom of the bag. I can't leave them. His cold fingers twist around mine, and I press myself against him, craving the distraction of him, craving him because he doesn't seem to completely crave me. I pull him to his feet while Lil remains still beneath my plush duvet and lead him through the living room, the kitchen, until we get to the bathroom. Indifference is a vicious aphrodisiac. I click on the light and don't look at my reflection but at his, instead. His skin is paler, something I didn't think possible. The shadows beneath his eyes are delicate thumbprints of exhaustion. He looks haunted too. Placing both of my hands against his cheeks, I feel the bones jut, trailing them down to the fullness of his lips.

"Is this okay?" I search his eyes for the want I desperately seek. He nods as if in a trance, and I wonder if that's all we are—a dream, a spell.

He kisses me gently from a hesitant mouth. I can feel his fear, how his shaking hands hold my wrists.

"I've been reading," he says, his words reverberating off of my teeth, "there's some correlation with sex."

I look up at him with pleading, watery eyes. I want to tell him it will all be okay, but I don't know that. I don't know anything.

From across the apartment, we hear Lil's scream.

He kisses me once more, as tender as someone who could love you, before we run towards the sound.

I can hear Cedar, her steady repetition of, *No, no, no, no.*

Lil's legs twist amongst the duvet, twisting, twisting, twisting, her nails digging into the sheets. She sobs and clenches her teeth. Her cries match Cedar's. Can she hear her? Feel her? Are they somewhere together?

"Lil?" I hurry to the bed even though my legs feel like cement, even though I want to turn around, slam the door. She moves and I see it, the crimson on the covers. She parts her legs, a red sea expelling her clotted dreams.

I'll never understand how an early miscarriage contains so much blood, as if the body of an adult has been sloshing around inside of her, twisting and forming and changing its mind.

Her eyes stay tightly shut. I search the sheets for a small creature, its snout upturned, sharp teeth hungry for her breast, but there is nothing. She is left with nothing.

I wonder if we should have left sooner. If the waiting, these four walls, Derek decomposing on the other side of the door have made things worse.

"I'll run you a bath," I whisper, hand to her forehead, hoping she'll open her eyes. She doesn't. She just grits her teeth.

I bring her water and the rest of our crackers. I link a hand through her elbow and pull her up, up, up, leading her from the stain on the mattress. Elijah grabs the blankets and sheets, balling and tucking them away out of sight.

Steam floats atop the water and the mirror is fogged. I help her take off her T-shirt, toss the boxers in the trash as she submerges. I made the water too hot. The kind of temperature that convinces you that you can be stripped of experiences. The kind of bathwater that feels like rebirth.

I get the last of my wine and pour us two heaping glasses. She refused to take a sip before, but now she tips the glass back fully until droplets pour out the corners of her mouth and into the pinkish water that surrounds her.

"Derek only ever wanted to fuck me in the same position," she says, eyes glued straight ahead to the soap scum-tinged wall. "Only missionary." She laughs, a barking, biting laugh, and takes another gulp. "He wanted me beneath him. Always."

"Even in the beginning?"

She laughs again, shakes her head. "You're right. No, in the beginning he wanted whatever I'd give him. Lapped me up like a man dying of thirst. Beamed with gratitude with whatever scraps I'd throw. In the beginning he begged me to ride him—he said he'd die for me, that he wanted to die beneath me."

My pussy flinches, moistens. I sit on the toilet seat, to stop it or give in to it I'm not sure.

She laughs again. "How long have we been here?"

"Three days."

"It feels like months, doesn't it?"

I think of her stroking her stomach, smiling upon it in peace, seemingly unbothered by the burden, the poor timing.

I nod.

"Ian changed," I whisper. "Ian changed too."

"I know," she whispers. "I saw him in the club as Derek and I ran to the car. I saw him slither around the building. He always moved like that, didn't he? Even before the sickness. He slithered." She takes a deep breath before continuing. "I thought I was going to lose you. Derek said there was nothing we could do."

I take another sip, wondering if he was right, if I'm a mere carcass on the floor of the bar, my flesh prodded and picked at, left to spoil; this is nothing but a dream, the DMT exploding in my brain as it dies.

"We got home that day and he was ready. He was prepared for the end. Jugs of water. Canned food. Weapons. He never ..." She laughs that biting laugh again. "He never for a fucking second suspected that he'd change."

Her breasts float in the water as her hand prances in the air from point to point as she talks. "And the stupid thing?"

I wait.

"I didn't either. I pictured us holed up as the world crumbled around us. And the things we fought about, me making money off of these"—she grabs a boob, flops it in her hand before letting it splash back into the water—"his issues would disappear because I couldn't work anymore and he hadn't gotten away with stopping me. The world had stopped me. So I couldn't be mad, I couldn't be resentful. I couldn't continue to ask him what he wanted from me when we first met, when he'd hung around the club every weekend begging to take me out. I couldn't hound him about whether or not he planned on treating me as if I was less than later." She polishes off the glass, and I pour half of mine into hers.

"I loved him." She dunks her head beneath the water letting it cover her entire face, comes up and slicks her hair back, pauses in contemplation. "I loved him the way you loved Ian."

I take another gulp as I remember Ian, in this room, my palms pressed firmly against the ceramic wall above Lil's head. His body jokingly nudging mine out of the way so he could fully stand in front of the mirror as we brushed our teeth. Our laughter leaving splatters of toothpaste on the glass.

"When you knew they had the potential to be someone good," I whisper. We used to talk about this, our horrible knack for extracting the goodness of men. We blamed ourselves. Our smart mouths and languid bodies. We blamed ourselves.

"We really fail that Bechdel test every time, don't we?"

I laugh, shaking my head. "I think, if there's ever a time for an exception, it's now. Besides, are they even men anymore? Are there rules pertaining to monsters? We are two women speaking of monsters, aren't we?"

She laughs again but I've lost her. She's picturing him. Derek. What he became.

"Do you think the baby would have been okay?"

I don't know what answer would comfort her more, so I settle on the truth.

"I have no idea."

She sinks deeper into the water.

When I lost a baby, a medium told me that spirits never truly leave; they wait around, watching, until the time is right.

"The spirit world," she said, frizzy blonde hair blowing in the wind, "is better than here. There's no pain. She'll come back." And it soothed me, how she felt the little girl too. This little girl who, for a couple weeks, made me want to believe in love even though I wasn't sure I wanted her. I hoped I'd see her, in the corner of my eye, cradled with Cedar, but I never did. The medium charged me one hundred dollars. She didn't bring up Cedar, who sat cross-legged in the grass in the corner of my psyche the entire session, and when I called to book another reading, her number was no longer in service. I could tell Lil what that woman told me, that her baby is still with her, waiting in the wings, but I don't know how to bring it up without bringing it all up so I don't mention it.

"I'll leave you be, if you want," I say, gently touching the top of her wet head.

"Please don't," she says, turning to look at me fully. "I think I'm losing my mind. I keep seeing this shadowy figure of a little girl. I keep thinking …" She stops, takes a deep breath. "I keep wondering if I'm seeing my daughter."

I plop back down onto the toilet, again afraid of fainting. Cedar has a vice grip around my psyche. Her small, raspy voice asks why I must always hide her away, when she's shaped me so much.

THIRTY

T HE KITCHEN IS EMPTY WHEN I LEAVE THE BATHROOM. I close the door softly and hear the calming sounds of Lil splashing and then the unmistakable sound of a sob. I don't go back in.

"Lij?"

Elijah doesn't answer. I grab a knife from the butcher block beside the stove, the blood rushing from my face as I think of his last temperature read, how there was nothing unusual. It feels foolish—I don't think I'd be able to kill him even if I had to. Am I putting us at risk? Cedar snickers, a quick little giggle from the other end of the apartment.

"Do you want to trust him?" she asks.

"Elijah, you're scaring me." I keep my voice steady, as quiet as possible, hoping that Lil cannot hear me, that she's underwater, her eyes shut tight.

There's a shuffling sound. I take a deep breath, searching the air for that sickly animal scent that sometimes wafts towards me as I'm sleeping. It's lodged in my memory or maybe Ian is stopping by, trapped somewhere between life and death. The air still smells of the sage I burned yesterday afternoon, thick and slightly stale, its sweetness dissipating yet still able to soothe.

I whisper to Cedar. *Show me. Show me what's happening.* She giggles again.

In my room, Elijah is sound asleep on the bed, his face as smooth and expressionless as a child.

I look in the mirror and don't recognize my reflection, but I suppose it's my own. I lie down beside him and try to sleep. I watch Elijah, hoping the curve of his cheek, the gentle coo of his breath will comfort me, but I can't slow the pounding of my heart.

SOMETIMES HATRED FEELS LIKE MY BIRTHRIGHT. THE points that have led me to this state are all true and tangible. Men kill us in all ways, big and small. Great, bloody deaths and gentle, nonviolent deaths that leave us breathing, over-thinking, timid, insecure yet full of rage. For some, that rage looks like self-hatred. This society makes it easier to blame ourselves. I blame the Bible. This man-made guide that taught men we are little more than subordinates. Don't tell me that their actions don't make us dim our lights or look at ourselves the way they do: as little more than objects, little more than vessels of pleasure and comfort, control and betrayal. Men will suck us dry.

Men leave a legacy of pain in their wake. I think that we inherit their selfishness. They make us crave the ability to inflict pain before we ourselves are indeed hurt. Each morning I wake begging the universe or something within my brain to make me only attracted to women, but then I get coffee and I catch an aloof, unassuming man at the side of the room waiting for his order and he looks like hope. And I won't realize that he's not until it's too late.

Maybe my mother stayed because compared to the other men she's known, her own father, my father looked like safety. Amongst the bad, he was better, even when he proved time and time again that he wasn't. Maybe she dug her heels in the way a child does when they so desperately want something to be true, the way I tricked myself into believing in Santa Claus long after I knew he was a fabrication. Santa was my favourite part of my childhood, the magic of half-eaten carrots and cookie crumbs, the presents sprawled across the living room floor. Presents that my mother meticulously wrapped and my father hefted on his back and carefully placed around the tree. I remember hearing about Santa and thinking of The Tooth Fairy and The Easter Bunny and knowing, pointedly: *everything is a lie.*

Maybe it's the lies we tell ourselves that make life bearable.

It's painful to think of my father when I was a little kid. When he was present, he was so present. Chasing Theo and I around the house while we squealed with laughter, enthralled by every single story that fell from our lips. I suppose it was always as if there were two of him. The good twin and the bad, like the true Gemini that he is. It was mostly the good. At least it always seemed like it. Maybe my memory casts a golden hue. Maybe I wear rose-coloured glasses in retrospection.

It was early spring, the air still chilly at night and in the morning but as warm as a promise in the afternoon. Theo ran ahead of me after we got off of the bus. I pictured him telling my parents about the girl who sat behind me and slammed my face into the window, her fist clenched around my hair for leverage. When I first got inside, I thought he had. Everyone sat stone-faced and Theo, only ten, looked like he could burst into tears. I hoped, for his own sake, that he wouldn't. My father said crying was for *fucking sissies*.

Everyone sat at the dining room table, reserved only for stuffy dinners with my dad's family or more often a workspace where I could spread out all my books with ample enough room to study for exams. Years later, when I'd become who this world made me become, I slid to the very edge of that cursed table and fucked my high-school boyfriend when no one was home. He was a sweet Pisces. I was already broken. I chewed him up and spit him back out.

My parents were on one side, my brother on the other. Theo barely looked up at me as I walked in. I plopped myself down into the empty seat beside him as if I was late to Sunday school. I wanted to nudge him with my elbow: *What the heck is up with these two, eh?* But his eyes remained downcast on his hands neatly folded in his lap. When I asked later if he already knew, he said, "I just read the room, Delilah." My father's anxiety-inducing rage and my mother's guilt-inducing passive aggression had taught us that coping mechanism from before we could talk.

It's crazy to think I was in the final moments of normalcy, of blissful ignorance, of trust.

"I'm having an affair." His voice felt oddly formal and removed, bad acting.

My mother's breath heaved from her lungs, clearing the way for a sob, all high-pitched and pathetic. I glanced at Theo, saw how his soft waves hung even lower as he refused to raise his head. I watched the tears silently splatter against his pale blue jeans. I wondered if, like me, he was hoping that instead of this they were sitting us down to tell us someone was dead. Later, I'd wish I didn't think that. My mom's guffaws were all-encompassing. She orchestrated the family meeting; she already knew, but looking back I think she was waiting for us to be there to fully cry. She knew, that unlike her husband, her children would be there for her. Or maybe she wanted to hear him tell the family they'd made together that it was he who set fire to it. My father looked as if it was taking everything in his power not to smirk, so pleased to be clutching the gas can and a match.

"Who is she?" My shoulders pressed back against the hardwood of the chair. I grew up in that moment. My hatred felt ancient. I visualized grabbing my father by the hair and slamming his face against the dining room table, covered in dull green remnants of my water colour painting accident of '97. I could hear the wet *thwop* sound of his face hitting the wood, again, again, again until there was barely a face left. I knew he wouldn't fight me back. He looked like a stranger sitting in front of me in a tight black T-shirt, eyes free from guilt as if he were merely bored. Bored with the entire life he'd created for himself.

"She's a dancer."

"How old is she?"

"Twenty-six."

I was only twelve and twenty-six seemed so far away, but I'm older now than she was then and it seems so, so young. My father was forty. They say it's a tough year for a man.

"Do you love her?" I didn't know why I had to ask it, but I did, unsure what answer would hurt more.

"Yes, I do." After he said it, I realized either answer would hurt equally, each in their own way. The no would seem selfish, careless. The yes would explain why his eyes were so empty. Why he seemed to be done with all of us already. This stranger was a gateway to a completely different life, a better life—the youth he missed out on because of all of us.

Theo must have felt it too, my father's absence even though he was sitting right there. His sobs rattled from his chest, but his head remained lowered. He hadn't cried in front of my father since he was six or seven years old, and his embarrassment mixed with his anguish was tangible. He aggressively wiped the tears from his blotchy cheeks as if he could forcibly stop them from falling. His breath kept catching in his throat in this horrible, painful little rush like that of a baby who's cried itself into a state of exhaustion. He was architecting a room within his mind, a room to rot in. It was then that my mother let out the deep groan of a dying animal.

"Get out!" The words came from far down in my chest and sounded much older, as if the last ten minutes had aged me ten years. The sobs of my mother and brother, the two people I loved most in this world, rattled around me as I steadily repeated myself. "Get the fuck out."

My mother's groans were replaced by a high, childish voice. "No, no, no, no." And I watched as she clutched onto my father's arm as if he was her ticket out of this sinking ship. As if he wasn't the one who crashed it.

Later, when all was forgiven and my mother dolled herself up like a prized poodle and pranced towards him whenever he entered the room, he referred to his transgressions as "being bad."

She stayed, or rather, she didn't kick him out. She tried, when there were more women and no hint of falling in love with any of them, but he didn't stay away longer than a week, blowing up her phone with texts and calls and sneaking around the house so she could silently let him into their bedroom as if they were teenagers. He only wanted her when she was done with him. He wouldn't leave her the fuck alone. Wouldn't let her heal. He wore her down. His pawing attention made her feel giddy, wanted—as long as she didn't look into it too deeply: he was yet again creating a situation where he'd have his cake and eat it too.

They stayed together and when I look at her now, I see a different brand of dying. She kills parts of herself every day. Before the first affair she was fiery, alive with laughter and wit. Now, when he's around, I can tell she tries not to listen to him bragging about women whose eyes lingered on him at the grocery store. Her smile no longer reaches her eyes. Does he pat himself on the back for taking a thumb tack to her balloons? For conditioning her to accept a joyless existence where she smiles at him with only her lips as he calls her mine?

I've always wondered if getting away with some horrible betrayal is what joy looks like to my father, like a child sneaking a cookie before dinner and not getting caught. Like a lingering glance with a twenty-something-year-old woman in the checkout line while he buys the groceries for a dinner he can suck the air out of by bragging about how he was sure he made the young woman flustered. Letting us all know that it is her he thinks of when he takes a bite of the food my mother so tenderly prepared for him. He can't seem to help but allude to his "transgressions" with a twinkle in his eye as if they are his life's greatest work, what *really* shaped him as a man.

Yet all the while I know. I know that there was a man or a series of men who ruined him for the rest of us. Thoughts of his own father still able to instill tight-lipped beady-eyed rage. Thoughts of his own father still able to make him weep like a *fucking sissy.*

He let his pain manifest in us instead of looking it directly in the eye. I hope he hates himself when he's alone. I hope he knows what I know: that he's a coward.

Years ago, when I couldn't fight the venom in my voice, when I couldn't hide that his mere presence filled me with disgust, he'd say, "Cut me a fucking break! I do so much for this family!" For a moment I dissected his words, thought of the food on the table, the bills paid, the car rides to school functions. I would have traded it all for someone I could trust. For someone that didn't lose himself to his moods, who didn't ruin everything without a second thought or a moment of remorse. He says we should be thankful he didn't abandon us. But for some reason that's always been worse—that he is delusional enough to believe his presence has ever been beneficial. I see him as a grovelling little man biding time to build the courage to destroy us all. The long con.

What hurts most is he doesn't even seem to realize the relationship Theo and I could have had with him had he not done what he did. Now, our relationships are constantly marred by the doubt of not really knowing who he is. Of wondering if he's happy now, if he was ever happy. My mom calls him a master chess player, and whenever she does, I think, *But you don't know how to play chess. You're always going to lose.*

Sometimes it terrifies me that my mother might never feel truly loved ever again, that all of her wonderful moments will be diluted with doubt. When I think of how my father hurt her and then later how he wouldn't let her go, part of me wants him dead. Part of me hopes he's somewhere shaking with fever, a horrible ache in his shoulders and neck. I hope he'll be on the receiving end of his final betrayal, that he'll feel powerless. That he'll finally feel remorse.

I used to feel a little twinge of jealousy when I thought of my parents' love story and how I'd never find someone to love me the way my dad loved my mom. Now all of his actions appear performative: his arms around her waist in public, the kiss on the cheek before he heads out the door, the way he speaks of her and says that she is the most beautiful woman in the world, that all other men must be jealous of him. It all sounds like someone grovelling, covering their ass. None of it captures her essence. He doesn't talk about how when she laughs her eyes sparkle like a child's. How she can look at you when you're upset and you will suddenly feel safe to be yourself. He doesn't see her.

He calls her a fox. He talks grossly about her "huge, white ass" and once asked me if I was upset that I didn't inherit her big boobs. Instead of stating the obvious: that I stunted my puberty with a horrifying eating disorder, I said, "The men I sleep with love my little tits." The memory will forever make me cringe, how I needed to prove my worth in the eyes of other hungry men hoping that he'd see it in me too.

I stormed away from that horrible family meeting and said, "I'm calling Cedar." Initially my mother told me no, but my father stopped her, waving a hand towards me in dismissal.

"Don't tell her what happened," my mother said quickly as I was on the outskirts of the room.

When I turned and met her eyes, my own filled with a snarky preteen rage, hers were welled with tears. A small tether of control she gained by making her pain a secret, by tucking it deep inside of herself with all of the other heartbreaking moments that have defined her.

"I won't," I said before I began to dial, yet still she watched me with her shoulders pulled back and lips set as if it were my actions that had the power to ruin her life.

The dreams of what she thought her life was.

My foot repeatedly tapped the linoleum while Nan's phone rang and rang and rang. I could see my mother peering at me from where she still sat at the dining room table beside my father.

Nan answered the phone with her classic, homey, "Yeah?"

I asked for Cedar and looked away from my mom. Even over the phone I could tell that Nan knew that something was wrong.

"You all good, honey?"

For some reason, being talked to like a child for the first time since my reality had been turned upside down nearly pushed me over the edge. I swallowed hard, biting back the impending crack in my voice that would give it all away.

"Oh yeah, I was just wondering if Ceeds wanted to go for a bike ride." I looked back at my mom, felt the wave of pride as her shoulders relaxed by way of my nonchalant tone. Theo remained at the table, as still as a statue, eyes glued to his chubby hands curled in his lap. My mother's eyes remained on me, but my father stared straight ahead, already elsewhere, maybe a beach with his girlfriend, a fancy hotel suite, a parking lot. I couldn't understand how it was possible for me to hate someone so much, how it was possible for him to hate us. It had always been us four against the world, hadn't it?

"Wait!" I could hear Nan hefting herself up from her chair, the tile floor creak beneath her slippered feet. "Cedar isn't with you?"

"Ummm …" I gave myself away in a second, twirling the cord around my fingers and staring at the chipping yellow paint on the kitchen walls.

"That little shit," Nan muttered under her breath.

I thought of hanging up. I didn't.

"We musta just got our wires crossed, Nan." I thought of how Cedar was slipping away from me, our two-year age difference suddenly an ocean filled with bottom feeders and tentacles that threatened to curl around my legs. It was April 7 and Cedar had just come back from spending spring break with her mother. She was different, in her After, and would never be the same.

"I thought we were meeting there, but she probably thought we were meeting here."

Nan tutted twice, and I could picture her staring out her front door at the softening ground outside, thinking of what she'd say when Cedar got home.

For a moment, I was distracted from the smog clouding the dining room, the hazy aftermath of an explosion. I didn't risk looking at my father again, of tearing into the wound that I had haphazardly bandaged. I avoided my mother's eyes too, betrayed by her lack of self-respect, by the *stand by your man* clench of her jaw. Her defiance, I thought, only benefited this traitor, my father.

I can see now that she didn't want the humiliation of being spit out into the world, abandoned for a younger woman, her life left to rumour and speculation, biting opinions that said that she deserved this. Because when we are betrayed, there are always those that say it's our fault. I didn't realize that then. I was just a kid.

"Let's go for a bike ride," I muttered to Theo.

My hand on his shoulder made him jump, and I was met with bewildered eyes as if I had woken him from a dream. He looked back down at his hands, wet tear marks on his jeans, and solemnly nodded. He cleared his throat the way our father did when he was embarrassed by his own portrayal of emotion. It made him sound so much older than ten. We'd both aged in the last hour. Fairy tales take years to build but can be destroyed in an afternoon. The look on my father's face was one of impatience, as if getting through this conversation was just a mundane task before he could walk out of the door and into his bright and shining future. As if we were little more than a sacrifice made for a better life. I wondered if walking into the strip club made him feel powerful in ways that caring for us never could. I know now, from all of those other men, that it does. No part of his expression said that he felt pathetic. No part of my mother's showcased the anger I felt she was owed.

I kept my hand on Theo's shoulder as he got up from the chair. He didn't raise his eyes. I swallowed the urge to scream about what a great fucking example my dad had just set for his son, what a great fucking example my mom was setting for me. They grounded me when I swore, but I didn't think today would count. Instead, I kept my eyes glued straight ahead, my palm pressed firmly into Theo's shoulder as I led him out of the room and into the yard. The only sound was the slamming of our own front door.

Through the picture window I could see my parents still sitting at the table, each staring at the wall in front of them, the shelves with family photos, an antique teapot my mom got from a thrift shop, wine glasses from their wedding, baby books with blurbs on their first date, positive pregnancy tests and blurry black and grey ultrasound printouts. They were surrounded by the silent debris of their lives. All these mementos, in the end, were powerless.

You can spend a lifetime building a home. You can set fire to it in a matter of minutes.

Nan used to always say that bad news came in threes. The knowledge of my father's affair was only part one. I didn't realize that then either.

By that night I would regret asking Theo to go for a bike ride. I'd regret calling Nan's looking for Cedar. I'd regret, I'd regret, I'd regret.

THIRTY-ONE

He's over me when I stir. Richard. Sneering. I can smell his cologne. I can shut my eyes, but I cannot move.

He leans in closer, his breath against my cheek.

"Delilah. Delilah!" I pull away, suddenly shocked by my ability to move.

I clutch both hands above my head, holding my neck forward as I curl against the wall, still hearing his laughter. I wait, picturing Richard climbing onto the bed behind me, crawling over to me slowly, slowly, slowly as if he's trying not to wake me. I can't bring myself to turn my head, to face him. He's never gotten this close to me before. *I'm sorry. I'm sorry. I'm sorry.* Am I saying it out loud or merely thinking it? His hand rests lightly on my shoulder.

"Is she okay?"

It's Lil's voice that brings me back. I turn over, meeting Elijah's frightened eyes. His hand hangs in the air in front of me.

"Sleep paralysis." I force a laugh.

Elijah sits beside me on the bed, rests his hand just beside my thigh as if he is nervous to touch me. Lil sits on the floor, her eyes concerned, biting her bottom lip as if she wants to say something but stops herself.

The room is silent except for my slowing breaths. I look to the window. The sky is still dark yet without the pitch fearfulness of midnight.

"It's four o'clock," Elijah whispers, following my gaze to the window. "We haven't heard anything for the last couple of hours."

"You didn't get any more sleep?"

"Shifts, you know?"

I rub my eyes and look at the room around me, the duffel bag is half full of only the necessities—somehow, I have to find a way to pour in the Polaroids. I debate doing it nonchalantly, as if they are little more than keepsakes, what you'd grab in a house fire.

"How are you feeling?" I ask Lil, hating the question as it leaves my lips. She nods and shrugs. I wish I would have said anything else.

"Did you sleep?"

"A little." She shrugs again, averts her eyes. Like me, she prefers to keep her pain to herself.

The first hours of morning always feel like hope.

"Let's pretend we're going on a road trip," I say, sitting up, trying to interject some semblance of positivity into this shit bag of a situation, trying to shake the feeling that Richard ... Richard is here. I glance around the room again, expecting to see him looming in the corner.

Elijah squeezes my hand, looks up at me until my eyes focus on him. I smile, pulled from the hauntings of my own mind.

Hi, he mouths, running his thumb over the top of mine.

Hey, I mouth back.

I've lived in this apartment for five years and now that I'm leaving, I have this sick feeling I'll never return. That the dust will gather and these walls will weaken, that rats—or something worse—will take it over as their own. That in the future, if there's a future, someone will walk in and wonder about the girl with the old Hollywood mirror, the pretty bottles of perfume, the grimy sink. I think of a girl standing in the centre of the orange shag rug, taking a deep breath, trying to feel how I felt. I figure she'll assume that I'm dead, one of the many lost to society's After. I don't know whether or not she will be right. I want to leave Cedar, but I can't. She's kept safe, sealed tight, haunting a compartment of my mind.

I pass Elijah a two-litre water bottle and tell him to fill it up.

"Go for safety pees too," I say to both of them, feeling like my mother before road trips long ago. Lil rolls her eyes, but regardless, they leave the room. I hustle to the closet, dropping to my knees and extending my arms, always afraid that something will grip my wrists from the darkness. My fingers caress the hard edges of the shoebox. The shoebox will have to stay. Instead, I pour the photos, cocks and shoulders, arched backs and strong jaws, into a plastic dollar store bag as if they are little more than dirty laundry. *Dirty laundry.* The thought makes me chuckle. I bury the bag beneath a sweatshirt, tuck three pairs of socks, underwear, another pair of jeans on top.

"Got everything?"

Elijah's voice makes me jump. My head snaps up as I look at him over my shoulder, trying to rid my expression from hints of guilt.

"I think so." I try my best to keep my voice light, hoping whatever fear detected is considered only because of the state of the world. "You startled me," I add with a soft giggle.

He walks over to me, his body arching over where I sit on the floor, looks down into my open duffel bag that I begin to zip. His body slinks like a cat, sinewy shoulders and long legs. I shudder. I want to take off his pants. I want to witness how he moves.

"You ready?" My voice comes out huskier than intended. Is it the potential danger of him that makes me want him? The sudden chance that he could wake up monstrous?

He nods.

THIRTY-TWO

The early morning air is cool, but the scent of acrid piss and human shit overpowers the fresh morning dew. I dodge a pile, mucky and fresh, and fight the urge to laugh. If I laugh, I fear I'll scream. I keep my car key clenched between my index and middle fingers, reminiscent of the days of walking through parking lots late at night, when the men you feared still resembled men.

It's easier now, isn't it? Cedar whispers. *They reveal themselves now.*

I shudder again and unlock the car, the interior light casting a glow into the back seat that I peer into, picturing a creature hunched on the floor waiting to pop up like a depraved jack-in-the-box as soon as we enter. There is nothing but a discarded cardigan, empty coffee cups, the plastic wrap and aluminum paper from packages of cigarettes.

"Lock the doors," I whisper as we all get in, pushing mine down with a satisfying click. The panic still lingers in my chest as I look to Lil beside me, as I look back at Elijah in the back seat, immediately wishing I would have told him to take the front.

The car starts with a rumble and a nearly full tank of gas. The headlights come to life and I stifle a scream as the warm yellow lights catch a creature in their glow. He's hunched forward, waiting to pounce, eyes dedicated, froth dripping off of fangs. Lil lets out a small whimper that she stops with her knuckles. The eyes. I think of his eyes reflected in my bathroom mirror, dedicated and hungry. The eyes catching the early morning sunlight on my front porch, confident and satiated. The creature has Justin/Jamie/Josh's eyes. I think of the photos, behind us all, buried deep within the duffel bag. I think of the photo that Deb waved at me in the convenience store parking lot. I didn't think he would change. I didn't think he was any worse than most: entitled, horny, a little dumb. I glance at Elijah in the rear-view mirror, hoping that I can trust my gut. His dark eyes are wide, focused on the creature before us.

"It's okay," I say to no one in particular.

I rest my palm on Lil's thigh, steadying her, and I place my foot firmly on the gas. A quick acceleration knocks Justin/Jamie/Josh off of his feet. I wish more than ever that I knew for sure what his name was. I press my foot down more firmly, biting my tongue for comfort as he *thumps* beneath my tires. I turn on the radio and drive. The car is silent except for Lil's soft cries. I can't look at her. I can't look.

WE'VE LISTENED TO THE RADIO FOR HALF AN HOUR. NO broadcasting. Only classic rock. Music has the power to transport you somewhere better. I can feel it putting us all at ease, giving us a moment's peace. We are in the last scene of a horror movie.

"I've wanted to see where you grew up for forever," Lil says, face turned towards the passing trees.

She grew up in the city. A series of foster homes and then a series of homes belonging to older boyfriends. Men like Tony. Men, I suppose, like Derek.

"It's … quaint," I say, thinking of summers spent splitting milkweed and searching for crayfish, scrapes from falling off of bikes onto gravel roads. A blissful element of untouchability, of freedom.

"I can see that. I haven't seen a house in like twenty fucking minutes."

We laugh, but it's half-hearted. Reality always has a knack for slamming against the door.

"I didn't realize you lived out this way," Elijah's voice is somewhat solemn, and I wonder what memories play in his mind, what the countryside inspires in him.

"Have you been here before?" I ask, glancing in the rear-view mirror before letting my eyes fall back to the road. I wonder if he's wishing he were with his mother and sister. I wait for him to answer. He doesn't, just keeps his eyes set on the passing trees. I roll down the window, breathing in the scent of wet earth and pine. It dulls the panicked sweat and stale smoke scent of the car.

The smell of half-decomposing bodies and filth has yet to permeate. The sky is a cloudless baby blue. The boons still look untouched, wild, beautiful. I feel the ever-constant sensation of being pulled in two directions. On one hand, the open space of the country finally makes me feel as if I can breathe, but on the other, the knowledge that I am nearing a place where I'm known makes me feel suffocated. There's this fear of never truly being able to hide from my mother, residing in her silent judgment. She'll disprove of Elijah, a stranger, think me foolish after her lifetime of warnings. And bringing Lil will inspire a sense of jealousy.

My mother has never been the type to seek comfort amongst other women. Instead, she feels scrutiny in their presence. When Theo and I were little, she was very insistent that I not have friends over very often, whereas our house was always awash with the laughter of Theo's little friends. "Girls are judgy. They notice when things aren't clean, when I'm not wearing makeup," she'd say when I brought up the double standard. "Boys are just happy to be here."

We're less than twenty minutes away, and I feel as if coming here was a huge mistake. We have a car; we could go anywhere else. If I were by myself, I would turn around. I would never mention the trip at all. I open my mouth to tell them that I can't do it, I can't go home, but I lose the nerve. I don't want to frighten them. I want them to believe that I'm confident, in control. Still, I slow down, pretending to be in awe of the swaying fields, the bright flowering sumac. I can feel Cedar pent up and buzzing. Coming home makes her feel the same way, equally free and trapped. There's a raw, unkept beauty to this place that reminds me of being young, careless, alive. It juxtaposes against an ugliness of reality, of death looming from every shadow. My stomach quivers.

In the rear-view mirror I notice Elijah, his face cast out the window, tears streaming down his porcelain skin.

We're less than ten minutes away.

It's easier to talk when you're driving, when you don't have to make eye contact, when you can pretend that you're alone. I debate asking if he's okay, but I don't, remembering the days I'd silently cry in the back seat of my parents' car with my eyes glued to the window. If someone would have noticed, would have asked what was wrong, the spell would have been broken. There is something about being in the back seat of a car, the world blurring past, the radio a soundtrack.

"It's strange to go back to a place that killed you." I permit myself one line. No one answers and it's fitting. We're all locked somewhere within our own psyches, dreaming of futures or coughing up pasts. I watch birds flutter from trees, unbothered, in love.

We're less than five minutes away.

I light up a cigarette and try not to look down the road where all of this pain was born, but I do. And I swear I can hear Theo, his voice still high and sparkling, his laugh slightly chaotic.

I can feel it. I can feel how we felt on that day when our world changed. How it was shaping us for cynicism, yet how we had never felt closer. I can feel it. I can feel it.

A large wooden sign has been tacked to a telephone pole, its message spray-painted in bright red: STAY OUT OF THE WOODS. The message strips the scenery of its serenity, makes the shadows between the trees loom large and dangerous. I think of the children lured from their homes with the thrill of a dare. I think of Theo, hoping that wherever he is, he's warm, he's fed. Even if he's a monster. We can never fully see the monstrosity in those we love. And even when we can, how we beg for them not to suffer. If Theo were to be trapped somewhere, would it be here? Where it all began? Where it all ended? I inhale deeply, smoke dispersing in thin threads out the window, dancing away. I used to tell Ian we could park anywhere but here. Not this road. He'd laugh, squeeze my thigh with his large hand that always made me feel claimed, chosen, wanted—even when I knew I was nothing. Even though he told me to tell anyone who asked that he picked me up hitchhiking when we showed up at a party together, his cum crusted in my underwear. I swallow hard, a weak attempt to stifle the nausea oozing from my stomach making me feel feverish, exhausted. We are about to pass Theo's apartment, and I can't bear to stop.

Two deer burst from the tree line, a doe and a fawn, speckled and small. I hit the shoulder as they cross, running flat out, not looking back. The tires squeal slightly, the car jerking before it connects with the gravel and careens to a stop. I lean forward against the steering wheel as if I'm alone. I chuck the butt of my cigarette out the window, roll it back up. I sob.

Lil's gasp pulls me back, back, back to the tip of her delicate finger as she points to the trees. A man, or what once was, emerges and follows the deer to where they have disappeared amongst the thick brush. I long to pray, to search for a faith I can believe in.

Static cuts through the radio.

Cedar says, *Can't you see what I've done?* Lil presses her fingers to her temples.

THIRTY-THREE

THIS ROAD. THIS FUCKING ROAD HOLDS ALL OF THE memories of that day. The worst day. April 7.

The gravel spit up at mine and Theo's legs. It was a warm day for the beginning of April and it felt like a small gift. That we could escape, he and I, into the sunshine and pretend that nothing had changed since yesterday. That we weren't suddenly altered forever.

For the first fifteen minutes, we pedalled in silence, our minds separately racing, coming up with scenarios of what this unexpected future might hold. I pictured my father introducing us to this woman and only then noticing that her stomach was swollen with life; I pictured spitting in her face even though it wasn't her fault, and she owed us nothing. Later, my mother would say that my father behaved for thirteen years—didn't he deserve some credit for how long he stayed faithful? Unwaveringly, I always tell her no. The longer you wait to cheat the more time you've spent building the fantasy, the larger the wreckage. A single home lot becoming sprawling grounds of ash and rot and the never-ending question: *was any of it real?* It always makes me think of fireworks over The Magic Kingdom, when I looked up at a shimmering Tinker Bell shooting across the sky and asked my father if it was magic. He said it was an optical illusion of lights. Maybe he was always preparing me for the death of a dream. Maybe I should show him some respect. *Thank you, Daddy, you made me a realist.*

"Do you want to scream?" I asked Theo as I pedalled up beside him.

He released a loud "ahhhhhh!" bellowing over the cornfields that surrounded us.

His voice was still high and childlike, dirty blonde curls blowing in the wind.

"Fuuuuuuuuuuck youuuuuuuuuuu!" I screamed, my words accented with a whooping laugh as the tears cascaded down my cheeks. "Fuck ... YOU!" I repeated.

"Whatta bastard!" Theo yelled next. "Whatta fucking douche!"

Theo and I so rarely swore at home, hearing him yell curses at the bright blue sky filled me with glee. It was only my father who really swore, constantly muttering *fuck* or *cocksucker* beneath his breath.

"Let's go to the creek," I shouted over the wind.

We'd been coming to the creek for as long as I could remember, leaving our socks and shoes on the shore and wading in to catch slippery minnows and crayfish. In my mind's eye, it was always noon at the creek, the sun at its highest point glimmering through the trees while we unpacked bologna sandwiches with processed cheese slices and lots of mustard and drank juice boxes or chilled bottles of water.

I knew I'd made the wrong call as we dropped our bikes by the chipping stone of the bridge and walked to the shore. The creek felt like our father. I could see him helping Theo jump from rock to rock to get to the other side. I could see the sun falling atop of his head, his squinting eyes as he smiled and hollered for us to come and see the turtle or snake he found along the shore. His hushed voice as he pointed and told us to be quiet, to step lightly as not to scare any of the critters away.

"I hate him," Theo said, picking up a too large rock and chucking it into the shallow water.

"Me too," I muttered, squatting to search for snakeskin, translucent and paper-thin. Dark grey clouds seemingly came from nowhere and covered the sun, and I wondered, fearfully, if this wouldn't be the way I'd forever picture the creek in my mind: forest ominous and shadowy, the breeze coming off the water bitingly cold instead of comforting. I vowed then to never return to my favourite places when I was upset—it would only tarnish them.

"Should we go find Cedar?" I asked, kicking at rocks, the shoreline free of gifts.

Theo was halfway across, jumping from stone to stone. I shouted to him again.

Finally, he turned to look at me. Across his face he wore a huge smile, the creek still holding its magic as he pointed to a fish. He jumped in, nearly slipping as he did but remaining steady as the water splashed up at his ankles.

"Get back in here. You'll get sick!" I yelled as he trudged back to shore. His cheeks were pink from the breeze.

"Was it super cold?" I looked down at his pale toes.

"It wasn't too bad," he said, stomping his feet in the grass a couple times before tucking his still damp feet back into his socks.

"Do I have to go with you to Cedar's?"

"You want to go home?" I asked in disbelief, picturing my parents still seated at the dining room table. Or worse, my father flipping through the channels too fast to even register as my mom scrubbed dishes too quickly in the next room, her eyes glazed.

"I don't want to talk to him," he said, looking off in the distance in the direction of our house, "but I want to check on Mom."

I wished right then that I was more like Theo—his ability to put others before himself while I angrily internalized everything, always thinking of how others would affect me, rarely how I would affect them. But when I thought of my mother sitting at the dining room table, eyes crazed and desperate and unable to stand up for herself, no part of me felt the urge to comfort her. I knew if I was there, I wouldn't even know how to approach her warmly. Even if I tried, it would come off forced, rendering it brutally obvious that the longer my father stayed in the house, the faster I told myself that I didn't need either of them.

Maybe it was different for Theo. A son. A boy who wouldn't see his future reflected in his mother's. Whose fears wouldn't be based on what she let herself endure. He could look at comforting our mother as something separate from himself. Maybe, he'd tell himself he would never ever be a man like my father and being there for her would prove it to himself in some way: *I will never be a man like him*. To my father's dismay, even at ten, Theo already wasn't shaping up to be a man like him. He wasn't afraid to be silly or cuddle or fart in the car. He was very much himself. Despite my father's booming rage or condescending talk, Theo remained soft. That scared me too, hearing my dad mutter beneath his breath about sweet, gentle men who he deemed useless. I worried how much longer Theo had of this childish blissful ignorance. This inability to internalize the horrible things spoken by the one man who was supposed to help build us. I couldn't remember exactly when the curtain had fallen for me, when all of the awful things my father said about women began to rest between my skin and bones.

I hoped Theo would never change.

"Are you sure you don't want to go and find Cedar with me?" I asked again, a little more hopeful as I dreaded the idea of going home and walking into that now haunted house.

"I really want to go see Mom and Sadie," he said, and I thought of how our dog would have her chin rested on the floor, head atop her paws, eyes nervously looking up at the thick tension around her. I thought of how my dad would yell at her to move if she decided to seek security beneath the footrest of his La-Z-Boy.

I looked at the sky. The clouds were moving fast, their edges dark grey.

"You don't have to go with me," Theo said.

"Come on, Thee, it looks like it's gonna rain. Why don't you come to Nan's with me?" I thought of piping hot orange pekoe tea and oatmeal chocolate chip cookies in their bright yellow bag. The smell of the wood stove that Nan would insist on running until mid-May.

Theo just wrinkled his nose and shook his head. "I'll be fine, really."

I tried to remember if I had been coming to the creek by myself at ten. It seemed I did nothing alone, always with Cedar or Theo. Being alone had frightened me since infancy; I could never seem to shake the feeling of being watched—or worse, monsters freeing themselves from the shadows and revealing themselves to me. Nan said I had a gift, but it felt like a curse, this imagination.

"Go straight home," I said as he grabbed his bike and began to walk it up the gravel slope leading back to the road.

"I will," he said nonchalantly as I watched him climb onto his bike and peer down at me.

"I love you, Delilah!" he yelled as he began to pedal away, and I felt it immediately, this fear of being alone.

THIRTY-FOUR

There's a sob still trapped in my throat. I swallow it down, feel its pressure within my chest as if it's going to tear it in two. I've been driving slower for the last five minutes, stretching out the time it takes to get to my parents' house.

I call from the driveway, not wanting to scare my mother. Wishing I would have called when I left. Wishing I wouldn't have left at all.

Her hello is rushed—expecting news, positioned for the worst.

"I'm outside, Ma."

"I'll unlock the door," she says, her voice sombre, yet within seconds I see the curtain move and her face peek out.

"Do you mind staying in the car for a second?" I say quickly. Lil nods but I feel her fear, the fear that I've taken her far away from home, that I've taken her somewhere she isn't welcome. Elijah grips my shoulder, squeezes ever so gently.

The air outside is humid, but inside the house is cold, as if I'm stepping into an unfinished basement. The chill soothes me. I still expect Sadie to run to me, but she's been dead for years. My mother looks as if she hasn't slept in months. Her always glowing skin is sallow, the circles beneath her eyes a dull grey brown. Her hair, usually shiny and styled, needs to be washed; it hangs in strings. All of the curtains are drawn, and I see the snowy sparkle of dust in the air as I shut the front door, shrouding the hallway again in darkness.

"I've been hoping it looks as if nobody's home or maybe as if we're all dead in here." Her words are hoarse like she hasn't spoken much lately. She musters a half-hearted laugh.

"Dad?" I ask, my eyes taking their time to adjust to the shadows after the bright daylight. She looks down at her feet, stays silent. "Theo?"

I go to the kitchen, fill the kettle, set it on the stove and make a mental note to take it off the burner before it begins to squeal. I look down at my body, the track pants, baggy sweater, my own dirty hair pushed back into a messy bun. For a moment, I experience a shard of happiness that my father isn't here. That I will be free from him weighing my worth with his eyes. I don't know if I could take a moment of his judgment. It might be the thing that pushes me completely over the edge. One look of his disapproval erases all of my praise—his unmoving mouth says, *You could have done better* while his eyes say, *I expected more from you.* It's tough knowing you'll never be enough for the one person who you just want to be enough for. It makes you desperate.

"Men are starting to pray," my mother says, her eyes glassy. She chooses not to focus on mine.

I step into the doorway of the living room, expecting to see my father in his chair, the steam from his coffee cup wafting up into the shadows. The room is empty. There is only the glow of the TV, the shot of a busy church parking lot, men crowding the front doors. Sombre-faced teenagers to young fathers carrying small sons. The camera pans to faces wet with fevered sweat, for some maybe only tears.

The screen splits: live footage from the church on one side, the newsroom on the other.

"Three weeks ago, the internet became littered with confession videos of men beginning to change. Today, the sick are taking to the streets, uniting together to demand forgiveness in groups."

"We want to warn our audience of severe subject matter, references to sexual and physical violence. What you're about to see is believed to be the first recorded confession. It was uploaded on April 7 of this year."

The screen goes black for a moment before the shaky clip begins to play.

"Ma? Come here." My voice is jittery, sounds alien to my ears. It sounds younger. I will watch it this time. I pinch my thigh. I will watch it.

I hear her chair screech across the linoleum.

On the screen, a sixty-something man crosses his chest before looking directly into the camera. His face is beginning to change, only slightly, a jutting of the jaw. The shock that I experienced seeing it for the first time has worn off. Now, I can home in on the new wrinkles around his eyes, how he tries to open them wider, how he tries to induce sympathy.

"What is this?" Mom asks, stepping closer to the screen as if he's looking back at her.

"Seventeen years ago," Glen's raspy voice cuts through the room. "I raped and murdered a young lady." A groan hums through my lips, these grandfatherly terms, this weak attempt at absolving. I can see him, years before, on my TV screen talking about his rough childhood. I can hear the newscaster—young, trim, blonde—asking him about his goals when he was just a boy, commending him for his talents as the best hockey player in his small town before the drugs and misdemeanours got in the way.

"I'm begging. I'm begging God for forgiveness. I'm sorry. I'm so, so sorry."

Glen's eyes are filled with tears, lips quivering in attempted remorse or perhaps a very real fear.

"I want to swallow my pride and beg God for forgiveness. Please, God, have mercy on me. I've suffered with this for so many years."

He lets out a wail, his voice changing to a squeal halfway through, his mouth unnaturally large, neck strained with taut muscle. He tries to speak again, but his voice can no longer formulate words. His eyes are terrified. The phone clatters to the ground.

"What—what the hell is this?" Mom continues, her voice slick with disbelief.

I hear crows, squawking outside my window. They caw, *LIAR LIAR LIAR*.

He was a truck driver. I think of the footage with Cedar and her bike. I think of her killing time, getting a bag of cheesy popcorn, a blue slushie, not quite ready to go home and confront the fact that I had accidentally spoiled her alibi with Nan. Or worse, that I had hurt her feelings with the last words I ever said to her.

Don't worry, he's long gone now, Cedar whispers.

The camera pans back to the church parking lot, a fresh sea of guilty men in early stages of changing. The newscaster, a pretty young woman who's free from makeup and clothed in grey from neck to ankle, holds the mic from a distance as if she'll be able to drop it and run whenever she needs to.

"Please, God!" a young man shouts, coarse hair beginning to bristle from his ears and along his jaw. He falls to his knees, startling the reporter who quickly steps back, the camera jostling slightly, the arm of whoever is behind it reaching out to steady her.

"A recent scientific study has correlated the virus with individuals who have perpetrated sexual assault. All of these men are seeking absolution for their sins."

Her voice is peppy, but it's forced, straining to be objective, her arm gently shakes.

"I want to say I'm sorry." The words are muffled by the wet, sopping mouth of a man in his mid-twenties. "Ashley? Ashley, I know that I told you if you ever came out about me raping you that I'd kill myself. I know that was wrong. All of it. All of it. I hurt you, I'm sorry."

"You've got to be kidding me," my mother whispers beneath her breath as we watch man after man step forward and state their acts of violence through tears and anguished sobs. She wraps me in her arms, and I could die. I begin to cry. I always felt as if there was a part of her that was slightly afraid of getting too close to me. I lean into her body, realizing how much I missed being held in her arms.

They're animals. They're animals, Cedar whispers. *They're all going to turn into animals.*

Nan used to call men animals too, but with more acceptance than loathing. She'd say it as if they couldn't help themselves. As if they were only about as smart as a puppy. Cedar and I would cringe, only girls, but still aware of this double standard that we were somehow in control whereas boys, grown men, somehow were not. We'd roll our eyes. It seemed "boys will be boys" never expired.

Boys will be boys. Men will be animals, Cedar whispers now.

SHE'S WHISPERED IT MANY TIMES DURING GROGGY mornings as the wine pounded in my temples and my stomach churned. When all I had to show were pictures: broken, fractured, fragmented.

"Have you heard of the Polaroids that have been popping up in the city?" my mother asks. I try not to straighten my spine, try to leave my body slack as I lean against her chest.

"I have," I say, scrambling for more words, wondering if my response was enough.

On the TV screen, all of the men begin to fall to their knees, hands raised in the air or clutched together in front of their faces, eyes tightly squeezed or cast upwards towards the sky. Their lips move rapidly as they murmur their sins.

"Please, God, please!" they begin to chant in unison.

And it seems real, or rather, I suppose it is. These men, who are only truly sorry once they're face-to-face with the consequences of their own actions.

The squealing starts and my mother and I gasp in unison and then laugh. I forgot about the kettle. I run to the kitchen, pull it from the stove as I hear a knock at the door. My mom looks at me with frightened eyes, her fingers gripping the back of the kitchen chair. I'm transported to when I was four years old as she tells me to stay quiet while we wait for the shadow at the front door to give up and go. But I'm not four, and it's not my grandfather at the door. It's not a stranger. It's Elijah. I can see the top of his head through the delicate stained glass.

"It's okay," I say. "I know him."

And the words sound strange, as if they are a lie or only a half-truth. Maybe they are.

"Honey, I don't think it's safe." Her voice is slightly whiney at the end, childlike. Fearful.

"Trust me, he's on the right side of things," I say as I unlock the door and let him in.

For a moment I think of Elijah up all night, scouring the internet for some semblance of a cause, some semblance of a cure, a fear lodged deep within his gut that he'll change too.

"Lil," he says, his eyes panicked as he points a long, thin finger back towards the car.

The bleeding that seemed to have stopped has started again.

"Delilah?" she asks, her voice small, frightened.

I hush her as Elijah carries Lil into the house.

My mother watches us all with a kind of removed caution.

And Cedar whispers, *Can I meet her?*

THIRTY-FIVE

Lil sits in the tub, the lavender scented bubbles up to her neck. The cramps come in waves. She sips chamomile tea. I bring her a cigarette. I watch as she takes long drags with her eyes closed.

"Are you sure it's okay that I'm here?"

I nod, lightly touching her shoulder.

"My body had a spontaneous abortion," she says with a biting laugh. "I'd feel lucky if I was one of the thousands of women who needed one."

I don't say anything, thinking of the women carrying babies that they are in no way prepared to care for. Burdens for the end of the world. Thinking of Wade, an ex—one I swore I loved with every cell of my body—who told me I was lucky when my body did the same as Lil's, rid itself.

He had knocked me up when I was on the pill. I know the exact night it happened because I had asked him to wear a condom, and he whined and scoffed and prodded at me until I gave up. It wasn't long before my breasts ached, water from the shower making me wince as it hit my swollen nipples. He had been shopping for engagement rings, and during late nights we'd lie together beneath the covers and talk about our children. We called them by their names and told stories about them as if they were already there, this girl, this boy. We loved the idea of making a family better than the ones we'd come from.

I was always a woman who said I would have an abortion if an oops happened without a plan, but this, this felt different. As my stomach twisted in nausea and my face became a map of acne, I had an initial shock of wanting to protect this life with my own. I felt animal. Aggressive. Feral. Dogs that had once lain before me on their backs lashed at my throat with sharp teeth and low growls.

Before, I had looked at motherhood as docile, submissive; the raging hormones taught me that it was something else entirely. I had never felt stronger. I told him that I might want to keep it. That I at least wanted to discuss the pros, the cons.

I suppose I expected him to feel torn the way I did. I was convinced he loved me more than anyone in my life ever had— even more than Cedar, who had been slipping from me, slipping because of my joy. His eyes burned as he told me that I was crazy for even considering keeping it, that I would ruin all of our lives. All I heard, despite all of the dreamy talk we had about a future family, was: you will be a horrible mother.

This man, who knew my darkness acutely, was he right?

I sobbed, my body sinking to the floor just outside the bathroom. I wanted the cheap tile to crack open, to pull me down, down, down. I'm not even sure that I wanted to keep it. I knew it was only a cluster of cells, barely anything yet. I think I just wanted compassion. I wanted him to apologize for not listening when I asked him to please put on a condom. I wanted accountability. I wanted him to hold space for my confusion, for how my hormones raged, how I was becoming something else.

"You're a stupid fucking whore," he said, ten feet from me as if I was contaminated.

I cried harder than I ever had, fingers spread out on the floor in front of me, body curved inward seeking comfort that wouldn't come.

I thought of the word whore, how it had now been applied to me for polar opposites of the same subject. The word, like cocktease, like slut, bitch, it's a means of control.

The next morning I awoke with a stabbing cramp and I knew. I knew, I knew, I knew that the life had left me. Wade told me I should thank him. "I stressed you out so bad that your body made the decision for you. You should thank me."

I want to tell Lil that this is no world for a baby. That this is no world for a pregnant woman. It's no place to be vulnerable. But I know those words wouldn't help so all I say is, "I'm sorry." I think of Wade and I know that he's a monster now. He was a monster then. All of them who were monsters then are monsters now.

All of them who were monsters then are monsters now, Cedar repeats.

"I know why Ian changed," I whisper to Lil.

She looks up, forehead damp with sweat.

"Why?"

"He was a rapist." The words feel heavy as they leave my lips. Unbelievable. Wrong. Words I swore I'd never speak. Yet here they are, fitting in place.

Ian knew it too, what brought on his initial fever. They all must. Why else would they ever confess? I think that's why Ian came back for me. Not to save me, but to see if I could save him. The way those men are kneeling outside of churches worldwide, shouting for mercy. The reason Glen uploaded his crimes to the internet. Ian wanted to know if I could extract him from guilt. I couldn't. He brought this on himself. They all did.

THERE WAS A PARTY, DOWN A WINDING ROAD, ALONG the water, during the summer before I moved away for college. It's crazy to think that by that time I had been fucking Ian for two years. And no one knew. It's easy to live in the shadows. It's easy to be a dirty secret. Somewhere during those years, I had told myself that we each got the same thing out of it: no-strings-attached sex. No complicated conversation. We were free of feelings. We were just for fun. We could date other people. We were free to fall in love. We could meet up on sticky summer nights, lonely little liars. There had been times where I sat upon the laps of other boys and watched his eyes narrow in jealousy. But he was never jealous enough to act. Never jealous enough to tell me that he cared. I'd put on a show for him then, I suppose, the way I did in the club. One where he coolly watched, knowing all the while he could have me the second he made a move.

It's strange, thinking of him now that he's gone. In a lot of ways it's easier now that all hope is lost.

The table was a mix of different conversation when Ian raised his lanky arm in a cheers. The condensation on his bottle of Blue glistened in the moonlight.

"I'd like to cheers myself," he said, "for taking Delilah's virginity." The table became a cluster of laughter from the men, murmurs from the women. I looked down at my hands, my vision darkening around the edges as the bottles clinked. When I looked up no one would meet my eyes. I'd told my mom I'd be fine to stay the night, but after the conversation moved on and tension settled around our bones like dust, I got up and walking away from the table. Out of eyesight, I held my flip phone to the sky, searching for a bar.

The text fluttered and failed.

I went into the empty cottage, placed my hands on either side of the counter, and breathed in and out slowly. One of Ian's friends, not much taller than me, nondescript with kind eyes, came inside, and I stood up straight. His name was Will and it was his uncle's cottage. I hoped he hadn't noticed my glassy stare, my deep breaths.

"He can be a real fucking jerk sometimes," he said. My eyes softened, and I begged myself not to cry as I nodded.

"Do you want a drink?" he asked.

There were bottles covering the counter. Blue curaçao, vodka, lemonade, rum, sour puss, sprite, diet coke. I said sure. The other boys came into the cottage then, and I could tell they felt uncomfortable meeting my eyes. Their eyes held the shame of someone who'd gotten caught watching porn. I could see it, how they each played out what that night, that first night, must have looked like. If they hadn't thought of me naked before, they were thinking it now. I could hear them kicking themselves, seeing me for the first time as something sexual, something that they could have had for themselves. It's strange how a man's cock can do that to a girl, put her on the table. They thought fucking weird girls would have lost them their popularity; realizing Ian had been doing it for years made them feel slighted.

The drink was blue and sweet, and the screen door slammed when Ian entered the room. The girls were still outside with the boys they were dating, getting into little drunken spats, skinny dipping.

I walked up to Ian and asked, "Can you drive me home later?"

He looked through me. I heard the others snicker again, picturing my chest curved over the gearshift, head in Ian's lap, legs sprawled in a back seat. I took another sip, pulled my phone from my pocket. The texts all had little *x's* beside them. Failed.

Two years of wanting to be claimed finally coming to fruition and showing me that I never wanted to be claimed at all, I felt so fucking stupid. I had been so convinced that night was the night that I'd feel it, I'd feel special. A night that I told myself I earned, after two years—over two years—of shameful disregard.

"I just want to go home," I said, suddenly not caring how immature I sounded. Tears stung the edges of my eyelids, the sound of clinking bottles, the murmurs, the laughs deafening.

"I'm tired." I leaned back against the counter, knocking a plastic Solo cup to the floor with a splash.

"It's okay, Delilah." Will looked at the mess on the floor, left it sprawling across the tile, as he took my cup and set it on the counter. "You can sleep in my room. You'll feel better in the morning, k?"

There was a murmur of voices from the others. Ian stayed silent.

The bedroom smelled like wood stove smoke, and I thought of my nan's house. My stomach churned. Will handed me a pillow, and I clutched it like a life raft, curling around it in fetal position. He turned off the light. The darkness was comforting after the shame of all the eyes on me around the picnic table, of the bright kitchen lights and murmurs. I felt so warmed by his compassion. For years I've looked back upon that night and thought of how special I felt as he led me to the room, as he offered me that olive branch of kindness when he didn't have to. He told me to sleep tight and that everything would be better in the morning. As he lightly shut the door, I felt cared for and began to cry, eyes shut tight, face pushed hard against the pillow.

I heard it then. The creaking of the hinges, socked feet shuffling upon hardwood, a stifled laugh, the jingle of a belt buckle. My body felt heavy as I was rolled onto my back, the pillow taken ever so gently from my arms. Ian's face was close to mine, and I tried not to breathe as I waited for his apology, for a kiss that would somehow make up for it all. I was so accustomed to small moments of tenderness after gutting moments of carelessness. But his eyes … his eyes were still cold.

We wait for apologies that will never come. We wait and wait and wait and then tell ourselves that we don't need them. We are steel. We are untouchable.

My eyelids were heavy, but I could see them—the others—a bare shoulder, a muscular thigh, a hard cock pushed up against my slack mouth.

"She's heavier than she looks," one of them said with a grunt and a chuckle. Where did my clothes go? I heard the moans, nervous laughter. Felt pressure. Sharp teeth to my tits, rough hands on my hips. I woke up alone, my naked body curled around the pillow. I wondered who placed the pillow back into my arms, if it had been Will again. I put on my clothes and tiptoed out of the room, out into the quiet cottage, careful not to creak the floor with each of my steps. The screen door latched behind me with a small, satisfying click. I began to walk. I began to run. My cell didn't work until I got half an hour down the road.

When my mom picked me up from the dusty shoulder, I said I had a good time and had just started walking because it was such a nice day. In reality, the sunshine felt like another attack. I worried she could smell them on me. I bit my tongue as we drove by the hospital. I scalded myself in the shower when I got home. I didn't look down at my body, but I felt it more than ever that it no longer belonged to me. That whatever was left of her was gone.

Later, Cedar said at least I was alive.

But I didn't want to be. I wanted to die.

I started fucking older men soon after. After the cottage, after all of those nights I wouldn't mention to anyone. Men rarely asked my age. The number didn't matter to them, not as much as my knee socks and messy hair. Once, I ran into my parents when I was at the mall with one; I expected my father to grab me by the arm, to puff out his chest as he asked the man, "What are you doing with my daughter, buddy?" But instead they chatted and after, the man—I don't remember his name—told me how nice of a guy my dad was. I wondered if it took away a bit of the conquest for him, that my dad didn't care enough to ask too many questions. Instead, I think it only ramped him up. My issues were authentic; I was the real thing. He told me to call him Daddy that day. He bought me a sweater, cream-coloured, demure. I liked his quick intake of breath when the words left my lips: *Daddy*. I liked how he looked at me, like I was something precious that he was going to devour. A fine cut of meat, a threat. My favourite part about fucking him was the sense that he felt a little disgusted with himself. I liked the quick dart of his eyes, how he wasn't yet sure if he was ashamed or powerful. Is that what I liked about Ian too?

Lil looks at me as if she's seeing me for the first time. She reaches out a wet hand and clasps it around mine.

"Derek must have been too."

"Not to you?" I ask, thinking of nights with men who said they loved me, how they pushed against swatting hands, how they didn't seem to notice my corpse-still body, how it felt as if I wasn't even there as they thrust faster, faster, fastest.

"Not beat you down, drag you out, but there was coercion. There was a lot of coercion."

I wish it were me, who cursed them all on that walk home after Richard—when I prayed to Marybeth. The thought gives me a shiver of pride. But I know that the pride belongs solely to Cedar.

You're welcome, she singsongs. *Justice only comes from our swift kicks.*

THIRTY-SIX

When Lil is out of the tub and tucked tight into Theo's bed, I wander back downstairs. My mom is where I found her this morning, seated at the kitchen table waiting for a call. Elijah takes the bathroom next. Our hands touch when I hand him two towels, and I want to run away with him. I want to tell him everything that has made me who I am, and I want him to say, "I'm sorry," and "I'm here for you." I want him to say, "But look at you now, a killer."

I am not a victim or a survivor. I am just a woman in this world.

"Have a nice shower," I say softly, wandering back down the stairs.

I can tell by my mother's posture that she's upset with me. I've been able to do that since childhood, read body language like a book.

"What do you know about him?" she asks, her voice hushed even though we can both hear the running water from the shower upstairs. I think of leaving the room. Of joining Elijah. Of slitting my wrists over the kitchen sink.

"He saved my life."

She raises her eyebrows.

I don't repeat what Kyle said to me, but I can still feel him, his shoulder pressed tightly into mine.

"How long have you known him?" she asks, her head absentmindedly turning so she can glance up the stairs as if the shower is all a ruse, as if he's gearing to attack.

"Not long." I try not to think about it too deeply.

"Delilah, you do this. You pass over your trust as if it's nothing."

I snort and meet her eyes. "I don't have any trust left."

She rolls hers. "I just want to make sure we're safe." She pauses, looks up at the ceiling. "What do you know about him? What's his last name?"

There's an edge to her voice when she asks the last question. I think of the men I've fucked whose names are a blur. I feel like a slut and wonder if that is her intention or if I just think it is because of my own internalized shame. I can't tell her that I don't know, that I've never asked. I think back to the days with a smartphone, when I knew people's last names only if they were part of their handles.

"Ma, he's nice. He's a good guy, I promise. I've noticed no unhealthy curvature of the spine." I laugh—it's empty. I hear the click of the shower, picture his wet hand pushing in the knob, his body wrapped in a plush, white, bleach-scented towel.

"We'll go to the station, okay?" I add, looking her right in the eyes. I think of Theo. I know that filing a missing person's report is laughable, foolish. I'll do it anyways.

"Your father is looking for him. He'll find him."

I thought he was already gone. But who am I kidding? If my dad changed, she would let him kill her. I should know that. Of course she would. She has let him kill her spirit for years, and when your spirit is wounded, losing your body barely hurts. I imagine my father with his hunting rifle and a thermos of coffee. His mouth muttering in rage. Body riddled with fever. He can't survive this, can he?

"Do you believe it's rape that causes it?"

I watch her face closely as her eyes fall to her hands, looking at them as if they don't belong to her.

"I've heard many different things."

I think of the men we saw on TV. They know what causes it. They can feel it now. It's why they're sorry. She's told me how my father treats her sexually: heavy-handed aggression, how he calls her a dirty whore. When I said, "Atta girl, Ma," she said, "But I don't like it at all."

"It's not steroids or saliva particles," I say, thinking of Ian, of the cottage, feeling my stomach churn as I remember how black and blue my nipples were. How I winced as I pissed for three days. How I blamed myself, erasing any of their agency, their guilt as I messaged:

What happened last night? I must have gotten too drunk.

I knew I'd only had one wine cooler before Will's drink, but my temples throbbed as if I'd had a dozen.

And then came his quick reply:

I don't know, man. I can barely remember.

He never called me man. I read it over and over and over again.

I typed:

Did you guys rape me?

I stared at the words until they no longer looked like words at all.

Before logging off, he responded:

Haha no.

And you know what? The no looked better than the truth. The no looked like a warm comforter I could crawl inside. No, no, no, no. La, la, la, la. The no, for a moment, erased the sensation of feeling my body sloppily passed, poked and prodded, flipped over. The no let me ignore the pain. The no felt like hope. Later, I wanted to ask him why he bragged about taking my virginity years after the fact, what that moment meant to him. I wanted to ask if what happened was planned, if that's why he invited me in the first place.

I fought the urge to apologize for even asking and replied:

Okay haha.

It sat unread for two weeks.

"It's karma, Ma," I say, pulling myself back, back, back. "It's karma. There was no justice and now, the universe, something, I don't know, is creating it. Predators are having to pay. Finally."

I watch as she stands, walks to the drawer beside the stove, pulls out a pack of cigarettes. She slides the pack to me as she flicks one to life and inhales deeply, too tired to hide her habit.

"And you know for certain that he'll be okay then?" She looks up the stairs to where we can hear the tap turning on and off, the *thwack thwack thwack* of a toothbrush against ceramic. Will seemed so sweet that night and even years later when I met him in the park with a thermos of whisky. He was sweet then too.

"I'd say if he's fine so far, then he will be."

We think of Glen. I know it. We think of him on his knees, beginning to change yet still recognizable, confessing the ways in which he ruined not only one life but every other one surrounding it.

"Do you still have your nan's old camera?" she asks, staring at me straight on, and I know she knows. She knows, she knows, she knows.

I think for a minute, but not long enough.

"Yes," I say. "I bring it with me wherever I go."

THIRTY-SEVEN

"ARE YOU OKAY?" ELIJAH ASKS, HIS HAIR STILL DAMP from the shower.

My childhood bedroom feels preserved. A crypt.

I look at the T-shirts still hanging on the back of the door, the Lip Smackers on the desk now tinged a disturbing brown. It reminds me of how much time has passed. It reminds me that I'm still stuck there; the past is a place. Time has carried on. I've swerved and swayed with the motions of life, yet still, I'm there.

"No, but is anyone?" I ask, sitting down hard on my bed. My own damp hair drips onto my oversized T-shirt, decorated with an animated version of my nan's old poodle, George.

"Come here," he says, sitting down beside me and opening his arms like an invitation. I lean into them, breathe in the scent of Dove soap and my mother's Pantene shampoo.

I can feel Cedar, uncomfortable but still present. I ignore her.

"I wish I could tell you that things will be okay," he says with a sigh, a small half-hearted chuckle.

"I wish you could too." I pull back to look up at him. He's so beautiful that having him look directly at me makes me fidget. I wonder if he's dissecting all of my flaws or if I'm just so used to men dissecting my flaws that I figure he's doing it too.

"I'm really glad I met you." No one has ever said that to me before. Instead, I've heard the contrary tons of times: *I wish I never would have fucking met you.*

"You don't really know me," I whisper, averting my eyes, twisting a small loose thread on the neck of his T-shirt. He wouldn't be here if he knew.

"You don't really know me either. But this feeling ... it has to count for something, doesn't it?"

I drop my head then, watching fat tears splatter against his grey track pants, waiting for him to push me away for my gentle weakness, but he doesn't. He holds me tighter, his hands rubbing against my shoulders soft and slow.

"I'm a mess." I look up, smiling through my tears.

"No, you're not," he says, his olive eyes unwavering from mine.

"You're like the night."

I stare at him, unsure of how to respond.

"I want to get lost in you, but I can't help being afraid of the dark."

My hungry lips meet his, his breath hot, his tongue surprisingly cold. My limbs feel weak but my conscious feels clear. I want to love him. I want to know what happiness feels like, what trust feels like.

For a moment, my mind is free from the crumbling world. From the people I've lost, the people I'll lose. For a moment all I feel is him, his tongue swirling with mine, our breath ragged in unison. His hands slip beneath my T-shirt to pull it over my head. He looks at me as if I'm something truly beautiful.

I want him. I want him to get lost in me.

THIRTY-EIGHT

We learn about the prosecution the following morning over coffee. Even as men devolve and women disappear, there are still men in power. And the men in power say that something has to be done for these creatures who have been killed. Their families need answers. I realize, the sip of coffee in my mouth suddenly shit-bitter, that the creatures hold more value than women in the eyes of men.

I watch rapt as the Polaroid of Kyle flashes back across the screen and is then followed by his grad photo, a fresh clip of his crying mother. I feel both Elijah and my mother look at me, but for different reasons.

"That's the guy, right?" Elijah says quickly, his voice has an edge of awe.

I nod too quickly. "I think so."

Lil is still sleeping in Theo's old room upstairs. It's equally preserved: N64 games and a Metallica poster, Dragon Ball Z figurines and a gigantic stack of Pokémon cards. I saw her for a moment in the hall when I got up to pee. She said she tossed and turned all night, that she was afraid. I thought of myself, how I sleep better once the sun is up. I told her to go back to bed.

"You knew him?" Mom asks, eyes still set on the screen.

"He's—that's who was following me when I first met Elijah." Elijah places his hand across mine on the table. I resist the urge to jerk my hand away, to show him that I'm not dainty, I don't need saving.

"I'm sure he deserved whatever came to him," Elijah says.

"Yeah." It's half-hearted. I can feel my mother's eyes on me, measuring my expression, the curve of my smile the way she used to when I was a child, trying to tell whether or not I'm lying. Following Kyle there is another trigger warning and after it clips of five new Polaroids, the subjects all dead. Two of them are mine, the other three from an Instax Mini: new, trendy, vicious.

My father has yet to come home. We don't speak about it, which feels odd, his looming presence just gone.

The remaining cops, mostly women, but some men too, have coined *The Polaroid Killer* a threat to the justice system. I can't help my laugh. My free hand slaps the table, making both my mother and Elijah jump as I shout, "There *is* no justice system!"

Swift kicks, Cedar whispers.

I look to Elijah, embarrassed, fearful if now that he has me, he'll start backing away, slowly and then all at once. That he'll be like the others with their indifference that I've met with desperation—weak attempts at capturing that initial spark, that long-gone level of attention. Horrible moods that make me nearly impossible to deal with once all else has failed so I can say that I pushed them away instead of acknowledging the truth: they were already on their way out the door.

I think of April 7. That fucking day and all of the men who marred it.

First my father. Then a wealthy drunk named Kent Philips. And then, worst of all, Glen Belvedere. I don't even like saying their names. I prefer them nameless, these monsters who ruined my life. Nan was right. Bad things come in threes.

I take a deep breath. My mother watches me as if I'm a wild animal. The panic crawls up my throat in that old familiar way, shortening my breath, tunnelling my vision, deafening my ears.

I know she wants to ask me: *Who are you?*

She doesn't.

I want to tell her of all the things that have shaped me, but I don't. She knows, doesn't she?

The clip rolls again of Glen, then of another dark web confession, before it lands on the group of devolving men praying, screaming, squealing. Elijah lets out a puff of breath. A camera pans overhead as the changing attack the unchanged. The area is no longer safe for reporters. The men can no longer speak. Soldiers swarm the parking lot, fully equipped with riot gear, assault rifles. They fire, killing as many creatures as they can. It seems violence is only deemed justifiable if the call is made by a man.

"Have you heard anything? From Dad? From Theo?"

My mother hangs her head. When she looks up at me, her green eyes are slits of anger. They ask: *What do you think?*

"I'll look for him today, Ma. I'll look."

I think of the signs beside the road, the warnings to stay out of the woods. I think of the club. The church parking lots. I think of the deterioration and shiver.

And like always, I think of that day. That worst day. That day that would make everything else dull in comparison. That day that prepared me for sorrow, that taught me to expect it.

After Theo left the creek, I didn't initially go to Nan's. There was too much of a chance Cedar wasn't yet home, and I thought if Nan saw my face without the distraction of Theo beside me, she would be able to read that something was terribly wrong in the set of my jaw, how I anxiously pinched my bottom lip between index finger and thumb.

And I wouldn't be able to stay silent, the words would rush from my mouth: my dad is having an affair.

I pedalled fast, unsure of where I was going but basking in the sensation of propelling myself further and further from home, the ability to rely on my own strength.

Once I found Cedar and told her all that had happened, she would ask me to sleep over. I wouldn't call my mother, instead letting her pace the front hall, peering into the slipping day and worrying that I wasn't ever coming back.

In my twelve-year-old mind, I pictured hating my mother forever. Of casting her into the same hellish pit along with my father, of laughing snarkily whenever they spoke to each other or shared a tender moment. Of asking questions like, "Do you miss your girlfriend?" just to see my mother's face drop and my father's face morph into a grimace, knowing that he would have no right to say a word. I pictured staying at Nan's forever. I would become sisters with Cedar, and we would invite Theo over for Indian tacos, pizza, slumber parties where we'd set up our tent in the backyard and tell ghost stories until the early hints of dawn.

Back then I didn't realize how easily our lives could become ghost stories of their own.

I rode my bike into the small stretch of what resembled downtown, the convenience store and skatepark, post office, and cop shop, to look for Cedar. Maybe she'd be leaning against the wall of the store, lips tinged blue from her slushie. Or maybe she was sitting at the top of the ramp as her friends from high school did kick flips and ollies. Part of me hoped I'd find her alone, just having parted with her friends who looked at me like I was a little kid. Cedar talked to me differently when they were around, her sentences shorter, voice a little bored. Upon seeing me she would know that the cat was out of the bag, that I knew she'd used me as an alibi. She'd done it once before, but she'd warned me ahead of time; I felt sad to be excluded but happy that she had given me an important task. I figured that if I lied successfully, it wouldn't be long before she'd begin to include me, that she'd begin to see me as cool.

I didn't find her and was just beginning to worry, the anxiety twisting my stomach like someone wringing out a rag, when I spotted her at the edge of the soccer field with a group of people I'd seen from afar but didn't know.

Cedar's going to be trouble, my mom's words repeated in my head, and I hated that I would always be the good one, too anxious to rebel. I stopped quickly and wiped my eyes, hoping there were no remnants of emotion on my face. I thought of turning around, pedalling home or to Nan's before she saw me. But I couldn't go home. I couldn't go to Nan's. I hopped off of my bike.

There's a way to approach people you hope to impress and it's slowly. You never want to seem overly eager. I'd seen it my entire life, my parents' voices getting higher, their conversation style changing whenever a new person came around. How they'd never say what was on their mind but instead turned extremely agreeable, saving their personalities for the car ride home. I cursed myself for not wearing lip gloss, for wearing a bright teal windbreaker while all the teenagers wore only hoodies.

"Hey," I said, walking up and tossing my bike so it tipped over onto its side in the grass.

"Delilah!" Cedar said from where she sat cross-legged in the grass, her voice dreamy, purple hood of her polyester sweatshirt pulled low on her forehead, concealing her recently chopped hair. She cut it the week she got back from her mom's—I understand it now; she didn't want to see the same girl when she looked into the mirror.

She covered her mouth with her hands and peered at me with twinkling, glassy eyes.

"Did you blow my cover?"

"I think you're good," I said, chuckling as if I was older. "I told Nan there was a miscommunication. I thought we were meeting at yours, you thought we were meeting at mine."

"Gah!" Cedar let out a dramatic whoosh of breath. "You're amazing."

I grinned and sat down next to her, finally getting the courage to look around at the others. I had never met any of them before, these boys with longish hair and a couple other girls wearing tight pants and talking only to each other. There was one boy in particular with dark blue eyes and a lip ring, who watched us from where he stood leaning up against a tree trunk. I saw her eyes flicker from mine to his as I spoke, and I immediately felt othered. A childish third wheel, an imposter. Ian had that dark draw to him even then.

"Cedar, something really bad happened. Do you think we can go somewhere else?" I asked her in a half-whisper.

Her voice was much louder than mine when she responded. "Oh my God, what? Did you get your period?"

I felt my ears redden as a couple of the guys snickered. I kept my eyes glued to hers, pleading.

"Sorry—" she muttered, nearly under her breath, expression touched with a hint of remorse. "What's wrong?"

She pulled a long white cigarette out of the front pocket of her sweatshirt.

"Can I have one?" I asked, imagining her sneaking them from Nan's red plastic case when she fell asleep in her chair.

Cedar raised her eyebrows and handed me the cigarette before fishing out another. She leaned in close with a clear lime green lighter, and I coughed upon the first inhale but liked the sting of smoke against my throat. It felt fitting, that slightly painful burn.

"She's an old pro!" Cedar sang gleefully as she took a long drag herself.

Conversations continued around us and within minutes I was old news, sitting beside Cedar with my second cigarette between my fingers and a sickness in my stomach.

"My dad's fucking a twenty-something-year-old," I said finally, flicking pieces of black and silvery ash into the grass beside me.

"What the fuck!" Cedar laughed, and I couldn't help laughing too, at the absurdity of it all—my father in his tighty whities that hung from his ass, his belly that subtly protruded through the thin cotton of his well-worn T-shirts that would ride up when he was sitting down and yet he somehow wouldn't feel the cool air on his stomach; he'd just sit there like Winnie the Pooh.

"Yeah," I said, the laugh catching in my throat as I took another drag, my mouth dry and bitter.

Cedar had never known her father, and I knew that sometimes she envied mine. How when I was small, he'd perch me up on his shoulders so I could feel like a giant. How he brought me chocolate bars or McDonald's breakfast some mornings on his drive home from work. How he taught me how to ride a bike, and throw a punch, and had been letting me drive the car on the backroads even though I was only twelve.

"Does Auntie know?" Cedar smooshed the butt of her

cigarette into the ground. Nan would scoff, watching us use Mother Earth as an ashtray.

"Yeah." I held my elbows as I looked out across the field.

"Shit," Cedar muttered, her voice small. "Do you think he's going to move out?"

I thought of my house without my dad's slippers beside the front door or his whistle in the kitchen while he made his morning coffee. I thought of my house without slamming doors and screamed *fucks* directed at no one and everyone all at once.

I thought of how embarrassed my mom would be if she didn't kick him out and instead he chose to willingly leave, packing up all his belongings some afternoon that Theo and I were in school.

"I don't think so. Mom is hanging off of his side and he says he's sorry." I looked at Cedar, at how her dark eyes rolled and her lips parted with an *umph* of disbelief. It was a little lie. He hadn't said sorry.

"My mom would have at least bopped him one."

I watched as she turned out a slender wrist and shot it out into the air. Auntie had a lot of boyfriends—none of them lasted more than a few years. I never told Cedar that I knew about what the current one had done to her. I figured one day she'd tell me herself, but maybe she wouldn't have. Her mother didn't bop him one; she didn't kick him out.

"Can we go back to Nan's?" I asked her then, my voice sounding even younger than my twelve years.

"Come on," Cedar said, looking out at the other teenagers even though none of them were looking at us. "One of these dudes is bound to find us beers." She said *dudes* loudly so they'd hear her. She was always good at that, getting attention when she wanted it.

I thought of the blurry sickness that had violently shook

through me when Cedar taught me how to chug two weeks before, how even the scent of the stuff had the power to turn my stomach. I felt childish and small. Cedar seemed so grown-up.

"Please?" I asked her, making my large eyes larger, my voice cute. Cedar looked over my head and as I nervously followed her gaze, I realized that lip ring dude was standing behind me, wearing a sly grin. I felt a red-hot blush creep up my neck. I recognized him from Cedar's Facebook, realized she was acting this way all for him. His presence immediately infuriated me. I could feel Cedar slipping away as her voice changed slightly and her eyes no longer locked with mine when she spoke.

"Wow, Lilah. Your dad fucking sucks. It's more reason to have fun."

I stared at her lips in disbelief, my stomach sinking. This was not the girl that tickled my back until I fell asleep. She met my eyes for a split second, and I swore hers held a silent apology. It only made me angrier. I wanted to yell that everyone was a fucking liar. *Everyone is a fucking LIAR!* I wondered what would happen if I publicly spiralled out of control. If the surrounding teenagers would come closer and laugh or if they would back away slowly, murmuring amongst themselves, careful not to make eye contact, to engage.

The longing to violently erupt in public had been growing subtly over the last two years and then quickly over the last month, and today it felt as if it had reached its peak. So far, the only scenes I had caused were storming out of a family function and violently sobbing in the car or slamming my bedroom door and wailing. Although loud and obnoxious, they had all still held their realm of privacy; they were easy to ignore. Later, when I'd calmed down, my mother would talk in hushed tones as if I wasn't there and say, "PMS. She's going to be an early bloomer like me."

I wanted to scream and pull out clumps of my hair, throwing them at the unsuspecting audience. I thought of walking out into the woods and disappearing. Instead, I sat still, feeling the early stirrings of sadness creeping up my chest, my throat, until my bottom lip began to involuntarily protrude. I tried to clear my head, but the little voice kept saying that Cedar had finally realized I was a loser too. That my worst nightmare had finally come true: I had no one. I would always have no one. I wanted everyone to die. I tried to push the thought from my mind, but it got louder and louder and louder until I was doing it … I was crying in public. I could feel the snot thick above my lip, my cheeks and chest covered in bright red blotches.

Cedar grabbed me by the shoulders then, meeting my eyes with an ice I had never before seen. "Get yourself together."

My face got warmer as the sobs barked from my throat, escaping my mouth more as I willed myself to stop. All eyes were on me. Faces twisted in pity and disgust, surprise and laughter. Cedar's hands were still curled around my shoulders, but her eyes were once again looking past me, over my head. Her mouth danced in a smile before she met my eyes again, hers filled with mock sympathy. She looked like a liar too.

"I fucking hate you!" I yelled, jerking out of her grasp, my mind racing with words that I could say to hurt her back. I had never wanted to hurt her before, but I had never wanted something more as she let out a piercing cackle.

"At least my dad cares about me enough to actually be in my life," I said loudly, my voice also changing to something else once it was intended for everyone around us. I wanted to make her feel small. My eyes were still full of tears as they met hers, the eyes I loved more than anything. Her hurt reflected my own, and it didn't feel the way I hoped it would. I turned away quickly, no longer wanting to stare into the face of pain that I'd inflicted.

I yanked my bike from the grass and hopped on with a kick of my foot to propel me forward. As I sped away from the park, I passed a man. He was sitting on a bench, smoking a dart. My embarrassment kept my eyes from meeting his.

It's okay, Lilah. It's okay, she says now, her voice softer than usual. *You didn't mean it.*

That was the last time I saw Cedar alive.

THIRTY-NINE

There's a knock on the door and despite the broad daylight, despite the fact that the creatures cannot knock, we all stoop down into our seats, eyes darting back and forth. Elijah pushes his chair from the table. My mom places her hand on his forearm, urging him to sit back down.

We wait for a key in the lock. We are waiting for my father.

The pounding continues. Four hard knocks.

Part two of the worst day of our lives sounded like these knocks. Is my mom thinking of that too? That horrible day? On that day there were four knocks and two officers with hat in hands telling them that their little boy had been hit by a drunk driver, that he had been rushed to the hospital. My mom went in the cruiser. My dad followed behind, and I've always wondered if he thought this was his karma.

I wasn't home yet.

They didn't leave a note, and when I got in, face still blotchy, I felt a level of abandonment I never had before.

Two more knocks snap me back to reality, Elijah's curiosity, my mom's indifference. I get up, wandering slowly to the door. It's Deb standing there in uniform. She looks as if she has aged twenty years. I open the door quickly.

"Hi."

I can hear nervous murmurs from the kitchen.

The relief rushes into my lungs, even as my eyes begin to water. Standing tall beside Deb is my first best friend.

"Theo." My voice breaks as I open the door wider, as I pull him into my arms. He's thinner than I've ever seen him. His eyes are shadowed with exhaustion, but he's okay, he's okay, he's okay.

Mom pushes past me, pulling him from my grasp, kissing his hair.

I shut and lock the door behind them, peering down the driveway, expecting monsters to jump from the bushes.

"He was out by the creek," Deb says to me. I think of telling her of that last day, that horrible day. Does she know? That it was my idea to go for a bike ride in the first place?

"I was looking for Dad," Theo interjects. "I wanted to make sure he didn't get too cold."

My mom's voice cracks in a whimper. She pulls him closer to her chest.

I think of Theo's apartment overturned. It wasn't him who changed.

"Dad said he wasn't feeling good when he got there. His teeth were chattering." He looks at me. "You thought I'd changed," he says, pulling me into a hug.

My body melts into his—my brother, my Theo.

"I was so angry, for a long time," he whispers against my hair. "But I didn't change. I didn't change. Is it anger? That causes it?"

I think of his life after the accident. Those first two years where he had to leave his friends and join a remedial class. The friends who no longer knew how to speak to him, whose energy had become uncomfortable whenever he was around, who showed him without meaning to that he was different. He was in an After of his own. Then there were those evenings, those evenings where my mother told him to eat one more bite, as if he was a toddler, as she retaught him everything she'd taught him years before. Cooing, "It's okay, honey. It's okay," as his fury consumed him, as he slammed his fist against the kitchen table, her eyes soft and only hardening when they looked at me as I lingered at the edge of the kitchen.

"Evelyn, can I speak with you in the other room?" Deb asks my mother, extending a hand to lightly touch her forearm. Theo looks at me, lightly shakes his head.

"I'm Elijah." I watch his arm extend from a step behind me. For a second Theo steps back; we're all afraid of men now.

"Theo," he says, attempting to make his voice jovial.

My mother's cry cuts through from the other room. Theo locks my gaze for another second before dropping his eyes to his muddy boots. I hear the slamming of my mother's bedroom door. The walls rattle.

"He was already gone," he whispers beneath his breath. "I thought—I don't know—I thought maybe he could come back. I don't know, it's stupid."

I shut my eyes tight. In my mind I can see my father when I was only two or three, his smiling face as he tossed me in the air above his head, his firm hands as he caught me. I can hear the shriek of my laughter. I was loved, wasn't I?

When Deb comes back, she rests a hand on my shoulder. I think of the Polaroid. I think of Justin/Jamie/Josh, now roadkill. I think of Kyle, the news. I think of that drive home when I first became a killer, my damp, bloodied jeans, the Polaroid of Richard that I untacked from the wall beside my bed and tucked away in the back of my drawer. How it now rests in the duffel bag with the others. I think of Cedar.

Cedar's rage that never dissipates. Cedar's rage that never lets me go.

"I'm sorry, Delilah," Deb says. "For everything."

"Do you want to stay here?" I ask, thinking of her large empty house, all of the places where creatures could hide. She shakes her head.

"She'd be proud of you. She always knew you could be tough as nails."

Does she know?

She pats Theo on the shoulder. Looks to Elijah.

"Deborah Hurston," she says, hand extended. "Wish it was better circumstances."

Elijah nods, shakes her hand.

Deb's eyes flit to mine. I can't tell if her expression is one of judgment or concern. "I'll be back later. Talk to your mother," she says as I close the door behind her, as I slump down against the door. As I miss my father for all of the things he was, for all of the things I wanted him to be.

My mother lets out a howl. How much grief can four walls take before a house is truly haunted?

FORTY

"Who was the officer talking about, when she said, 'She'd be proud of you?'"

We sit in the silence of the living room, curtains drawn, Elijah and I.

I stab my fingernails into my thigh. I can barely feel her anymore.

"Cedar," I say, waiting for the flickering of lights, for her little voice in my ear. She's dissipating.

"My cousin. She went missing …" I stop, take a deep breath. I can hear my words to her, on that last day, that worst day. Words I never meant. *I fucking hate you, I fucking hate you, I fucking hate you.* It plays on a loop in my head, shrill. "There were witnesses who said that they'd seen her. There was even video footage of her arguing with this man outside of the convenience store. That man. That man from the first video."

I shake my head, seeing Glen. Hearing his voice too, years ago, pleading innocent. I can see him beaming as he left the court a free man. I think of him now, sinewy flesh tearing as his body painfully morphs, gnarled mouth begging forgiveness, running free like an animal.

The stairs creak and I turn to see Lil standing in the doorway. For a moment I think she's sleep walking, the way Cedar used to, her eyes large and haunted.

"Babes?" I ask as her hand lightly grazes the wall as she walks down the hall. I look at Elijah. I can tell his mind is jumping to symptoms and side effects as mine jumps to insanity. It's this house. It's this fucking house. My car keys jingle in her left hand. I think of my how my nan would pull Cedar out of her spells, a gentle hand on her shoulder that sometimes would make her twist in fright. Her voice calmly cooing, *"Honey, honey, honey."*

I look into the oval mirror hanging from the wall. I look like me.

At the door Lil slides the deadbolt. She doesn't look back as she steps out onto the porch.

"Don't," Elijah says, hand on my wrist. But I can't. I can't let her leave. I can't let her die. When I catch up to her and touch her shoulder, she looks at me and nods. She smiles too wide.

"Lil?"

"It's okay," she says, her husky voice soft and sweet. "Come with me."

She sounds like Cedar. I sit beside her in the passenger seat as she starts up my car, the smile never leaving her face. Elijah stands on the porch. I place my palm against the passenger window, an order to stay, a goodbye. She begins to drive.

Lil careens down the dirt road, slowing for the fork, turning at the soccer field, the grass overgrown, speckled with litter. I watch as it passes by. She looks at me, nods, reaches out a cold hand to rest on my thigh. I close my eyes.

I listen for Cedar, her little whispers inside my brain. I hear nothing but the tires against gravel, the cawing of crows. Lil squeezes my leg, her stare glued to the road ahead. She slows, turning down a dead-end road.

"You'll have to turn around," I say, but she doesn't listen. She just keeps driving past the private property signs. Cedar and I used to dare each other to ride our bikes down here. Neither of us ever did. There were myths of a flying head, a man with hooves for feet. The road is surrounded by swamp, spindly trees crawling up from the muck like the arms I used to see reaching up from the darkness at the foot of my bed. I roll down my window and breathe in the wet scent of decaying plants. I hear the hiss of vultures flying just above the decrepit trees. They remind me of being in the back of Carl's car, of the slideshow that I begged Cedar to stop. When we get to the end of the road, Lil pulls the car onto the soft shoulder and cuts the ignition. She hops out. I shiver as I look out the windows, searching for the creatures of the myths Nan used to tell us of around campfires—or the men that have become monsters. Lil begins to walk into the trees. I bite my tongue for comfort and follow.

"Don't be scared, La-la-la-lilah."

"What did you just call me?"

Lil giggles, skips into the muck of the swamp. I watch the brownish water speckle her white socks, bleed through her white sneakers. It's the sensation of déjà vu that I feel first. I look around as if in a dream and pinch my thigh. The mud suctions around each of my steps with a gurgle. Lil carries across the swamp too fast, her feet barely making a sound. I struggle to keep up, not wanting to be left alone in the heavy silence. The trees creak in the gentle wind, a slow ache. She rounds a bend and is out of sight. I look back towards the car, how it sits near the edge of the muck and looks like a safe place to watch a nightmare unfold. Do the men—the creatures—do they come out this far?

I think of Elijah in my room. Has my mother left hers? Is she back at the table, a smoke burning down to a long ash as she stares into a better life, memories past? Does Theo feel grateful to not be one of the *real* men with their racist jokes and hungry eyes? The ones my father always praised. The ones he emulated.

"Lilah!" Her voice whistles through the trees.

I follow. I follow even though I don't want to.

I can't see Lil. I can't see her.

The muck nearly trips me, the glug of the mud the only sound I can hear.

"Lil, please." My voice is small as I round the bend.

When I spot her again, she's on hands and knees in the swamp, her neck craned forward as if she's trying to see her reflection in the murky water. My mind is a mix of rapid whispers, thoughts spewing too fast to be articulated, blood pumping in my wrists, my temples. But the whispers? The whispers are all my own.

I hear Cedar's giggle, entertained and proud of herself. One she reserved for the moments where she truly had me terrified. I want to turn around. I need to turn around, but I don't. I can't. I reach out a hand, feel Lil's boney shoulder, see where her sights are set as she begins to pull something from the mud. It's half-decomposed and dark. I reach for it with her, feeling the synthetic fabric beneath my fingertips, it gleams a dark purple in the dwindling sunlight.

"He dumped me here," Lil says. "He left me here, Lilah. I've been trying to tell you."

She's so young yet the wisdom in her is ancient. Jet-black and honest. A lifetime spent in the shadows, she says men are brought up promised milk and honey. We're brought up begging for scraps of recycled love. She says all they've really mastered is the act of taking whatever they feel is owed to them. She says we must be the remorse. We must be the redemption. We must be the swift kicks. She never used to have a saviour complex, but then again, she used to believe she didn't need one. She is everything I want to be. She is dead.

I close my eyes, fall to my hands and knees beside her, letting my fingers twist into the cool sludge until I feel it, hard and smooth, slightly curved. I can hear my ragged breath. I raise the rib into the light and Lil lets out a gasp, falls further forward into the water as if she's just woken up.

For the first time since she's died, I can hear my nan humming "Please Mr. Postman." The air around us wafts with the candied scent of sweetgrass. Cedar unlocks herself from a compartment in my mind. I can feel her getting smaller. I can feel her saying goodbye. *O:nen ki'*.

Lil looks up at me with wide, startled eyes. She begins to shake as a whimper rattles through her.

"When we get back to the car, the house, don't look in any mirrors, ok? She'll come back."

Lil vomits into the dark water.

As much as I'll miss Cedar, I don't want her to return.

The darkness falls around us, the sounds of our feet in the water echoing, the creak of the trees sounding like aching joints. We hurry.

I clutch my car keys in my palm, afraid to drop them, to lose them, to be stuck in the inky blackness of night. In my other hand I keep a firm hold on Lil.

"It's okay," I whisper when she begins to slow.

"Do you think we all go there?" she asks. I remain silent. I don't know. "I want to go there. It's more peaceful than here, wherever they went," she says, her voice solemn. I nod. I've heard that before.

"She took her," she says. "She took my baby." Her skin glistens with tears. I can see the car and when we reach it, I turn the mirrors so they face the ground. When I get in, I close my eyes, reach out my hand in the darkness, turn the rear-view mirror the other way. I inch out of the soft earth, careful not to get stuck. I turn on the radio, filling the car with the sound of The Marvelettes. I don't look back.

"She wanted me to tell you something, Delilah. She made me promise that I'd tell you. She wanted you to know that you'll be okay without her, that you know what to do. That you've always done the right thing. She says it's over now. The sickness is over." Lil pauses, her voice breaking. "She says it's time that you forgave yourself."

FORTY-ONE

The front door to my parents' house is open when we pull into the driveway. Lil is beside me, body slouched against the passenger side window, sleeping like a child after a long day in the sun.

Leaving her to sleep, I lock the car doors and run.

The table at the front, with its decorative bowl of potpourri that has always been a bed for our car keys, lies toppled on its side. The sour animal stench hits me at once, reminding me of the club.

"Ma!" I yell, feeling stupid as I look into the kitchen.

She sits there, smoking a menthol, and coolly asks, "Do you want to say goodbye to your father?"

I stare at her, eyes blinking like an idiot. Hair that was slicked in grease now shines brightly; she must have had a bath while I was gone. Her skin, lighter than her mother's, her sister's, mine, gleams with her ivory foundation, covering her freckles, her cheeks rosy with raspberry blush, lashes elongated with jet-black mascara, lips a deep burgundy. She's dressed in a black shirt, low cut, a black lace bodice pushing up her enviable cleavage.

"Mom, you look radiant." The words don't fit the scene, but they are true nonetheless.

She smiles wickedly. And I don't think I've ever seen her look this powerful, this terrifying.

I smell of swamp and panicked sweat.

"He's downstairs," she says, taking another drag, the smoke swirling above our heads.

I leave the kitchen at the sound of the red-hot butt of her cigarette being put to death in her emerald green ashtray.

"The boys are there too," she adds, and I think of Elijah, of Theo.

My blood runs cold as I step into the hall. The basement light glows yellow beneath the closed door. I've always hated it, our basement, unfinished and too cold. I want to tell her that Cedar is gone, set free, but the expression on her face silences me. It makes me feel as if she already knows.

There's a sound of metal against smooth cement as I approach the door. I turn the knob, the entire time wanting to turn back, to leave the house without a word, to get into my car with Lil, to drive and drive and drive, to start fresh somewhere far away. But I turn the knob, leaving the door open for her as I descend the rickety wooden stairs.

The basement is illuminated with a single pull-string bulb, and I see Theo first, seated in an old plastic chair from a set we used to have in the backyard. My brother looks up at me, sweat on his brow, scratches on his arms, his chest heaves with exasperated breath.

"I brought him down here when Deb dropped him off. Elijah helped me secure him."

Secure him. The words hang in the air, and I don't want to look. I don't want to look into the shadowy corner of the basement, but I do. I thought Deb had killed him. I thought that was the reason for my mother's howl. How often do we do that? Assume we know the reasons for our mother's agony? Does it make it easier for us to dismiss it?

Deb's steely cuffs are clenched too tight around my father's pink flesh. He's bound to a support beam with an old dog chain. He makes a whining sound, clothing torn, flesh blistering.

There is nothing more heartbreaking than seeing your father for who he truly is.

I don't let my eyes linger on the monstrosity of his body. I wonder if Elijah finally wishes he never met me.

The stairs creak and I turn as my mother descends slowly, slowly. In her hand is the muted grey kettle and a knife. I understand why she has the knife, but not the kettle. I think of the tea parties she and I and Sadie would have when I was a girl; even the dog would sit in a chair, attempt to lap milk from a tiny cup. Mom let me feed her gingersnaps and triangles of egg salad sandwiches.

"Say goodbye to your father, kids," she says, and I open my mouth but I can't find the words. I can hear Theo's breath, quick, panicked.

She steps close to him. I hear the scrape of the dog chain against the floor. I look at the snarl of his mouth, the deformation of his once perfect nose. The animal in his eyes, his squeals a language none of us can speak as she pours the scalding hot water over the top of his head in a wicked baptism with a calm voice, a cooing, "It's okay, it's okay."

I think of lobsters trying to climb from a vat of boiling water, of being disoriented by the sharp pain. She drops the kettle with a clang, something so soothing and maternal causing immense agony.

"All you had to do was love us," she says.

I flinch as she takes the knife, looks him straight in the eyes like something she was stupid to ever love, and slits his throat.

There is nothing more liberating than seeing your mother for who she truly is.

FORTY-TWO

We sit around the kitchen table with a bottle of wine, which we each grab to refill quickly emptying glasses. In the centre rests Cedar's rib. The thick scent of sage fills the air, an attempt to clear the space, to rid us all of the darkness.

But I can still feel Richard, and without Cedar he feels more frightening than ever. I strain my ears to hear her, but she's gone. She's finally gone.

I went and got Lil from the car shortly after we ascended the basement stairs, after I covered all of the mirrors in the house with bedsheets, towels. I couldn't help it—I looked into one, hoping that I would see Cedar's eyes reflecting back from mine. But she was gone. I repeated my own name three times into the glass. I have never felt more myself. I didn't tell Lil what happened in the basement. I couldn't tell her, yet I wonder if she knows. I wonder what Cedar would have said. I long to know. I miss her, the way I always have.

Lil sits hunched over in a wooden chair, her skin greyish, eyes brimming with exhaustion. I want to ask her what it was like, the spirit world, but she just looks so tired, so empty. I'll ask her tomorrow or maybe the day after. I'll ask her when she once again seems like herself, when the longing to slip somewhere else has dissipated. I've never seen the other side. I never want to. Like drugs, I'd be lost to it.

I want to ask her what she meant, about the sickness being over. But I know that can wait too. It all can wait.

The sound of the breaking news jingle chimes from the living room, the TV still turned up too loud. We all follow the sound, standing in the light of the TV to see what fresh hell awaits.

"Worldwide, the metamorphosis of men has been dissipating. There seems to be no reversal of those who are already changing, but no new cases have been reported anywhere in the world over the last four hours—a first, since this all began earlier this month."

Lil looks up at me, and for a moment, I swear I see Cedar in her eyes. Eyes shining with I-told-you-so energy. Eyes proud and self-assured and free.

"Scientists are still conducting research and autopsies on the bodies of the changed. Those still living are being used for analysis purposes and will be culled after all information has been gathered. If you see one, you are not to approach. But the aggression of them seems to be miraculously lessening. Many, worldwide, have taken to the woods to die alone. The uploading of confession videos and men taking to the streets to speak openly about abuse has been hugely beneficial to the understanding of this virus. So far, all of those affected have been perpetrators of sexual violence. In a bittersweet way"—the anchor stops, looks off camera before turning back with a huge grin—"this marks a huge win for all victims of sexual abuse. Justice, it seems, has finally found a way. The head of the investigation unit has stopped the search for The Polaroid Killer. The case is being closed, referred to as vigilante justice. It's suspected that all victims were people who would have changed anyway."

Lil is holding Theo's hand. I watch them from the corner of my eye as they cry for different reasons. My mom leaves the room, and I follow her back to the kitchen table. Her hands no longer shake, and I wonder if any ounce of guilt she held onto has vanished, knowing that either way, Daddy was already gone. I watch her as she walks to the counter, opens the third drawer, and pulls out a thick stack of papers. She tosses it onto the table with a thump.

"Deb dropped this off for you," she says, eyeing me knowingly. "I don't know how much good they'll be anymore."

I squirm in my seat but still reach out my hand, pulling the stack towards me. I glance quickly, flicking my finger through them all too fast to register individual names, but they're all the same. All mug shots with lists of crimes. Each of them specifying some form of sexual violence. Will's file rests on top, and I feel a pang of guilt that I didn't get him sooner.

"She seemed to think they would be useful to you."

Deb's green light: *Go on, honey, kill them all.*

Cedar made it easy for me, but the monsters, there will always be monsters. Yet maybe not for a while.

My eyes are glued to the pages, trying to figure out how long Deb has known. Was it when she saw the Polaroid first flash on the news or did she know earlier? Did she know when I was still only a girl myself? Has she always protected me in a way that only a woman would know to protect another woman? Has she always known, like my father said, that a woman needed a good reason to kill?

And this world, this world has given us plenty.

Perhaps all of us left will have to become killers one day, utilizing whatever tricks we've learned to survive. Perhaps we will begin to understand them, these men, how they clutched onto power with bloody hands.

I long to hear Cedar. The cliché rings true: you really don't know what you have until it's gone. My tears splatter against the black-and-white pages.

Tomorrow, Theo and Elijah will drag what's left of my father out of the basement. We will bury him in the backyard, beside Sadie. We will play his favourite songs and drink Busch Lights and talk about the good times, the times where he made us feel loved and protected and excited for the future.

I take a gulp of wine and stand up. Theo and Lil sit side by side in the living room. I plant a kiss on each of their heads. When they look up at me, both sets of eyes say that everything will be okay. Cedar was right. Everything will be okay. She's given us a gift. She's given us the gift of revenge.

I leave the room, climbing the stairs of this progressively haunted house. I can feel him. Richard. Angry and abrasive. Sad. I wish Cedar would have taken him with her too. But he belongs here, stuck in his everlasting limbo. Stuck in his own regrets. He wants me to feel guilt that I can't bring myself to feel. I think he's angry with himself—for choosing the wrong troubled girl, for underestimating me.

The Polaroids, once carefully tucked into the bottom of my bag, have been carelessly spilled across my unmade bed. The image startles me, my secrets spread. I look up quickly at the creaking sound of my bedroom door, jumping as Elijah enters the room with an expression I have yet to see. I'm tired. I'm so tired of men revealing themselves to me.

"I lost my father too, you know," he says, pulling my oldest Polaroid from the pocket of his blue jeans.

He tosses it onto the bed. It's Richard, with his arm outstretched blocking his face from the flash.

And I see Elijah as a little boy, Elijah Clark, waiting by a picture window for a daddy who will never return. And I see him growing up around a lack of influence that has worked to save him. Yet his eyes, his eyes are still filled with remorseful rage.

"He loved you," I say, hearing a loop of Richard's panicked voice. "He just didn't love you more than himself."

"Thank you," Elijah says, closing his eyes tightly, tears brimming around his beautiful, dark lashes. And I can taste the pain in his kiss. I can taste how he misses his father the way I miss mine. His hands rest tenderly on my hips. Tears dampen my cheeks. He has been spared from the hands of men.

"I love you," I mutter against his lips.

"I love you more, Delilah."

Richard hovers in the corner of the room, along with all of the others that I've trapped, stuck forever with the consequences of their actions. I like to think Richard's grateful for me too, for showing my strength, for saving his son.

This is the world we live in; this is how it shapes us.

A world where grown men are hungry for young girls.

And fathers cheat.

Where men hop into cars when they're already piss drunk.

And little boys pedal fast and reckless instead of permitting themselves tears.

One where boys you desperately want to love you spend a lifetime just giving you enough sustenance to keep you from starving—where they inflict further damage just because they can.

It's a world where even the best have this insatiable urge to dominate and the worst have this insatiable urge to kill.

A world that doesn't want to stop policing our bodies.

A world that doesn't want to stop making excuses for male violence, until maybe now, now that they can actually feel the consequences in the crippling of spine, the protruding of teeth, the incessant fever and rage, their bodies' betrayal. Now that they can feel that loss of self. Maybe now they'll care, now that it affects them. Now that it's led to their own demise.

Pray for us, pray for us. Please, God, help us.

I can hear them all around me, these lost creatures.

There is one woman to every one hundred men, hair long and wolfish, eyes hungry, lips set into a sneer. The ones who tried to get power back the same way they lost it. Coercive, aggressive, violent.

It's true what they say.

Karma's a bitch.

ACKNOWLEDGMENTS

Thank you to Max. BABY. This has been a journey that I wouldn't want to trek with anyone else. Your belief in me from day one has instilled so much confidence during times of doubt. Thank you for popping back into my life when I needed you most. For always hyping me up, for tirelessly polishing and re-organizing and designing this stunning cover. You are courageous and bold and brilliant. I love you.

To my Momma, thank you for teaching me that nothing matters more than the truth. Thank you for reading every single draft. For validating that my voice is important and needed in this world. For showing me strength. For loving me so fiercely. For being my best friend. I love you more, today and tomorrow too.

To my Daddio, thank you for valuing that I'm tough as nails. For teaching me to be driven and dedicated. For all of our conversations on the atrocities of this world. For being there for me whenever I call. I hope I'll always be the apple of your eye.

To my Tiko. Your laugh will always be my favourite sound.

To Tommy, I value that day that we sat on the floor, drinking wine, and I read you the entirety of that whopping first draft more than you'll ever know. Thank you for putting in such effort to grow and change and holding space for me to do the same. You are a wonderful man and partner. You my bestfraaaaand. I love you the most.

To my Beppe, for teaching me to chase my dreams. Nothing from nothing is nothing.

To Johnny, the best example of a father and grandfather. I was so lucky to be loved by you.

To all of my best friends & cute boys. You fill my world with happiness. Thank you for being you.

To Duska, thank you for taking my author photos and always making me feel like a goddess.

To Dana & Kate, your insight and enthusiasm has meant so much to me. Can't wait to hug yas! (Also a Texas-sized thank you to Randy for the boar jaw)

To all of the women, enby, trans, and 2S folks in my life, you inspire me daily. Thank you for your depth, your courage, your tough tenderness. We are powerful.

To everyone raising awareness, fighting for action, and demanding justice for MMIWG2S. Nyáwen'kowa.

To everyone living in Afters that they never asked for, I see you, I hear you, I love you.

To all of the cis, het men, if you've gotten this far you must be one of the good ones. Remember that you have the power to influence others, please use it to help create a better society.

ABOUT THE AUTHOR

Gin Sexsmith is an Indigenous writer and musician from Tyendinaga Mohawk Territory living in the under-land-claims town of Deseronto, Ontario. Obsessed with the darker sides of our psyche, Gin's work explores love, loss, sexuality, and mental illness.

9 798986 466187